# Sensible Shoes

A STORY ABOUT THE SPIRITUAL JOURNEY

Sharon Garlough Brown

An imprint of InterVarsity Press
Downers Grove, Illinois

*InterVarsity Press*
*P.O. Box 1400, Downers Grove, IL 60515-1426*
*ivpress.com*
*email@ivpress.com*



*InterVarsity Press® is the bookpublishing division of InterVarsity Christian Fellowship/USA®, a movement of students and faculty active on campus at hundreds of universities, colleges and schools of nursing in the United States of America, and a member movement of the International Fellowship of Evangelical Students. For information about local and regional activities, visit intervarsity.org.*



*Cover design: Cindy Kiple*
*Images: small girl sitting on suitcase: susan.k./Getty Images*
*group of women holding hands: JupiterImages/Getty Images*
*Interior design: Beth Hagenberg*

*ISBN 978-0-8308-4305-3 (print)*
*ISBN 978-0-8308-6453-9 (digital)*

*Printed in the United States of America* ♾

*InterVarsity Press is committed to ecological stewardship and to the conservation of natural resources in all our operations. This book was printed using sustainably sourced paper.*

**Library of Congress Cataloging-in-Publication Data**
*Brown, Sharon Garlough, 1969-*
*Sensible shoes: a story about the spiritual journey/Sharon Garlough Brown*
*348 pg; 21 cm*
*ISBN 978-0-8308-4305-3 (pbk : alk. paper)*
*1.Christian women—fiction. 2. Spiritual retreats—fiction. 3. Friendship—fiction.*
*PS3602.R722867 S46 2013*
*813/.6*

*2012045854*

**P** 39 38 37 36 35 34 33 32 31 30 29 28 27 26 25 24 23 22 21 20 19
**Y** 40 39 38 37 36 35 34 33 32 31 30 29 28 27 26 25 24 23 22 21 20 19

*To the ones who have walked with me*

*And to the Holy Spirit, gentle revealer and faithful guide*
*With deep love and gratitude*

# Table of Contents

1

# Invitation to a Journey

*Stand at the crossroads, and look, and ask*
*for the ancient paths, where the good way lies;*
*and walk in it, and find rest for your souls.*

JEREMIAH 6:16

## *Meg, 1967*

*A solitary little girl in a gray wool coat and red knit cap flitted through the snow, searching for a glimmer of gold. Someone had given the jingle bells to Mama for Christmas, and Mama had smiled when she hung them on the front door. So when the wind snatched the bells and spirited them away, five-year-old Meg was determined to find them and make Mama happy again.*

*Meg hummed as she searched around bushes in the yard. She loved hide-and-seek. She wished Mama or Rachel would play hide-and-seek with her; but Mama was too busy to play, and eleven-year-old Rachel always said she was too big for baby games. If only Daddy hadn't gone to heaven to be with Jesus! Daddy had been very good at hide-and-seek.*

*Meg patiently pursued the lost bells for almost an hour, finally spotting one of them peeking out from a snowbank near Mrs. Anderson's garage. Clutching her prize, Meg skipped down the driveway and up the front steps.*

*Mama was standing at the door, scowling and scolding. "Margaret Fowler! Didn't you hear me calling for you?"*

*"Mama, I found them!" Meg beamed as she offered her gift.*

*Mama stripped off Meg's hat, revealing thick blonde curls. "How many times do I have to tell you? Take your boots off outside. I don't want snow messing up this floor."*

*Meg left her boots on the porch and danced inside, jingling the bells. "Look, Mama! I found your bells!"*

*Mama frowned as she shut the door. "What bells?"*

Meg Crane stepped across the threshold of her childhood home in Kingsbury, Michigan, the jingling of her keys echoing in the foyer. Though she had spent almost forty of her forty-six years in the Fowler family's large Victorian house, it had never felt this cavernously lonely. Shutting the door behind her, Meg sank slowly to the floor and leaned her head against the wood paneling.

Gone. Becca was gone. Her beloved daughter had flown away.

Meg wished they could have had more time together. The fourth of August had arrived too quickly, and now her only child was on a plane to London, where she would spend her junior year of college.

Becca's lively presence at home had kept Meg happily preoccupied. There had been so much to do together, so many preparations to make for the overseas adventure. Becca's joy and enthusiasm had temporarily buoyed Meg's spirits above her own grief.

But now the empty house engulfed her with dreadful stillness.

Mother was also gone. Still gone.

Months after Ruth Fowler's death, Meg was still fighting the impulse to call out a greeting to her mother whenever she arrived home. She still expected Mother to appear at the dinner table. She still listened for her footsteps on the staircase. She still paused by the bedroom door, stifling the urge to say goodnight.

Meg supposed she would be slow to process Becca's absence too. She imagined she would still look for Becca's pink water bottle on the kitchen counter. She would still listen for her daughter's cheerful voice humming along with her iPod. She would probably still awaken around midnight and expect to hear Becca arrive home safely after an evening out with friends.

But now the only sounds in the house were the melancholy sighs of an antique grandfather clock and the low hum of the refrigerator.

Meg Crane was alone. Truly alone.

*Now what?*

Slumping forward, Meg cradled her head in her hands and wept.

On Saturday night Meg dutifully set her alarm. Though she would have preferred to stay in bed on Sunday morning, she arrived at Kingsbury Community Church during the opening hymn. For years she had faithfully practiced the safest way to avoid interacting with other worshipers: arrive while everyone was singing, sit in the far back corner of the sanctuary near the exit door, and leave before the benediction. At five-foot-two, Meg had a singular advantage for slipping in and out of places without being seen. Most Sundays her invisibility strategy worked flawlessly.

On this Sunday, however, Pastor Dave's wife, Sandy, happened to be standing in the narthex when Meg exited. Meg walked as if she were in a hurry, hoping her determined gaze and stride would give the impression she had other commitments to keep. But when Sandy smiled and greeted her by name, Meg knew she had been thwarted.

"I was hoping to catch you this morning, Meg. I haven't seen you the last few months. How are you?"

"Fine, thanks, Sandy. And you?"

"We're doing well. Enjoying this great weather. Michigan summers are beautiful, aren't they?"

Meg could hear the choir singing the final response and knew she didn't have much time before the narthex filled with people she didn't want to see. It took so much effort simply to keep from bursting into tears. One look of compassion, one word tenderly spoken, and she was likely to disintegrate.

She inched her way closer to the door.

"This came in the mail the other day, and I thought of you." Sandy handed her a plum-colored flyer. "It's about the fall programs at the New Hope Center. You know about New Hope, right?"

Meg had never visited the retreat center, but as a lifelong resident of Kingsbury, she had driven by the building and grounds many times. "I—uh . . . I know where it is, but that's about all." The sanctuary doors were getting ready to open, and soon she would be surrounded.

Sandy clearly did not share her sense of urgency. "New Hope's a wonderful place," she went on. "I've gone to lots of programs there, and this particular one is really good."

Meg brushed her ash blonde curls away from her eyes and feigned interest as Sandy showed her the paragraph about a "sacred journey."

"It's all about deepening your relationship with God through prayer and other spiritual disciplines," Sandy explained. "And with the changes you've gone through the past couple of months, I thought this group might help you find your way."

Meg bit her lip. Evidently, the pastor had spoken to his wife about how hard she was finding the grief process.

Sandy continued with a gentle voice. "I remember how I felt after my mom died, and I know how close the two of you were."

*Close?*

Meg felt heat rise to her neck and face. The scarlet blotches consuming her fair skin were giving her away. Tattletales. She resented those blotches.

"Thank you so much for thinking of me, Sandy," she said, wrapping her icy hand around her throat to cool it down. "Please tell Pastor Dave what a meaningful sermon he preached today."

Then she quickly slipped out the glass doors before anyone else could smile and call her by name.

## Hannah, 1976

*Seven-year-old Hannah Shepley loved Brown Bear, her faithful steward of secrets and sorrows. When one of his gentle eyes fell off and disappeared, her heart broke. Miss Betty, their elderly neighbor, patted Hannah's head with her arthritic hand and told her not to worry. She could fix Brown Bear's eyes. Hannah tearfully entrusted him to Miss Betty, who promised to return him soon.*

*When Brown Bear came home two days later, Miss Betty beamed and said, "Here, Hannah. See? Good as new!"*

*But as Hannah looked into Brown Bear's eyes, she did not recognize him. She knew that he did not recognize her either. The all-knowing, tender expression was gone, replaced by the blank, amnesic stare of large plastic buttons. Hannah had lost her best friend and confidante.*

*Her mother was embarrassed by her silence. "What do you say, Hannah? Miss Betty worked hard fixing your bear for you."*

*"Thank you, Miss Betty," Hannah whispered. But when she was alone in her room, she burst into tears.*

"I always feel so much better after I talk to you," said the tearful female voice on the other end of the phone.

Thirty-nine-year-old Hannah Shepley smiled to herself. She loved her job. For fifteen years she had served as an associate pastor at Westminster Church in Chicago, and she still loved her work.

"Let's get together to pray," Hannah said, pulling out her planner and scanning the details of her schedule that day: Tuesday, the fifth of August. She was booked straight through a dinner meeting. "Is eight o'clock tonight too late for you?" she asked. "I'm happy to come to your home, or you're welcome to come to my office whichever is better for you." They made arrangements to meet in Hannah's office.

Hannah had never regretted her decision to furnish and decorate her office far more comfortably than her house. Not only did the warm ambience provide a safe haven for people in crisis, but she spent most of her life there. In fact, she had once calculated the number of waking hours she actually spent at home, only to discover it ranked a distant third.

Behind hospitals.

Hannah looked at her watch and grabbed her keys. She needed to be at the hospital by ten o'clock to pray with Ken Walsh before his open heart surgery. And while she was there, she could check on Mabel Copeland, who was recovering from a hip replacement. If she hurried, she would still have time to pick up flowers on the way.

She nearly bumped into Steve Hernandez, Westminster's senior pastor, in the hallway. "Racing off again?" Steve asked.

"Pre-op this morning and then a bunch of pastoral care appointments." Hannah tucked her chin length, light brown hair behind her ears. "I've got another one of those days where I need to be in three places at once. You know how that goes."

"Is there anything I can help you with today?" Steve asked.

Steve always asked, and Hannah always said no. She had everything covered. Even so, she was grateful he made a habit of inquiring. Many senior pastors took their associates for granted. Not Steve. He tried to keep his finger on the spiritual pulse of his staff, and they loved him for it.

"Make sure you take some time to breathe today, Hannah."

She laughed. "I've got breathing time scheduled for a week from Thursday."

The next morning, just before eight o'clock, Steve knocked on her open office door. "Another early start?" he asked, glancing at his watch.

Hannah looked up from her reading and stifled a yawn. "I was at the hospital to pray with Ted and his family before his surgery this morning. I wanted to stay and wait with them, but I've got a nine o'clock meeting. I'll go back later, though, to make sure he's doing okay." She motioned to her brown suede couch. "C'mon in, Steve. Have a seat."

He moved aside a pillow and a blanket. "Did you go home last night?"

"I'll grab a power nap later." She took a sip of coffee. "What's up?"

She heard Steve take a deep, preparatory breath. "Hannah, the elders and I have come to a decision I know you won't like, but I'm hoping you can receive it as a gift."

Hannah clenched her jaw and immediately began scanning for possibilities of what he might say. Amazing, how many divergent thoughts could sprint through her mind in five seconds. With a single shot fired into the air, she was off and running. Were they restructuring the staff? Canceling one of the ministry programs? Giving her another team to oversee?

"We're giving you a nine-month sabbatical," he said. "Starting in September."

She skidded to an abrupt stop. "I don't understand," she said, studying his face for non-verbal clues.

"I know. But some of us have been talking about it for a while now, and it's time. You've been here almost fifteen years without a break. You're way overdue."

"But lots of pastors go a lot longer than that and never get a break," she countered. "Besides, I had six weeks off last year!"

Steve laughed. "So you could recover from major surgery! And if I remember correctly, you kept working from home."

She shook her head emphatically. "I don't need a sabbatical. I love my work, and I'm doing okay."

"You can't argue out of this one, Hannah. It's already been decided. And to express our love and appreciation for you—and to help you relax—some folks have given donations to cover all of your living expenses."

Hannah had never heard of an associate pastor being given such a generous sabbatical, and she was suspicious. She knew she didn't have control over her facial expression, so she looked away, fixing her gaze on the potted plant and "Get Well Soon!" balloon she would be delivering later that day.

Steve read her reaction and responded to her unspoken fears. "You're not being fired, Hannah. I promise. Your job performance is outstanding, the congregation loves you, and you're a wonderful colleague."

She still wouldn't look at him. She didn't trust herself. Out of her peripheral vision she saw him lean forward on the couch, plant his elbows on his knees, and clasp his hands together. This was Steve's earnest pose, reserved for particularly treacherous moments of pastoral care: couples on the verge of divorce, teenagers threatening suicide, parents losing their faith after the death of a child. Steve would dig his heels firmly into the ground and tug on the invisible rope, pulling a teetering soul safely away from despair's precipice and into the strong arms of Jesus.

Clearly, Steve thought she was hovering on the brink. What brink? She couldn't remember him ever using the rope with her. She didn't need the rope. Didn't, didn't, didn't.

"Remember that great sermon you preached just a few months ago on John 15?" he continued.

Hannah did not reply. She had a sinking feeling that her words of wisdom about Jesus as the vine and the Father as the gardener were about to come back and bite her.

"You told the congregation that pruning isn't punishment—it's improvement. You reminded us that pruning is God's way of shaping us to become even more like Christ. Jesus said the branches that get pruned are the ones bearing fruit. And you're bearing fruit, Hannah. Lots of it. This sabbatical isn't punishment—it's pruning. It's time to let God care for you and shape you so you can become even more like Christ."

"But September?" she exclaimed. "That's impossible! I've got all these fall programs already planned. There's no way I can wrap up everything here that fast. And who would even cover for me?"

Steve hesitated, and in his hesitation, Hannah discerned the truth. They'd had this planned for a while. They had just avoided telling her until now. Why hadn't they given her more warning? Why hadn't they included her in the planning? More than that, why hadn't they consulted her to begin with?

"We've got everything covered, Hannah. You don't have to worry about anything. I promise."

This was crazy. Absolutely absurd. How could this be happening?

Steve spoke with a low, reassuring voice. "You've done a great job here at Westminster—the staff and elders all think so. But I also think you need some time and space to disentangle your personal and professional identities. You don't know who you are when you aren't pastoring. You don't know what to do when you're not being needed. And you have no idea how tired you are. Trust me. I've been there."

Even though his voice was gentle, she winced.

"Years ago my senior pastor had the same talk with me, Hannah. He saw warning signs in my life that I didn't see, and he took action. His intervention saved my ministry, my family, and my health. It was a huge blessing to me, and I hope this will be a blessing to you."

She didn't want to hear it. She wasn't burned out, and she wasn't on the brink of disaster. She didn't have a family to worry about, and her health was fine. She didn't need a break. Didn't, didn't, didn't.

"Can't I just take a month off?"

"No."

"Three months then? I'll go on a guided retreat somewhere and come back renewed and refreshed."

Steve was immovable. "This is radical pruning we're talking about. If we only give you a couple of months, you'll just mark time until you can come back and pick up right where you left off."

"But an entire school year! What am I possibly going to do with all that time off?"

He smiled gently. "Don't worry about trying to figure out the whole thing right now. We can talk later about some ideas for how you might want to spend it. The priority is getting you to a place where you can shift gears into real rest, and we're going to do everything we possibly can to help make that happen for you." He stood up. "Nine months, Hannah. Just give God nine months."

She knew there was no use arguing. They had made the decision without even consulting her—without her knowledge or approval—and it was out of her control. As she watched Steve leave her office, Hannah couldn't help feeling resentful. She didn't need an intervention, and she didn't want his gift—especially a gift that was intended to be so outrageously generous. Not only did she feel resentful, but now she felt guilty over being ungrateful.

She hated feeling that way.

## Mara, 1968

*Mara Payne bit her lip and fixed her eyes on her saddle shoes as she kicked up little clumps of dirt and grass. She had played this role countless times, and she knew the script by heart. One by one the fourth grade team captains would call out the names of her classmates. One by one the chosen would saunter to their respective sides, congratulating each other and whispering recommendations for the next pick into the captains' ears.*

*Mara didn't have to look up to know what was happening. The feet next to hers were Eddie Carter's. She knew his sneakers: blue stripes, muddy laces, and a small tear where a big toe wriggled in the sock. Eddie was always second-to-last pick, but at least he was chosen. Mara was just the leftover. When the sullen captain finally groaned her name, she would take the walk of shame and tell herself she didn't care. But her tearstained shoes told a different story.*

Mara and Tom Garrison sat on the metal bleachers on a warm August evening in western Michigan, eating hot dogs and cheering on their sons' baseball team, the Kingsbury Knights. Fridays were one of the few evenings the family spent together. Most weeks Tom traveled Monday through Thursday, leaving Mara to manage the precisely choreographed steps of the single parent dance. But when Tom was in town, he was devoted to their two teenage boys.

"Go, go, go!" Tom jumped to his feet and shouted as fifteen-year-old Kevin drilled a hard line drive deep into center field, rounding first, rounding second, and sliding into third base. "Safe!" Tom yelled along with the umpire. "Yeah! Way to go, Kev!" He sat down again, still clapping enthusiastically. "I tell you what, Mara—that boy's got talent. You watch! He's gonna end up with a scholarship somewhere. Baseball, football, basketball—you name it, he can do it."

Mara sipped her diet soda and scanned the dugout bench for thirteen-year-old Brian. When she finally spotted him, she stood up. She was hard to miss in her oversized lime green tunic and large-brimmed straw hat; but if Brian saw her waving to him, he didn't acknowledge her. She sat back down and stared at her shoes, hoping no one else had seen him look her direction before turning away.

"So," she began, rubbing her palms back and forth along her considerable thighs. "Do you know any more details about your plans with the boys tomorrow?"

Tom did not reply, choosing instead to concentrate intently on the pitcher's windup and Kevin's lead at third base. Mara waited for the batter's swing and miss before she tried again. "I was just wondering if you guys are planning to be gone all day or if you'll be home for dinner?"

"Don't know. We'll play it by ear." He was still watching the mound.

Mara removed her hat and smoothed her freshly colored, dark auburn hair. She could still smell the ammonia. Someday maybe she'd splurge and treat herself to color from a salon instead of from a box. Unfortunately, the copper highlights had turned out to be far more orange than she'd wanted, and she was going to have to try to fix them without making things worse. She supposed she could always go back to a boring shade of brown. Or maybe she'd make an appointment with a hairdresser. She figured that at fifty, she was entitled to a little more attentive pampering than she normally indulged in, even if Tom disagreed.

She sighed. "I'm happy to cook something for us, if you think you'll be back from the game by then."

Tom took a bite of his hot dog and waved to Brian. Brian waved back. "I said I don't know. We'll play it by ear."

"It just helps me plan my Saturday if I know what to expect—"

"Enough, Mara!" he barked, rubbing his hands over his gray crew cut. "Wouldya just let me watch the game?" He jumped up to cheer again as Kevin raced home on a ground ball to the shortstop. "Way to hustle, Kev! Keep it up!" Kevin turned his freckled face to the stands and high-fived toward his dad.

Mara put her hat back on. "I just—"

Tom spun around, glaring at her. "Do whatever you want, okay? If we get hungry, we'll stop and get something to eat on the way home. Just quit naggin' me!"

Mara saw one of the other mothers turn and cast a sympathetic glance in her direction. Knowing their conversation had been overheard, Mara forced a broad smile and a lighthearted chuckle. "Men!" she mouthed to the woman, rolling her eyes and shaking her head.

For the next three innings she ignored Tom and pretended to be interested in the lives of the other families sitting in the bleachers. The other Perfect Happy Families. After the game ended, she stood in the stands and watched Tom embrace the boys on the field. Then she shuffled slowly across the parking lot to her black SUV, fighting back her tears until she was safely out of sight from any spectators.

When Tom and the boys arrived home after their customary post-game celebration at Steak 'n Shake, Mara was already in bed, pretending to be asleep.

On Monday night Mara sat on her king-sized bed pairing socks. She'd heard other women talk about leaving clean laundry in baskets for husbands and kids to grab what they needed. But Mara had never minded sorting laundry. There was something particularly satisfying about matching socks together. When she couldn't find a mate, she'd put the lone sock in her top dresser drawer and wait for the missing one to surface. In fact, her top drawer was crammed with unmated—no, once-mated—socks she couldn't bear to throw away.

There ought to be a country and western song about that.

Maybe there already was.

Kevin appeared in the doorway just as Mara was putting away the last of Tom's undershirts. "Dad says to tell you he won't be home until late Thursday night."

Ever since Kevin got a cell phone for his fifteenth birthday, Tom had made a habit of communicating most of his messages through him. Or by text. These days Mara had very little voice-to-voice contact with Tom when he traveled. Or when he was home.

Having delivered the message, Kevin was already headed down the hallway.

Just once, she wished the boys would linger long enough for a meaningful conversation—something other than the typical grunt or shrug whenever she asked about homework or friends. The only time she received actual sentences was when they were asking for food or laundry or taxi services.

"Kevin, don't forget you've got an orthodontist appointment tomorrow!" Mara called after him. He didn't reply. "Kevin!"

"I know!" he yelled from his room.

"Where are my jeans?" Now Brian was in the doorway.

"I put them away in your drawer."

"No—my black ones."

"I haven't seen your black ones."

"I put them in the laundry like a week ago!"

"I don't know, Brian. I emptied the basket this morning and washed everything that was in it."

"So where are my jeans?" The freckled dimple at the left corner of his mouth was beginning to twitch. He looked just like his father as he stood there frowning, arms crossed over his chest.

"Check the floor in your room. I saw a pile of stuff by your desk."

Dawn, her counselor, had told her to stop picking up after the boys. *They need to take some responsibility,* Dawn said. *They've got to learn to live with consequences.*

Brian disappeared and came back with the jeans crumpled into a ball. He tossed them at Mara.

"I need these for tomorrow," he said, and left the room.

Mara exhaled slowly and put the jeans into the empty laundry basket. Someday maybe things would be different. *God, please.* She wasn't sure how much longer she could go on like this.

## Charissa, 1990

*The Goodman family always chose the first row pew right in front of the pulpit, where everyone could see them. Eight-year-old Charissa would sit between her parents, feigning close attention as the Reverend Hildenberg preached. Even when her tights itched and her taffeta sash was cinched uncomfortably around her waist, Charissa was determined not to fidget.*

*She was a statue—still and stoic like the ones carved centuries ago by Mother's Greek ancestors. Daddy's ancestors were still and stoic too; but they were British. Maybe even royalty. Charissa liked the idea of being a princess. Daddy always said she had a face that could launch a thousand ships, like Helen of Troy.*

*Charissa of Kingsbury.*

*She liked the sound of her name, even if she always had to correct people who mispronounced it. "It's 'Ka-Rissa,'" she would say. Her name meant, "grace," and Charissa liked that too. She practiced being as graceful as possible.*

*Most weeks Charissa spent the worship service sitting still on the outside while moving fast on the inside. Mother did not allow her to bring books to church or to the dinner table, so Charissa hid them in her head. She had a whole library of books stored inside her, and she could read them whenever she wanted. No one ever knew she was just pretending to listen to the sermon. In fact, every week the Reverend Hildenberg would shake Charissa's hand and tell her what a joy it was to see a young lady paying such careful attention. And Mr. Goodman would put his arm around Charissa's shoulders, smile, and say, "Thank you, Reverend. We're very proud of her."*

Twenty-six-year-old Charissa Goodman Sinclair leaned back to stretch her tight shoulders and then stood up at her desk. Only the doctoral students at Kingsbury University had private study cubicles in the main library, and hers was stacked high with English literature classics. She scanned the shelves, trying to decide which books to take home. She was definitely going to be spending the evening with Milton again, and she would need her resources on culture and society in Elizabethan England. Of course, she could also get a head start on her Shakespeare paper if she finished her analysis of *Paradise Lost*. The fall term had only just begun, and she was already swamped.

She pulled her long dark hair up into a clip and looked at her watch. John was supposed to pick her up on his way home from work. Maybe she should call and tell him that she'd be spending the night at the library instead. Then she would have easy access to all the books she might need.

But no—that wouldn't work. She would have to get home to shower and change in the morning before her eight o'clock class, and she didn't want to awaken John to come and get her. She hated having only one car. It was so inconvenient.

At least their skimp-and-save lifestyle was temporary. John was working his way up at the marketing firm, and Charissa would be an English literature professor someday. Just four more years of graduate school. Her father didn't understand why she would invest six years of her life in acquiring a graduate degree from a non-prestigious Christian university when she could have had her choice of Ivy League schools. At Kingsbury, however, Charissa's reputation in the English Department was well-known. Having graduated *summa cum laude,* she relished the distinct advantages of being a big fish in a small pond. Although Daddy would have preferred her pursuing a more profitable career in law or business, he loved telling people that his little girl was getting her Ph.D. And Charissa didn't mind him telling.

She packed up her laptop and a stack of books before heading out to the parking lot to wait for her husband.

On Tuesday evening Charissa was on her way to her library cubicle when she noticed plum-colored flyers posted on a bulletin board. Since there were multiple copies, she removed the thumbtack and slipped one into her backpack.

Normally, she wouldn't have paid any attention. She had never been to the New Hope Retreat Center, and she didn't know anything about its programs. But Dr. Allen, who taught her *Literature and the Christian Imagination* seminar, had been urging his students to find ways to deepen their life with God.

"I know I'm sounding like a broken record," he said at the end of class the next day, "but if you truly want to understand the literature we're reading this semester, you'll need to do some extra-curricular work. You'll need to make a commitment to pay attention to the path and contours of your own spiritual journey."

Removing his glasses, he ran his hand across his face and through his salt and pepper hair. "The poets and authors we're studying wrote out of the depths of their personal experience with God," he went on. "Their work reflects their wrestling with who God is and who God created them to be. If you don't do some wrestling of your own, the texts will have little meaning for you. So I encourage you again to explore your own spiritual formation this semester—to be intentional about how you are being shaped to become more and more like Christ. If you find ways to cooperate with the Spirit's work of transformation, these texts will spring to life for you."

Charissa wondered if New Hope's program would qualify as an appropriate spiritual formation experience. She could manage six Saturday sessions spread over three months. Maybe the New Hope course would be the perfect way to fulfill Dr. Allen's request.

She waited for the room to clear before she approached his desk to ask if he knew anything about the "sacred journey" group advertised on the flyer.

"Walk with me," he said, picking up his briefcase and his travel mug.

She followed him down the crowded hallway toward his office. "I'm just wondering if this is the sort of class you were talking about—something that would supplement the work we're doing in your course."

"Absolutely."

"And the director, Katherine Rhodes. Do you know anything about her?"

He nodded. "I know Katherine well. She's been at New Hope for a long time."

Charissa hesitated, trying to find the right way to phrase her next question. "And theologically . . . I mean . . . "

Dr. Allen interrupted, chuckling. "Worried about orthodoxy, Charissa? You're far more likely to hear heresy in these classrooms than from her. You'd be in good hands." He took a sip from his mug. "Apart from the spiritual formation recommendations I made in class, why are you interested in going?"

She thought for a moment and then answered, "To learn."

He stopped walking and turned his riveting dark eyes upon her. "Wrong answer," he said, smiling enigmatically. Was he teasing her?

Though she was several inches taller than her professor, Charissa suddenly felt rather small. Lowering her gaze away from his eyes, she focused instead on his neatly trimmed goatee and waited for him to explain himself.

"Go to encounter God, Charissa, or don't go at all."

## Hannah

Just one month after Steve broke the news of her unsolicited, unwelcomed vacation, Hannah Shepley relinquished her keys to Heather Kirk, the twenty-something pastoral intern that Westminster had hired to try to fill her shoes. Heather, who had graduated from seminary in May, was thrilled to have a nine-month internship before she sought a more permanent call elsewhere. Fresh-faced and eager, she was full of audacious hopes and plans for "doing ministry."

As Hannah looked into her replacement's sparkling eyes, she caught a glimpse of her former self. She had been young and eager once too, arriving at Westminster fresh from seminary—a twenty-four-year-old sparkplug, ready to ignite the church into action. But the last fifteen years had taken their toll. These days when Hannah looked into the mirror, she hardly knew herself. Her brown hair had streaks of silver which took too much effort to conceal, and her eyes were tired. So tired. In fact, her aging seemed to have accelerated ever since Steve had told her she needed to rest. Or maybe she had merely become more aware of her weariness once she had stopped moving quite so fast.

"Don't worry about anything," Heather assured her, jingling Hannah's house and office keys. "I've got everything covered. And if I've got any questions about the house, I'll e-mail you." The intern smiled knowingly. "Pastor Steve doesn't want me calling you with questions about anything else."

"Well, God bless you, Heather." Hannah's heart was so disconnected from her lips that she didn't recognize her own voice speaking the polite benediction. "I hope it's a fruitful time for you." *Really?* Did she actually want this fresh-faced neophyte to thrive as her surrogate? Or was she secretly hoping her substitute would flounder so miserably that Westminster would be clamoring for her immediate return?

She didn't want to answer that question.

Sneaking one more furtive glance at her house, Hannah followed her friend Nancy Johnson out to the car. Hannah had loaded her ten-year-old Honda with as many books from her office as she could manage. If she was going to be forced into time away, she could at least make her sabbatical as productive as possible.

Clothes were an afterthought. Hannah often joked that she could get dressed in the dark with her monochromatic wardrobe. In fact, she often did throw on clothes in the middle of the night for emergency hospital visits. Everything she owned was easy care and travel friendly, and she had stuffed the essentials into a single suitcase and a duffel bag: her sheepskin slippers and flannel pajamas, a few pairs of jeans and sweats, some casual tops and travel knit pants, a winter coat and fleece pullover, comfortable shoes and boots. She'd pick up clothes for warmer weather in the spring. That way she would have an excuse to go back home.

"I know this must be hard for you," Nancy said quietly.

*You have no idea,* Hannah replied to herself. She still couldn't believe this was happening.

She shoved the last box onto the floor behind the driver's seat, hoping Nancy hadn't glimpsed its bulging contents when the lid popped off. The box was full of old journals and other personal mementos Hannah hadn't wanted to risk leaving behind. She didn't know how nosy Heather would be, or who else might be wandering through her house while she was away. Even if she never opened the box during the sabbatical, she didn't want anyone else discovering it.

"Doug and I are praying you'll be able to rest and meet God in new ways," Nancy said, reaching into her pocket to pull out a key. Nancy and Doug had generously given Hannah their Lake Michigan family cottage for the next nine months. Though Hannah had never been there, she had seen pictures. It was beautiful.

"This is for the front door," Nancy went on. "It sticks a little bit, so you have to fiddle with it. And here are the directions for how to get there. Let's see—what else? Oh—make sure you drink the filtered water. The well water doesn't taste very good. I left a binder for you on the kitchen counter with all the other details you might need to know, but if you have any questions about anything, call us. And remember, we're only three hours away."

"Thanks, Nancy. Thanks for being so incredibly generous." Hannah sighed and tucked her uncooperative hair behind her ears again. "There must be something seriously wrong with me. Who wouldn't want nine whole months of paid vacation? I must be crazy."

Nancy wrapped her arm around Hannah's shoulders. "You're not crazy, just driven. Passion about your work is a good thing. It's one of the things we love about you! But Pastor Steve is right. You've been carrying the weight of the world on your shoulders. It's time for you to rest." Nancy kissed her furrowed brow. "Besides, it's a special work of grace when God helps us shift from being the giver to the receiver. At least, that's what you told me after I had surgery."

Hannah laughed ruefully. "I hate it when my wisdom comes back to bite me!"

Hannah arrived at the Johnsons' Lake Michigan cottage just in time to watch the September sun descend with crimson pageantry. Seating herself in a weathered gray Adirondack chair on the deck, she stared across the shimmering lake and breathed deeply.

The simple poetry of dwindling daylight stirred her. Something she had yet to understand or articulate was setting beneath a horizon in her life too, and she had no vision to imagine what would rise in its place.

*Help, Lord,* she prayed, watching fiery ribbons unfurl across the sky.

The last splashes of color were fading when Hannah crossed the threshold into her borrowed home. A single whiff of the damp mustiness, and she was eight years old again, skipping through the cottage her parents had rented for a week on the California coast. "Daddy, look!" she'd squealed, surveying her kingdom. "Bunk beds! I've always wanted bunk beds!"

Now she wandered slowly from room to room, trying to decide where to land. The cottage was at least twice the size of her two-bedroom house in Chicago, and even though it was decorated simply, it still felt far too luxurious. Nancy had finely tuned, elegant taste. This wasn't one of those cottages furnished with thrift store knickknacks and cast-off wedding gifts. This was the sort of place where Hannah would be reluctant to put her feet on the furniture—except Nancy had specifically commanded her to put her feet up.

Hannah sighed as she removed the pink cellophane from a large wicker gift basket overflowing with cookies, chocolate, homemade strawberry preserves, and a dozen varieties of tea.

Tea. That's what she needed—a cup of tea to soothe and settle her. Then she could begin organizing books on the shelves Nancy had so thoughtfully cleared.

She chose a packet of decaf vanilla chai, filled the electric kettle, and read the note on the counter: "This is your home, Hannah. Rest and play here with joy!"

Rest, play, joy.

Those weren't words Hannah ever strung together. Not for herself, anyway. Her joy was her work. Her joy was being useful and productive. She could still see the intern standing there on her front porch, blithely jingling the keys to her life.

How could Steve do this to her?

As she waited for the water to boil, she thumbed absent-mindedly through a stack of Michigan travel and event brochures. A plum-colored flyer finally captured her wandering thoughts. The New Hope Retreat Center in Kingsbury sounded familiar, and then she remembered that Nancy had attended a prayer group there during the summer. Hannah paused to read: "Jesus says, 'Are you tired? Worn out? Burned out on religion? Come to me. Get away with me and you'll recover your life. I'll show you how to take a real rest. Walk with me and work with me—watch how I do it. Learn the unforced rhythms of grace. I won't lay anything heavy or ill-fitting on you. Keep company with me and you'll learn to live freely and lightly' (Matthew 11:28-30). We invite you to come take a sacred journey."

Hannah stopped reading. The words from *The Message* paraphrase gripped her, bringing a well-known passage to new life. Tired? Worn out? Burned out? Steve had answered for her: yes, yes, yes.

And Jesus offered an invitation to the weary: Come. Get away. Walk with me. Work with me. Watch. Learn. Keep company. Live freely and lightly.

*Come take a sacred journey.*

With a cup of tea in hand, Hannah settled onto the couch to pray. As she tried to focus her thoughts, however, she realized it wasn't just the stress of packing or the three hour drive from Chicago that had worn her out. She was tired. Truly tired. Fifteen-years-of-uninterrupted-ministry tired.

Before the tea was gone, Hannah was asleep.

## Charissa

*The eighth grade honors math teacher always returned tests the same way: highest scores first. On the day he returned Charissa Goodman's test second, there was a collective gasp in the room. He raised his eyebrows and handed an externally composed Charissa her exam. "First time for everything, eh? Not so perfect on this one."*

*Charissa stiffened and sat even more uprightly in her chair. Sensing the riveted gaze of her classmates, she scanned the paper for red. There it was—a ridiculous mistake she hadn't caught in her double- and triple-checking. How could she have missed that? She took the offending paper and slid it out of view into her binder.*

*She would have to be more careful next time.*

John Sinclair arrived at the Kingsbury University library right before eight o'clock, just in time to meet Charissa after her evening class. He had spent the past two hours at their apartment, carefully preparing his wife's favorite meal: lemon herbed chicken with tomato and feta salad. He had even stopped by the bakery after work to pick up a fresh loaf of focaccia. Wednesdays were long days for Charissa, so John always tried to do something special for her when she got home.

As he watched her approach the car, he couldn't suppress a low whistling, exhaled breath. Even from a distance Charissa was strikingly beautiful: her flawless Mediterranean olive skin, her sculpted figure, her silky jet-black hair. Everything about Charissa Goodman was perfect. Absolutely perfect. People were often surprised that John and Charissa were married. He was so "boy next door" with his thin brown hair and small brown eyes—the type of guy whose high school yearbook was filled with inscriptions about his "sweet personality" and "great sense of humor." Charissa, on the other hand, turned heads wherever she went. It wasn't just her statuesque beauty that attracted attention. She had a certain grace about her, carrying herself with practiced poise.

John's friends had discouraged him from even attempting to get a date with her when the two of them first met as sophomores at Kingsbury University. "The Ice Princess doesn't condescend to anybody," they warned him. "Give it up, John."

But John had never been one to give up. Though he hadn't been granted his desire for an athlete's body, he had the heart and determination of an Olympic champion; and he had been determined to make Charissa Goodman laugh. Even the Ice Princess eventually thawed in the warmth of John's good humor.

He grinned as he called through the open car window. "Hey, gorgeous! Want a ride?" Charissa tossed her bag of books into the backseat and then slid in beside him. "How about a kiss for the guy who loves you?" he asked, leaning toward her.

She kissed him on the cheek. "Sorry. Distracted."

"I can tell. What's up?"

"You know that Saturday morning class I mentioned to you?"

John nodded as he turned left out of the parking lot. "Yeah. What did Dr. Allen say about it? Is it safe?"

She laughed. "He says I'm already surrounded by heretics."

"Cool! I'd love to meet some! We can have them over for dinner, now that we actually have a table. I'll even cook."

"You always cook."

"Well, we need to eat. Hey! Ouch!" He beamed as Charissa punched his arm playfully. "I'm only saying you have different gifts, honey. Great intellectual gifts, just not culinary ones." She pretended to pout. "So," he continued, "is it worth giving up two Saturday mornings a month? And before you answer, remember that class competes against my famous chocolate chip pancakes."

"I know. I'm counting the cost." She fiddled with her long dark hair. "Anyway, Dr. Allen asked me why I was interested in going. I said, 'To learn.' And he stared at me with those penetrating eyes and said, 'Wrong answer.'"

"My wife? Wrong answer? Impossible. Gimme his phone number."

"John!"

"Sorry, Riss. Go ahead. I'm listening. Really."

She sighed. "He said if I went for any reason other than encountering God, then I was going for the wrong reason. And I can't stop thinking about it. I mean—he's the one who told us we needed to find something to supplement his class. And if the goal of all of this isn't learning, then I don't get it. I just don't get it."

John had spent the first year of their married life trying to perfect his Greek mother-in-law's recipes, and he was becoming increasingly proficient in the kitchen.

"Well, what do you think of my lemon chicken?" he asked, watching Charissa from across the candlelit table.

"Mom would be impressed. It was great, John. Thanks." While he cleared away dishes, she went to her backpack and pulled out her laptop and some books. Flipping on the overhead light, she seated herself at the table again and began to work.

"Can I get you anything?" he called as he loaded the dishwasher. She was so focused, she didn't hear him. He came out from the kitchen and stood behind her, wrapping his arms around her. "Need anything?" he asked, kissing her neck. She shook her head and kept typing as he massaged her shoulders. "You're tense," he commented, pressing his fingers more firmly into her smooth skin. "I've got a remedy for that, if you're interested." He breathed in the citrus fragrance of her hair.

She spoke without looking at him. "I'm totally swamped. I'm already going to be pulling an all-nighter just to get this paper finished by tomorrow morning." He gently released her.

"I know," said John. "The work of a grad student, right? It's never done." He kissed the top of her head before he blew out the candles.

When Charissa finished her Shakespeare paper at 4 a.m., she was far too caffeinated to sleep. Since it was too dark to take her morning power walk, she started cleaning. Cleaning was one of her favorite forms of stress relief, and she cleaned frequently.

She had promised their irascible neighbors she would only vacuum between 9 a.m. and 9 p.m. Not that there was much to sweep: only a small family room and dining area off the kitchen, one bedroom, and a narrow hallway. But Charissa often said that a carpet swept in a precise sawtooth pattern did wonders for her mental health. Sometimes she vacuumed twice a day.

Because it was too early for carpets, she blitzed the pantry. Organizing shelves was not a high priority for John, and since he did all their cooking, the pantry rapidly deteriorated into disorder. At least once a week she imposed her will: cereal boxes in descending height, spices in alphabetical sequence, grains and pasta grouped by color.

"A place for everything and everything in its place."

That was Charissa's rule of life. If she hadn't decided to become a professor of literature, she would have excelled as a personal manager. She had never understood how people tolerated chaos.

While she segregated the tomato, Alfredo, and barbecue sauces, she pressed the replay button on Dr. Allen's rebuke. Wrong answer. Wrong answer. Wrong answer. Why was "learning" the wrong answer?

Charissa hated being corrected. Usually she managed to correct herself before anyone else had the opportunity. And now Dr. Allen—whose good opinion was crucial to her academic success—had offered a mysterious reproach instead of his customary praise. She couldn't fathom what he had meant. She also wasn't going to ask for clarification. Charissa rarely called attention to her ignorance by asking anyone for help. She would simply go to the class and fulfill his recommendations for the semester.

She finished ordering the chaos, picked a piece of stray fluff off the carpet, and tried to decide what else she could clean before her regularly scheduled quiet time.

## *Mara*

Mara Garrison took a mug of peppermint tea from Dawn and eased her plus-sized body into the familiar armchair. What pounds of pain should she talk about today?

Every month she sat in Dawn's counseling office, going round and round on the same issues. Trust. Shame. Rejection. Self-worth.

Circles. She was walking in circles.

"I feel stuck," Mara said, shaking her head. "I feel totally stuck. It's like I understand how I ended up here, but I don't know how to move forward. I'm fifty years old, and I'm starting to wonder if I'm ever gonna get anywhere."

"You've come such a long way, Mara. Truly."

Dawn was always so encouraging. Mara wished she had a friend like Dawn—someone she could sit and share a cup of tea with, without having to write a check at the end of the visit. Dawn knew Mara more intimately than anyone had ever known her. The only thing Mara knew about Dawn, however, was that she had two beautiful, brown-eyed, ebony-skinned daughters who looked just like her: Kendra and Essence. Mara knew them from the smiling photos on Dawn's desk. Such lovely girls.

*Essence.* Mara wondered if her life would have been different if she'd had a name like Essence. *Essence Payne Garrison.*

Probably not. She supposed she would have been teased and rejected with that name too.

*Mara Payne.* She had always disliked her last name, enduring its cruelty for thirty-five years before marrying out of it. Of course, by marrying Tom Garrison she had just exchanged one kind of pain for another. But she wasn't going to talk about Tom today. She was tired of talking about Tom.

"You've done the hard work of exploring the reasons behind some of your struggles," Dawn was saying. "Maybe now there's a deeper level of faith and spirituality for you to explore—an opportunity for you to lean not on your own understanding, but to trust God in a new way."

Mara ran her index finger round and round the rim of the mug. Circles, circles, circles.

"I'm actually glad you're this frustrated," Dawn said.

Mara stopped circling. "Whaddya mean?"

This wasn't what Dawn usually said. Usually Dawn tried to convince her that her circles were ascending spirals up a mountain, not endless cycles leading nowhere. Usually Dawn tried to help her see that just because she was revisiting an issue didn't mean she had gone backwards. She was simply viewing it from another vantage point, from higher up the mountain.

"You've reached a place of holy discontent," Dawn said. "The frustration you're feeling can actually be a gift to nudge you toward something deeper. I'm hearing restlessness in you, and restlessness is movement. You may feel stuck, but your spirit is moving."

"But I feel agitated, not peaceful. I thought the Christian life was all about peace and joy, and I don't have it. I swear I must be doing something wrong."

Dawn leaned forward in her chair. "Agitation is also God's gift to us, Mara, strange as that sounds. Imagine yourself standing in a doorway, at a threshold. Your discontent can move you out of the old and into the new. When you reach the end of yourself and say, 'I'm tired of living this way. I want something more!' then God is there, helping you to let go and move forward. Does that make sense?"

Mara thought carefully. "I just want peace," she finally said, chewing on what was left of a fingernail.

"What is peace?" Dawn asked.

*I know, I know.*

They'd had this conversation many times, and Mara knew the script by heart. Dawn would remind her that peace wasn't the absence of conflict, but the presence of God in the midst of the storm. Dawn would tell her that peace wasn't dependent on her circumstances—that true peace was about wholeness and being at one with God. Dawn would say that peace was a gift, the fruit of intimacy with Christ, flowing out of God's love for her.

Though Mara understood what peace was, she had never *known* it.

"I'm tired," she breathed. "Tired of the constant battling. I just want a rest."

Dawn sat a long time without saying anything, and Mara wondered what she was thinking. Maybe Dawn was finally giving up on her too. Maybe she was hopeless.

She stared at her shoes and braced herself for the verdict.

Dawn stood up and went to her desk, pulling out a plum-colored pamphlet from a stack of papers. "You've heard me mention some of the groups and programs at the New Hope Center," she said, handing the paper to Mara. "They offer what they call a 'sacred journey' group, exploring ways to encounter God. A group like that would give you a place to connect with other people walking the same kind of spiritual path. I think it might be a good thing for you to do."

Mara skimmed the description quickly, looking for a reason to say no.

> The sacred journey is a pilgrimage for those who are thirsty for more of God. This journey is for all those who are dissatisfied with living on the surface and who want to travel deeper into God's heart. We invite you to come and explore spiritual disciplines as we seek to create sacred space for God.

Mara stopped reading. There. She'd found it. "I hate the word *discipline,*" she said. "I already feel guilty, and I haven't even gone yet."

"I know," said Dawn. "Lots of people have the same reaction. But spiritual disciplines aren't laws or rules to follow. They're tools that help us create space in our lives so God can work within us. We can't transform ourselves. That's God's work, by God's grace. But disciplines help us cooperate with the work of the Spirit."

Mara communicated her cynicism with a frown.

"Think of it this way, Mara. We don't have the power to make the sun rise, but we can choose to be awake when it happens. Spiritual disciplines help us stay awake."

Mara kept examining the flyer, looking for more reasons to say no. Over the years she had completed plenty of personal Bible studies and had the workbooks to prove it. Even though she knew she didn't want another fill-in-the-blank, do-it-yourself study, she wasn't sure she was ready to explore her spiritual life with other people. "I'm not sure about the group thing," she confessed.

"Why?"

"Because at least by doing things on my own, no one has the chance to reject me." There. She'd said it.

"Look how far you've already come," Dawn said gently. "You've been able to disclose lots of things you'd never been able to talk about before, and I haven't rejected you."

Mara smiled slightly. "I pay you not to reject me." She reached into her oversized bag for a tissue.

"Mara, I wouldn't recommend this group if you weren't ready for something more. This kind of group is a first step toward deeper things. This is a group where you have anonymity. You're free to disclose what you want. But at least you'd be walking the path with others. You can't keep living on your own, Mara. It's not good for you to be alone. And you've been alone for most of your life, even when you've been with other people."

Dawn was right. Mara surrounded herself with people who didn't know her: casual acquaintances who shared common interests, people she met at the boys' extra-curricular activities, even friends at church. Mara had constructed a persona that functioned reasonably well. But deep within her defenses was a little girl who was terrified that if other people discovered who she really was, they would walk away.

She left Dawn's office not sure what to do. Yes, she was captive to her fears, but at least her captivity was familiar. What would she discover if she stepped through the doorway into the unknown? Was her discontent strong enough to propel her forward? More than that, did she actually trust God enough to let go of the past and stride into something new?

She didn't know. She honestly didn't know.

Mara waited until the boys had gone upstairs to finish homework on Thursday night before she tried to broach the subject of the New Hope group with Tom. He had arrived home early from his business trip, and he seemed to be in a relatively decent mood.

"Dawn gave me some information about a group at the New Hope Retreat Center," she said casually, spooning leftover mashed potatoes into a plastic container.

He didn't look up from his *Sports Illustrated.*

She finished putting away the food and then tried again. "When I saw Dawn this week, she recommended a group for me. She thought it might be helpful."

He continued to read. "What's that gonna cost?" he asked. Mara had known he'd be interested in that detail.

"It's by donation."

"How much?" He still wasn't looking at her.

"I don't know. Whatever someone wants to give, I guess. It goes to support the ministries there."

He turned a page. "Then why don't you chuck the counseling and go with the freebie?"

They'd had this argument before about the cost of her counseling appointments. Tom had never understood why Mara needed to pay someone to listen to her.

"Seeing Dawn helps me keep everything together." She hoped that Kevin and Brian weren't eavesdropping.

"Keep what together? It's not like you've got a particularly rough life. Look around you." He waved his hand around their newly remodeled kitchen, expanded to accommodate two teenage boys. "There are people in this world who have real things to complain about, you know."

She stared into the gleaming sink, chewed her nail, and counted to ten.

Tom wouldn't refuse to pay for the group. He would just make her feel guilty for needing it. Or rather, as Dawn often said, Mara would choose to respond to Tom by feeling guilty.

She grabbed a pint of double fudge brownie ice cream from the freezer before retreating to their bedroom, where she soothed herself with her tonic of choice: reality television. Watching other people's drama and conflicts usually made her feel much better about her own.

Usually.

## *Meg*

*Meg Fowler soared as she hurried home from school. Jim Crane had asked her to the Valentine's Day Dance! She had been saving her babysitting money for months, hoping he would ask, hoping she'd have enough to buy a dress. THE dress. The most beautiful gown she had ever seen: sky blue chiffon, just off the shoulders, with airy ruffles at the neckline. When the weekend came, she begged her mother to take her to VanKammen's Department Store so she could try it on.*

*Meg eyed herself approvingly in the dressing room mirror, twirling this way and that. The gown was even prettier than she'd remembered, a perfect complement to her blonde hair and fair complexion. Beaming, she floated down the hallway to show her mother.*

*"That's the dress you've been fussing about?" Mother asked, frowning. "You cer-*

*tainly don't have the figure for that. Of course, it's your money. Do what you want."*

*Meg returned to the dressing room, removed the gown, and put it back on the rack.*

Meg almost threw the New Hope flyer away. Instead, it landed on the kitchen counter with a pile of other things she didn't know what to do with. Passivity was her instinctive way of decision-making, especially when she felt overwhelmed. If she just waited long enough, decisions would be made for her.

But no matter what pile she put it in, the plum-colored paper kept catching her eye, beckoning her with its simple invitation: "Come take a sacred journey."

Although Rachel, her older sister, wasn't particularly religious, Meg finally called and asked her for advice. "Well, you need to do something for yourself, Megs," Rachel said. "With Mother gone, you're rattling around alone inside that big old house. Besides, I know you don't have piano students on Saturday mornings. What's your excuse?"

Meg pondered those words long after she hung up the phone. "There are good reasons and real reasons," Pastor Dave was fond of saying. Meg had run out of good reasons. And the real reason?

She was afraid.

But Rachel wouldn't understand that, so Meg didn't try to explain. She was tired of trying to explain. This was one of the many arguments she simply could not win. Rachel had always been the fearless, adventurous one, off exploring faraway places with delight in the unknown and the exotic. Rachel was the daughter with wings. Meg was the daughter with roots.

Meg had always been the one with roots.

The one time she had spread her wings, she hadn't flown far from home. Meg married her high school sweetheart, and they moved into a house two miles away. For six and a half years she was Mrs. Jim Crane, and life was blissfully happy. Then on a gray and grimacing November afternoon, when Meg was seven months pregnant with Becca, a stranger's voice on the telephone brought news that obliterated her. *So sorry to have to tell you. Your husband. Highway accident. Ambulance. St. Luke's Hospital. Mrs. Crane? Hello?* Meg didn't get to the hospital in time to say good-bye.

That night she packed as much as she could carry of her life with Jim into two suitcases, locked the front door, and staggered back to her mother's house. Six weeks later she was at St Luke's again, giving birth to their daughter on Christmas Eve.

For months after the accident, Meg was a stranger to herself. No longer "Jim's wife," she had to learn how to be "Becca's mom." Most nights she cried herself to sleep after Mother went to bed. Though Mother had been widowed when Meg was only four, she had no patience for tears and did not tolerate self-pity. "I never had the luxury of feeling sorry for myself," she often scolded Meg. "And neither do you. You've got a baby to take care of. You're going to have to be a grown-up and move on."

So Meg had wept in secret.

Now, more than twenty years later, the disequilibrium of grief had returned for another season, even bleaker, harsher, and more annihilating than before. Mother was gone. Becca was gone. And Jim was back.

After years of silent absence, Jim was with her again in dreams. As Meg slept, her subconscious mind raised him from the dead, and she only had the power to bury him when she was awake. Even that power was weakening. New grief had moved the immovable, breaking the seal on her old sorrow and rolling away the stone she had tightly lodged against the tomb of her memories. Now Jim leapt forth into resurrected life, always just beyond her reach. She could not follow. She could not hold him. And she didn't have the strength to miss him again. *Please, Lord, don't make me miss him again.* At least Becca was away in England. Meg wouldn't want her daughter to know about her torment or her tears.

So she wept in secret.

"You're forty-six, Megs," Rachel reminded her on the phone one night. "It's time to figure out who you are when you're not being Ruth Fowler's daughter. Go to the group. And for cryin' out loud, get a pet or something, will you?"

Meg knew her heartache was far more complicated than her mother's absence, even if Rachel didn't understand. Her grief was deeper than the loss of her identity as "daughter." Mother's death had simply been the crowbar, prying open an old box of sorrow.

*Time to figure out who you are.*

Maybe Sandy and Rachel were right. Maybe it was time to venture beyond the walls of her lonely house. Maybe it was time for a sacred journey after all.

If only she could find a way to put one foot in front of the other.

2

# The Pilgrimage Begins

*Blessed are those whose strength is in you,*
*whose hearts are set on pilgrimage.*
*As they pass through the Valley of Baka,*
*they make it a place of springs;*
*the autumn rains also cover it with pools.*
*They go from strength to strength,*
*till each appears before God in Zion.*

Psalm 84:5-7

## New Hope

When Meg arrived at the New Hope Retreat Center on the second Saturday of September, she instinctively looked for the parking space farthest away from the building entrance. After circling a bit, she chose a spot partially shielded by small shrubs. *Help,* she breathed, turning off the ignition. Her hand was on her seatbelt, half poised to remove it, half clinging to it for security. From her semi-secluded vantage point, she watched a small group of people gather outside the main entrance. She wondered if any of them had wrestled with demons that morning. The sacred journey hadn't even started, and she was already exhausted.

"Just remember the old saying," Rachel had told her. "'A journey of a thousand miles begins with a single step.'"

As Meg stared at the ivy-covered brick building, she tried to rouse enough courage simply to walk one hundred yards across the parking lot. *Help, God, please,* she prayed. Though her high heels clicked a steady tempo on the pavement, her insubordinate heart raced uncontrollably. By the time she reached the portico, her chest was pounding in her ears.

A tiny, silver-haired and round-faced woman greeted her at the door. "Welcome! I'm Katherine Rhodes," she said, extending both her hands. Meg was expecting a flimsy, delicate handshake from the five-foot-nothing sprite—not a firm, steadying, two-handed grip. This was a woman of sturdy resolve, like Meg's mother. But unlike Ruth Fowler, who had been determinedly wintry, Katherine radiated summery warmth. "Are you here for the sacred journey group?" Katherine asked.

"Yes," Meg squeaked. She felt her face flush with color. Why was her face always hot when her hands were always cold?

"So glad you're here," Katherine said. "Just make your way to the end of the hallway and turn right. And help yourself to coffee and bagels."

Meg ducked into a restroom off the hallway, relieved to see she was alone. Scrutinizing herself in the mirror, she turned this way and that. No use. Each angle merely gave her new inspiration to find fault. She experimented with pulling her shoulder length blonde curls away from her face, but that was too open. The red blotches were still visible on her neck. So she let her hair down again, opting to shield herself with a veil.

And what about her skirt and blouse? Too dressy? Katherine and the others had been casually dressed. What if she discovered she was the only one in church clothes? She licked her finger and rubbed it feverishly over a small black spot on her sleeve, becoming increasingly irritated with herself.

When a woman wearing jeans and a sweatshirt opened the door, Meg knew she had run out of time to make herself right. There would be no pleasing her clamoring inner critic today, no quieting Mother's voice inside her head. Or was it her own voice? She wasn't even sure anymore.

The sunlit, sage green room was filling slowly with casually dressed people when Meg entered. She scanned the desk for her name tag, then made her way to the far back corner table near an artificial ficus tree and an exit door. She wondered if anyone had noticed her hand trembling when she scribbled an illegible signature on the group roster.

She felt sick to her stomach.

What in the world had she been thinking, signing up for something like this? She should have signed up for a women's Bible study at the church instead. At least she would have recognized people there. But this? If she hadn't been so eager to please her pastor and his wife, she wouldn't have come. Meg wasn't sure which would be more painful: disappointing them or giving herself an ulcer. She reached for her purse and was about to take flight when someone approached the table, cutting off her escape route.

"Mind if I sit with you? I like back corners too." The heavy-set woman winked conspiratorially. "Makes it easier for me to watch everything that's going on."

*Makes it easier for me to run to the bathroom if I need to throw up,* Meg answered. But only to herself. She forced a smile and motioned to the empty seat next to her.

"Thanks," the newcomer replied, setting down her coffee mug, a bagel, and an oversized embroidered bag. Clothed in loud floral prints and bold, jangling accessories, she had the appearance of a free-spirited non-conformist. Even her short, wavy hair was colorful: reddish brown with brash copper highlights.

*Wish I could wear bright colors with confidence,* Meg thought, looking down at her tan skirt.

The woman exhaled slowly as she squeezed her matronly figure into the seat. "These chairs aren't built for large women, are they?" she commented dryly, observing Meg's petite frame. "Not that you've got that problem." She extended a steady hand. "I'm Mara Garrison."

"Meg. Meg Crane. Sorry for the cold hands." Meg's voice was barely above a whisper.

"Warm heart, I bet," Mara said, fiddling with her colorful bangles and large-beaded necklaces. Was that a tattoo on her wrist? Meg couldn't tell for sure and didn't want to stare. "So, Meg—you ready for a 'sacred journey'?" Meg shrugged and managed a weak smile. "I'm not sure either," Mara went on, reaching into her bag. "But a friend thought I needed this, so here I am. How 'bout you? How'd you find out about it?"

"I . . . um . . . " Meg felt color rushing to her face. If only she had worn a turtleneck. But it was still too warm for turtlenecks. "My pastor's wife recommended it because it helped her after her mom died. And she thought maybe it would help me now that my mother's gone." Too much. She'd said too much. She hadn't planned on revealing herself. Now she was going to cry. She bit her lip and willed back the tears.

Mara stopped putting on her bright red lipstick and looked up from her compact mirror. "Oh, I'm sorry," she said, offering a tender look of compassion that threatened Meg's already fragile nervous system.

"Excuse me," Meg mumbled. She grabbed her purse and slipped quickly out the exit door, leaving her Bible behind.

Mara wasn't sure if Meg had left for the restroom, or if she intended to go home. *Poor thing.* Meg looked as anxious on the outside as Mara felt on the inside. Instead of running after her with the Bible, Mara decided it might be good if Meg had a reason to come back. For Meg's sake.

No. For her own sake.

If Meg didn't return, Mara might end up all by herself at the back corner table, and there was nothing lonelier than being by yourself in a room full of people. She knew that from experience.

She broke off a piece of her cinnamon raisin bagel and chewed slowly, surveying her fellow travelers. Most of the thirty pilgrims were women. A few twentysomething guys with backpacks stood near the front, drinking out of water bottles and chatting comfortably. Several couples sat close together, arms draped loosely around one another's shoulders. Mara wondered if the men had come willingly. And if they actually wanted to be there, did those women appreciate the blessing they'd been given? Or did they take their spiritual partnerships for granted?

Mara tried to squash her feelings of envy, but she couldn't help herself. She had spent years wishing Tom would show the faintest interest in spiritual things. Years. But the harder she prayed, the more resistant he seemed to become. So she walked the road of faith alone. Always alone.

At that moment Meg returned to the table, looking sheepish. Mara wasn't sure if she had come back to pick up her Bible or to sit down. Meg seemed uncertain too, with one hand hovering over the Bible and one hand touching the back of the chair.

"Welcome, everyone! I'm Katherine Rhodes."

Meg plunged into her seat, gripping her purse tightly.

"I'm noticing we've got a few tables without many people," Katherine said, scanning the room. "I'm wondering if a couple of you would be willing to move to that back table in the corner, and maybe another couple to the table up front here. Let's aim for four or five per table. Then go ahead and take the next few minutes to introduce yourselves. Maybe say why you're here."

Mara watched as two women approached their table from the opposite side of the room. One was tall and sylphlike, elegant in a plum top, black denim jeans, and gold hoop earrings. She looked like she had stepped off the front cover of a magazine—the sort of magazine whose airbrushed women taunted Mara with tips for sexually satisfying men, keeping fit, and maintaining youthful skin. Mara preferred magazines offering real-life glimpses of celebrities with cellulite.

She had long ago given up any hope of satisfying Tom or keeping fit. As for maintaining youthful skin, her cupboards overflowed with anti-aging, wrinkle-firming, collagen-enhancing, antioxidant-ing products. She was determined to preserve by rigorous regimen the only physical asset for which she had ever been commended: Mara had "nice skin." Though she knew it was the sort of compliment people often offered to overweight women, Mara did have a dewy soft complexion that invited speculation about what her skin care secrets might be. Someone had also once told her that she had "lovely feet." But in a world obsessed with faces and figures, beautiful feet didn't get you very far.

As she observed the covergirl's diamond wedding ring and glossy manicure, Mara suddenly felt very self-conscious over her nail-bitten stubs. She closed her left hand into a fist to hide the offending fingers and tried not to think about all the other pretty and privileged girls who had made her life miserable. The rich, stuck-up, judgmental—

*Stop it!* she commanded herself. *You don't even know her. She hasn't spoken a single word, and you're already judging her.*

Why, why, why? Why, after all these years, why did those same buttons still get pushed?

She wished the nine-year-old girl who lived inside her menopausal body would just grow up.

Trying hard to ignore the olive-skinned beauty, Mara eyed the other newcomer. She was about Mara's height—maybe five-five or five-six—but she was average weight, without any visible curves. Nothing about her attracted attention: no color, no makeup, and no jewelry, except for a cross necklace. It required a certain measure of courage not to fuss over a middle-aged face, and Mara supposed she was either confident in her unremarkable, simple features or one of those rare women who simply couldn't be bothered to fret about her appearance.

She certainly didn't seem to fret about her hair. Her chin length, light brown hair was damp, hanging limply around her face. Mara decided she could benefit from a few layers and a blow-dryer—and perhaps some overall color and highlighting to conceal the streaks of gray.

The woman's wrinkles were prominent, aging her face. She wore the brow of a deep thinker. Or a worrier. Or maybe both. And her dark eyes were ringed with weariness. Mara had never seen such dark circles. Beyond the weariness, however, was a knowing look which would have been unnerving if not combined with soft gentleness. There was something trustworthy and true in her eyes that invited confidence, even secrets.

Or maybe it was Mara's imagination. Maybe it was the cross she wore that made Mara instinctively trust her. She had never seen a cross like it—fashioned from nails and dangling from a black cord. She couldn't help staring at it.

The woman met her gaze and smiled. Mara liked her.

"Hi, I'm Hannah Shepley." She looked at Mara's name tag. "Nice to meet you, Mara . . . and Meg . . . and . . . sorry—I can't quite see your tag."

"Charissa Sinclair," The Model replied.

"Charissa?" Mara repeated. "Haven't heard that name before. It's pretty."

It figured. She even got the glamorous name. Maybe she had made it up. Did real people actually have names like *Charissa Sinclair*? Mara watched her pull a laptop out of her backpack and tried not to feel resentful.

"So, why don't we each say a little bit about why we're here?" Hannah suggested, folding her hands in front of her as if she were getting ready to pray.

Meg lowered her eyes. Charissa turned off her cell phone. The rest of the room was buzzing with indiscernible conversation.

"I'll go ahead," Mara offered, glancing around the table as she cleared her throat. "I'm Mara. Mara Garrison. I'm married and have three boys. Brian is thirteen, Kevin is fifteen, and Jeremy is thirty with a baby on the way. Don't know how that happened. Time passing, I mean, not the baby part." She giggled with a kind of chortling unrestraint that always embarrassed the boys and amused her friends.

Hannah grinned while Charissa shifted in her seat.

Mara continued, "So anyway, I've been feeling totally stuck in all sorts of areas of my life. I've never done Bible studies or prayer stuff in a group before, and I'm pretty nervous about being here. Don't know what to expect, you know? But my therapist suggested that this group might help me dump some of my junk, so here I am. Ready or not."

Crap. Had she just said that out loud? What was wrong with her? "TMI, Mom," the boys would say. Way Too Much Information. Charissa was regarding her with scrunched up eyebrows.

The Model probably didn't have a therapist.

Hannah's voice broke the awkward silence. "I'm sure you're not alone in that, Mara. We've all got burdens we need to unload so we can travel more 'freely and lightly' with Jesus, right?"

Mara inwardly thanked her, grateful for the effort to ease her discomfort. Maybe she had a therapist too.

"I guess I'll go next," Hannah said. Charissa was concentrating on her computer screen, and Meg was gazing longingly at the exit door. "I'm Hannah. I'm up here from Chicago, staying at a friend's cottage at the lake for the next nine months." Charissa raised her eyebrows, and Mara wondered if Hannah were an unwed mother, seeking anonymity. Maybe that's why she looked so weary and sad.

"Are you a writer?" asked Charissa.

*Huh,* thought Mara. *That never would have occurred to me. Shows you where my mind goes.*

Hannah smiled wryly. "No. I'm a pastor who's been forced against my will to take a long sabbatical in an absolutely gorgeous place. And I don't have a clue what to do with it."

That explained the weariness, then. Compassion had carved the indelible lines on her forehead. She wore a pastor's brow.

"Have you got family with you?" asked Mara, embarrassed over imagining her with a therapist or a love child. *Too many tabloid magazines.*

"No," Hannah replied. "No family nearby, anyway. My folks live in Oregon, and my brother and his family live in New York, and I landed in the middle. That's about it. Just waiting to see what God has for me."

Though Hannah's lips formed a smile, Mara noticed her smile didn't light her eyes. Those dark, tired, sorrowful eyes. Mara wondered what her story was. What kind of woman wouldn't want a long rest in a lakeside cottage? She wished she could have a sabbatical from a husband and teenagers. She wouldn't need nine months. She would be happy with a few weeks of not having to take care of anyone but herself. Pure bliss.

She looked at Hannah and tried not to feel jealous.

Charissa's voice interrupted her wandering thoughts. "I'm Charissa Sinclair. My husband, John, and I celebrated our first anniversary last month." The others murmured their congratulations. "Thanks. I'm currently working on my Ph.D. in English literature at Kingsbury University. I've always had a passion for learning, and when I saw the flyer for this class, it looked interesting. One of my professors knows the director, and he highly recommended it."

Great, Mara thought. Beautiful *and* smart. What if she was surrounded by really smart, super-spiritual people? Did anybody else have as much baggage as she did? Anybody? Everybody seemed so put together. Well, almost everybody. Meg looked pretty freaked out. But a pastor and a Ph.D. student? If Mara had known it would be like this, she wouldn't have come. She was obviously in way over her head. What was Dawn thinking?

*Help.*

Katherine's voice spoke above the noise of animated conversations in the room. "Go ahead and start wrapping up," she said.

"How about you, Meg?" Hannah asked. "Don't want to leave you out."

Mara saw Meg swallow hard. "Not much to tell," Meg's soprano voice quivered. "I've got one daughter, Becca, who is spending her junior year abroad in England right now. She's a literature major."

Mara felt strangely comforted as she watched a red band of fear become a choke chain around Meg's neck. At least Mara could conceal her fingernails. Meg was a neon billboard for anxiety.

*Poor thing.*

"Glad you're here, Meg," Hannah said.

*Bless her heart,* Mara thought.

Just then Katherine extended both her hands and invited everyone to bow their heads to pray. Closing her eyes, Mara wondered if Meg would still be there when she opened them again.

Katherine's voice had the gentle, soothing flow of rippling water as she led the group through a Scripture meditation as part of their opening prayer. "I'm going to read a text from the beginning of Mark's gospel," Katherine said. "As you listen, imagine you're part of the story. What do you see? Hear? Feel? Where are you in the story? Then simply sit with God and pray through what you noticed."

Mara listened with eyes closed while Katherine read. Jesus was beside the Sea of Galilee, calling disciples to follow him. Mara imagined herself on the beach, watching from a distance, a warm breeze on her face and sunlight in her eyes.

"Follow me," Jesus was saying to the others.

Mara watched with envy, aching to be one of the Chosen Ones. She witnessed their joy as they got up, one by one, and left work behind. They dropped nets and waved good-bye to family and friends, their faces full of light and life.

Bitter tears stung her eyes as the scene unfolded in her mind. Jesus was not going to choose her. He was going to pass by and keep on walking. Mara couldn't bear to watch him leave with the others, so she stared at her feet.

Suddenly, there was a touch on her shoulder. She looked up, and she was face to face with Jesus. He was smiling. She had never seen a smile quite like it—welcoming her into his circle of light. "Mara, come with me," he said. "I choose you. Come walk with me."

Immediately, Mara saw how much she was carrying. She was surrounded by trunks, bags, suitcases. How could she follow him?

Jesus grinned. "Just leave it," he said, chuckling. And the chuckle crescendoed to the most lyrical laughter she had ever heard. He threw back his head, looked to the sky, and exclaimed, "Thank you, Father!" Then he took her hand, and they walked away together.

Mara pressed her palms firmly against her eyes to drive back the onslaught of emotion. She had never experienced anything like that before. Of course, she had never imagined herself in a Bible story before. So what was she to make of it? She certainly didn't trust her imagination. She had simply projected her own wishful thinking and longing for attention onto the text. *Right?* It was like a waking dream—some kind of processing of her subconscious thoughts and hopes. Or maybe the result of reading too many romance novels, imagining herself being loved and chosen by the hero.

But it had seemed so real. If only it had been true. *If only . . .*

She reached into her bag and fumbled around for a tissue, trying not to disturb anyone with her sniffling. A light touch on her shoulder, however, revealed she had already given herself away.

Hannah was offering her a pack of tissues and a pastor's smile.

Hannah's thoughts were clamoring so loudly in the hovering silence, she wouldn't have been at all surprised if someone had overheard.

Mara. Something was going on with Mara. Why was she crying?

Hannah hoped Mara wasn't upset about revealing she had a therapist. Though Hannah had tried to soothe the palpable tension at the table, one didn't need to be an expert in the subtleties of body language to interpret Charissa's reaction. Her stiffened posture and cocked eyebrows had spoken volumes of disapproval. *Poor Mara.* She didn't seem the type to be reckless or nonchalant about personal disclosures. Her crimson blush after her confession revealed that her lips had spoken without her mind's consent. *Help her, Lord.*

And Meg. *Poor Meg.* Hannah tried to catch a covert glimpse of her, but Meg had drawn her blonde curls like curtains around her face, and Hannah couldn't see anything. *Please help Meg, Lord. Please give her peace.*

Katherine's voice broke the stillness of the room and momentarily silenced Hannah's internal noise. "The psalmist sings to God, 'Blessed are those whose strength is in you, whose hearts are set on pilgrimage.'" Katherine was smiling warmly as she looked out at the group. "It's a joy to welcome each one of you to a sacred journey."

Hannah scanned the room, wondering about the circumstances that had brought each of her fellow travelers to this place. Transition? Loss? A desire for a deeper life with God?

Hannah had come because of Nancy's prompting and encouragement. "I left that New Hope flyer for you on purpose," Nancy had said when the two of them spoke earlier in the week. "It's a bit of a drive from the cottage—maybe forty minutes or so. But I loved the prayer group I went to over the summer, and some of the women were telling me about the sacred journey group. It just sounds like it would be a wonderful experience. I'd like to do it someday. Maybe next summer."

"Have you met the facilitator?" Hannah had asked.

"A couple of times. Katherine seemed like a really neat woman—she just had this soothing sort of presence, without having to say too much."

Though Hannah had tried to gather information about Katherine Rhodes, her Internet search yielded nothing except a few entries about Katherine's position as director at the retreat center. Hannah did find a discussion forum on the New Hope website, however, where a number of people had commented on their experiences in the sacred journey groups. The testimonies intrigued her:

"The sacred journey helped me understand and navigate the landscape of my inner world so that I could walk more closely with God."

"I started to see the things that move me toward God and away from God."

"I grew, not only in intimacy with Christ, but in intimacy with my own self."

"I learned new ways to be with the God who is always with me."

Perhaps the sacred journey was an opportunity for Hannah to learn how to lead a new kind of spiritual formation group at Westminster—something other than the Bible studies and small groups she had been coordinating for so long. It had been years since she had enrolled in any kind of continuing education for herself, and maybe this was a chance to sharpen her own pastoral skills so she would have more to offer others. She could go back to Westminster even better equipped for the work of ministry. If she was going to be forced to rest, at least her resting could be productive.

Very productive.

Hearing Katherine's voice shift into a storytelling mode, Hannah tuned in to listen. "I have a three-year-old granddaughter named Morgan who is a little butterfly of a girl," Katherine was saying. "She loves to talk—she chatters constantly—especially when she's in her car seat. She's always telling my daughter, Sarah, to look at things. And Sarah will often respond rather absent-mindedly, 'Yes, honey, I see!' or 'Wow, Morgan, that's great!'

"One morning last week, while Sarah was driving her to preschool, Morgan said, 'Look, Mommy! Look what I have in my lap!' Without turning around, Sarah replied, 'Yes, honey, I see! That's great!' Little Morgan didn't miss a beat. 'Mommy,' she said sternly, 'we do not look with our mouths! Turn around and see me with your eyes!'"

Hannah wasn't sure if Meg was smiling shyly at Katherine's story or at Mara's boisterous laugh. Maybe both.

"The spiritual life is all about paying attention," said Katherine. "The Spirit of God is always speaking to us, but we need to slow down, stop, and give more than lip service to what God is saying. We need to get off autopilot and take time to look and listen with the eyes and ears of the heart."

Katherine paused, letting the room fill again with pregnant silence.

"Now, I'll caution you right from the beginning," she said slowly. "Walking the path toward freedom and deep transformation takes courage. It's not easy. It's not linear. It can seem messy and chaotic at times, and you're likely to lose your sense of equilibrium as old things die and new things are born. You may feel disoriented as idols you once trusted and relied upon are revealed and removed. But don't be afraid of the mess. The Holy Spirit is a faithful guide, gently shepherding and empowering us as we travel more deeply into the heart of God."

Charissa had stopped typing. Mara was fiddling with her bracelets. Meg was staring toward the exit door. Hannah didn't realize she was gripping her cross until she felt the blunt tip of the nail dig into her palm. She let go.

Katherine was right. Hannah had enough experience shepherding others through life change to know what kind of courage and perseverance that journey required. She hoped Meg and Mara would be able to manage it. In fact, maybe they were the reason Hannah had signed up for the group. She could be alongside them if they needed encouragement. By the look of things, they were going to need all the encouragement they could get.

Katherine continued, "The most important notes you'll take are not notes on what I say, though I hope you'll glean a few helpful nuggets here and there. Your most important notes will be on what you're noticing about your own life with God. Plan to keep some kind of journal—words, images, prayers, art, photos—something that will help you record what God reveals to you. You won't need to share your reflections with anyone else unless you choose to do so. But give yourself the gift of documenting your journey.

"As we walk together the next couple of months, we're going to explore some spiritual practices that have helped Christians throughout the centuries pay attention to the movement of the Holy Spirit. While there are many rich and fruitful spiritual disciplines that help us love and serve God's world, we're going to explore disciplines that focus on the transformation of the inner life so that we're then set free to love and serve others in renewed ways. We'll engage in practices that help us cultivate a deeper attachment to Jesus. We'll look at ways to create sacred space in our lives so we have more freedom to say yes to God."

*Freedom to say yes to God.* Hannah wrote that down. She could use that in Chicago. She had a feeling she would be able to adapt and use a lot of what Katherine would be presenting. Good. Very good.

Hannah watched Charissa's hand shoot up when Katherine asked if anyone had any questions. "Are you going to give us a syllabus and a supplementary reading list?" Charissa asked, enunciating her consonants with careful precision.

The corners of Katherine's mouth curled into a slight smile. "I know this will be frustrating to some of you, but I won't be assigning readings or using a syllabus. For the most part, I won't even tell you ahead of time what to expect, though you'll have personal reflections to do in the weeks between our sessions."

Charissa threw her shoulders back.

Katherine was scanning the room as she continued. "One thing I've learned to pay attention to over the years is my impulse to want to control my life. We can be so quick to take the reins and charge ahead of what God is doing in us and around us that we miss the gentler promptings of the Spirit. It's not that I won't be giving you tools to help you encounter God in the journey," she explained. "It's just that I don't want to give you anything right now that might tempt you to rely on your own understanding. I want to help you respond to the Spirit in deeper freedom and trust." She brushed a wisp of silver hair away from her cheek. "Any other questions?"

Hannah cast a sideways glance at Charissa, who was drumming her fingers on her laptop, looking irritated. Charissa spoke fluent Eyebrow, and Hannah had no difficulty interpreting. She hoped Katherine wasn't being intimidated or affected. Hannah knew from experience how distracting facial expressions could be to a speaker, and Charissa was a seasoned professional. At least Charissa hadn't sat near the front of the room. Maybe Katherine couldn't see her. *Please don't let Katherine see her, Lord.*

"To get you started on your sacred journey," Katherine went on, "we'll begin with a mini-pilgrimage. Have any of you walked a labyrinth before?" A few hands went up around the room. "The one you'll be walking today is the same pattern as the thirteenth-century labyrinth on the floor of Chartres Cathedral in France." She paused, looking intently at the group. "Now, I'll be honest with you. Some Christians get nervous about labyrinths because they're found in many cultural and spiritual traditions. After all, the circle and spiral are ancient symbols for wholeness and transformation, and some people claim that the labyrinth pattern itself is mystical."

"Fabulous," Charissa muttered.

"I don't believe there's anything inherently mystical about the labyrinth," Katherine said. "Transformation and healing come as gifts from meeting with the living God—not from walking along a particular pattern or path. The labyrinth simply provides an opportunity for prayer. Remember, the intent of spiritual disciplines is to create space where we can encounter God—space where we can be deeply touched and changed by God's extravagant love for us. In walking the labyrinth, we deliberately slow down to give God our prayerful attention. We ask the Holy Spirit to help us be fully present to the One who is always with us. We quiet ourselves so we can notice the stirrings of God and respond in love, faith, and obedience."

Katherine picked up a stack of papers from her podium. “I’ll pass around handouts to your tables so you can read about the labyrinth in your groups. Then when you’re ready, head right out these exit doors and follow the path to the courtyard. Once you’ve finished walking and praying, come back inside, and we’ll share some reflections with one another, okay? And may you know God’s near presence as you walk together.”

**Sacred Journey, New Hope Retreat Center**
***Session One: A Path for Prayer***
*Katherine Rhodes, Facilitator*

---

Walking the labyrinth is a sacred journey of prayer. Unlike a maze, the labyrinth has a single winding path that leads to and from the center, with no obstacles or dead-ends. As you walk, there may be times when you'll want to stop, rest, and listen. Journey at your own pace. If you do get lost or confused, feel free to step off the path and begin again.

While there is no set way to walk the labyrinth, some people find it helpful to picture the journey in three stages: the trip inward, the time at the center, and the trip outward.

Just as pilgrims deliberately leave behind the cares of the world to travel freely and lightly, so God invites us to let go of the things that clutter our lives. As you begin the journey, notice what distracts and hinders you. Notice what competes for your affection and attachment to Jesus. The journey to the center is an opportunity to release burdens, identify fears, and confess sins.

The center of the labyrinth is a resting place where you are held in God's loving embrace. Linger as long as you wish, receiving whatever gifts of Scripture, insight, presence, peace, or revelation God gives. Simply enjoy being with God.

Then, whenever you are ready, begin the outward journey. Allow the Spirit to strengthen and empower you as you take God's presence and gifts out into the world.

## A Path for Prayer

"What is it—a maze?" Mara asked, looking at the picture of the labyrinth on the handout. "That's just what I need—to get lost the very first day. I could be wandering around in circles for weeks!"

Charissa appeared to be reading ahead. "You can't get lost," she said dismissively. "There's only one path to and from the center."

"Well, that's good news," Hannah said cheerfully, hoping Mara hadn't taken Charissa's irritated tone to heart.

Charissa did not reply, verbally or non-verbally. Not even in Eyebrow.

"It looks kinda like a flower at the center, doesn't it?" Mara commented, still studying the pattern. "Oh, I see. Here's the entrance at the bottom, and I guess that's the exit too, huh? One way in, one way out?"

Hannah followed the meandering path with her finger, trying to trace it along the many switchbacks to and from the rosette-shaped center. After a while she gave up. "Shall I read the paragraphs out loud?" she asked.

Mara was the only one who responded, nodding.

Clearing her throat, Hannah began to speak slowly and deliberately, allowing space for the words to breathe. She could hear Mara murmuring to herself as she tried to memorize the three parts of the journey; but Hannah couldn't tell if Charissa and Meg were listening. Charissa was staring at her laptop screen. Meg was staring at the floor.

"Well, shall we give it a try?" Hannah asked after she finished reading. Mara and Charissa rose from the table, but Meg stayed glued to her seat. "You coming, Meg?" Hannah asked gently.

Meg shook her head and pointed at her high heels. "I'm afraid I didn't wear very sensible shoes. Guess I wasn't taking 'sacred journey' literally, huh?" There was a flicker of life and humor in her eyes. Only a flicker.

"I like it!" Mara exclaimed. "Sacred journeys need sensible shoes! What shall we call ourselves? The Sensible Shoes Club?"

Meg laughed.

"C'mon, girlfriend," Mara insisted, grasping Meg's hand and pulling her to her feet. "Your high heels aren't gonna get you out of this one. You're comin' with us, ready or not." Hannah was surprised Meg didn't flinch.

Katherine was watching people exit. "You can leave your backpacks and purses at your tables," she said. "After all, pilgrims need to travel as lightly as possible."

When they reached the labyrinth courtyard, there were already a dozen people walking and praying. Some moved quickly, striding the path efficiently; others moved slowly, stopping frequently.

"Well, this wasn't what I expected," Mara said in a loud whisper. "I thought it was gonna be some kind of hedge maze or something. What is it? Just lines painted on the concrete?"

"Looks like it," Hannah replied with a low voice, not wanting to disturb any of the prayerful pilgrims.

"I seriously hope I don't get lost," Mara declared before she shuffled over to the entry point. Meg had chosen a bench at the far corner of the courtyard, semi-secluded in a bower of late summer roses. Charissa was circling the periphery, carefully scrutinizing those who were walking.

The movement on the labyrinth reminded Hannah of a slow English country dance without the chamber music: people weaving in and out along the twists and turns, walking close together and then far apart, side-by-side for a short time and then turning away from one another to follow the direction of the path. A few had already reached the center. One man knelt with his head in his hands; one woman stood with her arms raised, face to the sun.

As Hannah waited for more room to open, she prayed for Mara, Meg, Charissa, and Katherine. Then a tide of other faces rolled into her mind and would not recede, so she prayed for them too. At least Steve couldn't keep her from praying for the people she had been forced to abandon.

Hannah had reluctantly agreed to remove herself completely from the life of the church for nine months. Steve had directed her not to make any pastoral phone calls or send any work-related e-mail. Nancy had promised to let her know if anything significant happened.

Death would have been easier.

This was a sort of living death. Hannah lived on, but not in the same way she had known for the past fifteen years.

*Exile.*

That was the word to describe it. She had been exiled—except she had been sent to a beautiful, tranquil place. She ought to be grateful. But she wasn't grateful. And then the guilt started all over again. It was a vicious cycle.

Hannah watched Charissa begin her journey and wished Meg would join too. *Stop, stop, stop*, she told herself. Here she was, already taking responsibility for people she had only just met. Nancy was right. Hannah was so accustomed to carrying others' burdens that she didn't know how to lay them down.

*Help.*

By the time she finally stepped onto the path, many of her fellow travelers had completed their journeys. Meg and Charissa had gone back inside, and Mara was on her outward loop, passing Hannah on one of the switchbacks. Hannah found herself walking quickly and then remembered that being in a hurry defeated the whole purpose of the discipline. Or perhaps being in a hurry revealed something deeper about her pace of life. She slowed down and began to pray about letting go.

As she prayed, an image came to mind—something she had seen almost twenty years earlier. She was in college then, a young and passionate believer, striving to please God by serving other people. Often she was so busy with classes and work and ministry that she forgot to eat.

One day, while she was praying in her dorm room, she saw an image of herself as a little girl—maybe four or five years old. Little Hannah was racing in and out of the throne room of God to take flowers to Jesus. Back and forth she ran, in and out. Each time she raced in, she dumped more flowers at Jesus' feet. Then out she'd run to gather more. On and on it went until finally, during one rushing delivery, Jesus scooped her up into his lap and gently wrapped his arms around her so she couldn't wriggle away.

"Thank you for the flowers, Hannah," he said, smiling. "They're beautiful! But what I'd really love is to sit and hold you for a while."

Hannah sighed. Twenty years later, Jesus would probably speak the same exact words to her again. Why was it so hard for her to be still?

She stopped walking and stared at the center of the labyrinth, thinking about another woman who had struggled to be still: Jesus' friend Martha.

Hannah had always been sympathetic to Martha, who hospitably opened her home to Jesus and the disciples. She understood why Martha would become irritated and distracted by a sister who refused to help her get dinner ready for a house full of guests. Hannah pictured Martha banging the pots around and sighing heavily, trying to get Mary's attention. But Mary just sat there with Jesus, oblivious to—or ignoring—her sister's rising blood pressure.

Martha simmered, seethed, and eventually erupted, chastising Jesus for her sister's laziness, accusing him of not caring about her, and demanding he intervene. "Don't you care that my sister has left me to do all the work by myself? Tell her then to help me!"

What was Jesus' tone of voice when he answered? "Martha, Martha, you are worried and distracted by many things."

Worried and distracted.

How many times had Jesus spoken those same words into Hannah's life? "Hannah, Hannah, you are worried and distracted by many things."

She sighed again. Both sisters lived within her, and they had been arguing with one another for years. When Hannah sat still and attentively like Mary, listening to Jesus, her inner Martha would complain she was wasting time—especially since there was so much important kingdom work to be done. And when Hannah raced from one act of service to another, pouring out her life with multi-tasking efficiency, her inner Mary would cast one contemplative glance in her direction, and she'd feel guilty. Jesus was often left to referee the ongoing quarrel in her spirit.

"Only one thing is necessary," Jesus told Martha. Mary had chosen the better part of sitting still with Jesus, and Hannah had the same invitation.

In fact, now that all her opportunities for serving had been stripped away, Hannah had all the time in the world to sit and listen to Jesus with single-minded attention—with nobody clamoring for her help. Nobody.

So why did she resist the very thing she claimed she wanted? Why did she resist the invitation to sit with the Lord?

By the time Hannah reached the center of the labyrinth, she was alone. She intended to linger and listen for God's still, small voice. She intended to settle herself in God's presence and concentrate on the "one necessary thing." But as she sat, she became more and more agitated. She kept thinking about the others gathered inside.

*What had Katherine said about group discussion?*

Hannah tried to focus.

*But had she missed anything?*

She took a deep breath, trying to center herself for prayer.

*But should she make sure she was at her table just in case someone needed something?*

She glanced at her watch: eleven fifteen.

*What time had the others gone back in?*

She stood up. She could always come back to walk and pray when she wasn't so distracted.

Without bothering to make the outward journey, Hannah left the labyrinth and scurried back inside.

Charissa had left the labyrinth feeling provoked and resentful.

There had been no moment of inspiration, no sense of God's presence, no word of insight. Nothing. Silence.

Silence from God, anyway.

Her own thoughts had been loud enough, mostly second-guessing whether she was doing it right as she wandered aimlessly back and forth.

Charissa didn't like spirals. She liked straight lines and clear destinations. Walking in circles was pointless, and the twists and turns were frustrating. Just when she thought she was nearing the center, the path would hurl her to the outside again. It was extremely irritating.

As she walked, she wasn't able to think of anything she needed to release. No sins came to mind for her to confess. She tried to appear prayerful in case anyone was watching, but she was just eager to get to the end and be done with it.

Besides—with all the talk about "sacred journeys" and "knowing your inner world," she still wasn't convinced she hadn't landed in some sort of weird New Age group. Dr. Allen had assured her that the New Hope Center was theologically sound and that Katherine Rhodes was safe. But did Dr. Allen know about the labyrinth? Maybe Dr. Allen wasn't as orthodox as Charissa had thought. Maybe he'd managed to sneak under the Christian radar of Kingsbury University.

Now that she was sitting with the large group again, hearing testimonies about insights and discoveries from the prayer walk, she became even more annoyed.

One woman spoke about the gift of walking the labyrinth with so many other people. She said she was reminded that no matter how she was struggling, there were fellow pilgrims making the same journey toward the heart of God. The community of faith encouraged her and gave her hope.

Another spoke about his discovery that just when he thought he had reached the center, the path would whip him out again to the farthest exterior loop. He talked about noticing his strong desire to arrive at the destination and wondered if God was speaking to him about enjoying the journey, detours and all.

The personal reflections avalanched as people enthusiastically shared their spiritual insights. Charissa was glad no one at her table spoke up. At least her silence wouldn't be conspicuous. Or maybe she wanted to be conspicuously disapproving. She wasn't sure.

She shifted in her seat and fidgeted impatiently on her keyboard. *C'mon, c'mon.* Katherine Rhodes was yielding far too much control to tangential discussions. What a waste of a morning.

Just before noon Katherine wrapped up the discussion. "One thing I've discovered is that navigating our external world is often a piece of cake compared to traveling the labyrinth of our inner world. I'm glad to hear some of your stories about how the labyrinth became a metaphor and mirror for the Spirit's movement in your lives. Feel free to come any time to walk and pray in the courtyard.

"As I said at the beginning, you're likely to experience distractions and confusion as you journey. There may be times when you'll feel discouraged and be tempted to give up. But if you persevere—if you press on in hope and confidence that the Lord himself is directing your journey and is with you as you travel—it will be a marvelous adventure. It's also a special gift to walk with trustworthy companions. We need each other. God doesn't want us traveling alone. So I pray you'll come to know one another well, even as you come to know God better."

A marvelous adventure? *Not likely,* Charissa thought. Not if they would be sitting around, talking about flaky personal revelations from New Age practices. She couldn't believe they weren't getting a syllabus. How would she know if it was worth coming back?

"The early desert fathers and mothers retreated to the wilderness to find God and to know themselves," said Katherine. "We don't need to retreat to a far-off place or abandon our daily lives to encounter God. But we do need training in how to discern the movement of God's Spirit in ordinary and everyday circumstances. We need designated time for stillness and listening. It takes time to identify the baggage we've been carrying that weighs us down. That's some of what this journey will be about.

"Just one last practical bit before I offer a closing prayer. For the next two weeks, consider your images of God. Notice especially how your current images have taken shape and changed over the years. Who is God to you? And remember to keep a travelogue of your pilgrimage. I'm confident the Holy Spirit will be revealing many things as you take the time to slow down, be still, and listen." She paused. "My fellow pilgrims, the Lord is with you. May you find ways to be with God and with one another."

Charissa clapped her laptop shut and shoved it back in its case.

Meg lingered after the others left, hoping to speak privately to Katherine. When the room finally emptied, she approached tentatively. Katherine was cleaning up the back table, loading dirty plates and coffee mugs onto a pushcart.

"May I help you with that?" Meg asked.

Katherine turned around. "I'd be grateful," she replied, squinting to read the name tag. "Thank you, Meg."

While Katherine gathered her papers, Meg cleared the rest of the table. Even clearing dishes caused her to choke up, and she scolded herself. That was the thing about grief. It was so entirely unpredictable, launching stealth attacks through the simplest of triggers. How long had it been since she'd cleared away dishes in front of someone else? Though Becca had only been gone six weeks, it felt like a lifetime. And Mother—

"So, Meg, tell me. How did you find the morning?"

Meg quickly wiped her eyes. "I'm afraid I didn't come very well prepared," she said quietly.

"How so?" Katherine sat down and extended her hand, inviting Meg to sit beside her.

"I-um . . . I wasn't sure what to expect and didn't dress very suitably." Meg pointed to her high heels.

Katherine chuckled. "Not great walking shoes, huh? And I'm guessing by looking at you that you're probably not the type to throw off your shoes and go barefoot."

Meg smiled, shaking her head.

"So you have the labyrinth to look forward to next time. Come early enough, and there probably won't be anyone around to watch you."

Meg sighed. "Everyone had such profound things to say today. But I'm afraid I'm not very profound. I'm thinking maybe this group is too advanced for me."

Just speaking the words out loud caused her eyes to burn with tears again, and she looked away.

Katherine's voice was full of gentleness as she replied, "Jesus said, 'Blessed are the poor in spirit, for theirs is the kingdom of heaven.'"

The verse sounded familiar, but Meg didn't know what it meant.

"You begin the journey with a wonderful gift, Meg, if you already know you are poor in spirit—if you already see how desperately you need God. Humility is always the starting place for those who want to draw near to God."

Meg looked up and met Katherine's compassionate gaze.

"Of course," Katherine continued slowly, "there's also a disabling sort of poverty that sneers you're never good enough, no matter what you do or how hard you try. The right kind of spiritual poverty is a pathway to seeing God; the other kind prevents you from seeing who God has created you to be." She paused. "Perhaps your journey will take you from one to the other."

Meg shook her head. "I don't think I understand what you mean." There was so much she didn't understand. How could she be forty-six when she still felt so much like a child? Her age had crept up on her when she wasn't paying attention.

Katherine settled back into her chair. "I remember years ago when I was first starting in ministry," she said. "I had a dream I've never forgotten. In the dream I was applying for a job at a police station—of all places!—and the officer was really surly. He told me that if I wanted the job, I would have to lift three hundred pounds."

Meg laughed out loud.

"I know. Look at me!" Katherine chuckled, pointing to her thin arms. "So I told him I hadn't done anything athletic for a very long time. And he scowled and growled and said, 'Well, that's the job requirement, lady. Is it gonna be a problem for you?' And I looked him straight in the eye and said, 'No, it's not going to be a problem for me, because my Lord Jesus will do it for me.' Then he took me over to this enormous machine—it was absolutely monstrous—and he strapped me in. At first I could hardly move. But then suddenly, I was lifting huge weights high above my head over and over again."

Meg grinned, watching her demonstrate the weight-lifting motion.

Katherine's blue eyes were twinkling as she went on. "Sadly, I woke up before I found out if I got the job. But I knew the dream meant something important, so I asked the Spirit to help me understand. And when I prayed, I had the strong impression the Lord was saying, 'Kitty, this is humility. This is how I want you to live: knowing you have no strength on your own, but being absolutely confident that you can do everything through me.'" She paused. "Does that make sense?"

Meg spoke slowly. "I think so. My pastor often talks about coming to the end of ourselves and having nowhere to look but up."

"Exactly." Katherine clasped her hands together. "When Jesus spoke about the 'poor in spirit,' he was talking about people who were totally helpless and entirely dependent upon God to supply all their needs. That kind of weakness is a place of blessing, Meg. It's a gift to be able to say, 'I can't, but God can!'" Katherine peered intently into Meg's face. "Actually, that's one of my favorite prayers. I'll inhale saying the words, 'I can't' and exhale saying the words, 'You can, Lord,' over and over again throughout the day. Those simple words help keep me going in hope and faith when the way gets hard. And sometimes it gets very hard, doesn't it?"

Meg sat in silence, listening to the rhythm of her own breathing. Could prayer really be that constant? That simple? Her fears were like breath to her—frequent, regular, and so habitual, she hardly noticed. Could prayer become like that? Could her awareness of God's presence and power actually become life and breath to her?

Meg's voice was barely above a whisper. "I've had years to practice saying, 'I can't.' I'm not sure I can undo it."

Katherine smiled encouragingly. "Spiritual disciplines are all about forming new habits and new rhythms," she said. "If you've mastered the 'I can't' part, then you can start practicing the second part along with it: 'The Lord can.' God's grace is so big that even our weaknesses become wonderful opportunities for the Spirit to work in us. Our fears, our temptations—even our sins—can draw us closer to God."

Meg thought a few moments and then murmured, "My fears almost kept me from coming today, though."

Katherine had a knowing look to her. "And yet, God gave you the courage to come—and to stay." Meg felt her face flush, and she put her hand to her cheek. "I am absolutely confident, Meg, that the Lord will give you everything you need for walking the road to freedom. He'll be walking with you."

Meg tried to push down the lump in her throat. "Thank you," she breathed.

Katherine squeezed her hand and rose from the chair. "God bless you, Meg. I'll see you next time."

Meg exited through the courtyard doors and walked the tree-lined path to the labyrinth. When she arrived at the courtyard, she was surprised to find Hannah sitting on the rose-bowered bench. At first Meg considered trying to retreat unobserved, but it was too late. The click of her heels had given her away.

Hannah looked up from her writing and waved.

"Sorry," Meg said, pointing to Hannah's journal. "I didn't mean to interrupt anything."

"I'm almost finished anyway," Hannah replied, scooting over on the bench so Meg could sit down. Meg brushed some pink petals to the ground. "I was just writing some things down before I forget. Did you come out to walk?"

"No, I'll save that for next time. I just wanted to take another look."

They sat, listening to the wind whistling through the trees, until the sound of Hannah's protesting stomach disrupted the peace. Placing her hand on her abdomen, Hannah peered into her tote bag. "I should've thought to pack some snacks," she said. "Guess I'd better get something to eat before I head back to the lake. Any recommendations for something other than fast food? Maybe a place nearby where I could grab soup or a sandwich?"

Meg named the first place that came to mind. "Corner Nook. They've got great homemade soups and breads."

"Perfect! Is it easy to get to from here? That's the other thing I didn't pack with me—a map. I only printed out directions back and forth from here to the cottage." Hannah paused, smiling. "Not a very well-prepared pilgrim, am I?"

Meg pointed to her heels. "Join the club."

"Well, we both know better what to expect next time, don't we?" Hannah commented, putting away her journal. "So . . . can you point me in the right direction?"

"Actually, it's on my way home. Do you want to just follow me?"

Hannah didn't respond immediately, and Meg wondered why she was hesitating. She appeared to be thinking hard. "You might already have lunch plans," Hannah finally said, "but you'd be welcome to join me."

As she looked into Hannah's dark and weary eyes, Meg the Pleaser overpowered Meg the Griever.

There was no point in both of them eating alone.

The restaurant was buzzing with the hum of comfortable conversation when Meg and Hannah chose a corner table near the fireplace. "Hey! I haven't seen you for a long time!" the waitress greeted Meg.

"No, I haven't been here for a while," Meg replied. She and Hannah both turned down the offer of coffee.

"How's your mom doing?" the woman asked, filling their water glasses. "I haven't seen her for ages!"

Meg swallowed hard as her face flushed. "She passed away a few months ago."

Hannah immediately suffered a pang of grief for Meg and a knot of discomfort for the waitress.

"Oh, I'm so sorry," the woman said. "I remember you guys used to come in here a lot together. Your mom always ordered the same thing, right? Cherry chicken salad on wheat." Meg nodded, her large brown eyes brimming with tears. "Take your time," the waitress said, patting Meg's shoulder before she moved on to another table.

Meg looked down at the menu, attempting to conceal a trail of tears.

"I'm so sorry, Meg." Sorry on two accounts, Hannah thought: sorry for Meg's grief and sorry for the unintended role she had played in opening the wound. Feeling the familiar burden of responsibility bear down on her shoulders, she hunched forward. *Help, Lord.*

Meg shrugged weakly. "If my mother were here she'd tell me to just get over it. I hear her voice in my head, you know? Telling me I'm too sensitive. And she's right. She *was* right, I mean." Meg retrieved a tissue from her purse and tried to erase the tattletale marks of her sorrow, but her efforts only made things worse. Her mascara was now streaked in black across her face.

Hannah was just about to invite Meg to speak about her heartache—she was on the verge of trying to shepherd her through some of the grieving—when something caught in her spirit. A little nudge in a different direction.

Maybe Meg needed a friend, not a pastor.

"Well," Hannah said, "according to my baby book, my first sentence was, 'You hurt my feelings!'" Meg smiled slightly. "I guess I've had to learn to embrace my sensitivity as one of my greatest gifts. I wouldn't trade it for anything. But it's also a liability I have to manage. It's hard—exhausting sometimes. A blessing and a curse, huh?"

"Mostly curse for me," Meg replied. "Thankfully, my daughter, Becca, ended up with thicker skin." Under her breath she added, "And that's a good thing."

Again, the pastor within Hannah wrestled. She was ready to seize Meg's comment and explore the issues behind Meg's intense insecurities and undisguised low self-worth. Over the years Hannah had grown so accustomed to people disclosing their deepest struggles and most intimate heartaches that she half-expected to leave the Corner Nook knowing everything about Meg's past. Then she remembered that she hadn't entered Meg's life as Pastor Hannah Shepley. Meg wasn't seeking her out for advice, care, or support. Suddenly, Hannah heard Steve's nettling voice in her head. Again.

*You don't know who you are when you're not pastoring.*

Forget that. This woman clearly needed pastoral care, and Hannah wasn't going to miss the opportunity to provide it. While Meg excused herself from the table, Hannah ignored Steve's voice and let her thoughts run their race.

Meg wasn't wearing a wedding band. Was divorce another layer of her heartache?

And she had mentioned Becca a couple of times. Were they close, despite the miles between them?

And how would someone as timid as Meg decide to come to a group by herself?

That part didn't add up. Usually, someone had to be fairly self-aware and confident to join a group like theirs, or so desperate for transformation that discontent overpowered fear. Maybe that's what had pushed Meg—the disruption to her status quo. Grief always bore the potential for growth, and Meg was grieving. Old things had died, and the new was waiting to be birthed. Meg was pregnant with spiritual life, and maybe she didn't even realize it. But Hannah saw the signs.

Now she was even more impatient. She wanted to know Meg's story, and she wanted to help. She could be Meg's spiritual midwife, and Steve wouldn't know the difference.

Meg returned ten minutes later with her makeup carefully restored and her hair pulled back with a tortoise shell clip. "You okay?" Hannah asked, trying not to sound too eager or probing. Meg simply nodded.

Their conversation for the next hour was friendly and autobiographical without being revealing or transparent, much to Hannah's disappointment. She took the lead, speaking about her childhood, hoping her disclosures would prompt Meg to share intimate details of her story. Hannah talked about the trials of moving every couple of years when she was growing up. Her dad had been in sales, and they had followed his work. They stopped moving when she was fifteen, but she didn't talk about the reasons why—she never talked about that—and Meg didn't ask any questions.

Meg spoke about living in Kingsbury all her life, watching others come and go. She mentioned her love for music and her affection for the many piano students she had taught over the years. "Beginners," she explained. "I'm not good enough to teach the advanced ones." She talked about how her mother had helped her raise Becca after the death of her husband and how grateful she was that Becca was such a well-adjusted and confident girl. Hannah would have liked to have asked many questions, but she didn't sense an invitation.

No invitation at all.

She was kidding herself, wasn't she? She wasn't at the New Hope Center because of Meg or Mara or Westminster. When would she actually embrace the reality that this sabbatical was for her? Why was that so hard for her to accept?

As she drove back to the lake, she couldn't help thinking that the next nine months would prove to be even more difficult—and far more uncomfortable—than she had imagined.

3

# Exploring the Heart of God

*He said to them, "But who do you say that I am?"*

MATTHEW 16:15

## *Mara*

*Mara Payne sat quietly at her desk while the girls in her class chattered excitedly about Kristie Van Buren's upcoming birthday party. Kristie was the most popular girl in third grade, and she lived in a large house on Cliburn Avenue.*

*"Did you hear they're going to have pony rides in their backyard?"*

*"Kristie told me we can stay up all night, playing games and telling ghost stories!"*

*"Mrs. Van Buren told my mom that she's taking all of us to Henshaw's to buy makeup and perfume!"*

*Kristie had promised to invite Mara to her birthday party, if Mara helped her write a book report. Mara listened with wide-eyed anticipation as Kristie described in tantalizing detail all the activities planned for the celebration. "I'll even let you sit by me at the birthday table," Kristie pledged, smiling sweetly.*

*Mara had never been to a sleepover before, and her mother bought her a special nightgown for the occasion. But when the book report was turned in and the birthday invitations were handed out, Mara discovered there wasn't a pink envelope for her. Kristie shrugged and said, "My mom told me I invited too many people. Sorry! Maybe you can come next year."*

Mara drove home from the retreat center, her mind whirling with embryonic images and emerging insights.

She had spent her time in the labyrinth thinking about what she'd seen when Katherine read the Bible story. It had been so real: Jesus' voice, his eyes, his laugh. Especially his laugh. She could still hear his laughter ringing with delight and joy as if some great victory had been won: "Mara, come with me. I choose you. Come walk with me."

A flood of painful memories had besieged her as she traveled the path to the center: the panic over not being chosen, the fear of being left behind, the pain of being rejected. Mara was there again, reliving the scenes in high-definition detail. She watched her eight-year-old self playing alone on the playground, sitting alone on the bus, crying alone in her room. She viewed her sixteen-year-old self walking alone to class, eating alone in the cafeteria, lying alone in a bed after the neighbor boy had taken what he wanted—leaving her confused, afraid, ashamed, and more empty and alone than she had ever felt in her life.

Well, not quite empty and alone.

As the weeks went by, her nausea testified both to what the boy had taken from her and to what he had left behind. Her mother took her to the clinic before It became obvious to anyone else, and Mara only missed two days of school. They never spoke about It again. And the silence screamed.

Two and a half years later there was a different bed, a different man—a married one this time, promising her she was everything he'd ever wanted and telling her she would be his wife, if only she would be patient. So she gave birth to their baby, and he visited sometimes on weekends, and Jeremy called him "Daddy."

Mara waited and waited. But he did not choose her. When his wife finally found out about the mistress and the three-year-old boy, her threatened violence was terrifying. So was his. He shouted and raised his fist at Mara, commanding the No-Good Whore to disappear and take The Kid with her. A bus ride through the middle of the night whisked them away from Ohio to a city in Michigan where no one knew them. Kingsbury was the farthest Mara had ever traveled. It was as far as she could get with the bus fare money he had flung at her.

She had never forgotten the moment she stepped off the bus into a world reeking of cigarette smoke and sweat. She was disoriented and distracted, still reeling from the angry confrontation the day before. Jeremy was tired and hungry. "I want my bunny," he said, sucking his thumb.

"Bunny's not here. I'll get you a new bunny." How could she have forgotten to bring Jeremy's bunny? She had left the apartment in a panicked frenzy, grabbing only a couple of changes of clothes.

He stared at her with his father's hazel eyes. "I want my bunny!"

"I told you, Jeremy. I'll get you a new bunny." She tugged on his hand, and he tripped after her—her beautiful little brown-skinned boy with the dark curly hair, a spitting image of the man who had rejected them. Mara's eyes filled with tears.

Jeremy started to whimper. "I don't want a new bunny. I want Daddy's bunny."

"Well, you can't have Daddy's bunny, okay?" She looked around the bus station, trying to figure out where to go. Where could they go?

He cried harder. "I want Daddy! I want Daddy!"

She hit him. She actually slapped him across the face. "Shut up! You can't have Daddy! You can't have Bunny! You're never gonna see Daddy or Bunny again!"

Mara still couldn't purge the image of his small frightened face from her mind. To this day the memory haunted her, becoming only more resilient by her efforts to erase it. Jeremy had stopped crying, clutching her hand more tightly. Twenty-seven years later Mara could still feel the terrified grip of his chubby little fingers clinging to her hand with clammy warmth.

As she was wandering around the station with Jeremy, someone saw her crying—an angel lady named Jo. "You okay, honey?" the woman asked. "You look lost." Jo was large, round, black, and soft, and for a moment all of Mara's fears disappeared.

"I lost my bunny and my daddy," Jeremy said, looking up at the kind-faced stranger, his lip quivering. "And I'm hungry."

Mara never learned Jo's last name, but years later she still thanked God for her. Jo bought them breakfast and took them to the Crossroads House shelter, where other guardian angels gave them a safe place to stay, food to eat, and a new bunny for Jeremy. They also gave Mara hope. Their generosity pointed her to Jesus, and eventually she said yes to salvation. She knew how desperately she needed a new life, even if God only accepted her out of pity, out of mercy. At least God hadn't turned her away.

But now Jesus' words in the vision pursued her: *I choose you, Mara. Come walk with me.*

Mara had never been chosen for anything. Never. And she wasn't sure Jesus had chosen her either.

Not sure at all.

When Mara got home and checked her voice mail, she was thrilled to hear a message from Jeremy. "Hey, Mom! Abby's out of town visiting her folks, and I was wondering if I could come over and hang out for a while. I can bring Chinese or pizza. Your choice. Call me, okay?"

Mara chose cashew chicken with steamed rice and greeted Jeremy at the door later that afternoon. "Where are Tom and the boys this weekend?" Jeremy asked, kissing her cheek.

"Away on a camping trip. They'll be back late tomorrow." He followed her into the kitchen and sat down at the table with the wire-handled takeout boxes. "I'm glad you called, Jer," Mara said, removing plates and glasses from the cupboard.

"Well, you sounded kinda down the other night. I figured you might need some cheering up."

Mara wasn't sure how much to reveal. Dawn was trying to help her recognize the deep emotional attachments she had to her oldest son. It was true. She felt closer to Jeremy than she did to her husband. Jeremy held her heart in a way Tom never had, and she needed to find new ways to let go. But maybe not today.

She sighed. "Just feelin' kinda stuck."

"Tom?" he asked. She didn't reply as she took soda from the fridge and filled their glasses with ice. Jeremy shook his head. "Seriously, Mom. I don't know why you stay with him."

Mara knew why. It was a mutually beneficial relationship, at least for the time being. She figured they had five years left, max. They would see Brian through high school graduation, and that would be the end. Tom needed Mara to take care of the boys so he could be free to travel for business. Mara needed Tom to provide a house. She had never gone to college and had no means of earning enough money to support herself. The only thing she had ever known how to be was a mother. And as she often told herself, she certainly wasn't a great one. Most days she wouldn't even call herself "good." She knew which parent the boys would choose if she and Tom separated, and she wasn't ready to lose them. Not yet.

"Mom?"

"Sorry, Jer." She sat down at the table and started serving the food onto plates.

"I said I don't know why you stay with him."

"Financial security." Though it was an honest answer, it was not the truest one. "I've spent my life walking away from things when they got too hard," Mara added quietly. "If Tom decides to walk away, that's one thing. But I'm not leaving." Besides, she thought, God hates divorce. She wasn't going to do one more thing to make God disappointed. She changed the subject. "I don't want to talk about Tom. Tell me about you."

They spent the next several hours talking about Jeremy's new job and the baby girl who was due in January. As Mara listened to him, she couldn't help marveling that he had become such a healthy, responsible young man. She was just grateful she hadn't ruined him.

"I'm so proud of you, Jeremy," Mara said as they hugged good-bye at the door. "You turned out good, kid. Real good." *In spite of me,* she added to herself.

Jeremy put his hands to her face and kissed her forehead. "I had a mom who loved me," he said. "And that's a lot more than what some kids get."

Mara waited until he had driven away before she dissolved in tears.

## Charissa

*Charissa spent the summer before her junior year of high school as an exchange student in Greece. When she returned home in August after two and a half months of excitement and adventure, she was eager to reconnect with her childhood friend, Emily Perkins. She had so much to tell her.*

*Emily had also spent a few weeks of the summer away from home, undergoing treatment at a residential facility for teenage girls with eating disorders. When Emily came back to Kingsbury for a weekend, Charissa went over to her house for a visit. They hadn't seen one another since the end of the school year.*

*Nothing Charissa had heard about Emily's ongoing battle with anorexia prepared her for the altered appearance of her friend: hollow eyes, sunken cheeks, protruding collarbone. Emily's once luxuriously thick blonde hair looked as thin and brittle as her body. Though Charissa tried to hide her shock, she didn't think her face was cooperating, so she looked away. Emily had always been thin, but Charissa couldn't believe how rapidly she had deteriorated in just two months. No wonder her parents had finally decided to send her away for help. If she looked this emaciated after spending time at the clinic, what had she looked like before treatment?*

*"I'm so glad to see you, Charissa!" Emily exclaimed, embracing her with fragile arms. "I've missed you."*

*Charissa mumbled a reply and fought the urge to pull away.*

*"I want to hear all about your adventures in Greece. And I've got a lot to tell you too," said Emily, smiling. "I'm learning so much in some of my groups at the center, and I want to tell you everything. Come on. Let's go for one of our walks, okay? I've missed our walks."*

*Charissa stared at the friendship bracelet dangling loosely around Emily's wrist and wished she could think of something—anything—to say.*

Charissa had arranged to meet John in the New Hope parking lot at one o'clock, giving him time to enjoy his Saturday morning football league with a group of friends. Seating herself under a tree, she unpacked the lunch John had made for her and read his note: "Hope the first day of your sacred journey is fantastic! I love you!"

She exhaled slowly and leaned her head against the trunk. What should she do about the group? She didn't like the idea of not knowing where the class was headed. She certainly couldn't imagine leading her own group of students that way. And Katherine Rhodes's comment about wanting to be in control of her life had provoked her.

*I'm not controlling! I'm disciplined!* Charissa protested, removing her laptop. She supposed she might as well complete the assignment Katherine had given, just in case she decided to go back for the next session.

She opened a new document and stared a long time at the blank screen, trying to recall her earliest images of God.

*Grandfather*, she typed. Then she deleted it. That was a dead-end.

*Helper*. She often asked God for help and peace when she felt overwhelmed by stress, and it was no small miracle she hadn't collapsed under the weight of her own tyrannically high standards of achievement. Of course, her mother insisted that John was the one who had kept Charissa from developing ulcers. His lighthearted playfulness was a healthy counterpoint to her sobriety.

As Charissa took a bite of her veggie wrap, her mind wandered to their first date.

They were sophomores at Kingsbury. John had pestered her for months to go out with him, refusing to take no for an answer. He wasn't her type at all. For one thing, at five-foot-ten he was an inch shorter than she was, and she was determined not to date anyone under six feet tall. He also talked far too much about sports. Charissa had never met an athlete with a serious commitment to intellectual pursuits, and she was seriously committed to academics.

But he just wouldn't give up.

In exasperation she finally agreed to go on one date—*one!*—inwardly deciding to be so cold that he'd never ask her out again.

"That's fantastic!" he exclaimed when she rolled her eyes, scrunched her eyebrows, and said yes. He was like a small child who had just been promised a trip to Disney World.

On Friday night of that same week, promptly at six o'clock, John arrived at her dorm room with a box of chocolate covered cherries. Her roommate must have tutored him: Charissa didn't tolerate tardiness, and she loved chocolate covered cherries.

John said, "I probably should have told you that I'm taking you to a place where the food isn't great, but the atmosphere is fabulous." She pursed her lips.

"Great," she said, using her perfected sarcastic tone. She was masterful with single syllables. Much to her disappointment, however, John didn't seem to notice. Charissa threw her shoulders back and followed him down the hallway.

"Ohhh . . . " He reached into his pocket. "Sorry! I must've left my wallet in my room." He shrugged genially as she gave an exaggerated sigh and looked at her watch. "It's okay—my room's right upstairs. It'll just take a minute. C'mon." She was going to insist on waiting for him in the lounge but didn't want to waste her breath.

When John opened the door to his room, Charissa immediately recognized the swelling, soaring melody of one of her favorite pieces: Rachmaninov's *Rhapsody on a Theme of Paganini.*

"Hope Italian's okay," he said, ushering her inside.

In the middle of the tiny dorm room was a small round table set for two and covered with a red and white checkered cloth. The shelves and desks were lined with dozens of flickering white votive candles and small vases of red carnations. Just as Charissa was trying to comprehend the scene, John's roommate appeared, dressed in a black tuxedo.

"Welcome! My name is Tim, and I'll be taking care of you tonight. Can I start you off with a beverage?"

John was holding Charissa's chair for her, waiting for her to sit down. Dumbfounded, she stared at the table with her mouth half open. "Diet whatever," she finally mumbled, sinking into her seat.

"I'll take Dr Pepper," John said. Tim returned a few minutes later with hand-calligraphied menus and soda in plastic champagne glasses.

"I recommend the freshly microwaved lasagna," said John, perusing the menu.

Charissa couldn't help herself. She laughed. Lasagna was the only entrée listed.

"And the house salad is good, right, Tim?" John asked.

"It's excellent," Tim replied. "I'll bring fresh bread for the two of you."

John and Charissa spent the next four hours talking about music, movies, and literature. Charissa was surprised to discover that John was so knowledgeable about poetry. She was also surprised by his sense of humor. She had never met anyone who knew how to make her laugh. Over the next few years, John patiently chiseled away at her defenses until she finally said yes to his love.

Charissa pulled her drifting thoughts away from her husband and looked at her watch: thirty more minutes. That was more than enough time to finish the assignment. She drummed her fingers on her laptop keyboard. What were her images of God?

The memory that surfaced next took her by surprise.

She was sixteen. She had just returned from a few months in Greece, and her friend Emily was home from the clinic for the weekend. Charissa went to see her—she hadn't seen her all summer—and they went for a walk together around the block. As they walked, Emily talked about Jesus. Charissa listened with burgeoning discomfort, wishing Em would talk about something else—anything else. Jesus made her really uneasy.

Ten years later, something about Jesus still made her really uneasy.

It wasn't that she didn't believe he was the Son of God. Charissa was theologically orthodox, affirming all the fundamental tenets of Christian faith. But she was uncomfortable with people like Emily who had testimonies of conversion. After all, what kind of conversion experience could Charissa have had? She had been the model child and the model student. Yes, she believed Jesus died to save people from their sins, and she asked for forgiveness when she made mistakes. But she didn't fit into the category of "born again" believers. When people spoke about themselves as "sinners" and Christ as "personal Savior," she cringed.

*Helper.*

She supposed that image would suffice. She wrote a few paragraphs about Psalm 46, describing God as a "very present help in trouble," and she finished the assignment just as John arrived.

"Thanks for the lunch!" she said, sliding into the passenger seat. "What would I do without you?"

He grinned. "Starve."

She tousled his hair. "How was the football game?"

"Yours truly scored the game-winning touchdown."

"You missed your calling as a professional athlete, John."

"You're right. At least then we'd have two cars."

Charissa laughed.

"How 'bout you, Riss? How was the class?" John kept one hand on the steering wheel and rested the other on the back of her head, stroking her hair.

"It wasn't at all what I expected."

"Oooh . . . That doesn't sound good. So was it like a special kind of Bible study, or what?"

"No, definitely not a Bible study," she replied, communicating volumes of displeasure with her tone of voice. "The leader started off with a kind of meditation exercise. She read the text about Jesus calling the disciples and told us to imagine that we were there. What did we see? Feel? Hear? It was all very subjective. I guess we were supposed to experience the text in a fresh way. But I've heard that passage so many times before that I didn't get anything new out of it. Then she had us read a handout about something called a labyrinth. It's like this big maze marked into concrete, and you walk it and pray as you walk. I'm thinking it's some kind of New Age thing. And there's no syllabus and no assigned readings," Charissa harrumphed.

"That's a little weird, isn't it?"

"Well, *I* think it is. What kind of teacher doesn't give you a plan to follow? I don't get it."

"So what are you supposed to be learning?"

"No idea." Charissa twirled a stray strand of hair around her finger. "All she said was that she didn't want us charging ahead on our own. Then she gave us an assignment to think about our images of God. I got that done while I was waiting for you, even though I'm not sure I'll go back. I don't know what to do. Dr. Allen spoke so highly of her, and he really thought I'd get something out of this. But I sure don't see what that might be."

That night Charissa didn't sleep well. As she lay in bed at 2 a.m., listening to John's rhythmic breathing, she tried to remember the impertinent dream that had awakened her.

There was an attic room filled with books, and she was down on her knees unpacking them. She knew that if she could get all the boxes unpacked, she could put together a beautiful library. She carefully categorized and alphabetized all the titles, filling shelf after shelf. But just when she thought she had finished with the last box, more boxes would appear. As she tried to put the books away, someone was knocking on the door. She kept working without answering, determined to complete her project. But the knocking persisted, getting louder and louder. "Come in!" she called, still sorting. But no one entered, and the knocking continued. "What do you want?" she barked. "I told you to come in!" The door didn't open, and then she saw it was dead-bolted.

Charissa had awakened with the sound of knocking still echoing in her head. At first she thought there was actually someone at the door, and she sat bolt upright in bed. But there was only the steady tick tick tick of the wall clock, marking off the maddening minutes of insomnia.

Charissa had intended to sneak out of Monday's class before Dr. Allen could ask her any questions. But as she packed up her books, he managed to catch her eye. "Charissa, don't leave yet," he said, briefly interrupting the student who had stopped to talk with him.

She breathed deeply, finished packing her bag, and waited for him to end his conversation.

"Walk with me," he said, picking up his briefcase. "I want to hear about the sacred journey group."

She arranged her facial expression, disguising her irritation behind a calculated smile. "Well, it wasn't exactly what I expected."

"Go on . . . " He wasn't going to let her off the hook.

"I thought it would be an actual *class* on spiritual disciplines and prayer. That's what the flyer said, anyway. I was expecting a lecture with some discussion, and instead it was all very experiential. No syllabus, no assigned readings. No sense of direction for where it's going. Just not what I expected."

"I see."

She had a sinking feeling that he did. Dr. Allen possessed infamous skills in literary analysis, and suddenly, her life was his text. Charissa was accustomed to people seeing only what she wanted them to see, and now her professor apparently saw things that were concealed even from her.

She didn't like it.

"Remember, Charissa—the things that annoy, irritate, and disappoint us have just as much power to reveal the truth about ourselves as anything else. Learn to linger with what provokes you. You may just find the Spirit of God moving there."

They had reached his office, and he turned to face her. "True learning requires more than a syllabus," he went on. "In fact, sometimes a syllabus can get in the way, particularly if a student's primary goal is to master material." He hesitated, studying her carefully. "You're an excellent student, Charissa. You're conscientious, efficient, and skilled at doing things well. But there is more for you to see and to know." Although his compliments sounded like a rebuke, Charissa was determined neither to flinch nor look away. "Come in for a minute."

She followed him into his office. Setting down his briefcase, he picked up a photo from his desk and held it out for her to see. "You've heard me talk about my passion for sailing before," he said.

Charissa looked at the picture of Dr. Allen and some friends on a sailboat. Someone had managed to capture a moment of full sail—the wind ruffling his graying hair, his face glowing with joyful exhilaration.

"Have you ever sailed?" he asked.

"Only once with my dad when I was little. I just remember sitting on the water, waiting for the wind to come up. My dad was pretty frustrated, and I think it was the last time he went sailing. He bought a motorboat."

Dr. Allen laughed. "Exactly. Sailing isn't efficient. That's why I use it for my own spiritual growth and discipline." He paused. "For a Type A personality like me, it's hard not to be in control. I much prefer setting a course and getting there without detours or distractions—motoring through life, if you like. So sailing has been good training for me to learn how to be patient, to wait for the wind, and to discern how to set the sails to maximize the wind's power. Even though I have absolutely no control over the wind, I can respond to it if I'm paying attention."

He put the photo back on his desk. "Much as we might wish to direct our own spiritual journeys," he continued slowly, "growing in love for God and others is a lifelong process that can't be achieved by self-effort. We've got to learn how to cooperate with the Holy Spirit." He smiled enigmatically. "Perhaps God wants to reveal something to you about your frustration with the group."

His dark eyes were piercing, and she half-wished he'd go ahead and tell her what that revelation might be. But Dr. Allen knew better than to dispense information she needed to discover for herself. Self-restraint was the gift of a fine teacher, and at that moment she resented him for being a fine teacher.

That night she stewed in bed long after John fell asleep. *Learn to linger with what provokes you.* What in the world did that mean? Dr. Allen had certainly provoked her with his advice, but she didn't know what to do with it. What good was it? What good was any of it? She found herself wishing she'd never seen the New Hope flyer in the first place.

John had suggested she walk away and not go back to the group if it upset her so much. But Charissa had never been one to walk away from anything. Especially now that Dr. Allen was watching.

At 5 a.m. she gave up trying to sleep and went to the kitchen to make herself a cup of coffee. She might as well be productive if she was going to be awake. Since her Bible reading plan directed her to the Song of Solomon, she quickly skimmed through the pages. As a student of literature she knew she ought to appreciate the vigor and beauty of the ancient poetry. But as a student of Scripture she had never understood its purpose. It taught no doctrine and gave no precepts about how to live correctly. Frankly, the sexual imagery seemed wholly inappropriate for sacred text. Song of Songs was the sort of book teenage boys could read and enjoy, but Charissa had no use for it. She was just eager to be done so she could move on to the prophets.

She finished reading the Song in less than half an hour and ticked "quiet time" off her to-do list. Then she began organizing their walk-in closet, determined not to think anymore about Dr. Allen.

Or sailing.

## Hannah

*Mommy sometimes let Hannah play with the ceramic figurines from the china cabinet if Hannah promised to be very, very careful. "These are precious to me, Hannah. They belonged to Grammy, and they're very fragile."*

*Hannah's favorite was a little yellow bird with green and blue on its wings. One day she made a nest for the bird out of a small cardboard box filled with cotton balls. Then she climbed the tree oh-so-carefully and placed the nest on one of the branches. But before she could climb down and look, the nest tipped, and the little bird flew out onto the concrete below.*

*When Daddy found her, she was hiding behind the tree, rocking the shattered bird and crying. He took her in his arms and told her not to worry. He could fix the bird, good as new, and no one would ever know it had broken. Hannah stopped sniffling and handed over the bird.*

*Daddy was right. When he was done fixing it, it was as good as new. She could hardly even see the cracks.*

*In fact, if you didn't know they were there, you wouldn't see them at all.*

Hannah sat in a booth at Jill's Coffee House with her laptop open, checking her church e-mail. Nothing. In less than two weeks she had gone from complaining about having too many messages in her inbox to resenting that no one needed her.

At first she had tried to pretend she was on a luxury vacation. She read, walked, and browsed shops and galleries in the nearby town of Lake Haven. She watched sunsets and fed the birds. She perused the West Michigan tourist magazines, shopped at the farmers' market, picked her own apples at a local orchard, and attended an outdoor community band concert. But after a few days of relaxing, she was ready to go home.

She closed her empty inbox and checked Westminster's website for news: youth retreat, leadership training seminars, food pantry. Her replacement was leading a women's prayer group and a Bible study on Romans. No surprise there. Romans was a predictably ambitious choice for a fresh seminary graduate.

Steve was preaching a series called "Finding Hope Again," but the audio files hadn't been posted on the website. Maybe she should call the church office and see if they'd send her the sermons. She could use some hope.

She also wanted an excuse to call the church.

She dialed the number. "Good afternoon; Westminster. This is Annie." Just hearing the receptionist's voice was a way of connecting with her old life—her old life of two weeks ago.

"Hey, Annie, it's Hannah. How are you?"

"Hey! Fine, Hannah! How are you doing? How's your sabbatical going?"

*Terrible. She hated it.* "Fantastic!" she exclaimed. "It's beautiful up here. I miss everybody, though. What's new there?" Hannah tried to sound like she wasn't fishing for details. Which she wasn't. Was not.

"Oh, you know how September is with everything kicking off," Annie replied. "It's busy here. But Heather's doing a great job. She fits right in—lots of energy and passion. So you don't have to worry about anything! She's got it all covered."

Hannah had never been worried about Heather being incompetent. She was just disappointed by how easily she had been replaced.

"I guess you heard about George Connelly, huh?" Annie asked.

"Uh . . . no . . . What happened?" There was an awkward pause.

"Oh. I thought maybe that's why you were calling. George had a heart attack and went in for quadruple bypass surgery yesterday. I think he's doing okay, though. Steve's been at the hospital with Lindy today. Guess they'll send George home in four or five days if everything's straightforward."

Hannah couldn't believe no one had called her. Though she wasn't particularly close to George and Lindy, the Connellys had been members at Westminster for years. "Is Steve still at the hospital?" Hannah asked.

"No, he's back. I think he's in his office. Do you want to talk to him?"

"Yes, please." Hannah waited on hold while Annie transferred the call. Why hadn't Steve called her? It was completely inconsiderate of him to leave her out of the loop like that.

"Hi, Hannah." Steve sounded tired. Or was it her imagination?

"Hey, Steve." She wasn't going to waste time with small talk. "Annie was telling me about George. How's he doing?"

"He's hanging in there."

"How about Lindy? How's she holding up?"

"She's tired, but doing okay. Feeling grateful and relieved that the surgery went so well."

Mentally, Hannah already had her suitcase packed. She could be there in three hours. She was only three hours away from her old life. "How about if I come down for a couple of days, Steve, and help out with the hospital visits? I can be there in a few hours."

"No, Hannah." His voice was firm. "There's a reason why I didn't call you. We agreed to the boundaries before you left, remember?"

She sighed. "I know . . . but . . . I have nothing going on here, and if I could be helpful at all . . . "

"Hannah, I know how hard this is for you." *No he didn't. Not really.* "Having nothing going on is the point. You're supposed to be resting. More than that—I told you I saw warning signs that you've wrapped your whole identity around serving and being busy. Even now I'm hearing this compulsive desire to be useful, to be needed. It's not good, Hannah." She didn't want to hear this. She really didn't. "I'm hoping you can trust my heart enough to know that I'm for you, even when I say things you don't want to hear. Now—"

She recognized his tone of voice. There was no negotiating. No arguing. He was shifting gears.

"Tell me what you're doing for yourself while you're away. Did you sign up for that spiritual formation group you mentioned in your e-mail?"

"Yes," she said, trying to conceal her disappointment. "We had the first session last Saturday. I think it will be good."

"Fantastic." He paused, and she wished she could analyze his facial expressions or body language. Was he pulling on the pastoral rope again? "Hannah, I'm thinking it also might be helpful for you to connect with a spiritual director while you're up there. This sabbatical is radical surgery, and you can't operate on yourself. You're going to need some help." Hannah couldn't think of anything to say, so she stayed silent. "Maybe the person who leads your group can point you in the right direction. You've got some grieving to do, and that takes time. You know that. You'll need to walk through the same process you've shepherded so many others through. And you can't do it alone."

Hannah never did ask for copies of the sermon series. She already had enough of Steve's voice in her head.

September 23

7 p.m.

I'm sitting here on the deck, looking out at a shimmering lake and finding it hard to believe that I've only been here at the cottage for two weeks. It feels like a lifetime already. How in the world am I going to survive nine months? For one thing, I guess I'd better make a regular habit of journaling. Otherwise I just won't be able to process everything that's going on inside of me right now. And there's a lot whirling around.

I just can't get Steve's voice out of my head, telling me I have "a compulsive desire to be useful." Really? All I've ever wanted to be is a faithful servant. Nothing more. I've spent the past fifteen years pouring out my life for the church because that's what I'm called to do. I'm called to be obedient and faithful. I've wanted so much to please God—to hear the words, "Well done, good and faithful servant." It's been a blessing that I haven't had a family because the church has required every last ounce of my energy. Every bit of it.

Steve claims I need to go through my own grief process, and I guess he's right. I'll have to name the things that have died. I'll need to confront them in order to let go of them.

So here goes. I've been separated from my home, my friends, my routine. That's obvious. I've lost my work, and I loved my work. It was hard to hear about how well Heather is doing. I hate admitting that I feel threatened by her, but I'm admitting it. I feel jealous and threatened. I guess I'm grieving being so easily replaced. I'm not indispensable. Am I wrapped up in people needing me? I don't know.

Maybe Steve's right that I can't be my own surgeon. Maybe I'll ask Katherine on Saturday if she can recommend someone to walk alongside me.

I just don't know what to do.

When Hannah's cell phone rang Thursday morning, she was glad to hear Nancy's voice. "How's everything going, Hannah? Are you finding your way around? Is there anything you need?" Hannah stared out the large picture window, watching a spider dangling from the eaves by a gossamer thread.

"The cottage is wonderful, Nancy. Beautiful."

"Oh, good. I hope everything's comfortable for you."

*Physically, yes. Spiritually, no,* she thought. Aloud, she said, "You didn't miss a single detail, Nance. Thank you. I've got everything I need to relax." She just didn't know how to do it.

Nancy sighed. "Listen, Hannah . . . I promised I'd call you if anything significant happened down here." Hannah braced herself. "George Connelly passed away yesterday." A wave of nausea swept over her as she lurched forward.

"Oh, Nancy—"

"I know," Nancy murmured. "The church is rocked. I keep thinking about Lindy and those four little girls."

Hannah sped to her comfort zone. She knew how to be alongside grieving families. "I'll throw some things in the car and be there in a few hours. When's the memorial service?"

"Saturday." That was okay. Hannah could skip the sacred journey group. It was more important for her to be in Chicago. "Hannah . . . I've already talked with Steve this morning. He's got everything covered here. He thinks it's important for Heather to have a role to play in this, and she won't be able to do that if you're here." There was silence. "Hannah?"

"I'll call Steve."

September 25

9 p.m.

I spent all day walking the beach. I didn't know what else to do with myself. Nancy called this morning with the news that George died yesterday. He leaves behind Lindy and four little girls. I feel sick inside. Absolutely sick. The funeral is on Saturday, and I'm tempted to drive down for it. But Steve told me this morning he wants me to think long and hard about my reasons for wanting to come.

So I've been thinking about it today, and I realized that I'd only be going for myself. I'd pretend I was there for Lindy, but Lindy doesn't need me there. We have no deep personal connection to one another, and there's nothing I can offer her that other people aren't offering her right now. I hate admitting that. I hate admitting that my whole reason for going down to Chicago would be entirely selfish—a way of inserting myself back into that world for attention and affirmation. Like a drug. Steve was right. I have a compulsive desire to be needed.

When did I become a codependent pastor?

Nancy told me another bit of pastoral news. Mark and Christina Cooper found out yesterday that they've lost another baby. I did the funeral for Adelaide, their tiny stillborn daughter, just two years ago. Dear God, why? They've had hundreds of people praying for them for years now, and they keep having these losses.

I hate their suffering. Especially when it's in your power to give them a child, Lord. And that's my problem. If I didn't believe so passionately that you have the power to intervene in people's lives, then it wouldn't hurt so much when you don't.

There. I said it.

You know what I realized today? I realized that my very first image of God died a long time ago, and I didn't even know it.

My first image of God was the Father who fixed things. Like Dad. Nobody could fix things like Dad. I was thinking today about Brown Bear and how Miss Betty tried to fix him after one of his eyes got lost. I was so upset when she brought him back to me. He wasn't the same bear, and I cried and cried. Daddy found me crying in my room, and he wrapped his arms around me and said he would find eyes that recognized me. He promised me that everything would be okay. And he was right. I don't know where he managed to find eyes for my bear, but he restored him, good as new. There wasn't anything Daddy couldn't fix.

Until—

Until everything imploded, and I realized that even Dad couldn't fix it. Daddy didn't have the power to make it all better. And that's when I started looking to God to fix broken things. And slowly—slowly God mended things. And I trusted him.

I trusted you, Lord. I watched you heal, fix, and mend so many things that I came to believe there was nothing you couldn't do. You were my Heavenly Father, who faithfully fixed broken things. That was my first image of you.

But you don't fix things, Lord. You don't. I've watched young mothers die of breast cancer. I've buried children. I've wept with parents whose teenagers got killed by drunk drivers. I've sat with a front-row view into their grief and disappointment with you, Lord. I didn't realize until today how much all that heartache has actually affected me. The cumulative weight of other people's losses has steadily eroded my own hope and faith. I didn't even realize it until today. It's like the disappointment arrived so quietly, I didn't know it was there until I spoke it out loud.

I kept thinking about John 11 today. Mary and Martha send word to Jesus that their brother Lazarus is sick. "The one you love is sick, Lord," they say. They'd watched Jesus heal strangers. They'd heard about him speaking a word from a distance and someone getting healed. So certainly, Jesus would come and heal a friend, right? Or at least send forth God's healing power with a word of life, right?

Wrong.

Jesus loved Lazarus SO he stayed where he was. He didn't come. Yes, I know the punch line of the story. I know Jesus' delay was for God's glory to be made known in raising Lazarus from the dead. But today I was like Martha, confronting Jesus and accusing him with the words, "Lord, if you had been here . . . "

Lord, if only you'd been there for Mark and Christina. For George and Lindy. And for all the others I've wept with. Yes, I know this world isn't all we get. I know there's resurrection. I know you're there to comfort and weep with us.

But sometimes I feel so disappointed. So disappointed. It all feels heavy on me right now. Really heavy. And I don't know what to do about it.

Help, Lord.

Please.

## Mara

*Mara tried to hold on to Julie Conner's hand as tightly as she could. She knew the other team had identified her as the chain's weakest link, and they would be aiming their runner at her.*

*Again.*

*As Mara's team chanted the words, "Red rover, red rover, send Audrey right over!" Mara gritted her teeth and closed her eyes. When Audrey easily broke through Mara's defense, her team groaned. Mara felt her face get hot as Audrey chose Julie to take back to the other team.*

*"Okay, everybody!" the opposing captain yelled. "Brace yourself for The Whale! Red rover, red rover, send Mara right over!"*

*Mara lowered her head and shoulders and ran as hard as she could, straight for Denise and Kristie's clasped hands. But when she reached the other side, Kristie and Denise let go. Mara went tumbling face first into the ground, her dress coming up above her waist to expose dingy gray underwear. The other girls squealed with laughter.*

*"She's so fat I was afraid she was gonna break my arm off!" Denise exclaimed.*

*"Good thing you let go, Denise," Kristie said, still laughing. "You coulda been crushed!"*

*Mara picked herself up, smoothed down her dress, and trudged back to her team, bringing Kristie with her. If only Miss Pierce had been watching! But Miss Pierce was deeply engrossed in a conversation with another teacher over by the jungle gym, and they had their backs turned to the field. Mara wasn't going to tattle this time. That would only make things worse.*

*"Hey, Mara!" her captain sneered as Mara wiped her clammy palms on her skirt and gripped Kristie's hand. "I hope they keep asking for you. That's the only way you're ever gonna win us any points! Hey, you guys!" she called over to the other team. "Keep yelling for The Whale, okay? She's our secret weapon!"*

*And everyone laughed again.*

"So, Mara, tell me more about your image of Jesus choosing you."

Mara was sitting in Dawn's office, staring at a frayed patch on the armrest of her chair. She wondered if any of Dawn's other clients avoided eye contact by staring at the patch. "I don't know what else to say about it." She kept counting the individual strands of fiber. "I just wish it were real."

"What difference would it make to you if it really had happened—if Jesus really had chosen you to walk with him and be his disciple?"

Mara pulled at the strands, rubbing them between her fingers. "I'd feel special, I guess. I've never been chosen for anything my entire life." Not even by Tom, she thought. Most women could at least say they had been chosen by their husbands. But not Mara. When she became pregnant with Kevin, Tom had been worried that she would have another abortion. So he married her. He had chosen Kevin—not Mara.

"If Jesus didn't choose you, Mara, how did you become his disciple?"

Mara stopped fiddling with the upholstery strands and began spinning her wedding band. Round and round and round. "I chose him, I guess. And since Jesus never rejects anybody, he had to say yes." It was the first time she had ever been quite that blunt about it. "Doesn't Jesus say somewhere that he never turns anybody away?" She looked up to meet Dawn's gaze.

Dawn replied, "Jesus also said, 'You did not choose me, but I chose you.' Jesus *has* chosen you, Mara. You weren't just the leftover God had to take, simply because you were standing there. God didn't choose you out of pity. Jesus really has chosen you to be with him because he loves you and wants to be with you." Mara's eyes filled with tears, and she looked away. "The moment you truly believe that," Dawn said quietly, "is the moment everything shifts for you."

Mara pushed her shopping cart up and down the supermarket aisles, trying to process what Dawn had said about being loved and chosen. What difference would it make? How would anything change? She would still be stuck in a loveless marriage. She'd still be bearing the consequences of a lifetime of bad choices. What difference would it make?

As she reached for a box of Raisin Bran, something on her right wrist caught her attention. Over the years her tattoo had become such a familiar part of her physical features that she hardly noticed it. Or perhaps she had learned to ignore it. Now the image stared back at her, unblinking: the image of the all-seeing eye.

She had gotten the tattoo not long after she had come to faith—a reminder that the God she had encountered in her own wilderness of fear and confusion was the same God that Hagar, the slave-girl, had met in the desert.

*El Roi*, the "God who sees."

Hagar's story from Genesis had deeply resonated with Mara when she first heard it preached at the Crossroads House shelter. Hagar had been trying to escape too, running for her life from an abusive mistress. She was pregnant, frightened, and hopeless. But God found her in the desert wasteland and revealed his presence and his promises.

God had also found Mara and little Jeremy as they wandered in the Kingsbury bus station. God had stopped Mara along her escape route, speaking a message of hope through faithful servants at Crossroads.

*El Roi*, the God who saw her.

What began as a symbol of compassion, however, quickly deteriorated to a sign of judgment. She had marked herself with an indelible reminder that God was watching over her. But without her being aware of the shift, the image had morphed into a stern warning that a holy God was watching her every move, scrutinizing her life with disapproval. She began to hope God's eye would have the power to frighten her out of temptation and keep her in obedience. She desperately hoped the reminder of God seeing her would arrest her compulsive quest to find love and acceptance in the arms of men who knew the right things to say.

Instead, the eye accused, condemned, and shamed her whenever she stumbled.

So she married Tom when he suggested it, hoping Tom would be able to save her from her sin. But Tom had not been the rescuing messiah she had longed for.

Yes, he had provided a marriage bed, a house, and financial security; but Tom had no remedy for Mara's guilt, regret, and shame.

Though he knew the details of her past, he had never thought they were particularly significant. During their fifteen years together, Mara had lost count of the number of times he'd said to her, "Get over it, will you? Lots of women get abortions. Lots of people have affairs and sleep around. If your faith is making you feel guilty about everything, then I wish you'd just dump the God crap and be free."

Mara sighed as she loaded her grocery cart with things she shouldn't eat.

What did it really mean for her to name God, El Roi? Katherine had asked them to consider their images of God. Maybe she should read Hagar's story again.

The days went by, and Mara kept finding excuses. The busyness of the boys' extra-curricular activities kept her running. By the time she finished shuttling them back and forth between school and football and cross country and scouts, she was exhausted.

Dawn had insisted that her experience of imagining herself in the Bible story had been a God-sighting. "You encountered Jesus in a really powerful way as you listened to that story about him choosing the disciples," Dawn said. "Focus on what it means to be chosen by Jesus."

But Mara didn't have the energy for deep thoughts about God. She was tired. So tired. It took every ounce of physical, emotional, and mental strength just to keep the family going.

She sat one night on the couch after the boys went to bed, watching reality television with a tub of chocolate ice cream on her lap. What was wrong with her? If she could sit for hours in front of mindless entertainment, couldn't she find time for God? She ought to be reading, praying, seeking. Especially if Dawn was right about Jesus choosing her.

*If* Dawn was right.

Mara stared at the tattoo, and the tattoo stared back. Unwaveringly. Incessantly. El Roi was watching her every move, and El Roi was disappointed in her. Again.

She couldn't do it. She couldn't bear the guilt anymore. If the sacred journey was just going to make her feel guilty, then maybe Tom was right. She didn't need any more guilt.

Shifting her position on the couch, Mara reached for the remote and changed the channel.

## *Meg*

*When Meg got home from first grade on a bright autumn day, the house was locked. She called and called for Mama, but there was no answer. Not knowing what to do, she sat down on the front porch steps and began to cry.*

*Where was Mama?*

*As long minutes ticked by, she became more and more frantic. Maybe something had happened to Mama. Maybe something terrible had happened, and Mama was never coming back. Like Daddy. Something terrible had happened to Daddy, and Jesus took him away to heaven. She cried harder.*

*Just then Mrs. Anderson, their next-door neighbor, arrived home. She came over and sat down next to Meg, putting her arm around her. "It's okay, honey," she said. "I'm sure she's coming soon. Tell you what—let's go over to my house and wait together, okay? I've got some chocolate chip cookies I baked this morning, and I need someone to help me eat them." Still whimpering, Meg grasped Mrs. Anderson's hand and followed her to her house, where she kept vigil at the front window.*

*When Mama pulled into the driveway fifteen minutes later, Meg flew to her, sobbing. "What on earth is the matter?" Mama asked. Meg clung to her, gulping for air, unable to speak.*

*Mrs. Anderson came up from behind and gently patted Meg's head. "Meg was worried when you weren't here," she explained, continuing to stroke Meg's blonde curls.*

*Mama untangled herself from Meg's arms. "I was only at the store, Meg." She crisply thanked Mrs. Anderson for her help and then carried her shopping bags inside.*

*Mrs. Anderson knelt in front of Meg, wiping the tears from her cheeks. "It's okay, sweetheart. Everything's okay. How about if I talk to your mama later and set up a time for you to come over and help me bake? Would you like that?" Meg nodded, still sniffling. Mrs. Anderson drew Meg close and kissed her forehead. Then Meg dashed inside after her mother.*

Meg arrived at the New Hope Retreat Center at 8 a.m. on the last Saturday of September, wearing sensible shoes. When she reached the courtyard, she was relieved to be the only one there. She wanted to walk and pray before their ten o'clock group without being observed or scrutinized.

Standing at the entry of the labyrinth, she tried to summon the courage to take the first step. What if she did it wrong? What if she got lost and confused? What if she didn't hear anything from God? What if . . . ?

Unable to stem the tide of her anxious thoughts, Meg tried to pray one of the few Scripture passages she knew by memory: "The Lord is my shepherd; I shall not want. He maketh me to lie down in green pastures. He leadeth me beside the still waters. He restoreth my soul."

Her mind went blank, and she couldn't remember the rest. Mrs. Anderson had helped her memorize the Twenty-third Psalm when she was a very little girl, and now it was gone.

Meg stopped, overwhelmed by a sense of disappointment and disapproval. Without bothering to finish the path to the center, she simply left the labyrinth and went over to sit on the corner bench. She was pathetic. Absolutely pathetic. Why had she actually thought she would be able to take a sacred journey? Her mother had been right. There were so many things that were simply too hard for her. She was weak. Too weak. She buried her face in her hands.

"Well, Meg, here you are in your sensible shoes, ready to walk."

Meg was startled. She hadn't heard anyone approach. Wiping her eyes, she looked up into Katherine's smiling face.

"Forgive me," Katherine said gently, sitting down beside her on the bench. "My office overlooks the courtyard, and I happened to notice you didn't walk for very long." She handed Meg a tissue. "I wasn't going to interrupt, but as I watched you I had the distinct impression that you weren't meant to be sitting alone."

Meg blew her nose as delicately as possible. "I don't know what's wrong with me," she murmured. "I just don't know. I didn't know how to turn off all the voices in my head, so I tried to pray some Bible verses I learned when I was a little girl, and I couldn't remember them. For years I prayed the Twenty-third Psalm every night when I went to bed. And now I can't remember it past the first couple of lines. How pathetic is that?"

Katherine lightly touched her shoulder. "Not pathetic at all," she assured her. "Just take what you already have and meditate on that. Perhaps there's something in those first lines that the Spirit is inviting you to notice. What do you remember?"

Meg closed her eyes so she could concentrate. "'The Lord is my shepherd; I shall not want,'" she said. "'He maketh me to lie down in green pastures. He leadeth me beside the still waters. He restoreth my soul.' That's it. That's as far as it goes." She blew her nose again.

Katherine said, "You could spend a lifetime contemplating the beauty and richness of just those phrases. Which one speaks to you today?"

Meg immediately knew the answer to that question. Ever since she was a little girl, she had loved the image of God as a shepherd. She remembered looking at pictures in a children's Bible at Mrs. Anderson's house. Her favorite was a drawing of Jesus, the Good Shepherd, with a little lamb draped over his shoulders. He had left ninety-nine sheep to find the one that was lost.

"I think my first image of God was the Good Shepherd," Meg answered. "My neighbor used to sing me a song when I was a little girl, and for years I sang that song every time I felt afraid." She was surprised by how quickly the words came to mind, and she spoke them aloud. "'Jesus, tender Shepherd, hear me; bless thy little lamb tonight. Through the darkness, be thou near me; keep me safe till morning light.' I guess that's why I liked the image so much. Whenever I thought about Jesus as the tender Shepherd, I wasn't afraid anymore."

Katherine nodded. "Beautiful," she said, still resting her hand on Meg's shoulder. "So hold that as your image of God today. And as you walk, I'll sit here and pray for you."

Breathing deeply, Meg went over to the entry point of the labyrinth and stood still. *The Lord is my shepherd. The Lord is my shepherd.* She began to walk slowly and tentatively, concentrating on the winding path so she wouldn't get lost. *The Lord is my shepherd. I shall not want. He leads, guides, and protects me. He invites me to rest. He seeks me when I'm lost. I don't have to be afraid. Why am I always so afraid? Jesus, tender Shepherd, hear me. Help me not to be afraid.*

As she followed the meandering path toward the center, her imagination wandered. She saw a little lamb, lost, alone, and frightened, bleating piteously for its mother. But no one came. Darkness began to descend, and the lamb lay down, exhausted from calling out. How would the shepherd ever find it? In the distance Meg could hear the howling of wolves. *Come quickly!* she pleaded. *Come quickly!*

Meg heard him before she saw him: the shepherd was whistling as he came down the path. And when she heard the sound of his voice, her fear evaporated like fog in sunlight. She watched him pick up the little lamb and tenderly embrace it, nuzzling its nose and speaking softly and reassuringly. His voice sounded vaguely familiar as he spoke his words of comfort. "Don't worry, little one; you're safe. I have found you; you are mine. No one can snatch you away from my hand."

*You are mine. You are mine.*

What if she really believed she belonged to Jesus? What if the shepherd really did come and find her when she felt lost and afraid? What if the assurance of his presence really was enough to strengthen her and give her courage? What if . . . ?

She stood in the center of the labyrinth, contemplating the presence of God. She longed to believe God's promises. She longed for stronger faith. *Help me trust you, Jesus. Help me trust you. Please.* As she prayed, another verse from the psalm surfaced, and she held it for her outward journey. "Yea, though I walk through the valley of the shadow of death, I will fear no evil: for thou art with me."

*You are with me. You are with me. Help me be with you, Jesus. Please.* She wound her way through the turns and switchbacks. *You are with me.*

When she completed her journey, she went over to sit beside Katherine on the bench. Picking up a rose petal, Meg began to rub it slowly between her fingers.

The two women shared the hovering, prayerful silence for a long time before Katherine quietly asked, "How was your walk with God?"

Meg shook her head back and forth. "I'm not sure I did it right." She recounted how she had prayed and what she had seen. "It was all just my imagination," she concluded. "And I can't trust that. My imagination is always getting me into trouble."

"In what way?"

Meg let go of the rose petal and watched it flutter to the ground. "My mother always told me I had a wild imagination. I was always imagining bad things that might happen—I was always afraid. And then when terrible things did happen . . . " She took a slow, deep breath to still herself. "When terrible things did happen," she whispered, "I just became more afraid. And I've never stopped being afraid."

Katherine wrapped her arm around Meg's shoulder but did not reply.

Meg sighed. "I'd like to believe that what I imagined is somehow true. I mean—I know what the Bible says about Jesus being the Good Shepherd, but I haven't thought much about being like a lost sheep." She paused. "There was something so powerful and comforting when I imagined him finding me and rescuing me and telling me that I belonged to him. For a moment, it was like all my fears melted away."

Katherine squeezed her shoulder gently. "God gave you a wonderful gift, Meg. Your imagination is a wonderful gift—a vulnerability too—but a wonderful gift."

A gift? Meg's imagination had always seemed more of a liability than a gift—the vehicle through which she raced at breakneck speed to worst-case scenarios. She had lived in thousands of potential realities over the years, most of which had never materialized. It was exhausting.

"Jesus also had a wonderful imagination," Katherine continued. "He had an amazing way of inviting listeners to enter his stories and catch glimpses of who God is. That's what happened for you just now. You entered his story of the lost sheep. You walked in it and pondered it and prayed it, and the text came to life within you. That's a gift, Meg. You yielded to the Spirit's invitation and said yes to the gift of the Word made flesh. I'm proud of you."

*I'm proud of you.*

The words ricocheted in Meg's spirit as she tried to remember the last time someone had spoken them to her.

Years. It had been twenty long years.

Ignoring the stern voice inside her head commanding that she pull herself together, Meg buried her face against Katherine's shoulder and wept.

## Hannah

*Ten-year-old Hannah stood in the doorway, holding on to Daddy's waist and trying not to cry. Daddy kissed her forehead and spoke soothingly. "It's okay, Hannah. I'll be home in three days. And while I'm gone, you're in charge, okay? Take good care of Mom and Joey for me. And I'll call you when I get to California."*

*Hannah looked up into her father's eyes, her lips quivering. "Why do you have to go away so much? I don't like it when you're gone!"*

*"I know, honey. I know it's hard. But I've got to do my job, and you have a job too. Mom needs your help. I trust you to keep things going around here, okay?" Hannah nodded, sniffling. "I know that's a big responsibility, but I'm counting on you! I love you, sweetheart."*

*"I love you too, Daddy."*

Hannah arrived at New Hope just as Charissa was being dropped off near the entrance. "Thanks a lot, John!" Charissa said with a laugh. "I'll see you at one o'clock!" Then she hurried to the portico, where Hannah was holding the door open.

"Charissa, right?"

"Yes—you've got a good memory. And sorry—I know you're a pastor, but I've forgotten your name."

"Hannah." She smiled wryly to herself as they walked down the hallway and signed in. Wouldn't Steve say that was the whole reason for her sabbatical? To discover who she was when she wasn't playing a role?

While Charissa chose a seat at the front near the podium, Hannah took some coffee and scanned the room. Mara hadn't arrived yet, but Meg was sitting by herself at the back corner table near the exit door. Casually dressed in jeans and a navy blue turtleneck, she waved to Hannah when their eyes met.

"Nice to see you," Hannah said, setting down her coffee and her canvas tote bag.

"You too, Hannah."

Hannah was just about to engage Meg in conversation when Katherine gathered the group from the front. "Have you seen Mara?" Meg whispered.

Hannah shook her head and looked around the room. In fact, it appeared that several of the pilgrims had not returned for the second session. Hannah wasn't surprised. Intense and prayerful introspection wasn't for the fainthearted. To be honest, she was surprised Meg was there. And Charissa. Charissa had seemed so disapproving and provoked about the labyrinth.

Hannah sighed and looked at her watch.

Even as Katherine invited the group to still themselves in prayer, Hannah's mind kept whirling. People would be gathering at Westminster for the memorial service soon. She pictured Steve standing before the mourners, inviting people to share stories of how George had impacted their lives. She imagined Lindy sitting there in the front row, weeping at some of the memories, laughing at others. Steve had a real gift for personalizing funerals, and no doubt the intern would be learning a lot from him. Hannah hoped Lindy would be comforted by the outpouring of affection and gifts.

*Flowers.* Hannah had forgotten to send flowers. How could she have forgotten that?

She made herself a mental note to call a florist as soon as she got back to the cottage. Then again, maybe Steve wouldn't approve of her sending them. Would she be reinserting herself into the pastoral care process by sending Lindy flowers and a card? Hannah always sent flowers and cards to anyone who needed encouragement, and now she didn't know what to do.

She resented these boundaries. It didn't matter if Steve's intentions were good. She still felt like she was being punished. It wasn't fair.

She focused her attention on the group just in time to hear Katherine invite people to name their images of God. *Help me be fully present here, Lord. Please.* As voices from around the room spoke words and phrases, Katherine wrote them down on a large white board.

Jesus. Savior. Lord. Creator. Father. Provider. Healer. Spirit. Revealer. Good Shepherd. Lover. Physician. Tower. Rock. Door. Wind. Light of the World. Living Water. Teacher. Friend. Comforter. Counselor. I AM. Guide. Helper. Victor. Rescuer.

The words kept flowing.

Truth. Way. Immanuel. Redeemer. Artist. Author. Word. Treasure. King. Lamb. Host. Hiding Place. Love. Vine. Fire. Gardener. Builder. Resurrection. Life.

Katherine let each of the images rise and hover before she spoke again. "Maybe you've just heard a particular image that has caught your attention," she said. "Notice the things that attract and repel you. The Spirit of God speaks through both. Perhaps you heard an image that either drew you in or made you uncomfortable. Take the next twenty minutes or so to reflect in your journals on that. And if you don't know why you've responded in a certain way, ask the Spirit to show you."

While the room descended again into prayerful silence, Hannah studied the list of images carefully, listening for her own response to them. She knew which one unsettled her. She couldn't read beyond *Lover.*

God as Love, yes. But change that noun from an abstract concept into its active form, and she squirmed uncomfortably. Despite all the beautiful imagery in Scripture of God as the Lover pursuing his people and longing for intimacy and union, Hannah could not embrace the image for herself. That kind of intimacy frightened her.

She remembered one particular spiritual theology class in seminary. They were reading Christian mystic literature, full of erotic imagery about intimacy with God. One of her classmates had spoken up. "Sorry," he prefaced, "but all this lover imagery for God is kinda creepy. It's making me blush."

The class laughed, but their professor encouraged a willingness to be pushed beyond what was comfortable. "After all," he observed, "we do have books like Hosea as part of our sacred text."

Hannah supposed that if she were being psychoanalyzed, someone might probe her resistance to intimacy. Why was she afraid of being, as one mystic had expressed, "loved passionately, loved often, and loved long"?

What would she answer?

She knew her practiced response when people asked if she was married: "No. The right guy just never came along. Besides, my work keeps me so busy. I don't have time for a relationship." That was usually enough to shut down conversation. There was no arguing that Hannah Shepley was busy with her work. She wore her busy schedule conspicuously, faithfully attending every ministry meeting and every church event—always the first to arrive and the last to leave. Hers was the phone that rang with pastoral emergencies at 2 a.m. because people knew there was no family to disturb. She was always available, always willing.

But Steve had seen through her. "You hide behind your busyness, Hannah."

She hated admitting he was right.

Though Hannah knew many people thoroughly and intimately, very few knew her. She was skilled at disclosing just enough for others to believe they had connected with her in vulnerable places. But there were untouched layers—high security areas fenced off with barbed wire. No one had ever penetrated deep enough to glimpse the No Trespassing signs she had erected.

Except one. But that had been a lifetime ago.

One more thing she had been determined to forget. And right up until that moment, she had succeeded.

**Sacred Journey, New Hope Retreat Center**
***Session Two: Praying with the Word***
*Katherine Rhodes, Facilitator*

---

*Lectio divina* (sacred reading) is an ancient way of listening to Scripture, dating back to the early Middle Ages. It is a slow, prayerful digesting of God's Word.

In our information-overload culture, we have lost the art of lingering over words. Often when we read, we hurry through the material as quickly as possible, skimming for main ideas. But that kind of reading is counterproductive to spiritual formation. While it's essential to read God's Word, we must also allow God's Word to read us.

Many people study the Bible without ever being shaped by the text. When we come to the Word with our own agenda, we put ourselves in the position of control. We may look for what we get out of it rather than ever allowing the Word to get into us. We so easily forget that reading the Word of God is meant to be a supernatural act of cooperating with the Holy Spirit. We're meant to be listening to the Word with the ears of the heart.

At the beginning of his gospel, the apostle John wrote: "The Word became flesh and lived among us." This is the process of sacred reading. We read the Bible slowly and reverently, listening for the Word made flesh in our own lives. In sacred reading we aren't studying the Bible for historical, theological, or cultural contexts. We are looking to encounter the living God. *Lectio divina* invites the Holy Spirit to bring the Word to life in a way that grips us and speaks to us right in the midst of our daily lives. We let the word descend from our minds to our hearts where it can penetrate and transform us.

As Jesus often said, "Let those who have ears to hear, hear."

4

# Learning to Linger

*When Jesus turned and saw them following, he said to them,*
*"What are you looking for?"*

John 1:38

## Lectio Divina

If Charissa had not chosen a seat at the front table, she might have attempted an inconspicuous exit.

Was it her imagination, or did Katherine Rhodes look in her direction more frequently than any other? Not that she wasn't accustomed to being noticed. But Katherine seemed to possess an uncanny ability for zooming in on Charissa's face whenever she was feeling most provoked. Yes, Katherine saw her, but what exactly was she seeing? Charissa hated the thought of yet another person reading the subtext of her life without her permission.

As she listened to Katherine describe the process of *lectio divina,* she felt the impulse to leave, no matter who was watching or what they might think of her. Here she was again, listening to someone accuse her of wanting too much control. Ridiculous. This was not what she had signed up for. She wanted out. Maybe she could pull John away early from his football game to come and get her. But no, he wouldn't have his phone turned on. She sighed more loudly than she intended as she looked at her watch. One more hour. She might as well steel herself through to the end. For today, anyway.

"Picture lectio divina as a way of feasting on God's Word," Katherine was saying. "First we take a bite; then we chew, savoring the taste of it; and finally we swallow and digest it, and it becomes part of us. I'm going to read the same passage several times. Slowly. As I read the first time, listen for a word or a phrase that chooses you—something that catches your attention and invites you to linger with it. Don't analyze it. Just listen to it.

"Then, as you listen to the text again, ponder that word. Chew and savor it, letting the word descend from your mind to your heart. Why did it catch your attention? What is God personally saying to you? How does that word connect with your life? Don't be afraid of thoughts and feelings that arise around that word."

Charissa stiffened in her chair. Why should she be giving priority to feelings and impressions when she was reading the Bible? This sacred journey group was nothing but a collection of subjective exercises. What a waste of time. She wouldn't be at all surprised if Katherine had them all gather in a sacred circle, hold hands, and begin chanting some mantra together.

"After you've chewed on the word or phrase for a while," Katherine said, "begin a conversation with God. How is God inviting you to pray? Be honest. Allow the word you have been pondering to touch you at a deep level as you dialogue with God. Listen for the Spirit's gentle voice of reassurance as you talk with God about what you have heard. And then finally, simply rest in the Lord's presence. Let go of the need for words, and just enjoy being held in God's infinite love."

Katherine looked out at the group and smiled. "I can hear some of your thoughts racing, already worrying about whether you'll be doing it correctly. But lectio divina is simply a slow and prayerful reading with the heart. If you attempt to turn this into a method to master, you will have missed the point. Remember: we're looking to encounter God in his Word. And this is only one way to do it—not the only way. So don't worry. I'll guide you through the process with plenty of time for silence. Then, after I've given you time to rest in God's presence, I'll ring a chime to ease us back together.

"Go ahead and sit comfortably. Close your eyes, if you wish. Release the noise and distractions and chaos. Let go of everything that keeps you from being fully present to God right in this moment. Invite the Holy Spirit to open your ears to hear the Living Word."

Katherine's voice was becoming irritatingly soothing, and Charissa shifted her hips in the chair. *If she starts leading some kind of New Age breathing exercise, I swear I'm bolting out this door.*

Katherine said, "I'm going to read John 1:35-39, which takes place on the day after John the Baptist baptized Jesus. As I read the story, listen for a word or phrase that catches your attention. When you hear that word or phrase, just sit with it for a while." Charissa dutifully closed her eyes and listened as Katherine read slowly. Very slowly.

> The next day John again was standing with two of his disciples, and as he watched Jesus walk by, he exclaimed, "Look, here is the Lamb of God!" The two disciples heard him say this, and they followed Jesus. When Jesus turned and saw them following, he said to them, "What are you looking for?" They said to him, "Rabbi" (which translated means Teacher), "where are you staying?" He said to them, "Come and see." They came and saw where he was staying, and they remained with him that day. It was about four o'clock in the afternoon.

The room was still as each person presumably sat with the word or phrase that had resonated. The word *teacher* caught Charissa's attention. No surprise there. Now what? What was she supposed to do with it? She wasn't sure if the word had chosen her, or if she had chosen it. And since she didn't have any particular thoughts concerning it, she just waited until Katherine read the text again.

Long minutes passed. What was taking so long? How could they be meditating this long on such a short and simple passage? *C'mon, c'mon.* Charissa crossed her legs, uncrossed her legs, and recrossed her legs.

When Katherine spoke again, her voice was hushed. "Listen now for how that word or phrase connects with your life. What is God saying to you in this word?"

> The next day John again was standing with two of his disciples, and as he watched Jesus walk by, he exclaimed, "Look, here is the Lamb of God!" The two disciples heard him say this, and they followed Jesus. When Jesus turned and saw them following, he said to them, "What are you looking for?" They said to him, "Rabbi" (which translated means Teacher), "where are you staying?" He said to them, "Come and see." They came and saw

where he was staying, and they remained with him that day. It was about four o'clock in the afternoon.

This time something else caught Charissa's attention: What are you looking for? The teacher was asking his would-be students why they were following him. What did they actually want? The students didn't know. All they knew was that they needed time to investigate. They wanted to learn and understand. See? Why was "learning" the wrong answer?

Learning was her passion, an insatiable thirst. If Jesus had asked her the question, "What are you looking for?" her honest answer would have been, "To know more."

At that moment another verse came to mind. Charissa couldn't remember where it was from, and that irritated her almost as much as the verse itself: You search the Scriptures because you think that in them you have eternal life, yet you refuse to come to me to have life.

You refuse to come to me.

You refuse to come to me.

Charissa heard the refrain again and again. What did that verse have to do with anything? She sat up straighter in her chair, half-opening her eyes to glance around the room. Nobody else seemed to have their eyes open, and many of them were sitting with their faces upturned and their hands cupped, as if they were receiving something.

Like what?

She closed her eyes again and exhaled slowly. How much longer was she going to have to sit in the silence?

You refuse to come to me.

The silence wasn't silent at all. Not only was she hearing the swirling of words in her head, but now there was the sound of pounding in her ears. Pound, pound, pound. She pressed her fingers firmly against her forehead to try to stop the noise.

Pound, pound, pound. Like a fist on a door.

Katherine's voice spoke above the pounding. "Now listen for God's invitation to you," she said. "This is the time to talk with God about what you've heard and seen."

But Charissa did not want to talk to God. She wanted to disappear from the group and not come back. She hardly heard the words as Katherine read the text again because her head was still ringing with the fragment of the verse that had caught her off guard. *You refuse to come to me to have life. You refuse to come to me to have life . . . come to me to have life. Come to me to have life.*

Wait! Was that the invitation Katherine was talking about? "Come and see," she heard Katherine say.

*Come.*

*And see.*

See what?

## Drawing Near

"So, what are you looking for, Hannah?" Katherine asked as the two of them sat together at the back corner table just past noon. The room was empty except for Meg, who was clearing away coffee mugs.

"I'm not sure," Hannah replied. "I'm just not sure how to manage this sabbatical. I want it to be a fruitful time for me, but so far I feel like I'm not accomplishing anything. I'm just feeling sluggish and tired." She sighed slowly and tucked her hair behind her ears. "My senior pastor suggested finding a spiritual director, but I've never had a director before, and I don't know much about it."

Katherine smiled and handed Meg her coffee mug. "Spiritual direction is all about prayerful attention," she responded. "A director isn't there to solve problems or give advice. The director's role is simply to help you notice the movement of God in your life, to help you perceive the deep stirrings and longings in your spirit. And the Holy Spirit is always the primary director in the process." Katherine leaned closer, meeting Hannah's eyes. "Picture your life as a sacred text—the story of your life with God. By listening attentively to the Holy Spirit, a spiritual director engages in lectio divina, prayerfully reading the text of your life. It's a ministry of holy listening, with one ear attuned to the Holy Spirit and one ear attuned to your story. No agenda. No achievement plan. Just a time and place set apart for drawing near together to the living God."

Hannah thought for a moment before she replied. She wished someone would give her an agenda and an achievement plan, anything to help direct her time. Still, there was something attractive about the luxury of someone listening prayerfully to her life, and Katherine seemed like a trustworthy companion for the journey. "Maybe that's exactly what I need," Hannah said. "I feel like there's so much churning around inside me right now, and I'm not sure how to process all of it. It feels dark and chaotic, and I'm too close to it, you know? I don't have any perspective. No direction."

Katherine touched Hannah's sleeve. "It's hard to see light and hope when you're in the middle of all the stirring, isn't it? We need people hovering with the Spirit over our lives, watching for signs of life in the midst of the chaos and darkness. I'd be happy to explore that with you, Hannah."

Chaos, darkness, a hovering Spirit. Hannah hoped God would speak something into being. And soon. She was tired of the formless void.

"Are you sure you're up for lunch?" Meg asked as she and Hannah walked out to the parking lot together.

"Absolutely!" Hannah exclaimed. Though she had packed some snacks this time, she had eagerly accepted Meg's timid invitation. "How about if I follow you there?"

They were just getting ready to head to their cars when they spotted Charissa pacing, visibly agitated as she talked on her cell phone. Hannah couldn't help overhearing part of the conversation as they approached.

"I don't know, Mom. When I turned on my phone, there was a message from John's friend Tim, saying that the ambulance was taking him to the hospital. And now Tim's phone is off and I'm here without a car and I don't know what to do." Charissa started to cry. "No . . . no . . . There's nothing you can do. I've left messages for a bunch of people, but nobody's answering, and I just don't know who else to call . . . I know . . . okay . . . I'll call you later . . . Love you too, Mom . . . " Charissa slumped onto a bench, holding her head in her hands.

"Charissa?" Hannah said quietly, trying not to startle her. "Can I help you?" Charissa looked up and quickly wiped her nose. Meg reached into her purse and handed her a pack of tissues. "I couldn't help overhearing something about a hospital and needing a ride," Hannah continued. "If you can tell me where to go, I'll take you."

"It's my husband," Charissa answered. "I don't know what happened! He was playing football this morning, and he must've gotten hit hard. I don't know . . . They just said they were taking him to St. Luke's in an ambulance and that was almost an hour ago and I don't know what's happening!"

Meg extended her hand to Charissa, gently helping her to her feet. "It's okay, Charissa," Meg said. "We'll get you there." She looked at Hannah. "Maybe it would be easier if we all got in my car. I know how to get there."

By the time they reached the hospital, Charissa had regained her composure. Meg dropped them off at the emergency room entrance and went to park the car. While Charissa stood in line at the desk, Hannah sat down on an orange plastic chair in the waiting room.

"They've got him in for a CAT scan right now," Charissa informed Hannah when she joined her a few minutes later. "They'll let me back there as soon as they've brought him down from the radiology department." She breathed heavily. "I've never had anything like this happen before. I'm sorry I fell apart like that. I just didn't know what to do."

"Nothing to be sorry for," Hannah said. "Just glad to be able to help."

Charissa sat back in the chair, looking up at the cable news program on an overhead television. "I hope they let me back there soon. I hate not knowing what's going on."

Hannah followed her gaze to the television set and watched the closed captions scroll past. "I know," Hannah said. "Waiting is really hard." Charissa seemed lost in thought and did not reply. Hannah began to scan the rest of the room, trying to discern the stories behind the people sitting there.

The young mother wasn't difficult. Her face was clouded in apprehension as she rocked a lethargic baby, stroking the infant's head and murmuring, "You're okay, you're okay . . . " Hannah couldn't help thinking that she was whispering the words not only to comfort her child, but to soothe and reassure herself.

Then there was the gray-bearded man with shoulder length curly hair, wearing a leather biker's jacket and holding his arm gingerly. He had his face clenched like a fist, trying to look like he wasn't in pain.

The man reading a newspaper, wearing two different colored socks and drinking from a Biggby Coffee cup, gave nothing away. Hannah wondered if he was waiting for someone. He looked too calm and nonchalant to be waiting for anyone suffering a severe crisis. Then again, maybe he had put on two different socks because he was rushing to get to the hospital. Maybe the crisis had passed, and he was feeling relieved.

Meg's arrival interrupted Hannah's wandering speculations.

"Any news?" Meg asked.

"Only that they've got him in for a CAT scan right now," Charissa replied. "Sounds like it might be a concussion. I don't know. They said they'd let me back there soon." She looked at her watch and drummed her fingers on her lap.

Hannah reached into her tote bag and pulled out some trail mix and chocolate. "I remembered to pack some food today," she said, offering the snacks to the others. "Would you guys like something?" Charissa and Meg both chose chocolate. Hannah was just about to approach the woman with the baby to offer her a snack when the doors to the restricted area opened.

"Hey, Charissa!" a male voice called out.

Charissa spun around and exhaled in relief as a young man in muddy gray sweatpants and a navy blue college T-shirt approached her. "Tim!" she exclaimed.

He came over and gave her a friendly hug. "Did you just get here?" he asked. She nodded. "They took John up for an x-ray a little while ago, and then as I was heading out here to try to call you again, I ran into an old friend in the hallway. Sorry!" He rubbed some dried mud off his elbow.

"So what happened?"

Tim shook his head. "Oh, you know how gung-ho John is. What he lacks in muscle, he makes up for in heart."

Charissa flexed her eyebrows.

"He was going for a catch and collided hard with another guy," Tim explained. "He hit his head and got knocked out. He was conscious when the paramedics got there, but he was still pretty woozy, so they brought him here for observation. He should be done with the x-ray soon." He glanced at Meg and Hannah. "Hey, Charissa, if you've got friends with you, is it okay if I head home? I told Jenn I'd watch the kids this afternoon. Your car's still at the football field, though."

Meg spoke up. "I'll make sure you get your car. Don't worry."

"Are you sure?" Charissa asked, looking reluctant to accept the offer. "I don't have any idea how long we'll be here."

"I don't have any other plans today," Meg replied. "I can be here as long as you need me." Hannah saw the young mom glance anxiously at her watch and wondered how long she had been waiting.

"Thank you," Charissa said. "I really appreciate it. And thank you, Tim. Thanks for taking care of John for me."

He grinned. "I was taking care of John long before you came along, remember? Just call me and let me know how the all-star's doing, okay?"

Charissa nodded. "I should call my mom back to let her know I got here. She was worried." Charissa looked at Hannah and Meg. "My parents moved to Florida last year," she explained, "and it's hard being so far away, you know?" Finishing off the chocolate bar, she excused herself to make the call.

Meg waited until she'd gone and then turned to Hannah, apologetically. "I'm sorry, Hannah. I jumped in there to help without thinking about where you need to be. I can drive you back to your car, if you like."

"No, it's okay. There's nowhere for me to be." Absolutely nowhere. Hannah took a bite of her granola bar and glanced again at the mom. The baby was crying weakly. *Help her, Lord,* Hannah prayed. "Anyway," she went on, "I don't mind being back in a hospital waiting room again. Kinda feels like home."

Meg smiled. "We all have our gifts, don't we?"

"And I'd say you have a gift of compassion, Meg."

Meg flushed and put her hand to her cheek. "Oh, I don't know about that. I was just thinking how I would feel if I got a call from Becca and couldn't be there. I'd hope someone would take care of her for me." A nurse was summoning Charissa back to see John.

"Poor thing," Meg said gently, watching her stride through the doors. "You know, when I saw her crying and heard it was her husband, I had this sense of panic rise up inside of me. Like I time-traveled twenty years in a split second . . . " Her voice trailed off.

Hannah pulled her attention away from the mother and baby to focus on Meg. This was no longer casual conversation. She couldn't shake the sense that if she kept very still, Meg would continue to draw near. Hannah held her breath as she waited and prayed.

When Meg spoke again, her voice was trembling with emotion. "The day my husband died was terrible," she murmured. "I got the call at the house that there had been an accident, and the ambulance was taking Jim to the hospital. To this hospital, actually . . . " She looked toward the restricted doors. "But I didn't get here in time." Her voice was so soft that Hannah didn't dare breathe for fear of missing something. "They called me back through those doors, and a chaplain and a doctor were waiting to talk to me and—" Hannah reached for her hand. "And I didn't have anybody with me." Meg was biting her quivering lip.

"Oh, Meg, I'm so sorry."

Sometimes there just weren't any better words to say.

The doctors kept John for observation until four o'clock that afternoon and then released him with instructions to rest. As they walked across the parking lot to Meg's car, John responded amiably to Charissa's mild scolding. "Hey! How 'bout some credit for managing to hold on to the ball? You shoulda seen me! It was quite a catch!" He turned to Hannah and Meg. "Thanks for helping get Riss to the hospital. She's not used to being out of control, are you, Riss?"

Hannah noticed that Charissa's eyebrows were at a cool half-mast.

"Sorry to freak you out, honey," he said, taking hold of her hand. "I won't do it again."

Charissa did not reply.

John went on, addressing Meg and Hannah. "I'm sure this wasn't the way you guys expected to spend your day, hanging out in the ER. So, tell you what—how 'bout if we have you over sometime, and I'll make dinner for you?" His small brown eyes were twinkling with mischief. "'Cause it wouldn't be a 'thank you' to make you eat Charissa's cooking."

Charissa smiled slightly, shaking her head. "My mom also wants to thank you. She said what a relief it was to know somebody was taking care of us. I really appreciate it."

"Well, we all need 2 a.m. friends," Meg said, unlocking her car. "If you guys ever need anything, please call me. It sounds like I don't live too far away from you." She turned to Hannah. "Is it okay with you if I drop them off at their car first? Then I'll take you back to New Hope."

Hannah nodded. She was in no particular hurry to return to the cottage.

Hannah stared out the window as Meg drove to the New Hope parking lot. The signs of the season were everywhere: roadside stands overflowing with colorful gourds and pumpkins, U-Pick apple orchards teeming with families, hand-painted signs advertising fresh cider and brush hogging.

She sighed, thinking about autumn in Chicago. The burning bush outside her office window would become a fiery red. The maple trees at the church would be glowing in orange. The skyscraper windows would be mirroring the rosy glow of lingering sunsets. She wondered if Heather would plant mums in the pots on her patio. Hannah always planted purple and yellow mums in the fall. Maybe she should buy some flowers for the cottage to mark the changing of the seasons. Maybe that little bit of connection to Chicago would make the cottage feel more like home.

Or maybe not.

"One of these days, Meg, I'd love to have you come out to the lake," she said. "It's a beautiful, peaceful place. Great for reading or walking or praying."

Meg tilted her head slightly toward Hannah, keeping her eyes on the road. "I'd like that. I was wondering the other day how you're adjusting to being there. I mean—I think I'd find it hard to be uprooted like that. No matter how pretty it is."

"It takes some getting used to."

"Do you miss Chicago?"

"Some days more than others." That was an honest answer. "I miss the church. I miss my work. But I'm trying to leave my other life behind for now and trust that God is working out his purposes for me being here. I know there are some things the Lord wants to do in my life, and I want to be able to say yes to that work. It's hard, though. Change is really hard for me."

There. That confession might open up more conversation with Meg. Hannah always carefully calculated her disclosures for the benefit of those she pastored, deftly practicing benevolent manipulation.

For God's glory.

"Change is hard for me too," Meg said quietly.

Bingo.

They had reached the New Hope parking lot. Meg turned off the ignition but kept her hands firmly planted on the steering wheel. "You know," she said, staring at the windshield as she spoke, "when Katherine led us in that lectio divina today, I had such a strong sense of being right there with the disciples at the beginning of something wonderful. I heard John the Baptist say, 'There goes the Lamb of God!' and I wanted to leave everything behind and take off after Jesus. But then when he turned around and asked, 'What are you looking for?' I panicked. I don't know what I'm looking for. I wanted the others to give the answer so that I wouldn't have to speak up for myself. But listening to that text again and again, I kept hearing Jesus ask the same question: 'What do you want, Meg?' Not like he was frustrated with me, or anything. Just that it was really important."

Her voice caught, and Hannah watched Meg's large brown eyes brim with tears. "I can't remember the last time someone asked me that question," Meg said softly. "In fact, I can't even remember the last time I used the words, 'I want.' Or 'I need.' For so long it's been about what other people have wanted or needed. Don't get me wrong—I haven't minded! It's just that suddenly there isn't anybody wanting or needing anything from me." She turned and faced Hannah. "This is probably going to sound crazy, but I almost felt like I died when Becca and Mother were both gone, and no one needed me anymore."

"That's not crazy," Hannah reassured her. She knew exactly how Meg felt, but she didn't reveal it. After all, this wasn't about her.

"I've always thought it was selfish for me to worry about what I want or need," Meg said slowly. "But now I don't know. Today when I kept hearing Jesus ask that question, I wondered if maybe God wants me to think about myself right now. But that feels wrong. I don't want to become self-absorbed, you know?"

"I know," Hannah replied. "But it's like Katherine said on the first day. We have to know ourselves well if we're going to know God better, right? There's nothing wrong with taking the time to get to know yourself, Meg. Besides," she said, smiling. "Somehow I don't think you're in much danger of becoming a narcissist."

Meg looked pensive. "So I guess I've got to start at the beginning and ask the really simple questions like, who am I? And what do I want?"

Hannah shook her head slowly. "Just because something's simple doesn't mean it's easy."

There. A bit of pastoral wisdom.

For Meg.

5

# Come and See

*The angel who talked with me came again,*
*and wakened me, as one is wakened from sleep.*
*He said to me, "What do you see?"*

ZECHARIAH 4:1-2

## *Mara*

*Mara sat in the high school guidance counselor's office, staring at her feet.*

*"I'm looking at your grades," Mr. Graham said, thumbing through a file. "If you don't turn around these failing marks by the end of the semester, you won't graduate in May." Mara did not look up. "I know you're capable of doing better work than this. You've been a good student up until now. Is there anything going on that you'd like to talk about?"*

*Mara shook her head.*

*"I'd like to help you, Mara, but I don't know how if you won't talk to me."*

*Though Mara felt the sting of tears, she valiantly fought them back. Instinctively, her right hand shifted to her abdomen, where for a few weeks there had been life. But she was empty again. Empty and alone.*

*Mr. Graham rose from his chair. "If you change your mind, you know where to find me," he said. "I want to see you apply yourself again. You're a better student than this."*

*Mara nodded. Then she left the office, shuffled home by herself, and ate half a package of Oreos to fill the empty void.*

Mara sat in worship the last Sunday of September, half-listening to a sermon on Moses meeting God at the burning bush. She was thinking about the message Katherine Rhodes had left on her voice mail Saturday afternoon. Katherine said she was sorry Mara hadn't made it to the sacred journey group and that she would be very happy to meet with her privately. She also said she was praying for Mara, hoping she was all right.

Mara listened to the message with mixed emotion. She had expected to disappear from the group without being noticed or missed. It had never occurred to her that Katherine would take the time to call and ask about her. Now she was second-guessing her decision to quit. Was she that easily persuaded by a small demonstration of kindness and concern?

She tuned back in to Pastor Jeff just as he was talking about how God spoke to Moses. "Notice how things go down," Pastor Jeff said. "Something catches Moses' eye, and he looks. And when he looks, he sees it's something worth checking out. The Word says he 'turns aside' from what he's doing to go over and investigate. And that's when God speaks. Look how God waits to make sure he's got Moses' attention, and then he calls him by name and reveals his plan. Now Moses coulda just gone on with his daily business. He coulda just said, 'Hey, that's kinda weird over there, but heck! I got sheep to take care of! I don't have time to check that out.' Listen, folks. Many of you are livin' on autopilot, too busy to take time to notice what God's doing around you. You're sleep-walkin' and missin' what God's trying to say to you! Wake up, people!" Pastor Jeff had settled into his preaching cadence, and he was pacing back and forth, his whole body animated.

"Now I can hear what some of you are thinkin'. 'Hey, Pastor! If God put a burning bush near me, I'd pay attention too!' Listen, church! You're surrounded by burning bushes. God is constantly talkin'. The question is—are you listenin'? Ohhh! Preacher's meddlin' now!" There was a chorus of amens around the auditorium.

"You better ask yourself: how's God tryin' to get your attention? Maybe it's somethin' from the Word that's gripped you and won't let you go. Pay attention. Maybe it's a friend who's encouragin' you to take a leap of faith and trust God. Pay attention. Maybe it's somethin' that's really buggin' you, and

God wants you to pay attention so he can talk to you about why you're so upset. Wake up and listen! If you get a sense that the Lord Almighty is talkin' to you, I'm tellin' you, drop everything you're doin' and pay attention! Amen?"

A four-letter word other than "amen" came to Mara's mind, and she was grateful she caught herself before she said it out loud. *Fine, God!* she yielded. *I give. You win.*

She called Katherine first thing Monday morning and arranged to meet with her on Tuesday after she dropped the boys off at school.

Mara entered Katherine's office intending to pick up some handouts and maybe have a brief conversation. She had not planned to pour out her heart. But when Katherine asked her if she had given any thought to her images of God, Mara couldn't help herself. She started talking.

"I can't stop thinking about it. I try not to, but it's always there." She showed Katherine her tattoo. "El Roi, the 'God who sees,' right? The God who sees everything. I've spent my life disappointing God, and I'm so tired of it." She sat back on the green chintz sofa and crossed her arms.

"What do you mean by 'disappointing'?" Katherine asked.

"Letting God down," Mara answered. "I mean, it was one thing before I accepted Jesus. I understand getting forgiveness for my sin before that. But after I said I was a Christian, I kept right on screwin' up. I mean, bad stuff. Lots of crap."

Mara was tempted to divulge all the details just so Katherine would tell her she wasn't fit for a sacred journey. Then she wouldn't have to feel guilty for faking her way through it. Katherine could reject her, and that would be the end.

"But what does the word *disappointment* mean, Mara?"

Mara tightened her arms around herself and looked up at the ceiling, listening to voices out in the hallway: a man and a woman, laughing as they passed by Katherine's closed office door.

"Disappointment. I don't know . . . Like someone has certain expectations of you, and you don't live up to them. You fail." She could still hear laughter.

"And what are God's expectations for you?" Katherine asked.

"That I would be good. That I'd do things the right way. That I'd be faithful, you know? That I would be like Jesus. And I'm not. So it's like I've let God down. And I hate that feeling. It absolutely sucks." The hallway was hushed again, and all Mara could hear was the steady tick of Katherine's wall clock.

They shared the silence for a while. "What would you say if I told you it's impossible to disappoint God?" Katherine finally asked.

Mara laughed cynically. "I wouldn't believe you."

Katherine smiled with compassion. "But what does God know about you, Mara?"

Was that a trick question?

"Everything," Mara sighed. "That's the problem. I can't hide anything. He sees all my crap. Constantly."

Katherine never broke eye contact, and the intensity of her gaze made Mara feel vulnerable and exposed. "You're right that God knows everything about you," Katherine said gently. "God knows your weaknesses. Your frailty. Your imperfections. Your sin. Your humanity. And if nothing about you takes God by surprise, what expectations are you disappointing?"

Mara didn't reply. She wasn't sure.

"The only way you could disappoint God, Mara, would be if God had an unrealistic, idealized view of you. And God does not." Mara shifted position on the couch. "There are many things the Lord desires for us," Katherine went on slowly. "Many things. But his desires for us are rooted in his love and longing for us. Not in disappointment and condemnation."

"But if you knew the details about my sin, Katherine. If you knew about all my crap . . . "

Katherine said, "Tell me."

So Mara told her.

For the next hour she told her everything that came to mind: all the lurid details, all the shame, all the guilt, all the regret. Everything. She poured it out in colorful language with no attempt to edit, diminish, or conceal.

Katherine's eyes filled with tears as she listened, and her voice was low whenever she said, "Oh, my dear, dear child."

Mara finished telling her story and uncrossed her arms. "See?" she asked, wiping her face with her sleeve. Katherine handed her a tissue.

"I do see, Mara." Katherine's sapphire eyes welcomed Mara into healing pools. "The Lord also sees. El Roi is the God who sees you—who sees every detail of your life without condemning or accusing you. God's eyes are filled with tenderness and compassion. And El Roi watches over your life with far more love than you can possibly comprehend."

Mara stared at the tattoo. "Then why can't I get rid of the guilt?" she asked softly.

Katherine didn't speak for a long time, and Mara began to wonder what she was thinking. Maybe she was going to tell Mara she wasn't fit for a sacred journey after all. Maybe there was a different group for remedial Christians that Katherine would recommend. She braced herself for the verdict.

"You can't get rid of the guilt, dear one, because you're listening to the wrong voice and calling it the Spirit of God."

That wasn't the answer Mara had anticipated. "Whaddya mean?" she asked, mildly relieved that Katherine hadn't rejected her. Yet.

"You've turned to face your sin, Mara. You've had the courage to look at it, name it, and call it what it is. It's an offense against a holy God. But that's where you've stayed stuck. Instead of turning to face God to receive forgiveness, you've continued to stare at your sin and punish yourself. You've listened to the enemy's voice, accusing and belittling and shaming you, telling you that you've gone too far, telling you that you've gone beyond grace and that you need to make yourself right before you can turn back to God."

It was true. Mara was afraid to face God: afraid of judgment, afraid of rejection, afraid of condemnation.

Afraid.

"You can only turn to face God and receive his gifts when you're convinced that God is love," Katherine said.

Mara stared at her shoes. "I don't even know what love looks like." Her voice cracked with emotion as Katherine reached for her hand.

"I know, dear one. I know." The tenderness in Katherine's voice caused Mara to tear up again.

"So what am I supposed to do?" Mara asked. "How am I ever gonna get anywhere?"

Katherine leaned forward, clasping her hands together. "Start looking at Jesus," she said, smiling soothingly. "Start reading the stories of Jesus interacting with people just like you. Imagine yourself right in the middle of the story, experiencing grace, receiving forgiveness, seeing love. Let everything you see about Jesus begin to reshape your image of God and your image of yourself. God is love, Mara. And you are chosen, accepted, loved, forgiven, and treasured. That's how El Roi sees you. You are God's beloved."

Mara shook her head. "That's not the way I see myself."

"I know," Katherine said kindly. "But the Spirit of God is moving. The Holy Spirit is hovering over your life, speaking the words, 'Let there be!' And when the Spirit speaks those words of power—well, it's a whole new creation, isn't it?"

## *Hannah*

Mara was standing in the threshold of Katherine's office when Hannah arrived for her spiritual direction appointment. "Hey, Mara! We missed you on Saturday."

"Thanks." Mara fiddled with one of several oversized, brightly-colored bangle bracelets. "Katherine let me have a private session."

"I'm here for one of those myself," said Hannah, tucking her hair behind her ears.

Katherine appeared in the doorway, smiling. "I remember you two sat together at the back corner table the first week."

"Yeah—the Sensible Shoes Club," said Mara, still fiddling with her jewelry. "Poor Meg in her high heels. Did she come back for round two?"

"She did," Hannah replied. "In fact, I'm supposed to meet her here in an hour or so at the labyrinth." She hesitated a moment. "You're welcome to walk with us, Mara."

Mara stared at her feet. "You know," she said slowly, "I was gonna run some errands and get some things done before the boys get home from school . . . but maybe that can wait." She looked at Katherine. "I've got tons of stuff to think about, don't I?"

"If you'd rather be inside while you wait," Katherine answered, "we've got a beautiful chapel."

"Sounds like a plan!" Mara reached into her large embroidered bag and pulled out a notebook and a small Bible. "Ha! Never bothered to take 'em out after the first class. Guess I'm good to go!" She turned to Hannah. "I'll see you guys out there. Thanks. Thanks for inviting me." Then she headed down the hallway, jingling as her chains, charms, and beads jostled together.

Hannah sank into the sofa across from Katherine's tidy desk. For the first time since arriving in Michigan, Hannah felt a sense of kinship with space. Katherine's office was filled with potted plants, soft lamplight, and shelves stacked with books—not only theological and devotional works, but poetry, contemporary novels, and classical literature. Hannah saw some of her own favorite authors alongside names she didn't recognize. She wished she could spend hours browsing.

Just as she was thinking about how much she missed her office and her life, her eyes fell upon the Serenity Prayer framed on the wall: "God, grant me the serenity to accept the things I cannot change; the courage to change the things I can; and the wisdom to know the difference."

*Help, Lord,* she sighed.

Katherine took a single pillar candle from her desk and set it on the coffee table between them. "We light the Christ candle to remind us that we are in the presence of the Holy One," she said, blowing out the match as she sat down in an armchair and closed her eyes in prayer. "Jesus Christ, Light of the World, come and light the dark corners of our lives. Where we are blind, grant us sight. Where we stumble in darkness, illumine our path. Quiet us with your love, and enable us to hear your still, small voice. For you are our dear friend, Lord, and we long to be fully present to you."

Hannah kept her eyes closed, asking the Spirit to guide and direct her, to help her know what she wanted and needed, and to give her peace. She hadn't expected to feel anxious. Was this what people experienced when they came to her for help? It had been years since she'd sat on the receiving end of spiritual care, and despite Katherine's calm and trustworthy demeanor, Hannah felt uneasy. She preferred being The Pastor.

"So, Hannah," Katherine began, "why don't you tell me a bit about your own faith story?"

Hannah shifted on the couch, trying to find a comfortable position. "Like how I came to faith, you mean?"

Katherine smiled. "Anything you'd like to tell me about your life with God up until now."

Hannah took a deep breath. Where should she start?

Though she was tempted to launch straight into her current struggles over her sabbatical, Hannah knew she needed to provide a larger context. If Katherine was going to understand Hannah's journey forward, she would need at least a *Reader's Digest* version of Hannah's past.

Folding her hands in front of her, Hannah gave a rapid-fire, bullet point account of her childhood and adolescence: the frequent moves, her gradual awakening to her need for God as a teenager, her call to ministry. Hannah didn't supply many details, and Katherine didn't ask for any. In fact, Katherine didn't even ask a clarifying question.

Satisfied that she had given enough historical background, Hannah shared the words that had haunted her since August: *You don't know who you are when you're not pastoring.*

"It's true," Hannah said. "I feel like everything I've known and loved for the past fifteen years has been torn away from me, and I'm left feeling empty and sad. And I honestly don't know what to do about it. I want this sabbatical to be productive, and I just don't feel like I have any direction for it. No direction at all. I don't know what I'm supposed to be doing."

Katherine did not reply, and Hannah tried not to feel uneasy in the long silence. Shifting her gaze to the Christ candle, she watched the flame flicker and dance whenever she exhaled.

Katherine finally spoke. "So . . . as you think about this season of your life, Hannah, is there an image or a passage of Scripture that comes to mind? Anything that connects with your story?"

Hannah furrowed her brow in concentration. "Death. That's the only word I can think of. It feels like death. So I've been trying to name everything that's died so that I can grieve well."

She paused, thinking of all the things she had lost by leaving behind her life in Chicago: the familiarity of her home and neighborhood, the companionship of her friends and colleagues, the routine and reward of her ministry responsibilities. As she mentally reviewed the list, she knew which loss was most painful.

"I think what I'm grieving the most right now is the loss of my productivity. I love serving God. I love serving other people. I love being God's instrument in his kingdom work. And now all that has been stripped away from me. So I feel lost." Hannah looked out the window, watching orange and gold leaves flutter on the trees. "You know," she said thoughtfully, "it's funny that you used the word *season* just now. Because I think that's part of my problem."

Katherine waited patiently for Hannah to elaborate.

"I've always loved this time of year," Hannah went on, motioning toward the window. "I love the change of seasons, the change of colors. But for as long as I can remember, autumn has been a season of high activity for me—especially at the church, with all the fall programs kicking off. The run up to Thanksgiving and Advent is always busy. Really busy. And now this autumn is totally different." She paused. "I think the time of year is just underscoring my deep sense of loss, reminding me of all the things I'm usually doing in the fall—all the things I'm not doing now."

Her mind drifted again to Westminster, to the life she had loved and abandoned. The more she thought about it, the more she realized that autumn was the perfect image for describing her sense of loss. She had been forced into a season of transition, plunged toward winter's dormancy. Everything that had been fruitful and productive in her life had been stripped away. Everything.

Something Jesus said about his own death came to mind, and Hannah spoke the verse aloud: "'Unless a grain of wheat falls into the earth and dies, it remains just a single grain. But if it dies, it bears much fruit.'" She sighed. "I guess I need to trust that God is at work in this season of my life. If God is bringing things to death, then it will all be fruitful someday, even if I can't see how right now. I've got to trust that somehow invisible seeds are being scattered—seeds that will spring up into new life at the right time."

Katherine glanced out the window to the courtyard. "I confess I don't remember much from my science classes," she said, "but my granddaughter Jessica was telling me about photosynthesis the other day. Do you know why leaves change color in autumn?"

Hannah shook her head.

"Jessica explained to me that during the winter, there isn't enough water or light for producing food, so the trees take a rest. As they do that, the green chlorophyll disappears from the leaves, revealing bits of yellow and orange that have been there all along. We just can't see those colors in the summer because they're covered up by the green." Katherine paused, meeting Hannah's eyes. "Isn't it interesting how bright and beautiful colors emerge only when productivity shuts down?"

*Shutting down.*

Hannah chewed on those words a long time before she responded. "Shutting down," she echoed. "That's exactly what this sabbatical is all about." She exhaled slowly. "It's all about the death of my productivity. I've been cut back to a stump so that what's true about who I am can emerge, without me being so focused on my work."

She was right back to Steve's question again. Who was she when she wasn't serving? Who was she when she wasn't playing a role? Who was Hannah Shepley?

"You know the sad thing about all of this?" Hannah continued, staring at the Christ candle again. "For years I've taught people all about the 'false self'—all the ways we wrap our identities around how much we achieve, or how well we perform, or what other people think of us. All the ways we base our sense of significance and worth in all these secondary things. I've even led retreats on living out of our true self—living out of our true identity as children of God. And here I am, talking about how I'm grieving and struggling over not doing, not performing, not serving." She lowered her voice. "No wonder God had to strip everything away."

Katherine leaned toward her. "Hannah, the Lord is not condemning or punishing you," she said gently. "This is his love, pursuing you and enfolding you, tenderly drawing you near to heal and restore."

Hannah's thoughts were whirling and clamoring. She had been living as a hypocrite, teaching others what she had refused to embrace for herself. She hardly heard what Katherine said next.

"Hannah, Jesus loves you too much to let you root your identity in what you do for him, rather than who you are to him. He loves you too much to let you wrap yourself in anything other than his love for you—his deep, uncontainable, extravagant love for you."

Hannah pressed her palms against her eyes. "I can't believe I didn't see it clearly before," she murmured. "Steve saw it. He saw how I'd fallen in love with being used by God, how I was wrapping my life around my work. I just can't believe I didn't see it." She slowly shook her head back and forth, remembering Steve digging in his heels and tugging on the pastoral rope. "All this time, I thought I was loving God through my work. But honestly"—though it pained her to confess it, she spoke the fresh revelation out loud—"I'm beginning to think I started to love my work more than I loved God. Dear God—when did that happen?"

Hannah tried to swallow her tears. Since she couldn't bear the expression of deep compassion on Katherine's face, she looked away.

Katherine said, "Your true self will be emerging with new strength and even more beauty than before. I'm confident of that. That's the gift and promise when God strips away layers of the false self."

Hannah waited until she had control over her voice before she spoke again. "So where do I go from here?" she asked. "If this is all about shutting down my productivity so that I can refocus, then what am I supposed to do with my sabbatical?"

Katherine smiled gently. "Maybe the Spirit is inviting you to let go of your desire to make even your resting productive," she offered. "Let go of trying to purify your own love for God, Hannah, and just let this be a season of exploring how deeply God treasures you. Let this be a time of being open and receptive to Jesus pouring his love into you, apart from anything you do for him, apart from your work or your roles."

Hannah's recent conversation with Meg came to mind. Meg was asking the right questions: Who am I? What do I want? Hannah was going to need to ask herself the same questions. Was it going to take her nine months to answer them?

"It sounds like you've spent years calling yourself 'servant,'" Katherine observed quietly. "And Jesus calls you 'friend,' Hannah. More than that. You are the one Jesus loves."

As she sat in the silence of the room, Hannah remembered a women's retreat she had led years ago. She had finished the retreat by having the women gather in a circle. Then she passed around a mirror, inviting them to gaze at their own reflections and speak the words, "I am God's beloved, the one Jesus loves." When the mirror was passed to her, Hannah set it down on her podium without looking into it.

Funny. She hadn't thought about it at the time. She was just the facilitator of the exercise, not a participant.

She shifted forward on the couch and planted her elbows on her knees. "Thinking of all the things that have died," Hannah continued slowly, "I realized the other day that my first image of God died a long time ago."

Katherine was still leaning forward in her chair, listening attentively.

"My dad was a fixer. Whenever anything broke, I took it to him, and he fixed it. So when I first came to know God, that was my image: my Heavenly Father, the fixer of broken things. But I've watched too many people suffer to hold that image anymore. God doesn't fix." Her voice quivered, and she felt her eyes sting with tears. "And honestly, I'm not even sure what images of God I hold right now." They sat a long time in silence before Hannah spoke again. "You know how you listed those images of God on the board and asked us to pay attention to our responses?"

Katherine nodded.

"The one I had the strongest reaction to was 'Lover.' A really strong, negative reaction. God as Lover makes me extremely uncomfortable."

Katherine's voice was soothing. "Stay with what stirs you," she said slowly. "Our areas of resistance and avoidance can provide a wealth of information about our inner life. Don't be afraid to go deep, Hannah. It sounds like the Spirit is revealing something significant that's worth paying attention to."

*Pay attention. Pay attention. Pay attention.*

Hannah was hearing an echo in the room.

Meg and Mara were so deeply engrossed in conversation on the corner bench that they didn't hear Hannah approach. She greeted them just as Mara was showing Meg her wrist.

"I was just showing Meg my tattoo," Mara explained, holding out her wrist for Hannah to see. "I got it years ago to remind myself that God was watching over me. But then it started feeling like God was *watching* me and judging me. And I started feeling even more guilty. But something happened when I was with Katherine this morning. Like it all started to shift somehow. She was sitting there with tears in her eyes, listening to my story, and I started to think about how maybe God's eyes aren't eyes of judgment after all. I don't know . . . There's so much stuff I don't know. I feel like I've got to start over. Like I'm this little kid who doesn't know anything. 'Course, given where I've been, starting over's not a bad thing." She stopped to take a breath. "Is it really possible for a fifty-year-old woman to be born again, again?"

*Thirty-nine-year-old women too,* Hannah thought. *Dying, dying, dying in order to be born again and again and again.* But she didn't say that. This wasn't about her.

Instead, Hannah the Pastor replied, "Every day is a chance for new beginnings as old things die and new things are born. After all, that's what being born again is about, right? The old self dies, and the new self in Christ is given. And that doesn't happen only once, does it? The apostle Paul said he died every day. It's a lifelong process of dying to sin and self and rising again with Christ."

Mara whistled. "Too deep for me, Reverend," she said, chuckling. "Gotta keep it simple, or you'll lose me. Not that that's hard." She stood up and stretched. "So, are we gonna do this?" She looked down at Meg's feet. "Cute boots, sister! You look like you're ready for walkin'!"

Meg cast Hannah a distinctly perceptive glance and said, "Ready."

Hannah couldn't help wondering what Meg had seen.

## *Meg*

*Meg and Jim celebrated their high school graduation by having dinner at their favorite restaurant in Kingsbury—the Timber Creek Inn. As the two of them sat at the table, sipping soft drinks in the candlelight, Meg thought about their three years together. Jim was the light of her life, her dearest friend, her deepest joy. Her eyes welled up with tears as she looked at him.*

*"What's wrong?" he asked, taking her hand.*

*"Nothing. I'm just happy."*

*He smiled at her and reached into his coat pocket. "In that case . . . Will you make me the happiest guy in the whole world?" He pulled out the ring he had been saving for months to buy. "I love you, Meg. Will you marry me?"*

*Meg began to cry harder, unable to speak for joy. When the words finally came, she simply said yes. Again and again.*

Meg had spent the past three days contemplating two questions: Who am I? What do I want? Hannah had given her advice about how to seek answers. "Try to discover who you are apart from the roles you play or the relationships you have," Hannah had said.

Meg was confused. "But what does that leave me with? If you take away work and relationships, what do you have left? 'Woman'?"

Hannah had laughed without offering an answer.

Now as Meg traveled the inward path of the labyrinth, she confessed her frustration. She simply couldn't come up with any meaningful answers. Every time she tried to answer, *who am I?* she responded in the past tense. She had been Jim Crane's wife. She had been Ruth Fowler's daughter. Yes, she was still Becca's mom; but that relationship was shifting, and she hadn't found new equilibrium yet. She didn't know how to mother a daughter with wings.

Pastor Dave often described grief as amputation. Everything familiar in Meg's life had been hewn away, not with the careful precision of sterile scalpels, but with the raw violence of a chainsaw. Meg felt shaped only by what had been removed. She had been formed only by all the identities she had lost. Pastor Dave was right. She lived as an amputee, severed from herself. Some days the phantom pains of her former life were so strong they overpowered her.

As Meg followed the meandering path toward the center, her mother's voice rang in her ears: "You're pathetic, Meg. You just can't do anything on your own, can you?"

Mother was right. Meg had never been able to do anything without other people helping her, and now she couldn't even figure out who she was without wanting someone else to give her the answer.

*Who am I?*

How pathetic that the only word she could come up with was *woman*. Totally pathetic. But since she didn't know what else to do, she took Katherine's previous advice and waited to see if her single word would take her anywhere while she walked and prayed.

*Woman.*

It went nowhere. Absolutely nowhere.

Nothing clicked. Nothing.

But then—

*Woman. Woman. Woman I love.*

The small, incidental whisper of a single word crescendoed into a bigger, louder declaration as a long-forgotten, long-buried phrase rose from the depths of her subconscious. If she listened carefully, she could almost hear his voice saying it again: "How's the woman I love?" It had been his favorite description of her. Meg had been the woman Jim loved.

She stopped walking the path and stared toward the courtyard bench, where the pink roses were still in bloom. She and Jim used to sit together in a bower of pink roses at their little house. He had built the arbor for her on their first wedding anniversary, and he had planted fragrant climbing pink roses.

Her eyes filled with tears.

Could she really let Jim live a moment in her memory without trying to bury him again?

*Yea, though I walk through the valley of the shadow of death, I will fear no evil, for thou art with me.*

If she was going to walk through the valley of the shadow, she would need to do it now before her courage failed again. She glanced at Mara and Hannah journeying with her on the labyrinth and made her decision. She needed to stop listening to her mother's voice telling her she couldn't afford the luxury of grief: "You have a baby to take care of, Margaret, and I can only do so much. If you and Becca are going to stay here under my roof, you're going to have to act like a grown woman. I am not going to tolerate self-pity. You need to pull yourself together and move on."

*Pull yourself together and move on.*

Meg had needed her mother's help and approval, and her mother had not approved of weakness or tears. So Meg made her choice. She locked her husband away and chose her mother.

*Move on.*

But what if moving on now meant choosing Jim? Just for a moment. Just for one moment . . .

Just hearing his voice again after all these years caused her pulse to race: "How's the woman I love?" She remembered the depth of tenderness whenever he spoke those words to her. They were his first words of greeting when he got home from work; they were his gentle words of intimacy as they lay in one another's arms.

She remembered.

She remembered him holding her, comforting her, treasuring her, loving her. "You're mine, and I'll never let you go," he would say, pulling her tightly to himself. She had forgotten how safe she had been in Jim's arms. *Forgive me for forgetting.* She wasn't sure whose forgiveness she was asking for. She just knew she needed forgiveness.

By now Meg had reached the center. As she sat cross-legged on the cool pavement, she remembered the last time she'd walked the labyrinth. She had imagined the whistling shepherd coming and finding the little lamb. What had he said when he looked at her? "Don't worry, little one; you're safe. I have found you; you are mine."

*Mine.*

The single word danced about in her head until she realized why the shepherd's voice had sounded vaguely familiar.

The shepherd had spoken with Jim's voice.

*Why would she have imagined the shepherd speaking with Jim's voice?*

She wished Katherine were with her. Katherine would know why. There was something Meg was supposed to understand. She just didn't know what it was.

She looked up. Mara had already finished her journey and had left the courtyard, but Hannah was approaching the center. Their eyes met for a moment, and Meg was speaking before she could reconsider. "Hannah? Can you help me?"

As Hannah knelt beside her, Meg described the image of the shepherd with the little lamb, the memories of Jim loving and holding her, and her confusion about the connection. What was her subconscious trying to tell her? She waited breathlessly for Hannah's reply.

When Hannah finally spoke, her tone was hushed, almost reverent. "Maybe you heard Jim's voice in your memory because Jim was the one who made you feel safe and secure with his love."

Meg nodded. Hannah was right. That was true. Jim had loved her far more deeply than anyone she had ever known.

Hannah went on, her voice breaking ever so slightly as she spoke her next words. "Maybe it's about knowing that you're safe and secure with Jesus," she said. "Maybe it's about knowing that Jesus loves you with the same kind of love Jim had for you. Only more. I think God wants you to know that you really are the one Jesus loves, deeply and tenderly."

Meg's hand went to her heart, and she heard herself inhale. Long minutes passed before her mind caught up with the visceral, reflexive response of her body. Could she really fathom the depth of that kind of love? Could she really comprehend Jesus loving her more intensely than Jim had? If that's what the Lord was revealing, then everything changed.

Everything.

Suddenly, words Katherine had spoken on the courtyard bench winged back to her and rooted themselves within her spirit. "There is great love in God's heart for you, Meg. Love you have yet to experience. More than anything else in the world, God wants you to know that you are the one he treasures and loves. That's the heart of this journey. And I'll be praying for you as you walk that path."

*You are the woman I love. You're safe. I have found you. You are mine.*

Meg felt as if she were awakening from deep sleep. Suddenly, she knew the answers to the questions. She didn't yet know what the answers would mean or how her life would change with the knowing of them. But this was the beginning of a new journey. Yes, a sacred journey.

*Who was she?*

She was the one Jesus loved. Somehow—though she couldn't fully grasp it—somehow Jesus loved her even more deeply than Jim had.

*What did she want?*

As she knelt in the center, weeping, Meg discovered she wanted the same thing the would-be disciples had wanted.

She just wanted to be with Jesus.

## Charissa

*Mrs. Jackson's fourth grade classroom was quiet for the geography test. Charissa had studied hard and knew the state capitals by heart. She also knew the state mottoes and flowers, even though Mrs. Jackson had not asked for that information. Just as Charissa was wondering if she would get extra credit points for writing in the mottoes, Susie Winslow whispered from behind her.*

*"Pssst! What's the capital of Tennessee?" Charissa stiffened and did not reply. Susie tried again. "What's the capital of Tennessee?"*

*Without turning her head, Charissa muttered, "I'm not telling."*

*"What?" Susie hissed.*

*Charissa spun around. "I said, I'm not telling!"*

*Mrs. Jackson happened to look up just as Charissa was muttering to Susie. "Charissa, no talking during the test, please."*

*"But I—"*

*"Quiet, please."*

*Charissa fumed. She hated being scolded. After the test she marched up to her teacher's desk to explain what had happened. But Mrs. Jackson wouldn't listen. "Let it go, Charissa. It's not a big deal."*

*Charissa disagreed. And she wasn't going to let it go.*

It was getting dark when Charissa walked across campus after her last Wednesday class. As she passed by Bradley Hall on her way to the library, she noticed Dr. Allen's office light was on. She looked at her watch. She still had nearly half an hour before John would arrive—enough time for a brief conversation.

During her years at Kingsbury University, Charissa had taken several classes with Dr. Allen, including some undergraduate courses in medieval literature. She had always excelled, and he had often commended her for her aptitude in text analysis.

His *Literature and the Christian Imagination* seminar, however, was becoming increasingly obtuse. It wasn't that she didn't understand the poetry they were reading: she was well-versed in the writings of Milton, Donne, and Herbert. But Dr. Allen had begun pushing his students beyond simple text analysis into a realm of personal integration which she did not comprehend. He was asking probing questions about faith and practice, inviting them to reflect on how the literature was impacting their life with God.

For the first time ever, Charissa was measuring herself against her peers and perceiving some sort of deficiency. It puzzled her. She had spent years in church and had read the Bible cover-to-cover many times. She could have gone head-to-head with any one of them in a memory verse competition.

But as she sat in Dr. Allen's class, she felt as if she were listening to a foreign language. She wondered what kind of Bible training the other students had received. Her peers were speaking enthusiastically about the Spirit's movement in their lives, engaging with Dr. Allen in faith conversations that discomfited and provoked her. She seemed to have lost her edge as "most highly favored student," and she was determined to seek a remedy. She was equally determined to conceal her anxiety and her ignorance.

And then there was her experience at New Hope. She still didn't understand why Dr. Allen would have endorsed a class like that. In fact, perhaps the sacred journey group was the problem. Perhaps she should have signed up for a course in the Theology Department at Kingsbury instead—something with more direction and instruction. Perhaps things like labyrinth-walking and lectio divina were a waste of her valuable time, especially if there was a different course that would help her catch up with the other students.

Even as Charissa knocked on her professor's open office door, she wasn't quite sure what to say.

Dr. Allen looked up from his reading, removed his glasses, and rose from his chair. "Come in, Charissa."

"Am I interrupting?"

"Nothing that can't wait." He motioned to an empty seat. "What can I do for you?"

Charissa hesitated, not sure where to begin. She sat down on the edge of the chair. "Are you familiar with lectio divina?" she asked.

He nodded. "'Sacred reading.' An ancient way of savoring text. And one of my favorite spiritual disciplines. Why do you ask?"

She shrugged. "Mrs. Rhodes presented it on Saturday, and I'd never heard of it before." She still wasn't sure how to ask what she really wanted to know. "I've done lots of Bible studies, but this was different."

His lips curled into a cryptic smile. "Still worried about orthodoxy?"

*Yes,* she silently replied. *And I'm also interested in efficiency. I'm interested in the quickest way of learning what I need to know so I can excel in your class.*

Aloud, she said, "No—it's not that. It's just that the whole method seems so entirely subjective." *And a waste of my time,* she added to herself.

He was studying her carefully, and it was becoming unnerving. "Tell me more, Charissa."

"About what? Lectio divina?"

"Your experience of praying a text. Which text did Katherine give you?"

"Part of John 1, where John the Baptist points his own disciples to Jesus."

He nodded. "A great text for the start of a journey."

She did not respond.

"And where did the Spirit lead you?" he asked.

She wasn't sure the Spirit had led her anywhere. It was just her own imagining as she listened to Mrs. Rhodes read the same passage over and over again. That was her objection to the whole experience. There was no standard by which to measure personal thoughts and impressions; and without correct standards of interpretation, a person could easily drift into error. Even heresy.

Dr. Allen was still waiting for her reply. How much did she actually want to disclose to him about her personal response to the lectio divina exercise?

Charissa sat more erectly on the edge of the chair. "At first when she read the passage, nothing really struck me." She spoke slowly, weighing her words carefully. "Then the second time she read, I started thinking about how I would answer Jesus' question, 'What are you looking for?'"

He was leaning forward, listening attentively.

She forged ahead. "Anyway, when I heard that question, a memory came back to me. And then the Scripture and my own experience got jumbled together, and I went off on a tangent."

He wasn't saying anything. Why wasn't he saying anything?

"I don't know if you'll remember this or not," she went on, fiddling with the tendril of hair near her left ear. "But when I first talked to you about the New Hope class, you asked me why I wanted to go. And when I said, 'To learn,' you told me that was the wrong answer."

"I remember."

She sighed. "Well, when I heard the 'what are you looking for?' question from Jesus, it was like I was hearing your voice again, and I still had the same answer: to learn. And everything kind of spiraled from there."

Again, the enigmatic smile. "Are you saying you lost control over the text?"

Why did that same word keep coming up over and over again? She wasn't controlling!

"No, not control," she responded with a measured tone, determined not to sound defensive. "I just ended up thinking about some other Bible verses, and one thing led to another, and I ended up in a place I didn't expect."

He said, "'The wind blows where it chooses, and you hear the sound of it, but you do not know where it comes from or where it goes.'"

What, wind and sailing again? His response seemed a bit of a non sequitur, but he did not explain himself.

"I don't understand," she finally said, though she hated admitting it.

"From John 3, the story of Nicodemus," he replied. "Nicodemus didn't understand either. He was in the dark about Jesus, wasn't he? He knew he was attracted to Jesus' teaching, but he wasn't sure he wanted to go deeper than that."

Charissa wasn't sure she wanted to go deeper either. Then again, she was the one who had initiated the conversation. Why had she initiated the conversation?

She put on her engaged, eager student expression and let him finish. "Nicodemus was a teacher too," he was saying, "and no doubt he thought he had things figured out. But something about Jesus unsettled him. Then Jesus told him that his only way into the kingdom was to unlearn everything he thought he knew by being born again as a helpless infant. Well . . . you can imagine how bewildered Nicodemus would have been. And yet, light began to dawn in his darkness. He began to see."

*See what?* she fumed silently. What was she supposed to see? "So where am I supposed to go from here?" she asked, battling to mask her frustration.

"That's a good question to be asking."

She screamed, but only to herself. He was exasperating! "So are you saying I just have to start unlearning things? That's impossible! How am I supposed to do that?"

He didn't speak for a long time, and the silence became unbearable. She shouldn't have come. Why had she come? But she couldn't leave. Not yet. She had asked him a direct question, and maybe he was actually going to give her a direct answer.

Maybe.

"Charissa," he finally said, folding his hands in front of him as if he were going to pray, "if learning has become an idol and an obstacle for you—if your desire to learn is keeping you from encountering Christ—then the right place to begin is with confession and repentance. You begin by acknowledging the truth about yourself: you're a sinner who needs grace."

She knit her eyebrows together. *A sinner?* How *dare* he call her a sinner?

No one had ever—*ever*—called Charissa Goodman a sinner. It wasn't that she didn't believe she made mistakes. But there was a vast chasm between being intellectually aware of her need for forgiveness and actually embracing the identity of "sinner." After all, she strived to live as correctly as possible, eager to avoid reproach and error. Her friends would have called her a model Christian. In truth, it was how she viewed herself, though she never would have said so aloud.

She squared her shoulders.

He placed his elbows on his desk, still clasping his hands together. "Your desire for control is keeping you from entrusting yourself to Christ, Charissa. And your desire for perfection is preventing you from receiving grace. You're stumbling over the cross by trying to be good, by trying so hard to be perfect."

She did not speak. She would not look at him. She also found she could not get up, though she wanted to storm out.

"I'm not standing in judgment over you," he continued. "I'm not criticizing or condemning you. I only see your struggles because I have the same ones. It's hard for a good rule follower to be converted to grace. There are so many defenses we perfectionists hide behind, especially the impulse to trust our own efforts to live rightly and faithfully. Believe me. I know what it's like to try to add to Christ's work of salvation by striving to be perfect. But God doesn't need you to be good, Charissa. It's not your goodness that saves you. Or your performance. It's grace. All grace. And God wants to soften your heart and open your eyes so that you see how desperately you need that grace."

She clenched her jaw. He was still talking. Why was he still talking? She wished he would shut up.

"Your sin hasn't broken your heart," he said softly. "You haven't yet glimpsed the tremendous price Jesus paid to save you."

Enough. She'd had enough. She glared him down as she stood up.

"My husband's waiting for me," she said tersely, striding out the door.

Charissa's mother had once cautioned John about her daughter's power to bring her own weather system into a room. "I've never met such a wintry Greek girl," she said. "She didn't get my Mediterranean fire; she got her father's ice. Dress warmly, John."

When John picked up Charissa outside the library, the temperature inside the car plummeted. During the six years he had known her, John had become sensitive to predicting changes in Charissa's barometric pressure. But this unanticipated cold front took him completely by surprise, and no amount of warmth or humor thawed it.

"Is there anything I can do for you, Riss?" he asked as he sat on the floor in front of her after dinner, massaging her feet. She pulled away and kept typing. "How about something from the store? I'll run out and get you anything you want. How about some chocolate covered cherries?"

Silence.

"Strawberry cheesecake?"

No response.

"There's still some chocolate chip cookie dough ice cream in the freezer . . . "

Nothing.

"I wish you'd talk to me, Riss. I don't know how to help if I don't know what's going on. Please, honey, talk to me. I've run out of comfort food suggestions."

She scrunched her eyebrows.

"Okay . . . I'll be sitting right here, waiting for you to command me to do something. Anything!" He sat down in the recliner next to the couch, resisting the temptation to break the silence by turning on the television. Since he didn't want to do anything to aggravate her, he spent the next several hours aimlessly surfing the web and playing solitaire on his laptop.

At ten o'clock he gave up. "Love you," he said, kissing her on the forehead. "I'll see you in the morning."

John lay in bed, eavesdropping on one side of Charissa's early morning telephone conversation. "It's too late to change classes now, Mom." At least she was talking to someone. He just wished she would confide in him. "I know. It was totally inappropriate. I'm furious. But I also don't want to give him any satisfaction by walking away. And besides, I don't want to lose a whole semester." Pause. "I know. How dare he, right?"

How-dare-he-what? Who?

"No," Charissa went on. "I don't know what I'm going to do yet."

Pause.

John wished he could hear how her mother was responding. She usually had strong opinions to express. Charissa was silent a long time. And then, "I know, Mom. I don't have class again with him until next week, so at least I don't have to see him. I can easily avoid him until I figure out what to do."

Dr. Allen. It must be Dr. Allen. John couldn't think of any other professor who might provoke his wife like this.

Her voice trailed off as she slipped into conversation about something else. John waited until she was off the phone before he shuffled out to the kitchen to make coffee.

"Mornin', Riss." He kissed her on the cheek. She mumbled a half-hearted reply. "You want some coffee?"

"Already had some," she answered curtly, keeping her aquiline nose in a book.

He opened the fridge. "Can I get you some breakfast? I can make you some eggs or something."

"No-thank-you."

"Toast?"

"I'm not hungry."

John couldn't tell if she was actually reading or just pretending to read so she could avoid conversation. He poured some Cheerios into a bowl and sat down at the table, trying to figure out how to engage her. "Heard you on the phone with your mom," he ventured, swirling his spoon around in the milk before he took a bite.

She didn't respond.

"You wanna talk?"

No answer.

"Sounds like something happened with Dr. Allen?"

She looked up briefly from her book. "I'm done talking about it," she clipped.

John cleared his throat and took another bite. "You haven't talked to me about it yet. And I'm your husband, remember?"

Her eyes narrowed to steel slits. "So you're going to pile it on too, huh? Great."

"I'm not piling anything on. I just . . . I was just hoping you'd share with me about what's going on. That's all."

"I don't need you making me feel guilty." Her voice was ice. He wrapped his flannel robe more tightly around himself.

"No guilt, Riss. I was just trying to help." He finished his breakfast in silence. Not knowing what else to do, he hopped into the shower and prayed.

Dr. Nathan Allen was also praying as he sailed north along Lake Michigan early Thursday morning, skillfully tacking into the wind.

He had second-guessed himself a thousand times after Charissa left his office. Had he said too much? Had he pushed her too hard? Katherine Rhodes, his spiritual director, had once reminded him that two people could hear the same words in vastly different ways. "Depending on where they are in their walk with God," she said, "one person hears something as a tender word of grace and compassion, while another hears the same thing as a harsh word of rebuke."

He knew how Charissa had heard what he'd said.

Nathan had known her for a few years now, observing her in several classes and glimpsing her intellectual acuity. But he had never encountered a student who was wound up quite as tightly as Charissa Goodman Sinclair.

Charissa evoked his deep compassion. He recognized in his student many of the same sins and weaknesses the Spirit had aggressively pursued in his own life: the desire for control, the striving for perfection, the single-minded drivenness which had cost him so dearly in his own personal relationships. If he could help in pointing her to grace, then maybe he could spare her some of the pain he had known.

Then again, pain had been one of his finest, most reliable teachers.

*Help, Lord.*

Though he had been surprised when Charissa enrolled in his Christian imagination seminar, Nathan interpreted her presence in his class as a sign of the Spirit's stirring in her life—or, at the very least, he saw the opportunity for the Spirit to move her toward freedom from her captivity and rigidity. And then when she actually approached him and asked about the sacred journey group, he had inwardly rejoiced.

After weeks of fervently praying for her, he had finally discerned the Spirit's prompt to speak painful words of truth as she sat in his office. He knew what he'd said had wounded and angered her; he just hoped he hadn't caused her harm.

"Sometimes on the way to better, things get worse for a while," Katherine often said.

He adjusted the sails.

The encounter with Charissa had brought back the memory of another tense conversation he'd had with someone in a former life. How long had it been? Fifteen, sixteen years?

The two of them were in graduate school together, and she quickly became his closest friend. She was passionate about Jesus, full of love for God and other people. She had a light and spirit that drew him in, and during their two years of close friendship, her zeal awakened his faith and stirred his affections. Loving her made him love God more.

But she was so consumed by her desire to serve the Lord that she spurned his overture for something deeper than friendship. She did not believe there was room in her life for both Jesus and a relationship, and she refused to be divided and distracted. So she made her choice. She chose Jesus and rejected Nathan.

"You're hiding," he told her. "You're terrified of letting someone in. You've got secrets you won't even reveal to yourself. You've got things buried so deep inside of you that you've got no idea how to name the pain. But I would share the burden with you, whatever it is . . . whatever you're carrying . . . What if I'm part of God's plan for your life? What if God is trying to pour out his love for you through me?"

But he pushed too hard; he saw her too clearly. She walked away and never came back.

Nate passed the red lighthouse at the end of the channel and came about, changing course. As the wind filled the sails, he entrusted Charissa to God's faithful care. *Please don't let her walk away from you, Lord. Please.*

6

# Hiding and Seeking

*I myself will be the shepherd of my sheep,*
*and I will make them lie down,*
*says the Lord God.*
*I will seek the lost,*
*and I will bring back the strayed,*
*and I will bind up the injured,*
*and I will strengthen the weak.*

EZEKIEL 34:15-16

*Meg*

"Great lesson today, Ellie." Meg patted the blonde curls of her final Thursday evening piano student. "Keep working on those scales, okay? I know they're not much fun, but they'll help you with all of your songs." Meg smiled at her. "You're doing really, really well, honey. I'm proud of you."

Ellie wrapped her arms around Meg's waist. "Bye, Mrs. Crane. See you next week!"

Meg waved to Ellie's mom, who was waiting in the car. Then she closed the front door and sighed.

It was time.

She poured herself another cup of herbal tea before purposefully climbing the stairs into the attic. She hadn't visited the attic in years.

*Ready or not, here I come!* she breathed.

She knew exactly which box she was seeking: a small cedar hope chest she had hidden away after Jim died. She found it right where she had left it—tucked in a far corner beneath the eaves. Brushing off the cobwebs, she opened the latch. Meg hadn't seen his handwriting in two decades, and her eyes filled with tears as she read the words written on the very top envelope of the stack: *For Meg, the woman I love.*

Meg carried the chest down to her bedroom, where she sat at her desk for hours, reading all his letters. She had carefully preserved every one of them—from the very first note he had passed her in English class when they were fifteen to the very last card he had given her ten years later, just weeks before he died. Though her mother would have chastised her for being sentimental, Meg savored every word, reading the letters over and over again. She laughed and wept, sometimes simultaneously, as she heard Jim's voice speaking with love once more.

Meg took a single card to bed with her: Jim's last gift. She closed her eyes and remembered. They had gone out to dinner together at the Timber Creek Inn. She could see his face across the candlelight, his eyes brimming with joy and love. They'd had their first ultrasound glimpse of their baby that day, the baby they had longed and hoped and waited for. Jim reached into his coat pocket and pulled out the card, watching Meg as she opened it. "For the Mother-to-be," the front cover read. And inside: "God has hidden his special treasure within you, and angels await the unveiling."

Jim had written his own message on the inside cover:

*To Meg, the woman I love. How can words possibly express the love I feel for you and our baby right now? Suddenly it seems so real. I'm going to be a dad! Just watching our baby move and hearing the heartbeat—I can hardly believe it. So many dreams have come true, and I can't imagine there's a happier man anywhere in the world tonight. You are my special treasure, Meg, and I can't wait to be the happiest father as well as the happiest husband. You're going to be an amazing mother. I love you, and I'm so proud of you. Yours forever and ever, Jim.*

*P.S. I hope our baby has your eyes.*

Meg had later placed inside the card the only photo Jim had ever seen of their baby: the grainy black and white picture showing tiny fists and feet. They hadn't known if the baby would be Rebecca Grace or William Ryan when Jim died. But one of his hopes was granted. Becca had her mother's eyes.

*Becca.*

Meg's thoughts drifted to her free-spirited daughter a world away. There was so much Meg had never told Becca about her dad. Becca had learned early on that when she asked about Daddy, Mommy felt sad. So after a while she stopped asking.

*If only . . .*

If only Meg had possessed the courage to do things differently with her daughter. If only she'd had the determination to allow Jim's memory to live and breathe in their midst. If only she'd been stronger, less afraid.

As she gazed at the ultrasound photo, Meg knew what she needed to do. She needed to ask for Becca's forgiveness. But how? It certainly wasn't something she wanted to do by e-mail. It also didn't feel right to do it over the phone. No, she wanted to look into Becca's eyes and tell her how sorry she was for hiding her dad from her. She wanted to show Becca his beautiful card and tell her how much her father had loved her, even though he had never had the chance to meet her and tell her himself. She wanted Becca to know.

Meg thought back to their parting conversation at the airport in August. She and Becca were standing together at the security gate, getting ready to say good-bye after too short a summer. "Mom, I wish you'd think about coming to see me in England. I'm going to have all that time off in December."

"Oh, honey, you know me. I'm such a homebody. But I bet Aunt Rachel would come if you asked her."

"It's not the same. I just wish . . . " Becca's voice trailed off.

Meg stroked her daughter's short dark hair. "I know . . . I know."

"You don't have to stay trapped, you know," Becca said sternly. "You don't have to live with so much fear."

"I'm sorry, honey. It's just the way I am. The way I've always been."

"Well, you could learn another way. You're always talking about my wings and Aunt Rachel's wings. You could fly too, Mom. If you wanted to."

Meg sighed as she remembered. What was the verse Hannah had given her the other day? Something about perfect love and fear? She opened her Bible and looked it up. It was from 1 John 4:18: "There is no fear in love, but perfect love casts out fear."

Perfect love casts out fear.

Was this her journey? From fear to love? She remembered the image of the shepherd finding her and comforting her. She remembered thinking that if Jesus really walked with her, she wouldn't be afraid. Suddenly, everything seemed to fit together: her emerging understanding of God's perfect love, her memories of Jim's deep love, her longing and love for Becca.

A single picture emerged. She saw herself boarding a plane. Meg Crane had never traveled farther than four hours from home, and that was when she and Jim had driven north to Mackinac Island for their honeymoon.

But traveling across the ocean by herself? She had never flown anywhere—she had never set foot on an airplane. She couldn't. She couldn't fly to England.

*Could she?*

Remembering the simple prayer Katherine had taught her, Meg slowed her rapid and anxious breathing, inhaling, *I can't.* Exhaling, *You can, Lord.* Inhale. *I can't.* Exhale. *You can, Lord.*

*If only . . .*

*What if . . . ?*

The next morning Meg discovered that her desire to see Becca had only intensified. As she sat with her coffee, she debated calling her sister to tell her what she was considering. On the one hand, Rachel could quickly point her in the right direction for an expedited passport and travel tips. On the other hand, once she told Rachel, she would be committed to following through. Rachel certainly wouldn't let her back away. Maybe that was what Meg needed: someone holding her accountable so she wouldn't retreat in fear. What should she do?

It was a whispered thought that seemed to come from outside herself. *You can pray about it.*

But Meg didn't know how to pray about making that kind of decision. How would she even know how to hear God's voice leading and directing her? She had so many voices in her head. How would she know which one was God's?

Her familiar anxiety began to grip her, and she breathed slowly. *I can't. You can, Lord. I can't. You can, Lord.*

The next voice she heard in her head was Katherine's, speaking gently and softly as the two of them had sat together on the labyrinth courtyard bench. "It's a privilege to walk alongside you in this journey, Meg. If you need some help or encouragement, call me."

Before she could change her mind, she removed the phone book from the kitchen cupboard and dialed the number to New Hope.

Later that afternoon Meg sat in Katherine's office, drinking chamomile tea. "Tell me about your fear," Katherine said. "Are you able to name it?"

"I don't know. That's what's so silly. I don't even know what I'm afraid of. I'm so used to staying close to home, and suddenly I'm thinking about flying across the ocean by myself. It just seems way too adventurous for me. Way too impulsive and sudden." She breathed deeply. "How do I know if it's something I'm supposed to do?"

Katherine sipped her tea slowly before she replied. "One of the early church fathers wrote that the glory of God is revealed in a person who is fully alive." She set her mug down on the coffee table and leaned forward slightly. "I'm listening to you describe your desire to see Becca, and you light up when you talk about the possibility of spending time with her. You've come to life, Meg, just talking about visiting her."

Meg nodded. "I miss her. And I'm feeling an urgency I can't quite explain—just that I have things to say that I want to say face to face. And she won't be coming home until next summer. I worry that if I don't do it now, I may never get the same kind of opportunity again."

Katherine said, "Sometimes it's hard to pay attention to our own desires, isn't it? We start believing that God only wants us to do the things we *don't* want to do. But God also speaks through the deep desires and longings of our hearts. God invites us to pay attention to the things that bring us life and joy." She paused. "The Good Shepherd guides with a gentle hand, Meg. With a steady, gentle hand. And you'll come to recognize his voice. Jesus promises that."

Meg stared out Katherine's office window to the labyrinth courtyard, remembering the peace she had experienced when she imagined the shepherd finding her. She remembered the joy of hearing the words that she was safe, that she belonged to him, that she was loved.

"I know one thing I want," Meg sighed. "I don't want to be afraid anymore. But I've been afraid for so long, it's in the air I breathe. I just don't know how to get rid of my fears, Katherine. And I need to get rid of my fears so I can follow Jesus."

Katherine smiled kindly. "Lay that burden down, dear one," she said. "We'll always be a mix of fear and faith."

Meg furrowed her brow in bewilderment. That wasn't the answer she had expected. She had thought perhaps Katherine would give her a strategy for overcoming her fears so she would be able to travel more freely and lightly with Jesus. "You mean I'm not supposed to try to get rid of my fears?" she asked. That didn't make sense. Wasn't the Bible filled with commands about not being afraid? Meg had broken all those commands.

"Faith isn't about not being afraid, Meg. Faith means we trust God, even when we're afraid. Especially when we're afraid." Katherine peered at Meg with intense gentleness. "Don't worry about trying to rid yourself of your fears," she said slowly. "Instead, let your fears do the hard work of revealing deep truths about yourself. Our fears can be windows into the raw and unvarnished truth of our lives. We don't cling to them or feed them, but we do listen prayerfully to what they teach us. We ask God what the fear is revealing about who we are and what we lack. We bring our fears into the light of God's healing love, offering them up to God as an expression of our weakness and our need for him." She paused. "Even our fears become opportunities for encountering Jesus, if we let them draw us close to the Lord."

The silence in the room became a soft-knit cloak, wrapping and enfolding Meg in comfort. She had never once considered that her fears could be anything other than an obstacle to faith—a persistent source of shame and regret. She had never considered the possibility that her fears could actually become an opportunity for deeper intimacy with Jesus. "So I stop worrying about trying to get rid of my fears and just start focusing on God's love for me?" she asked quietly.

Katherine nodded. "Getting rid of the fears is never the goal," she said. "If we fix our eyes on that, then we won't be looking at Jesus. Drawing close to the Lord is what we're seeking. God is always our first desire. So we focus on the perfect love and faithfulness of God instead of the depth of our fear. We meditate on how big God is. How trustworthy God is. How loving and gracious God is. And slowly . . . Slowly we discover our trust growing, and our fears shrinking—all by God's gift and power. Always by God's gift and power—not by our own efforts."

Katherine reached for a well-worn leather Bible and flipped through wrinkled pages until she found what she was looking for. "Here," she said, pointing to Isaiah 43. She handed the Bible to Meg. "Read the first few verses out loud, and when it says 'Israel' or 'Jacob,' put in your own name."

Meg raised her eyebrows. "Am I allowed to do that?" She had never heard of personalizing Bible verses.

Katherine chuckled. "Absolutely! At the moment we're not looking at this text historically. We're reading it devotionally as prayer. As God's promise to you."

Meg cleared her throat before she began to read the verses aloud, slowly and prayerfully. "But now thus says the Lord, he who created you, Meg; he who formed you, Meg: Do not fear, for I have redeemed you; I have called you by name, you are mine."

She stopped reading. *Mine. You are mine.* It was the same promise of assurance she had heard in the labyrinth! The same exact promise. Had she told Katherine what she had imagined the shepherd saying to her? She couldn't remember, and maybe it didn't matter. It was still God's word: God's word for her.

She kept reading aloud, continuing to insert her name. "When you pass through the waters, Meg, I will be with you; and through the rivers, they shall not overwhelm you; when you walk through fire, Meg, you shall not be burned, and the flame shall not consume you."

*I have called you by name, Meg; you are mine. I have called you by name, Meg; you are mine. Mine, mine, mine.* The words danced in her spirit. She sat, savoring the promise, as if the Good Shepherd were speaking the words directly to her. God had created her, formed her, redeemed her. And God was calling her. *I will be with you, Meg. I will be with you.*

She looked up at Katherine, her eyes filling with tears. She knew what God was inviting her to do, and she was going to do it. With God's help, she was going to do it.

"I think I'll call Becca as soon as I get home."

"Are you serious?" Becca exclaimed. "You're actually coming? I can't believe it! That's the most amazing present ever, Mom. Thank you! We'll have the best time together!" For the next hour Becca spoke excitedly about all the places she wanted them to visit together: museums, tea rooms, art galleries, historic buildings. "You're not going to believe everything there is to do over here, Mom. You better plan on coming to stay for a few weeks, okay?" Becca's joy and enthusiasm buoyed Meg's spirits above her own fears, and by the time she hung up the phone, she was ready to pack her suitcase.

Just before midnight Meg fell asleep with images of castles, thatched cottages, and rolling hills swirling around in her head.

And all night long she dreamed she could fly.

## Charissa

Charissa laced up her shoes and waited for Emily to arrive for a Saturday morning power walk. At least they had good weather. She didn't like walking laps at the mall.

"You sure you don't need the car this morning, Riss?" John asked.

She shook her head.

"Say hi to Emily for me, okay?" He kissed her on the forehead. "And Tim wanted me to tell you that he'll make sure I don't do anything stupid. I'm just watching from the sidelines to cheer the guys on." He fiddled with his keys, looking hopeful. She turned away. "Okay . . . I'll be back about one o'clock or so. Love you."

She waited to get up until she heard the door close behind him. Then she went to her bathroom mirror to check her makeup.

What was she going to do about John?

After days of not communicating with him, it was becoming difficult to lay down her defenses. If he would just explode at her in frustration, she wouldn't feel so guilty for shutting him out. But he continued to endure her icy cold front with a sunny cheerfulness that was becoming increasingly irritating.

She was plucking errant eyebrow hairs when Emily rang the buzzer. "Be right there!" Charissa called into the intercom. Pulling her hair into a ponytail, she went downstairs to greet her friend.

"I've missed you!" Emily said, embracing her. "I don't know where the months go."

"I know. Grad school is keeping me really busy, and now with that Saturday class I'm doing twice a month, the weeks just slip by."

Charissa covertly scrutinized her friend. It had been several months since they'd seen one another, and Emily looked like she could benefit from working up a sweat. Her jeans were definitely too snug around her hips, and her belly folded over the waistband. It wasn't that Charissa would have wished her back into compulsive obsession over her weight. After all, Emily had spent years waging war against her physical, emotional, and mental demons. But as Charissa followed her to the car, she couldn't help thinking that Emily had gone to the other extreme. A little more effort regarding her physical appearance wouldn't hurt her. It might even help her in the world of dating.

"You still want to walk the loop at Castleton Park?" Emily asked. They had been walking the loop at Castleton since they were sixteen.

"Sure," Charissa said. "And I want to hear everything about what's going on in your life, Em." Then Charissa wouldn't have to talk about hers.

It was usually a strategy that worked.

"So, enough about me and my Internet dating disasters," Emily panted as they completed their second mile loop around the park's hilly terrain. "I mean, if the guy's only interested in me for the way I look, and he never sees the real me, then I don't want to be in a relationship with him anyway. Right? I'm just going to keep praying and waiting for the Lord. Jesus has never failed me, no matter how rough it's gotten."

Jesus. It always came back to Jesus with Emily. Charissa didn't know how to respond, so she picked up the pace and kept her eyes fixed on the freshly tarred path ahead of her.

"What about you, Charissa? What's the Lord doing in your life?"

Ugh. Why did Emily always ask that question? Charissa hated when she asked that question. If only she had rescheduled their walk for another day. Or week. Or month. She didn't have her usual margin for humoring Emily's Jesus-and-me theology.

"Oh, I don't know," Charissa said. "I'm just keeping busy with everything." She was still watching the path and listening to the sound of her footsteps pound the pavement. Right. Left. Right. Left. One in front of the other in a perfectly precise, brisk rhythm.

"And how's John?" Emily asked, visibly struggling to keep up with her. "I was worried when I got your message about his concussion. That was scary, huh? He hasn't had any more headaches or anything?"

Charissa drew in her breath. She didn't know. She had been so preoccupied rehearsing her anger with Dr. Allen, she had actually forgotten about the hospital visit. She didn't have a clue if John had been feeling well or not. She hadn't asked him.

No wonder he had promised her he wouldn't be playing football.

"He's doing great." She pumped her arms harder. "He's out with the guys again this morning, though he promised me he would just be watching from the sidelines." She laughed casually, hoping Emily wouldn't ask any other questions that might uncover the lack of spousal communication.

"I'm so glad he's okay," Emily puffed. "He's such a great guy. After all these years, I still just have to keep confessing how jealous I am. Guys like John give me hope, you know? Like there might be another diamond in the rough out there."

Charissa did not reply. She couldn't believe she had forgotten about John's concussion. How could she have forgotten about a trip to the emergency room? What kind of wife was she, anyway? And how could she possibly admit to him that she had been that self-absorbed?

Then again, maybe she wouldn't need to confess anything. She'd simply start talking to him again. That would go a long way. She could just pretend nothing had happened and move on. John wouldn't demand anything from her. He never demanded anything from her. He would just be grateful to have her communicating. He was so easygoing, so easily pleased. She could find a way of pleasing him, and it would cover up everything else.

Everything.

Emily was back to talking about Jesus again. If she kept talking about Jesus, then Charissa wouldn't have to worry about her asking probing questions. "Remember how I told you about that women's spiritual formation group at my church?" Emily was saying.

Charissa nodded, silently willing Emily to go faster. *C'mon, c'mon.* They still had three miles to go, and at this rate, she'd barely make it home before John.

Emily continued, "Well, we were talking a few weeks ago about how we all have this tendency to stuff and hide our darker sides—to think, 'Good Christian girls shouldn't feel that, shouldn't think that, shouldn't do that.'" Emily stopped walking and motioned to a bench beside the path. "You mind?" she wheezed. "My allergies have been acting up. I just need to catch my breath for a sec."

Charissa did mind, but she didn't say so. Smiling indulgently, she fought the temptation to keep stepping in place and instead bounced up and down on the balls of her feet, scrunching her toes. *C'mon, c'mon, c'mon.*

"Anyway," Emily went on, leaning back into the bench and breathing deeply. "One of the women came up with this really great metaphor. She said it's like we all have these toxic waste containers inside of us. We shove our junk in there and then put a doily on top, pretending to everybody that we've got everything under control. We're constantly hiding behind these happy Christian masks. And now that I recognize that, I keep discovering all these ways that I've been stuffing my junk and trying to make it all look pretty and presentable. But Jesus is inviting me to face it and confess it so I can let go of it. I can't even describe to you how freeing it is to confess my sins to a group of women—these sisters in Christ—and to quit pretending I've got everything all together. It's amazing. The freedom is amazing." She took a long sip from her water bottle. "When I think back to all the stressful years and all the pressure I put on myself and how sick I became trying to be perfect . . . Well, you remember, Charissa . . . " Her voice trailed off. "I'm just so glad Jesus found me. Where would I be without the Lord?"

Charissa didn't have an answer.

She was thinking about toxic waste containers with doilies on top.

"How was football this morning?" Charissa asked when John got home. She had changed into a cropped tank top that accentuated her figure and was reclining on the couch with her hair down. John liked it when she had her hair down.

"It was good. I coached. How's Emily?" He put his wallet on the kitchen counter and hung up his keys. She saw his gaze fall momentarily to her chest as he lowered himself into the recliner.

"She's Emily. Still no boyfriend. Still talking a lot about Jesus." John smiled and leaned back in the chair, pressing his hands to his forehead. "Headache?" Charissa asked, shifting position on the couch.

"Just tired." He yawned. "I think I'll go lie down for a while."

She pulled the tank strap below her shoulder. "Want some company?"

John was eager. Thirsty. Charissa knew how to give him what he wanted and needed. She held nothing back of her body, even while her mind and heart were miles away. She could make up for days of shutting him out by letting him in, and he would be satisfied. More than satisfied.

"I love you, Charissa," he whispered, pulling her to himself.

She flashed her whitened smile and did not reply.

When John awoke a few hours later, Charissa was sitting at the table, typing on her laptop. "Hey," he said, wrapping his arms around her shoulders and kissing the top of her head. "Do you want to go out for dinner tonight?"

"What for?"

"I don't know . . . I just thought it might be a nice change of pace . . . you know . . . give us a chance to talk without any distractions."

Talking was something she didn't want to do. "I don't want to take the time to go out, John. I've got a ton of work due on Monday."

He sat down across the table from her, looking disappointed. His expression irritated her. Couldn't he be satisfied with what she'd already given him?

"Then how about if I go pick up pizza or something?" he asked.

"That's fine." She kept typing, while he sat in silence.

"Riss?"

"Hmm?"

"Can you stop typing a sec?" She looked up. "I was just hoping we'd have a chance to talk. I still don't have a clue what you've been so upset about, except for what I've overheard you and your mom talking about. And I just don't want to keep walking on eggshells around you. I'm not sure what to say, or what to do, or how to help. I thought maybe—maybe after this afternoon and everything—I thought maybe you were ready to talk to me, you know?"

She tapped the keyboard in agitation. *Eggshells?* This wasn't about him. He wasn't the one who had been unjustly criticized and persecuted. "I told you before, John. I don't need you making me feel guilty. I'm allowed to get upset over stuff."

"I know. I just wish you'd talk to me about it." He paused. "C'mon, Riss," he said gently, reaching for her hand. "What are you so afraid of?"

"I'm not afraid of anything."

"Then why won't you talk to me?" She didn't know. She honestly didn't know. "Charissa?"

"Hmm?" Why did she feel like crying? She hated crying.

"What did Dr. Allen say to you?"

She sat a long time, rolling the words around in her mouth before she spit them out. "He called me a sinner. A hard-hearted Pharisee. A control freak. An angry, critical, judgmental, perfectionistic bitch."

John raised his eyebrows. "Seriously?" She did not reply. "Gimme that guy's phone number." John looked angrier than she had ever seen him. "Seriously, Charissa. Gimme his phone number. I wanna talk to him. He totally crossed a line. How *dare* he say those things to you?"

She felt her lips quivering, and her eyes burned. John came over to embrace her. "C'mere," he said, pulling her to her feet. She rose reluctantly.

"Don't worry, honey. We'll take care of this. We'll call the dean, the president. Somebody. That guy oughta be fired." Tears burst forth without her permission. "It's okay, baby. Everything's gonna be okay. Don't worry."

He was stroking her hair, kissing her forehead, whispering words to soothe and comfort her. His gentleness was suffocating.

"I need to go to bed," she said, pulling away. "And I don't want to talk about this again." She hated the wounded look in his eyes.

But not enough to change her mind.

## Sunday

Meg scooted out the back door into the narthex as soon as Pastor Dave pronounced the benediction, hoping to catch Sandy before she was surrounded by a crowd of people.

Pastor Dave had announced in worship that Angel Carpenter, a young mother in the church, had just lost her husband in a car accident, and the deacons were looking for people to cook meals for her and her two little girls. Meg never heard the sermon. She couldn't stop thinking about the young widow. She wanted to help. She had spent three years sneaking in and out of worship at Kingsbury Community, but something had shifted. She wanted to serve. She didn't have much to offer, but she knew how to cook; and she missed cooking for other people.

"I'd like to volunteer, Sandy," she said shyly, the heat rising to her face. "To help that young mom, I mean. I'd like to make some meals for her."

Sandy grasped Meg's icy fingers. "That's wonderful, Meg. Thank you. She's reeling, you know?"

"I know." Though Meg felt her eyes brim with emotion, she didn't look away.

"If you'd prefer," Sandy said, "you can drop the meals off at my house, and I can get them to her." It was a kind offer, and a month ago Meg would have accepted it. In her old life of a week ago, she would have said yes.

"Thanks, Sandy, but I think I'll take them myself. I'd like to meet her."

Sandy smiled. "Well, I know Angel will be grateful."

As she drove home, Meg was the one filled with gratitude.

Hannah spent Sunday morning in her robe and slippers, with her Bible and a pot of English Breakfast tea. Meg had invited her to worship, and she had been tempted by the offer. Not for her sake, but for Meg's. She wanted to support Meg and encourage her on the road toward overcoming her fears and timidity.

Hannah had already decided, however, that it was best if she simply invested in her own personal spiritual growth for nine months. She didn't need the distractions of corporate worship. It was one of the casualties of her seminary training: she couldn't turn off the incessant internal monologue. Even when she wasn't leading worship, she was constantly analyzing everything from the flow of the service, to the style of the music, to the content of the sermons. The prayers didn't escape her scrutiny either. There were just too many temptations to be critical, and she rarely entered into any sense of communion with God during corporate worship. If she avoided church, she could focus on encountering God without meditating on anything else.

So she prayed for Meg and stayed by herself at the cottage. It was easier that way.

Charissa awoke on Sunday morning with a massive hangover. After years of being intoxicated with her own goodness, she felt sick to her stomach, and her head was throbbing.

Though John had respected her request not to talk about Dr. Allen, his tenderness revealed just how strong an ally he was in the battle against her persecutor. John had always possessed an extravagantly large vision of her—almost as lavish a vision as she possessed of herself. But in the past twenty-four hours, Charissa had caught a glimpse of her own internal toxic waste container, and what she saw nauseated her.

"Can I get you anything before I go?" he asked, tying his shoelaces. She shook her head slowly. "You sure? I'd be happy to skip church and take care of you."

That was exactly what she didn't want. "No, you go," she said quickly. "I'll be okay. It's just a headache." She wasn't sure if he believed her or not, but he didn't argue as he kissed her good-bye.

Hearing the door shut behind him, Charissa settled back into bed and stared up at the ceiling. *C'mon, pull yourself together,* she commanded. She couldn't afford to waste her energy on futile introspection. She still had to figure out how she was going to handle Dr. Allen, and she was running out of time.

She got up, got dressed, and removed the vacuum from the closet.

It was time to clean.

Mara stood outside at the Crossroads House shelter, listening to the sounds of boisterously happy children at play. For the past year she had been volunteering two Sunday afternoons a month, helping to take care of transitioning and homeless kids while their moms attended a Bible study.

As she scanned the playground, she noticed one little boy—maybe four or five years old—hiding behind a tree. Every now and again he would poke his dark curly head around the trunk, looking to see if anyone was coming. But the other children didn't seem to be playing hide-and-seek, and Mara wondered how long he had been waiting for someone to find him. She strolled over toward the tree.

"I wonder if there's anyone hiding anywhere around here," she said with a loud voice.

The child darted behind the tree again and scrunched himself into a little ball.

"I have been looking and looking, but I just can't seem to find anyone," she said, stooping to look beneath a bush. "Nobody there! Well . . . I wonder if there's anybody over here under this slide." She went over to the slide and walked around it several times. "Nope! Nobody under the slide. I wonder if there's anybody over there near that tree." She heard him giggle. "I sure hope I find him soon!"

He jumped out from behind the tree. "Boo!" he exclaimed, throwing his hands up into the air and laughing.

"Oh! *There* you are!" She read his name tag. "I have been looking everywhere for you, Jay-Jay! You are such a good hider!"

He twirled his dark curly hair around his finger. "I know," he said, clutching her hand happily. "Let's play again! Close your eyes and count, okay?" Mara half-covered her eyes with her hand, watching him to make sure he didn't stray too far away.

Jeremy had loved to play hide-and-seek too. In fact, Mara remembered playing with him on the Crossroads House playground years ago. Years and years ago.

She could still hear her precious little boy squealing with delight whenever she found him. "You always find me!" Jeremy would exclaim, skipping around her.

"You're right, Jer. No matter where you hide, I'll always find you!"

"Because I'm your little boy, right?"

"That's right, honey."

"And you love me very, very much," he would say before shoving his thumb into his mouth.

Mara would embrace him and reply, "That's right, Jeremy! You belong to me, and I love you very, very much."

Mara watched Jay-Jay run and hide behind the same tree again. Smiling, she called out, "Ready or not, here I come!"

As she removed her hand from her face, her gaze landed upon her tattooed wrist: the eye. God's all seeing, unblinking eye. Mara stared at the tattoo, and the tattoo stared back. Unwaveringly. Incessantly. El Roi was watching.

That's when she heard it: a gentle, tender echo of words spoken with deep feeling and great love.

*No matter where you hide, I'll always find you. You belong to me, and I love you very, very much.*

As her eyes welled up with healing tears, Mara saw and understood. In that sacred moment, standing on a playground, surrounded by laughing children, she finally understood.

Love had been seeking and finding her all along.

## Charissa

*Nine-year-old Charissa sat defiantly with her arms crossed and her bottom lip protruding in a perfect pout. "I can't believe you acted that way," her mother said. "What will Mrs. Baker think of you?"*

*Charissa scowled. "I didn't do anything wrong."*

*"You were rude to her when she gave you that gift. It was thoughtful of her to buy you a Christmas present. She didn't need to do that."*

*"Well, I don't like that shirt. It's ugly."*

*Mother exhaled slowly. Charissa knew she was in trouble whenever Mother exhaled slowly. "I don't care what you think of the blouse, young lady. What matters is what other people think of you. You're going to say 'thank you' for the present, and you're going to tell her what a lovely gift it is. Because that's what good girls do. And you are a good girl."*

*Sometimes Charissa hated being good.*

By the time John dropped Charissa off on campus early Monday morning, she knew what she had to do. She had to apologize to Dr. Allen for reacting so badly in his office. She had to admit he'd perceived some bit of truth about her life. She didn't see any other way forward. Kingsbury's graduate program was simply too small for her to avoid him, and she needed to maintain his good opinion and respect if she was going to succeed—especially if she was going to pursue a dissertation in seventeenth-century literature.

Her mother had coached her about how to apologize. "If you're absolutely determined not to wipe the dust off your feet and transfer somewhere else, Charissa, then just tell him you're sorry if you seemed angry. 'I'm sorry *if* I seemed angry' is different than apologizing for *being* angry. And given how totally inappropriate he was with you, you certainly don't owe him any more than that."

Her mother was right. Charissa could admit to his perception of her anger and leave it at that. Good enough. Maybe he wouldn't notice her non-apologetic apology.

She was walking across the quad toward the library when she heard a voice from behind her. "Good morning, Charissa."

Startled, she spun around. "Good morning, Dr. Allen." She was determined to pitch her voice correctly: congenial, but not too friendly. She would control her tone, her facial expressions, her body language, and her tongue. She was not going to lose control like she did in his office.

He took a sip from his travel mug. "Did you have a nice weekend?" he asked.

"Yes, and you?"

He was smiling, amiable. Maybe he was going to let her off the hook and pretend they'd never had the conversation.

No. She knew him too well to believe that. Eventually, he would mention it again. At least if she spoke first, she could seize control. She waited for him to finish talking about his sailing outing before she launched her preemptive strike.

"I've been thinking a lot about what you said last week. About my perfectionism." She wasn't going to use the word *sinner.* She wasn't sure she would ever be able to use that word to describe herself. "You were right. I'm sorry if I seemed angry."

Amazing, the difference a little word could make.

"I've been a perfectionist all my life," she continued, trying to convince herself it wasn't noble, even as she said it. She was like a job applicant, insisting her greatest weakness was being a conscientious workaholic. "I've even been a perfectionist about my faith. I just can't believe I didn't see it before. I can't believe I missed it."

He was studying her face carefully, looking as if he wasn't sure how much to say. She braced herself. "The spiritual life is a journey, Charissa, not an exam." His voice was quiet. "I'm glad that something I said was helpful to you."

Wishing her a good day, he turned away to walk to his office. As Charissa watched him go, she felt her shoulders relax. It was done. Over. Nothing more needed to be said. She could move on after a painless conversation. It had all been much easier than she'd imagined.

So why did she feel compelled to dig deeper when everything was under control? Why couldn't she leave well enough alone?

Against her better judgment, she followed him. "Dr. Allen?" He turned around and looked intently at her. "Could I come and see you sometime?"

He thought for a moment before answering, "Walk with me."

When Charissa sat down in his office, she didn't know what she wanted to say. At first she thought perhaps she'd take the opportunity to try to manage his impression of her. She considered how she could best demonstrate that she had understood what he had discerned. In fact, she wanted to show him she had already fixed it. She wanted to prove herself an excellent student, even in matters of faith.

But after she described her revelations about her perfectionism, Dr. Allen asked a probing diagnostic question that changed everything.

"What troubles you about what you've seen in yourself, Charissa?"

She hesitated and then answered, "I just can't believe I was so blind. I thought I had things figured out. I thought I was living out my faith the right way and now . . ." Her voice trailed off. The power of his penetrating eyes had caused her to be far more forthright than she had intended. She sighed. "I guess I'm just disappointed in myself. And I hate that feeling."

"So you're disappointed by your own imperfection."

"Yes, I guess that's right."

He nodded slowly. "That's a start—it's an important beginning. But there's more to repentance than feeling shock or disappointment with ourselves. If we don't glimpse the pain our sin has caused to God's heart or to others, then our repentance is still very self-centered."

His words pierced her before she had a chance to arm herself. "I don't understand." Was that her voice? It sounded so small and far away. She waited forever for his reply.

"You may feel disappointment or shame when you fail or when you're corrected," he finally said. "That's part of being a perfectionist, isn't it? We perfectionists are governed by our fear of failure. We're controlled by our highly developed inner critics. So when we sin, the impulse is either to deny it, or beat ourselves up." He took a long sip from his travel mug before he spoke again. "When I hear you say, 'I can't believe I did that!' it's a clue that you're still trying to be good. You're disappointed in yourself because you didn't get things right. So you're still trying to be your own savior and sanctifier. Does that make sense?"

Did it?

As she stared into her professor's earnest face, she saw that everything hinged on understanding what he said. Everything. Intuitively, she knew that Dr. Allen had never taught her anything more important than this. But she was dizzy. He had turned the snow globe of her life upside down, and he was shaking it with gentle violence.

"Real confession is deeper than seeing our own failure," he said softly. "We need to see how our sin impacts our communion and intimacy with God and with other people. Sin should break our hearts—not because we discover we're imperfect—but because we see that our sin has destructive consequences. And the sins of the spirit are particularly treacherous because they can be so easily concealed."

His face was shifting in and out of focus. She was going to cry. She was actually going to cry in front of Dr. Allen.

But this time she wasn't going to walk away.

"Can we talk?" Charissa asked.

John had just finished brushing his teeth and was getting ready to turn out the lamp on his nightstand when Charissa sat down cross-legged on her side of the bed. He seemed startled when she reached for his hand.

"I had a long talk with Dr. Allen today."

John looked surprised. "Did he apologize?"

Charissa shook her head.

He bristled. "Then I'm serious, Riss—the next step is the dean's office. If you won't make that phone call, I will. This is too important to just let it slide."

Charissa was determined to make eye contact even when it would have been much easier to look away. "Dr. Allen never actually called me any names," she said softly.

"But you said—"

"I know. I lied." John looked utterly confused. "I mean—that's how I heard what Dr. Allen said to me, but he didn't actually call me a bitch, John."

"But I thought—"

"I know. I was really angry with him—I was furious that he'd seen some things in me that I didn't want to see. I didn't want to hear the truth, John, and he was just telling me the truth."

John shook his head. "But it just sounds like you're making excuses for him now. I don't get what you're saying."

Charissa breathed deeply, asking God to help her continue the conversation she'd been imagining in her head for the past several hours.

"I had gone to visit him because I was feeling really unsettled about his class and the sacred journey group, and he ended up talking about Jesus and

Nicodemus and the whole born-again thing. When I told him that I just didn't understand what he was saying, he started pointing out my need for forgiveness and grace. He did say I was a sinner, but it wasn't an accusation."

John raised a single eyebrow.

"We talked a long time today about sin and repentance," she went on. "And I saw some new things about myself. Some really ugly stuff."

Charissa could tell by the expression on her husband's face that he was ready to rise to her defense again, eager to protest any suggestion of imperfection. When he opened his mouth to speak, she swiftly interrupted. "I need to say I'm sorry, John."

He was taken aback. "For what?"

She repositioned herself and reached for his other hand. "I've been completely self-centered and self-absorbed, and I know I've hurt you."

He smiled and shrugged. "It's okay. Don't worry about it. You've been under a lot of stress lately."

"It's not just stress. And it's not okay. It hasn't just been the last week. It's been our whole life together. You've sacrificed yourself for me, and I've just taken from you."

"That's not true." He shook his head emphatically.

"No, John, it is. And I'm sorry. I have to tell you that it never even occurred to me to ask if you've been feeling okay, after the concussion and everything. It's not that I wasn't making conversation about it. I actually forgot you were ever in the hospital. I was that self-absorbed."

John's face had contorted into an expression Charissa could not identify.

She forged ahead, worried she'd lose her courage if she didn't speak quickly. "Even when we were in bed together on Saturday . . . I . . . I wasn't loving you then. I was manipulating you." She touched his cheek, her voice trembling. She had started the confession, and she needed to complete it. "I've been so afraid of losing control. I haven't given myself fully to you, and I'm sorry. I didn't even see until today how many defenses I've had, even with you."

She paused, lowering her voice to a whisper. "I want a different way forward, John. Please forgive me. I'm so sorry for any pain I've caused you. And please don't just say it's okay, that it doesn't matter. I need you to say that it does matter and that you still forgive me."

Charissa had never truly experienced heartache until she saw John's eyes the moment she confessed her sin. The depth of woundedness in those gentle eyes was beyond language. Entirely inarticulate. And yet, the most perfect articulation Charissa had ever heard.

She saw. She understood. She broke. She loved.

"I forgive you, Charissa," he said quietly, his eyes brimming with tears. "I love you, and I forgive you."

That night John and Charissa Sinclair explored the sacred space of union that opened once defenses were removed.

And it was good.

It was very good.

## Hannah

*Fourteen-year-old Hannah often babysat Joey, her five-year-old brother, when their parents went out to dinner with clients. "Here's the number at the restaurant," Daddy said, kissing Hannah on the forehead. "We'll be home about nine o'clock." He turned to Joey. "Be good, Joe! Do what Hannah says, okay?" Joey flashed his cherubic grin and nodded.*

*While Joey watched television, Hannah cleaned up the dinner dishes. "I want to go outside and play!" Joey called from the other room.*

*"In a minute, Joe. I need to clean up here first." Just then the phone rang. Hannah's heart beat fast when she heard the voice on the other end.*

*"Hannah?" It was Brad Sterling. "It's Brad Sterling . . . you know . . . from Mr. Godwin's class?" Hannah knew exactly what class he was from. She hoped she sounded more composed than she felt.*

*"Hi, Brad!" she said cheerfully. Too cheerfully?*

*"Hi . . . um . . . I was wondering . . . " She was breathless, waiting. "I was wondering if you'd like to go out to a movie or something on Friday night."*

*Her knees buckled, and she sank into the chair. "I'd love to!"*

*"Really? Awesome! My mom says she'll drive us. Maybe we'll pick you up at about seven o'clock?"*

*Hannah was so excited, she could hardly speak. "That sounds great, Brad. Thank you!"*

*She hung up the phone and hugged herself. Was it possible? Her very first date! Her mind wandered into daydreams, and she forgot about the dishes. She also forgot about Joey.*

*The sound of screaming jolted her back to reality. Stricken with fear, she raced outside, following Joey's cries. She found him lying on his back underneath his favorite climbing tree. Fortunately, the next-door neighbors also heard the screaming. Mr. and Mrs. Chen were there in an instant, kneeling beside her and trying quickly to assess Joey's injuries. Hannah was hysterical. "It's all my fault! It's all my fault!" she sobbed.*

*The next few hours blurred together. Mr. Chen drove Joey to the nearby hospital while Mrs. Chen phoned the restaurant to get a message to the Shepleys. It was well after midnight when Hannah's parents arrived home with her brother. Joey's leg was in a cast, but he had no other injuries. Luckily.*

*"It's okay, Hannah," Daddy reassured her. "Everything's okay. Joey's going to be fine." But Hannah could not be consoled, and she would not forgive herself.*

*She never told her parents about the phone call from Brad. And the next day, to punish herself for getting distracted, she told Brad she was sorry, but she couldn't go to the movie after all.*

*He didn't ask her out again.*

Hannah was surprised when Charissa called to invite her to dinner on Friday night. She had assumed that John's offer to cook for her and Meg had been a perfunctory and glib comment. She hadn't expected an actual invitation.

"John and I want to thank you and Meg for helping us at the hospital," Charissa said. "And he can't wait to have people over to enjoy his cooking."

Hannah was also surprised to hear that Meg had already said yes. Much as Hannah would have preferred to avoid a social evening out, she wasn't going to miss the opportunity to be alongside Meg. "Why don't you plan on staying overnight at my house after we finish dinner?" Meg asked, as the two of them arranged to meet at the Sinclairs' apartment at seven o'clock on Friday. "That way you won't have to drive back in the morning for the group."

Meg's offer confirmed Hannah's decision. She didn't imagine that Meg often invited people into her home. Although Hannah expected the evening with Charissa to be irritatingly superficial, a few hours of small talk seemed a small price to pay for the privilege of being welcomed into Meg's life. As Friday approached, she actually found herself anticipating the evening with a certain measure of eagerness.

Hannah handed Charissa an autumn bouquet as she and Meg entered the Sinclairs' apartment. "These are beautiful!" Charissa exclaimed, admiring the flowers. "Thank you!"

Hannah smiled and took off her jacket. "You're welcome. How's John?"

"Back to normal. For better or for worse." Hannah noticed a light in Charissa's eyes that she hadn't seen before.

"She still won't let me play football tomorrow!" John called from the kitchen. "So I was thinking of crashing your group. I want to walk that labyrinth thingy."

"I'm thinking I need to give the labyrinth another try sometime," Charissa said, ushering them into a sparsely furnished, but perfectly tidy living room. "I wasn't in a great frame of mind that first day."

"Neither was I," said Meg. "I didn't manage it at all, remember? I was in high heels."

"I'd forgotten that." Charissa stooped to pick up a stray red leaf from the beige carpet. Hannah removed her offending shoes.

"I can't believe it's only been a month since the group started," Meg commented, seating herself on the sofa. "So much is swirling around inside of me—like I've traveled miles and months already. I guess I'm just amazed by what God has already shown me."

John emerged from the kitchen and wiped his damp hand on his jeans before extending it in a firm handshake. "Nice to see you guys. About fifteen minutes until dinner, okay?"

"It smells great," said Hannah. "Thanks so much for having us over. You didn't have to do this."

"Well, I told Riss that I've been wanting to have people over ever since we got a dining room table. Of course, I was hoping for some heretics for lively conversation. You guys aren't heretics, are you?"

Hannah and Meg looked at one another in shared confusion while Charissa punched his stomach playfully. "He takes some getting used to," she explained. "He's teasing me because I wasn't sure at first if I should sign up for the group. I didn't want to land in anything unorthodox, so I talked to my professor about it."

"And Dr. Allen assured her it was safe, much to my disappointment."

They laughed. Charissa sat down in an armchair, tucking her long legs underneath her. She looked far more relaxed than Hannah had ever seen her before, and Hannah wondered if her ease were linked to anything other than being in her own home.

While the others chatted, Hannah casually scanned the room, trying to gather clues about who Charissa was. But there were no family photographs, no knickknacks, nothing extraneous. The only color in the room was a pair of black matching urns filled with red reeds, symmetrically placed on two matching end tables. On the glass coffee table was a single pile of neatly stacked poetry anthologies, but there were no magazines or newspapers in view. Not even a collection of music or movies to give anything away.

Was she this much of a minimalist, Hannah wondered, or was there a bulging closet somewhere, stuffed with clutter she had hidden away?

She tuned in again just as Charissa was answering a question Meg had asked about her studies.

"I tend to work a lot with medieval and early modern English literature—lots of seventeenth-century poetry. And since so much of English lit has deep roots in the biblical story, it helps me to be well-versed in Scripture." Charissa hesitated. "Of course, some of the ways we're experiencing the Bible at the New Hope Center are new to me; and to be honest, it's been kind of unsettling. I'm used to doing text analysis, and reading Scripture with the imagination is . . . well . . . different." She looked at John. "I'm a bit of a control freak. Just ask my husband."

Hannah decided she was a minimalist. She probably had an alphabetized pantry and a closet organized by color.

"You're a lovable control freak," John said, resting his hand on her shoulder.

"Sometimes." Charissa put her hand on top of his and squeezed it. There was something tender in the gesture, and Hannah observed a fleeting nonverbal exchange between them as they looked at one another. Lovers could do that.

"Thinking back to the labyrinth," Hannah said, changing the subject, "Meg and I plan on getting there by nine o'clock tomorrow to walk and pray before the group starts. I think Mara will be there too. If you're interested, Charissa, we'd love to have you walk with us."

"Thanks. I'll think about it."

Hannah recognized the polite, noncommittal tone. She used it frequently herself.

John beamed with boyish delight as they complimented him on dinner. "Thankfully, he loves cooking," Charissa said, passing around a plate of steamed vegetables. "Because he's right when he says I don't have the gift. Or the desire. Much to my mom's horror."

John took the plate from Meg. "Charissa's mom is Greek, and she's a fantastic cook! She makes these amazing Mediterranean dishes. Unfortunately, they moved to Florida last year, and we don't get to see them too often. But whenever Mom visits, I ask her to give me some tips. And I've got a bunch of her recipes."

"Well, this chicken is delicious," said Meg.

"Thanks. It's Charissa's favorite. And I'm getting better at it. Right, Riss?"

"As good as Mom's, John."

"I'm gonna call her tonight and tell her you said that!" He laughed and speared a piece of chicken with his fork. "So, Meg . . . Riss said your daughter is studying abroad this year. Did she tell you she spent some time in England too?"

Meg shook her head.

"She spent a year as a Fulbright scholar after graduation. Ditched me for an entire year to hang out with the Brits. I didn't think she'd ever come back. I thought for sure she'd fall in love with some genius with a sexy accent and forget all about me."

"But I didn't," Charissa said, smiling. "I absolutely loved the UK, though. I'd go back in a heartbeat. Will you get over to visit your daughter while she's there?"

"Actually, I booked my trip last week. I'm flying there after Thanksgiving to stay for a few weeks. We'll get to celebrate Christmas and her birthday together, which will be wonderful. Becca's studying right in London, but she's been traveling all over the country on weekends, and she absolutely loves it. She can't wait to show me around."

"I'm jealous!" Charissa exclaimed. "If you'd like some travel tips, I'd be happy to show you my photos sometime. It might not be great weather-wise that time of year, but there's still so much to see and do. The trains make it really easy to get around."

"That would be great!" Meg replied. "I'm nervous and excited all at the same time. This will probably sound crazy, but I've never even been on a plane before. So this is a huge leap of faith for me."

John smiled at her. "Good for you! That's awesome. I bet you and Becca will have a blast together. You may not want to come home!" He looked in Hannah's direction. "How 'bout you? Charissa was telling me how your church has given you a long sabbatical. That's so cool! Are you gonna do some traveling?"

Hannah was taken aback. It had never once occurred to her that she had the freedom to go and do whatever she wanted. She had been so focused on being at the lake—so absorbed in her own grief process over her exile—that she hadn't even considered traveling. She shook her head in bewilderment. "I have no idea. I don't have a clue where I would go."

In fifteen years of ministry Hannah had never taken an extended vacation for herself. She had used her time to visit her folks in Oregon and her brother in New York. She had even used vacation time to babysit her nieces so her brother and sister-in-law could travel together. But Hannah had never indulged herself with a trip. She couldn't believe it hadn't occurred to her. Was she that weary? That shortsighted?

John pressed her. "Boy, if I were you, I'd think of all the things you've always wished you could do and never had time for. What an awesome opportunity."

"I'm beginning to see it that way," Hannah said. "Katherine has been wonderful, helping me glimpse some of what God wants to do in me during my time off."

"Katherine's an amazing woman," said Meg. "I can't believe what the Lord has shown me through her. She knows how to ask the right questions, doesn't she?"

Charissa looked intrigued. "I've had a bit of that myself the past few days. From one of my professors, not from Mrs. Rhodes. But come to think of it, she's Dr. Allen's spiritual director, so I guess she's mentored him. Anyway . . . It's been an intense week for me." She was quiet, as if debating how much to reveal. Hannah was well-acquainted with that type of pause. "You know the most important thing I've learned the past couple of weeks?" Charissa continued. "Dr. Allen told me to pay attention to the things that make me angry, defensive, and upset. That didn't make any sense at first. But I'm starting to understand that when something bugs me, it might be God's way of trying to get my attention."

"Like a fever telling you your body's fighting off infection, or pain that reveals something's wrong." Hannah spooned more rice onto her plate. "We need people like Katherine and your professor in our lives, don't we? We all have so many blind spots. But if we could see everything clearly by ourselves, we wouldn't need the body of Christ."

Meg was listening with rapt attention. "I think I met your professor once," she said, turning to Charissa. "We had a guest preacher a few months ago—one of our pastor's friends. I remember thinking it was strange that an English professor would be preaching, but he was fantastic. I remember he talked about sailing and the spiritual life."

*Sailing and the spiritual life.* A memory stirred in Hannah's mind, and she quickly dismissed it. Impossible.

Charissa grinned. "That sounds like him. He used to be a pastor before he became a professor."

Hannah's fork was hovering midway between her plate and her mouth. "What's your professor's name?" she asked, trying to sound nonchalant.

"Nathan Allen. Why? Do you know him?"

Hannah set her fork down in case her hand started trembling. "I knew him a long time ago," she said casually, smiling even though the room was spinning. "Nathan and I were in seminary together. But I transferred to a different seminary for the last year of my studies, and I didn't keep track of what happened to people after I left." She took a long, slow sip of water, trying to buy time to pull herself together. She could feel Meg's gaze riveted upon her.

"Small world, huh?" John remarked.

"Very." Hannah dabbed her lips with her napkin.

She hoped the others hadn't noticed anything odd about her reaction to Nathan's name. She also prayed it wouldn't occur to Charissa to mention to him that they had a mutual acquaintance. She spent the rest of dinner putting all of her energy into appearing relaxed and engaged in conversation. But underneath her mask of tranquility was churning turbulence.

*Nathan Allen.*

What were the chances of her ending up less than an hour away from Nathan Allen? She hadn't seen him in sixteen years. She hadn't thought about him in a decade. No, that wasn't true. He had come to mind two weeks ago when she was sitting in the group, praying about her images of God. But she had pushed him away.

Again.

Meg and Hannah said good-bye to Charissa and John just after nine o'clock and walked down to the parking lot together. Hannah wished she had refused Meg's offer to stay overnight. It had seemed like a good idea to avoid making an extra trip, but now she wanted to be alone. Though she considered telling Meg she had changed her mind, she didn't want to call attention to how unsettled she was. Meg had been kind to invite her, and Hannah wanted to be a good steward of Meg's trust. After all, Meg needed encouragement.

"You okay?" Meg asked when they reached their cars.

Hannah was inserting her key into the lock and had her back turned toward Meg. "Absolutely."

"You sure?"

Of course she was sure. Why wouldn't she be okay? "Yeah, I'm fine. Just tired." Hannah kept fiddling with her key, unwilling to make eye contact until she knew she had control over her face.

"If you'd like to talk about Nathan Allen, Hannah, I'd be happy to listen." Hannah froze with her key in the door. *Was this really Meg Crane?* "You seemed upset when Charissa mentioned his name," Meg said quietly.

Hannah turned around. She wasn't upset.

"I was just surprised to hear his name after so many years." She spoke with determined carelessness, trying quickly to decide how much to reveal. "We were really good friends in seminary—we used to spend lots of time together in classes and in the dorm. And he . . . well . . . he fell in love with me, I guess, and I didn't want him to. It became awkward."

A cloud of pregnant silence hovered between them, and Hannah knew Meg was contemplating how much more to ask. After one bold question, Hannah wasn't sure she could count on Meg to be demure and self-conscious. Evidently, her timidity was no longer a guarantee.

"Was that why you transferred to a different seminary?"

Make that two bold questions.

Hannah wished she could hop into her car and drive away. Far away.

"There were lots of good reasons for me to transfer somewhere else," she said, using her best matter-of-fact tone. She hoped she could communicate her desire to shut down the topic without hurting Meg's feelings.

Meg appeared to catch the hint and asked no more questions. "My house isn't far from here," Meg said, gingerly rubbing her neck with her hand. "Just follow me."

Hannah stepped out of her car and looked up with surprise at the large three-story, turreted Victorian home. "I had no idea you lived in a place like this!" she exclaimed, meeting Meg in the driveway. "It's beautiful!"

Meg sighed. "You haven't seen it in daylight. It's pretty tired. Mother always prided herself on keeping up the appearance of it, but the past couple of years have been hard. I just can't keep up with the maintenance." She paused. "Much to my mother's disappointment," she added under her breath.

Meg flipped on the light when they entered, and Hannah found herself in a dark wood-paneled foyer. The permeating scent of a vanilla air freshener only made the mustiness of the old house heavier, and Hannah was immediately reminded of a turn-of-the-century funeral parlor she had once visited in Chicago. As she glanced into a front sitting room stuffed with antiques and period furniture, Hannah intuitively understood Meg's burden.

"Pretty dreary, isn't it?" Meg apologized as she gave Hannah a tour. "I don't know what to do. My sister, Rachel, keeps telling me to sell it. She says it could be converted into apartments. I'm torn. The house has always been the Fowler family home, ever since my great-great grandfather built it in the 1880s. But I never wanted it for myself. It's so big." She sighed. "This is going to sound terrible, but there's no life here. I feel trapped. And guilty for feeling trapped. I never thought I'd be forty-six and still living in this house. Never."

For a moment Hannah considered asking Meg why she had stayed. Why hadn't she and Becca moved somewhere else together? Why had she stayed with her mother? But as she followed Meg upstairs to Becca's room, she decided that was a conversation for another day. She was tired. Very tired.

"At least this room feels lived in," Meg said, turning on the light. "I hope it's comfortable for you."

Hannah set down her duffel bag. "Thank you. It's perfect."

Becca's room was an oasis of light and life compared to the rest of the house. Breezy fabrics, bright colors, and white Christmas lights around the window revealed a young woman's concerted effort to bring joy into an otherwise cheerless place. The walls were papered with artwork—Hannah recognized several Monet and Degas posters—and the desk was covered with photos.

Hannah picked up one of the frames. "Is this Becca?" Meg nodded. "She has your eyes. She's beautiful."

"She's a wonderful girl," Meg said. "She's got her father's spirit: kind, generous, full of life and laughter. And that says something about her because this house wasn't an easy place for joy. I'm just glad she didn't end up with my fears." Meg gazed at the photo thoughtfully. "But maybe there's hope for me too. At least, that seems to be what God is doing in my life right now—freeing me from fear."

"I see that," Hannah said. She could personally testify to the liberating work of the Spirit. "And I've only known you for a month."

"Thanks. That means a lot." Meg stood in the doorway, making sure Hannah had everything she needed. "I'm praying for you," she said quietly before closing the door behind her.

Hannah detected something decidedly bold in that declaration.

## *Mara*

*The cafeteria at Roosevelt Junior High School buzzed with conversation. Mara trudged through the lunch line, holding tightly to her tray, avoiding eye contact with the other students. Choosing her usual table in the far back corner, she sat down by herself. At least she had remembered to bring a book to lunch. She didn't read it. She simply stared at the pages as she ate. The book was a poor shield against her loneliness and isolation, but it was the only thing she had.*

*She listened as Kristie Van Buren and some other girls laughed together at a nearby table. At one point Mara thought she heard her name, and she looked up just as one of them was staring in her direction. "Such a freak," the girl said. "I heard she missed school last week because of lice."*

*"I know. It's totally gross," another added. "I've never even seen her shower after gym."*

*"Well, have you seen where she lives?" the first girl asked.*

*Kristie answered, "Yeah! My mom never let me go over there in elementary school. She came over to my house once because my mom felt sorry for her. But she was so dirty, she wasn't allowed to come over again."*

*Bitter tears welled up as Mara continued to stare at the page, and all the words blurred together.*

The second Saturday of October was a beautiful autumn day. Mara strolled across the New Hope parking lot, inhaling the scent of a wood-burning fire and listening to the crackle and crunch of leaves beneath her feet. The veil of early morning fog had lifted to reveal trees that had burst into vibrancy overnight. The colors of the season always surprised her, especially the reds. Red took her breath away.

Hannah had phoned earlier in the week to invite her to a picnic after their group, and Mara was glad she had somewhere to go with people who wanted her company. Tom had taken Kevin and Brian to their early morning football practice, and then the three of them planned to spend the rest of the day tailgating at the university. At least Mara wouldn't have to spend another Saturday alone. She was tired of being alone. *Thank you, Jesus. Thank you for new friends.*

Meg and Hannah were already in the courtyard when she arrived at the labyrinth. "Mornin'!" she greeted them. "Gorgeous day, huh?" *Was that Meg?* Mara had never seen her looking so relaxed. It wasn't just the jeans and red sweatshirt. Something else had changed. "You don't look anything like the terrified woman in a skirt and heels from a month ago," Mara commented, smiling at her.

Meg laughed. "I'm getting the hang of the pilgrimage thing. It's been a good journey for me so far."

"For me too," Mara replied. "Not easy. But good." She turned to Hannah. "You okay? You look tired." The dark circles beneath Hannah's eyes were even more prominent than usual, and her skin was pale.

"I'm okay," Hannah said, bending down to fiddle with a shoelace.

Mara didn't believe her but decided not to probe. Instead she silently prayed, asking God to give Hannah whatever help she needed. Then she stepped onto the labyrinth.

She knew what she wanted to pray about.

Now that she was beginning to understand how God loved her—now that she wasn't feeling afraid of judgment and condemnation—she wanted to meditate on something else Katherine had said in her office. Katherine had pointed out something Mara had never noticed before: both Genesis texts about Hagar in the wilderness mentioned a well.

"You've been so thirsty, Mara," Katherine had said. "And you've been trying to satisfy that thirst by drinking from so many different wells. But God invites you to drink deeply from one well—the well of Living Water. The Lord wants you to know that he is the Living One who sees you without condemning you."

With that theme in mind, Katherine had recommended another meditation text for Mara: the story of Jesus meeting the Samaritan woman at the well. Mara spent all week praying with the fourth chapter of John, having no trouble finding herself in the midst of the Samaritan woman's story. Mara knew all about being an outsider and an outcast.

She removed an index card from her pocket and read the verses she had written down: "Jesus said to her, 'Everyone who drinks of this water will be thirsty again, but those who drink of the water that I will give them will never be thirsty. The water that I will give will become in them a spring of water gushing up to eternal life.' The woman said to him, 'Sir, give me this water, so that I may never be thirsty or have to keep coming here to draw water.'"

*Jesus, give me this water, so that I may never be thirsty. Jesus, give me this water. Please give me this water. All my life I've been so thirsty. So thirsty for love. So thirsty for acceptance. So thirsty. And I haven't been drinking the water you give. I'm sorry, Jesus.*

As Mara walked the inward path, she confessed the different wells she had drawn from over the years.

She had drawn from the well of sexual gratification, but the water had been bitter.

She had drawn from the well of material possessions, but that well was filled with salt water, making her crave more and more.

She had drawn from the well of approval and acceptance, but that well was unpredictable. She never knew if there would be water or not, and even when she managed to draw some out, her bucket leaked. She couldn't hold it. It didn't last.

Katherine was right. There was only one well that truly satisfied, and Mara wanted to drink deeply.

She thought about the Samaritan woman running back to the village, so excited about meeting Jesus that she left her bucket behind. "Come and see a man who told me everything I ever did!" the woman exclaimed. She wasn't afraid. She wasn't ashamed. Somehow, the dark details of her life became a testimony to point others to the Messiah. "Come and see a man! Come and see!"

Was it possible?

If Mara could share her story of heartache and sin—if she could speak freely about the bitter water she had drunk and point others to the Living Water—was it possible that Jesus had work for her to do? Was it possible that Jesus called her to follow, not out of pity, but because he had a purpose and a mission for her?

Dawn was right. Mara hadn't understood the truth about Jesus choosing her. She had seen herself as the leftover one God had to take just because she was standing there. But what if Jesus chose her because he actually loved her and wanted her to be with him? What if Jesus chose her, not because he felt sorry for her, but because her life was precious to him? What if she was actually worth something to God?

Mara couldn't yet comprehend the difference that would make, but she sensed a seismic shift in her spirit. And her heart was trembling with joy.

**Sacred Journey, New Hope Retreat Center**
***Session Three: Praying the Examen***
*Katherine Rhodes, Facilitator*

---

The prayer of examen was developed by Ignatius of Loyola in the sixteenth century as a discipline for discerning God's will and becoming more attentive to God's presence. The following is an adaptation of his spiritual exercise.

Think of the prayer of examen as a way of sitting with Jesus and talking through the details of your day. In the examen we slow down and pay attention to the data of our lives. We notice our thoughts, actions, emotions and motivations. By taking time to review our day in prayer, we have the opportunity to see details we might otherwise overlook. The examen helps us to perceive the movement of the Spirit and to discover God's presence in all of life.

As you begin to pray, still and quiet yourself. Give thanks for some of the specific gifts God has given you today. Then ask the Holy Spirit to guide and direct your thoughts as you prayerfully review your day. Let the details play out like a short movie. Pay attention both to the things that gave you life and to the things that drained you. Notice where the Spirit invites you to linger and ponder.

These are some questions you can adapt and use in the examen:

When were you aware of God's presence today? When did you sense God's absence?

When did you respond to God with love, faith, and obedience? When did you resist or avoid God?

When did you feel most alive and energized? When did you feel drained, troubled, or agitated?

Having reviewed the details of your day, confess what needs to be confessed. Allow God's Spirit to bring you wholeness, grace and forgiveness.

Finally, consider these questions: How will you live attentively in God's love tomorrow? How can you structure your day in light of God's presence, taking into account your own rhythms and responses to the movement of the Spirit? Ask for the grace to recognize the ways God makes his love known to you.

7

# Walking Attentively

*Search me, O God, and know my heart;*
*test me and know my thoughts.*
*See if there is any wicked way in me,*
*and lead me in the way everlasting.*

PSALM 139:23-24

"I still can't believe what a small world it is!" Charissa remarked to Hannah as she unpacked her laptop at the back corner table. "Funny how you and Dr. Allen were in seminary together. What a coincidence!"

"It sure is." Hannah was deliberately cheerful as she discerned how best to exert control. "Of course, it's been so long. I'm sure he wouldn't remember me after all these years. I wouldn't want him to feel embarrassed at not recognizing my name."

Charissa raised her eyebrows. "You don't want me to mention that I know you?"

Hannah proceeded carefully with manufactured indifference. "I wouldn't bother. I just hadn't heard his name for so long. It's always interesting to hear where life takes people." She shifted gears as smoothly as she could. "You know, I really enjoyed dinner last night. Thank you again!"

"You're welcome. We had a good time too."

While Katherine called the group together, Meg and Mara settled themselves at the table with their cups of coffee. Mara offered a blueberry bagel to Hannah. "Want half?" Hannah shook her head.

"I want to give you some time to leave your distractions behind so you can be fully present to God," Katherine said. "So go ahead and make yourselves comfortable where you're sitting, and I'll lead us through a palms-up, palms-down prayer. Have some of you done this before?"

There were murmurs around the room.

"It's a simple way of praying," Katherine continued, "but I find the physical gestures help me focus on letting go and receiving. Think of the things that are worrying, troubling, and distracting you, and place your palms down as you turn those cares over to God. Then when you're ready, turn your palms face up to receive what God has for you. Feel free to release and receive as many times as you need to. Let's pray together."

The room was silent. Charissa followed Katherine's instructions, dutifully placing her palms down on her lap as she tried to think of things she needed to turn over to God. The very act of praying with her palms down was uncomfortable. More than uncomfortable. It was provoking. At first she was ready to dismiss her discomfort as something physical. *Probably just a wrist thing,* she thought to herself. Maybe she just didn't like turning her hands up and down. But then Dr. Allen's voice chimed in her head, "Pay attention to the things that provoke you."

So she paid attention. Why was she reluctant to pray that way? Was there something deeper behind her resistance? Then it occurred to her. It wasn't the physical action itself. Rather, it was what the action represented. Charissa was uncomfortable letting go. She smiled in spite of herself. *Guess letting go takes practice, huh?*

So she confessed her desire for control. She confessed her fears about letting go. She confessed her lack of trust.

Her confessions rapidly gathered momentum.

She confessed her pride and her self-centeredness. She confessed her critical spirit and her stubbornness.

Now that she was acutely aware of her sins, she wanted to be done with them. She wanted to be free. She wanted to be—

She sighed as the revelation hit her.

She wanted to be perfect.

She was right back at the beginning of the battle again, face to face with her perfectionist stronghold. Would it always be like this?

*Help, God,* she breathed, turning her palms face up. But she soon discovered she was just as uncomfortable with receiving as with releasing. She half-opened her eyes to scan the room, wondering if she was the only person struggling with such a simple act of prayer. But she was surrounded by saints. No one else appeared to be having any trouble with the exercise. So she closed her eyes and turned her palms up and down in prayerful gestures, just in case anyone was watching.

Hannah was relieved when Katherine rang the chime to signal the end of prayer. Though her watch insisted the silence had only lasted ten minutes, it had felt longer than that. Much longer. What was wrong with her? She ought to treasure and savor silence as a way to listen for God's voice. Instead, silence scared her.

Especially now that Nathan Allen had resurfaced after so many years of absence.

Every time Hannah put her palms up to receive, Nathan intruded again. So she would go back to palms down, asking God to remove the distractions and take away the memories of him.

Why now, God? Why now? Why, when she was already feeling vulnerable and weak? Why, when this season of grief was already so painful? Why did she have to be distracted by something from her past?

Why, God, why?

What a cruel twist of fate. But then, she didn't believe in fate. So was she prepared to say that Nathan Allen's proximity was somehow part of God's plan? Or maybe a design to test her again after all these years? Or merely a coincidence?

Hannah didn't know. All she knew was that the thought of him was an unwelcome intrusion, and she didn't know how to make it—*him*—go away.

And now—of all the disciplines Katherine could have presented, why the prayer of examen? And why today? As she sat staring at the handout and listening to Katherine explain the prayer, she became more and more restless.

She didn't want to review the last twenty-four hours in attentive prayer. She wanted to forget about them and move on. Just when she was beginning to feel grateful for the sabbatical—just when she was beginning to glimpse some of the work God wanted to do within her during her forced rest—Nathan Allen had reappeared. It wasn't fair.

"I first started using the prayer of examen about twenty years ago," Katherine was saying, "and it has been one of my most important daily disciplines. The examen helps me slow down and see the opportunities for transformation that God is constantly giving me. Remember: the spiritual life is all about being awake and attentive to God, and the examen helps us stay alert. God speaks through the things that stir us. God speaks through the things that excite and energize us as well as the things that depress and deplete us. So pay attention to your strong reactions and feelings, both positive and negative. The Spirit speaks through both.

"Imagine, for example, that as I review my day, I remember how irritated and defensive I became when someone criticized me. I pay attention to that, asking the Lord what he wants me to see and know about my response. How was God present to me right then? What are God's invitations to me? As I pray it through I may discover that what the person said was true, and now I can explore what I'm protecting by being so defensive. Are you with me?"

There were murmurs and nods around the room.

"In the examen we ask the Spirit to search us and know us. The Lord invites us to perceive his constant activity in our lives, to notice the things that move us toward God and away from God. This kind of praying takes us deeply inward—not so we become self-absorbed and self-centered, but so that we can truly know ourselves. After all, self-knowledge and humility are pathways to knowing and loving God more and more. And the Holy Spirit's desire is always to draw us more deeply into intimate life with God. Now . . . what questions do you have?"

Hannah didn't bother listening to the questions or the answers. She didn't want to pray about why she felt so agitated. She also knew exactly what Katherine would say about her reluctance. "Your areas of resistance and avoidance can provide a wealth of information about your inner life. Pay attention to what the Holy Spirit might be revealing to you."

Why did it matter? Why did his name, spoken aloud for the first time in sixteen years, have the power to unsettle her? It was ridiculous. She ought to be stronger than that. She had gotten over him years ago. No—she had never needed to "get over him." She had never loved him—not really. At least, not like he had loved her.

See? This was exactly why she had said no to him years ago. Hannah hated distractions, and he was a distraction from her single-minded pursuit of Jesus. He was a distraction from her call to ministry. He was a distraction.

Now here he was again, a distraction from the work of healing and pruning that God was doing in her life. All the forward progress she had managed to make had been wiped away with the mention of his name. She felt disappointed that she could be so easily derailed.

Hannah tried to shift her attention to moments when she felt energized. What could she actually celebrate from the last twenty-four hours? Meg came to mind. Hannah was certainly grateful for the work the Spirit was doing in Meg's life to free her from fear, even if that meant that Meg was bolder in asking penetrating questions. Hannah thought about Meg's years of repressed grief over Jim. Meg had confided that she had only recently started feeling free to remember him again. *Imagine stuffing grief like that for so long,* Hannah thought.

Then Charissa came to mind. Charissa hadn't given specifics, but she had mentioned at dinner that the Spirit was revealing truth to her. Hannah could rejoice that Charissa was growing in her knowledge of God. But then she remembered what an important role Nathan had played in Charissa's spiritual growth, and she was back to being distracted again.

Maybe what Hannah needed was some perspective and distance from her own struggles. How would she advise someone who complained about battling distractions in prayer? How would she counsel someone about a Nathan Allen?

The answer that came to mind surprised her. *Maybe what you call a distraction is exactly what the Spirit wants you to see.*

But that didn't make sense. What did Nathan Allen's intrusion have to do with any of the work God was doing in her? She couldn't see it. She just couldn't see it.

Closing the pages of her journal, Hannah shut her eyes tight and pretended to be deep in prayer.

## Together

*Charissa sat in her high school cafeteria, listening to the girls at her table gossip about Teresa Gallagher. "I heard she's keeping the baby," one of them said.*

*"Seriously?" another asked.*

*"I heard she doesn't even know who the father is. She's slept with so many different guys."*

*Charissa glanced over to the table in the corner where Teresa sat alone, reading a book. Their eyes met for just a moment before Charissa looked away.*

*She could remember when she and Teresa were in elementary school together. Teresa was always trying to join Charissa and her friends at recess, so they would tell her to hide. Then they would all run away to find another game to play, leaving Teresa waiting in her hiding place until the bell rang. Teresa eventually figured out the rules of the game and stopped asking if she could play. Charissa was glad. Teresa wasn't the sort of girl she wanted to be seen with. When Teresa began to mix with the wrong crowd in junior high, Charissa wasn't at all surprised.*

*"Be careful who you associate with," Mother always told her. "If you lose your reputation, you lose everything."*

John was waiting near the portico when Charissa, Meg, Mara, and Hannah exited together at noon. Charissa kissed him and then turned to Mara. "Mara, have you met my husband, John, yet?" John smiled as he shook Mara's hand.

"Nice to meet you," Mara and John chorused.

"How was the pilgrims' progress today?" he teased, wrapping his arms around Charissa's waist. Charissa shrugged a reply.

Meg said, "Sometimes I feel like I'm not getting very far. Or like I'm traveling around in circles. Then I look back at where I've come from, and I guess I should feel encouraged."

"Man!" Mara exclaimed. "I thought I was the only one who felt that way! I get dizzy, walkin' around in circles."

Hannah decided to change the subject before they asked her any questions about her own experience with circular motion.

"Are you sure you two won't join us?" she asked Charissa and John.

Hannah had invited all of them to the lake for a picnic. Of course, she had extended the invitation before she found out about Nathan Allen. Much as she wished she could just go back to the cottage by herself, she was determined to be a gracious host.

"I don't want to crash the girls' day out," John said. "But hey! Why don't you go, Riss? You won't get many more days like this to be outside." Charissa looked tempted. "Go on, hon. I'll survive a few hours without you. Maybe I'll head over to the university for some tailgating. It's a great day for football!"

"As long as you're not playing! If I have to worry about you throwing a ball, John, I'm not going anywhere. I'm serious."

He kissed her. "Don't worry. I'll be good." She scrutinized him. "I promise! Go have fun!"

"It is a perfect autumn day, isn't it?" Charissa said. "And I haven't been on a picnic since I lived in England."

"Fresh bread, imported cheeses, fruit, cookies. I've even got English tea," Hannah said, reaching into her bag for her car keys.

"Okay, sold!"

"Wonderful! You can ride with me if you'd like." Hannah looked at Meg. "Have you guys got directions if we get separated?"

"All set," Meg answered, turning toward Mara. "You're riding with me, right?"

"You bet, girlfriend!"

"Be good, John." Charissa kissed him before he got into the car.

"Yes, ma'am. I'll keep my phone on so you can check up on me. Have fun!"

Hannah hadn't intended to talk with Charissa about Nathan Allen. That wasn't why she had invited Charissa to ride with her. *Definitely not,* she told herself. But as she listened to Charissa talk about her studies, all of Hannah's thoughts swirled around Nathan. She began to wonder if Charissa suspected something. Was that why Charissa wasn't mentioning him by name? Hannah decided it might be better if she expressed casual interest in an old peer. Maybe she could find out information without seeming too eager.

"So what kind of teacher is Nathan?" Hannah finally asked. It wasn't what she most wanted to know, but it seemed a safe place to begin.

"He's really gifted," Charissa replied. "He has this amazing way of bringing texts to life—he just sees things most people don't see. And not just on the written page. He also has this uncanny gift for reading people."

Hannah hoped she appeared more composed than she felt. She waited to respond until she thought she could modulate her voice correctly. "Sounds like he would have made a good pastor. Has he ever said why he switched to literature?"

Charissa shook her head. "Not to me, anyway. I just know he's been at Kingsbury for a few years now—since my junior year."

The car filled with silence. Hannah didn't want to call attention to herself by asking more questions, and Charissa seemed to be debating whether or not she should give unsolicited information.

"I don't know much else about him," Charissa finally said. "Except that he's divorced." Hannah inhaled. "And he's got a teenage son." Hannah stopped breathing.

"A teenager! Really?" Had her tone given her away?

Charissa said, "His name's Jake. I've met him a couple of times. Nice young man."

Hannah was worried that her face wasn't cooperating with her mental command to appear nonchalant. "That doesn't seem possible," Hannah mused, trying to adjust her expression to easygoing curiosity. "Are you sure his son is that old?"

Charissa shrugged. "I know he's in junior high, so I'm thinking he's thirteen or fourteen."

Hannah felt herself grow faint, and she gripped the steering wheel hard. Maybe it was a different Nathan Allen. It had to be. But everything she had heard about him pointed to her former friend: the sailing, the seminary training, the gifts of discernment and teaching. Hannah directed all her effort into sounding detached and disinterested. "I wonder if I've got the wrong Nathan Allen. What else can you tell me about him?"

Charissa thought for a moment. "He's shorter than I am—maybe five-eight or so? He's got dark hair, starting to gray a bit. What else?" Charissa appeared to be concentrating hard. "Oh—I know! He was an English major at Kingsbury. And he spent a year at Oxford before he went to seminary. He specialized in spirituality and literature."

Hannah's whole body constricted. Of course. How could she have forgotten that piece of his story?

It was definitely her Nathan Allen.

Meg followed the others down the stairway access from the cottage to the beach, gripping the handrail tightly. She didn't want to lose her balance and go tumbling with the picnic basket, so she stepped carefully.

Something was strangely familiar about this scene—the staircase, the sand dunes, the water, the wind. Though Meg had lived her entire life less than an hour away from Lake Michigan, she had spent very little time there. In fact, she couldn't remember the last time she had been at the lake.

As she pondered her sense of déjà vu, a single image materialized. She wasn't even sure it was an authentic memory. She was little—maybe three or four years old—and she was climbing down an outdoor staircase, tightly gripping someone's hand. She was worried about losing her balance, so she was concentrating intently on each step.

Then she heard a man's voice: "I've got you, Meggie. Keep comin'." Hard as she tried, she couldn't see a face. She only felt the grip of a hand and heard the sound of a voice.

*Was it her father?*

Meg possessed only shadowy images of him, and most of those had been influenced by photographs. She was only four when he died. Rachel, who was ten at the time, had many happy memories of "Daddy." Meg had always been jealous, though she had never confessed it aloud. Over the years Rachel had spoken happily, freely, even boastfully about their father and how he had loved her. Meg did not have the same gift.

But what was this image? Was she actually remembering a moment she had shared with her dad? Maybe she could ask Rachel if she remembered a trip to the beach before their father died.

"Hey! You okay?" Mara's shout interrupted her thoughts. Meg hadn't realized she had stopped halfway down the staircase. She waved to the others, who had already laid down a red tartan blanket near a sand dune.

"I'm coming!"

Hannah walked back over to the staircase and reached for the picnic basket Meg was carrying. "Here—let me take that for you."

"I'm okay. I've got it. Just had a weird bit of déjà vu—that's all."

"What about?"

"Something about coming down a staircase to a beach. I'm probably making it up."

"Making what up?" asked Mara as Meg and Hannah reached the dune.

Meg set the basket down on the blanket. "I was coming down the staircase, and something about the sand dunes and the lake felt really familiar. And then I saw an image of myself as a little girl, holding really tightly to someone's hand. To a man's hand. I'm wondering if it's an actual memory or just my imagination."

"Your dad?" Mara asked, unpacking some of the food.

"He died when I was four, and I don't have any memories of him: only stories my sister, Rachel, has told me. But I don't know. I guess it could be real."

Hannah said, "Maybe Rachel would remember a trip to the beach."

"That's what I'm wondering. But I don't want to plant a false memory in her."

"Ask her if your family used to go to the lake when you were little, and see what she says," Charissa suggested.

"It sucks growing up without a dad," Mara commented as she held out a loaf of bread to the others. "'Course, mine left before I was born. Abandoned us when my mom was six months pregnant. Cowardly son-of-a—"

Charissa narrowed her eyebrows and turned her back toward Mara. "What happened to your dad, Meg?" she asked.

Meg spoke the words matter-of-factly. "He was cleaning one of his guns, and it went off."

Hannah gasped. "Oh, Meg! I'm sorry. That's awful!"

"I guess it was." Meg took the bread from Mara. "But I don't remember any of it." She couldn't even remember missing her dad. Odd, how disconnected she felt from her own history. But Hannah was right. It must have been absolutely awful for her mother. Unspeakably horrible. Maybe that's why her mother had never talked about it.

The shock mirrored in Hannah's eyes unlocked something in Meg, as if Hannah were the surrogate, seeing and feeling what Meg did not. Could not.

Would not?

Meg wasn't sure she was ready for that kind of sight or feeling. Not sure at all.

"So, Hannah," Mara said, assembling another sandwich. "I'm kinda confused about this whole sabbatical thing. You're on a paid vacation because your church wanted you to have a break?"

"Basically." Hannah leaned back against the sand dune and stared up at the white underbelly of a gull hovering in slow motion above them. "They said I was overdue for one. I tried arguing my way out of it, but they won. So I'm here."

Mara whistled. "Man, I've heard of professors getting long sabbaticals, but not pastors. You must have a really generous church." Hannah did not respond. "And I've never asked you about the rest of your life," Mara continued. "I mean, life's more than the church and work, right?"

Hannah shrugged. "Not much to tell. For the past fifteen years the church has been my life."

"Married to the church, huh?" Mara pressed. "No husband? Boyfriend? Ex? Nothing?"

"Nope."

"Ah, it's not too late for that. You're still young, right? What are you? Forty?"

"Almost," Hannah said, smiling slightly. "Don't remind me."

"See, there's still time for you to fall in love and have a family. Right?" Mara turned to Meg and Charissa. "Do you guys know any eligible bachelors we could set her up with while she's here?"

"That's okay, Mara," Hannah said quickly, watching a pained and helpless expression flit across Meg's face. "I'm not looking for a relationship. I'm just not interested in falling in love."

"Seriously?" Mara seemed shocked. "Never?"

Hannah shook her head back and forth in a slow, definitive motion. She had given this answer many, many times before. "I made my choice a long time ago. I decided I couldn't serve Christ and have a family. Even if I wanted to change my mind, it's too late. For kids, anyway."

Mara wasn't going to give up that easily. "Oh, I don't know about that," she said. "I had a friend who gave birth to a beautiful, healthy boy at forty-three."

Hannah hesitated a moment and then replied, "I mean, I can't have children. I had a hysterectomy last year."

Meg leaned forward. Charissa cleared her throat. Mara turned crimson. "Oh, man—I'm sorry. I'm so sorry! There I go with my big mouth again. I just don't know when to shut it all off. I'm sorry, Hannah . . . So sorry . . . " She looked as if she wished the sand would part and consume her.

"No, it's okay. I get asked about it a lot. Don't worry." Hannah took hold of one of the long blades of reed grass and used the fine-tipped point to scribble in the sand. "It was all very straightforward," she said. "After years of trying all kinds of ways to control my symptoms, surgery became the inevitable solution. And I've felt great ever since. Really great. I'm grateful."

There was silence around the circle as each of them seemed to be searching for an appropriate response. "My mom had a hysterectomy a few years ago," Charissa ventured. "And she says she can't believe how much better she feels. Still, Hannah, I'm sorry. That must have been hard."

"Thanks." Hannah stopped scribbling and pulled some chocolate chip cookies from the picnic basket. "C'mon, guys. Eat up! I can't have all these leftovers to myself."

Confident that no one around the circle would have the courage to ask her any more questions, Hannah effortlessly steered the conversation for the rest of the afternoon. Mara eagerly divulged the details of her story, and The Pastor knew how to ask the right questions to keep her talking. In fact, Hannah was so skilled at manipulating that she was almost unaware she was doing it.

Almost.

"I talked too much," Mara despaired as she rode home with Meg and Charissa. "I'm so sorry. I completely dominated the whole afternoon. I just don't have an off switch, do I?"

*That's for sure,* Charissa thought. She was still trying to process everything Mara had disclosed about her past.

Meg kept one hand on the steering wheel and placed the other on Mara's shoulder. "I was so touched by your story, Mara," she said. "Thank you for trusting us enough to share what God's doing in your life. I wish I had your courage!" Meg turned briefly to smile at her. "When you were talking about the woman at the well, I started thinking about my own life and all the different wells I've tried to drink from."

"Really?" Mara asked, tearing up. "But you certainly don't have a past like mine, Meg." She wiped her nose on her sleeve as she fumbled around in her bag for a tissue.

Meg said, "We've all got pasts, don't we? Things we hide, things we're ashamed of, things we regret. I know I do." Charissa was mute. "You've given me something to think about today, Mara. Thank you."

In the backseat of the car, a battle was raging. Charissa had listened to the details of Mara's story with shock, horror, and disgust: the teenage pregnancy, the abortion, the affairs, the illegitimate child, the sexual promiscuity, the marriage of convenience, the expectation of divorce. Charissa had spent her life avoiding people like Mara, unwilling to be guilty by association.

But just when Charissa was beginning to congratulate herself for her own righteousness and moral purity, some words from Scripture came to mind. "It's not the healthy who need a doctor, but the sick," Jesus had said. She exhaled more loudly than she intended and drummed her fingers against the car window. She was still a Pharisee. Here she was, face to face with an honest-to-goodness sinner, and she had failed the test. She couldn't believe she had failed the test.

Then again, what had Dr. Allen said? "The spiritual life is a journey, Charissa, not an exam."

She sighed heavily.

If only she didn't have so far to go.

## *Meg*

*Nine-year-old Meg was awakened by the sound of a man's voice echoing in the foyer. Looking out her window, she saw a police car in the driveway. She tiptoed to the landing and sat down where she could hear without being seen.*

*Meg didn't understand everything the officer said, but his voice was stern. She caught the words "party" and "drinking." He said he was giving Rachel a warning; but if it happened again, he wouldn't be so generous. Mother's tone was icy as she thanked him for bringing Rachel home. When Meg heard the front door shut, she held her breath.*

*"How dare you!" Mother thundered.*

*"What's the big deal? I wasn't the only one busted, you know."*

*"You're fifteen! As if it's not bad enough that you're out drinking, you get dragged home here in a squad car for all the neighbors to see! How dare you! How dare you bring that kind of shame upon this family!"*

*"Oh, right! I forgot! The perfect Fowler family! Gotta make sure nobody finds out what really goes on around here!" Meg heard the slap of a hand against bare skin. "I hate you!" Rachel screamed.*

*Meg tried to scamper back to her room without being spotted, but she wasn't quick enough. Mother stormed up the stairs and saw her racing down the hallway. "Don't you dare take this out of the house, you hear me?" Mother hissed. Meg nodded and dove back into bed, pulling the covers tightly over her head.*

*She didn't sleep the rest of the night.*

When Meg got home from the lake, there was a message from Rachel: "Just checking in with you to say hi. I'll be home tonight. Call me!"

*Good,* Meg thought. Now she had an excuse to call and mention she had spent the day at the lake. Her heart was beating fast as she dialed Rachel's number. "Hey, Rache! Sorry I missed your call." Meg hoped she sounded relaxed. "I was at Lake Michigan with some friends."

"Wow! I haven't been there in ages. Where were you?"

"Near Lake Haven."

"I remember Lake Haven," Rachel said. "Cute town. We used to go there for ice cream after the beach, remember?" Meg didn't remember, and her chest was pounding.

"I guess I don't remember that," she said casually. "We used to go there with Mother?"

Rachel snickered. "Hell, no! Are you kidding? With Daddy! You think Mother would have anything to do with sand in her shoes?"

Meg gripped the phone. "And I went with you?"

"Well, you were really little, but yeah, you came with us a couple of times.

'Course, you were such a scaredy-cat, you wanted nothing to do with the water."

Meg was trying to figure out how much to ask. "I wish I could remember that."

"I haven't thought about those trips in a long time," Rachel said. "Those were good days, just being with Daddy. Of course, I liked them better before you came along." Meg couldn't tell if she was teasing or not.

"What do you mean?"

Rachel laughed. "You took his attention away from me!" Her voice was lighthearted. "Once you started coming with us, he couldn't play with me in the water. I swear you were scared of everything. And you were so slow! I always had to stop and wait for you."

Meg steadied herself. Was she on the verge of discovering if her memory was real?

"Come to think of it, I do remember a staircase on a beach." She waited to see if Rachel would supply any details.

"Yeah! I would race down to the sand and have to wait forever for you. And Daddy would tell me to be patient because you were little and needed help. I can still hear him too: 'It's okay, Meggie! It's okay! C'mon, Meggie, you can do it!'"

Meg gasped. "He called me 'Meggie'?"

"That's what I remember, anyway. I could be wrong." Meg could hardly take it in. "You know," Rachel continued, seemingly oblivious to the impact of her words, "there used to be photos somewhere in the attic. Next time I'm in town, I want to take a look up there. Who knows what we might find?"

"I'd love to see you. When could you come?"

"I don't know. I'm supposed to be in Detroit for business in a couple weeks. I guess I could tack on a day or two and come see you. Let me play with travel plans, and I'll let you know, okay?"

They chatted a few more minutes, and then Meg began to review her day in prayer.

She was spilling over with gratitude, pouring out her thanks for the gift she had been given. An authentic memory of her father! Not something she had imagined from photographs, but a real moment of presence with her dad. She played the scene in her head over and over again. Yes, Rachel had more memories, but Meg had a gift now too.

And yet there was a dark side to the gift which Meg did not want to examine, despite what Katherine had told the group that morning.

"For some of you," Katherine had said, "it will be easier to review the times when you were aware of God's presence. It will be easier to name the moments when you experienced joy, love and peace. You may be reluctant to confront the difficult struggles and darker feelings, but God is present in all of life. Our everyday lives are the raw materials for encountering God; so pay attention. Don't be afraid of asking what God is saying through the things you'd rather overlook and ignore. Often, that's exactly where the Spirit is moving."

Meg sighed. There were so many things she had refused to acknowledge: heartaches and disappointments, trials and pain. Meg had coped by packing difficult things into mental and emotional boxes. Then she had hidden them away in dark attic recesses, out of sight and out of mind.

Now that Meg had begun to unpack some of the boxes of grief and regret about Jim, it seemed no coincidence that a memory of her father had emerged as well. But if she accepted the joy of remembering her dad, wouldn't she also need to face the pain of losing him? Wouldn't she also need to address the heartache over how her childhood might have been different if Daddy hadn't died? And if she began to think hard about Daddy, she might also need to think hard about Mother.

She wasn't ready for that. She wasn't sure she would ever be ready for that.

She sat at the kitchen table, cradling her head in her hands. It was too much. Too hard. The journey to healing and transformation suddenly seemed even longer and more treacherous than ever before. She felt her spirit recoil in fear. *I can't do it. I'm sorry, Lord. I can't.*

That's when she heard her father's voice again. "I've got you, Meggie. Keep comin'."

Again and again the words rang in her head, and she felt the steadying grip of a strong hand, helping her walk forward. As the voice resonated in her spirit, Meg began to understand the meaning of the gift. These weren't just her father's words, were they? Her Heavenly Father was also speaking them tenderly to her, echoing the promises Katherine had given her from Isaiah 43: *I have called you by name, you are mine. When you pass through the waters, I will be with you; and through the rivers, they shall not overwhelm you.*

"I've got you, Meggie. Keep comin'."

As she continued to concentrate on the strengthening words of reassurance, Meg grew increasingly confident about one thing.

Her Heavenly Father wasn't going to let go.

## *Hannah*

Hannah didn't bother eating dinner Saturday night. She wasn't hungry after Meg, Mara, and Charissa left the cottage. So she went to bed early, intending to continue her daily discipline of lectio divina in John's gospel. Opening to the second chapter, she began reading prayerfully about the wedding at Cana, listening for a word or phrase that caught her attention.

> On the third day there was a wedding in Cana of Galilee, and the mother of Jesus was there. Jesus and his disciples had also been invited to the wedding. When the wine gave out, the mother of Jesus said to him, "They have no wine." And Jesus said to her, "Woman, what concern is that to you and to me? My hour has not yet come." His mother said to the servants, "Do whatever he tells you."

Do whatever he tells you. Do whatever he tells you.

Hannah couldn't get beyond those words. So she began to chew on them, inviting the Spirit to show her how those words connected with her life. Then she read the text aloud again.

> On the third day there was a wedding in Cana of Galilee, and the mother of Jesus was there. Jesus and his disciples had also been invited to the wedding. When the wine gave out, the mother of Jesus said to him, "They have no wine." And Jesus said to her, "Woman, what concern is that to you and to me? My hour has not yet come." His mother said to the servants, "Do whatever he tells you."

Do whatever he tells you. Why did those words choose her? Hadn't she already done what God had asked her to do?

She had left behind her work, her home, her friends, her life. She had obeyed, doing whatever he told her. Had she ever neglected doing what Jesus asked her to do? Ever?

Why, even when Nate—

No. She wasn't going there. She definitely wasn't going there. Was not, was not, was not.

*Isn't it enough for you that I walked away, Lord?*

She was not going to relive the moment. There was no point reliving the moment. She tried to distract herself from thoughts of Nathan by reading ahead in the text, but the words pursued her.

Do whatever he tells you.

*What, Lord? What do you want me to do? What haven't I already done for you?*

She read the text again, this time thinking about the wine that had run out. Is that what the Spirit wanted her to see? Is that what God wanted her to confess? That the wine of her life had run out and the joy was gone?

*Okay, Lord. I see that. Forgive me. The joy is gone, and I'm running on empty. Please fill me with living water that can become new wine.*

That's when it hit her with blunt force: Jesus' indifference, his reluctance to get involved, his insistence that it wasn't time for him to intervene.

It wasn't time.

*Well,* thought Hannah, *time ran out for me, and you certainly didn't do anything to help, did you?*

Wait.

Whoa.

Was that her voice speaking words of accusation against the Lord? She sounded so bitter. But she wasn't bitter. Was not, was not, was not.

*I'm sorry, Lord. Forgive me. I know I won't stay empty. I know you fill me with good things. Help me trust you. Please.*

Just then a memory from the picnic rose up again: the look of helpless sorrow that consumed Meg's face when Hannah mentioned the hysterectomy. But Meg didn't need to feel sorry for her. Hannah wasn't disappointed about not having a husband or children. Was not, was not, was not. People always presumed she was grieving, but she wasn't. *Was not.* She had never grieved over that. There was nothing to grieve.

She had no regrets—absolutely no regrets about the way her life had turned out. What she had gained in serving God was far greater than anything she had lost or left behind years ago. She had no regrets. None.

Then why did she feel sick to her stomach whenever Nathan came to mind? Why did the words of their ancient and painful conversation keep rising up to torment her?

"Isn't it possible that God wants to show his love for you through me?" Nathan had asked, his eyes brimming with deep emotion. "Isn't that possible? Why are you running away from love, Hannah? What are you hiding from?" He begged her not to walk away. He begged her to pray and seek God. "Please, Hannah. *Please . . .*"

She had told him she knew what Jesus wanted her to do. She was confident that saying no to Nathan was an act of obedience. But if she had known that she would someday be almost forty, single, and childless, would she have made the same choice? Would she have sealed off her heart and walked away? Suddenly, she didn't know how to answer those questions, and her uncertainty frightened her.

Not only had she lost everything she had known and loved in Chicago, but she had been thrust into a place where the past now returned to haunt her.

It all seemed like some sort of cruel, cosmic joke.

Hannah closed her Bible and turned off the bedside lamp.

What had Charissa said about how Nathan had helped her? "Dr. Allen told me to pay attention to the things that make me angry, defensive, and upset."

If God could use pain and agitation to uncover hidden hurts and reveal unresolved sorrow, then one thing was clear. The Spirit of God was moving.

Curling her body into a fetal position under the covers, Hannah wrapped herself in darkness and wept.

## Mara

Mara microwaved a frozen dinner and sat on the couch with the television off, waiting for Tom and the boys to get home. Her notebook was open so she could read what she had written that morning after she walked the labyrinth: "I'm getting it! I'm getting how Jesus sees all the crap in my life but doesn't condemn me. Like the Samaritan woman. She wasn't ashamed to tell people that the Messiah knew everything about her. Maybe I have a story that might actually help somebody. How cool would that be?"

As Mara examined her moments of gratitude from the morning, she was struck by how easy it was to forget what God had revealed to her—especially since she shifted so quickly into self-doubt. But here were her words on the page, serving as markers that the Holy Spirit had spoken to her. She wanted to remember. She needed to be deliberate about remembering so that she could move forward with faith and hope.

Katherine had said that some people would find it easier to focus on the negative parts of the day and lose sight of the blessings God had given. Mara was tired of being negative. Maybe the examen was a spiritual discipline to help her become more grateful.

Shifting her weight on the couch, she asked the Holy Spirit to give her courage to prayerfully review the rest of her day. She asked for light into the dark and difficult places, as well as vision to see the blessings and gifts. Then she imagined sitting next to Jesus, talking with him about what she had thought, felt, and experienced during the afternoon at the cottage.

She remembered the joy of feeling included and how grateful she was for her emerging friendship with Meg and Hannah. She closed her eyes as she pictured the scene again: warm sunlight on her face, wind in her hair, sand beneath her feet. She had tasted peace as she sat beside the shimmering lake, feasting on the good gifts of God.

Then she felt the searing pain of regret. She was so eager to connect with other women about their lives and relationships that she had pushed Hannah too hard. If only she hadn't asked about Hannah's personal life.

Mara had spent the rest of the afternoon trying to atone for her indiscretion. Determined to make amends for whatever sorrow she might have caused, Mara had willingly submitted to all of Hannah's probing questions about her life. She had made herself vulnerable, even as Charissa sat there screaming disapproval without saying a word.

Mara didn't care. She knew Charissa's type, and she was tired of having her buttons pushed. She had lived her whole life surrounded by little Charissas who grew up to be critical, judgmental, hard-hearted women. She didn't want Charissa's approval. *She didn't.* She didn't care. She didn't need approval or acceptance from shallow and superficial people. Charissa could reject her. Mara rejected Charissa. Her first impressions had been right after all.

The hum of the garage door interrupted her prayer, and she quickly wiped away her tears.

Tom and the boys were home.

## Hannah

Hannah awoke on Sunday morning, exhausted.

Over the years she had spent countless nights weeping for others in intercessory prayer. But she couldn't recall the last time she had spent a night sobbing uncontrollably for herself. As she lay in bed, she remembered something she had once read about tears being waters of the womb, breaking before the birth of something new. But her tears weren't the prelude to new birth. Her womb was gone. And there was nothing growing within her except disappointment: disappointment with herself, disappointment with her life, disappointment with—

Yes, profound disappointment with God.

There. She'd said it. *Happy now, Lord? Isn't that what you want? "Truth in the inner parts?" Fine. Take my truth.*

She rolled over and looked at the alarm clock: 11 a.m. When was the last time she had stayed in bed until 11 a.m.?

The second service would be underway at Westminster. The congregation would be gathered, singing the opening songs of worship, lifting their hearts and hands to the Lord. She was glad she wasn't there. She was glad she didn't have to sing praise choruses; glad she didn't have to fake joy and thanksgiving in front of anyone; glad that no one would be commending and admiring her for tireless servanthood to Christ and his church. Glad. She was tired of faking. Tired, tired, tired.

*I'm empty, Lord. Completely empty. And you know what? I'm not even interested in being filled. How's that for honest?*

She threw on her clothes, listening to the wind whip and lash a rope against the neighbors' flagpole. A storm was brewing. The gray sky was moody and menacing above the swirling, churning, crashing surf; and the sea had turned to slate. Good. She might have been soothed by a sunlit, sparkling lake, and Hannah didn't want to be soothed—not today. She skipped her morning cup of tea, braced herself against the wind, and headed for the beach.

*Do whatever he tells you. Do whatever he tells you. Do whatever he tells you.* The words still would not release her.

She had spent the night mentally rehearsing everything she had ever sacrificed for God. She had spent the night recounting every act of obedience, every denial to self, every detail of devotion: all the time, all the energy, all the strength. And for what? *For what?*

As she walked along the beach, she spit out her prayer through clenched teeth.

*What did I ever do to you to deserve what I've gotten? I gave up everything for you. Everything! And for what? I've given you a lifetime of total devotion—body, soul, mind, strength. What did I ever hold back from you? Name it! I tell people, "Oh, you know it's impossible to out-give God!" I'm such a liar.*

She shielded her eyes against a wind that was hurling stinging fistfuls of fine-grained sand into her face. The lid was off. No more stuffing and containing. The harder the wind blew, the more freely she voiced her anger.

*God is great; God is good, huh? No, you're not. Not to me. How's that for honest? How's that for truth?*

*You know what? I wish I had said yes to Nathan. I wish I hadn't cared about what you wanted because clearly, your plans for me weren't great, were they? Is this what you planned for me? That somehow it was good for me to be alone? This was the best you could come up with? Do you even care how much my heart broke every time I pronounced a couple "man and wife"? Do you care? I could've had a life with him! But no! I gave that up for you! Remember? I gave up EVERYTHING for you!*

She walked faster, boxing the air with her fists while a single gull kept pace, matching her forward, straining movement with playful backwards flight.

*And what about all those good gifts you promise to those who love and trust you? What about me? How many years did I cry out to you for healing? How many years did I beg you to touch my body and make me whole? Remember those prayers, God? The nights I would lie in bed and imagine I was reaching out to touch Jesus' garment so my hemorrhaging would stop? I didn't have any doubts you could touch and heal me. No doubts at all. But there was no answer for me, was there? One more dream laid down on the altar of sacrifice. One more disappointed hope. But what do I do? I smile and tell people that you're a faithful God, that you have a plan and purpose in our suffering and sorrow.*

*No. You. Don't.*

*Do you even care how much my heart broke every time I held someone else's child before you, speaking your words of promise and love over that family? Do you care?*

*You know what? I don't like the way you treat your friends. I've had enough. I'm done pretending I'm not angry and disappointed with you. I'm not going to fake that I believe your plans are always best—that you do everything out of love. I refuse to be a hypocrite.*

*Lover? You want to be my lover? I won't have you. You hear me? I won't have you. I'm saying no! Go pick on someone else. I'm done.*

Sinking to her knees, Hannah rocked herself back and forth in the sand, her sobs muffled by the plaintive shrieking of the gulls and the thundering tumult of the surf.

8

# Intimacy and Encounter

*Where can I go from your spirit?*
*Or where can I flee from your presence?*

Psalm 139:7

## Charissa

**Love (III)**

*Love bade me welcome, yet my soul drew back,*
*Guilty of dust and sin.*
*But quick-ey'd Love, observing me grow slack*
*From my first entrance in,*
*Drew nearer to me, sweetly questioning*
*If I lack'd anything.*

*A guest, I answer'd, worthy to be here:*
*Love said, You shall be he.*
*I, the unkind, ungrateful? Ah, my dear,*
*I cannot look on thee.*
*Love took my hand, and smiling did reply,*
*Who made the eyes but I?*

*Truth, Lord, but I have marr'd them: let my shame*
*Go where it doth deserve.*

*And know you not, says Love, who bore the blame?*
*My dear, then I will serve.*
*You must sit down, says Love, and taste my meat:*
*So I did sit and eat.*

George Herbert (1593-1633)

Charissa sat in Dr. Allen's class, listening to her peers discuss "Love (III)" with graphic intensity. They were probing Herbert's description of the Eucharist as an invitation to the deepest levels of intimacy and communion with Christ.

"The whole imagery of Love bidding welcome but the soul drawing back is a movement of passion, isn't it?" one of her male classmates commented. "Especially the lines, 'quick-ey'd Love, observing me grow slack from my first entrance in.' Herbert's playing with metaphor there."

Another one agreed. "God is Lover and Host here, and the distance between Lover and Beloved, Host and Guest keeps shrinking as the poem goes on," he observed. "Christ keeps welcoming, keeps inviting, until finally, the beloved and forgiven guest says yes and ingests God. 'You must sit down, says Love, and taste my meat: So I did sit and eat.'"

"We're in the realm of profound mystery here," Dr. Allen commented, sitting down on the edge of a desk and fastening his keen eyes on his students. "For the moment, let's set aside Herbert's theology of the sacrament so that we don't get drawn into a debate about how Christ is present in the Lord's Supper. Instead, I want to delve more deeply into your observations about the dance of movement between the soul and God, the movement of attraction and resistance. What's the connection between self-awareness and God-awareness for Herbert?"

One of the students spoke up. "It's all about the right kind of humility, isn't it?" she asked.

"Go on," Dr. Allen urged.

"I mean, the guest begins by recognizing his own unworthiness to draw near to Christ, even when the Lord is inviting and welcoming him to come.

The guest sees who God is and also sees himself clearly—and the gap between them seems too big to overcome." She paused. "And I suppose the guest could keep making endless excuses about why he can't say yes to God's invitation to intimacy and love. The wrong kind of humility—a kind of self-loathing and despair—could keep someone from saying yes to Love. And so could pride."

"Well said," Dr. Allen replied, nodding. "And that's a good segue into contemplating your own spiritual formation as a result of your reading. Where does each of you find yourself in the movement of attraction and resistance that Herbert describes? What do you notice within yourself as you read these lines? What's happening in your spirit?"

*What's happening in my spirit?* Charissa repeated silently. This was exactly the sort of questioning she hadn't comprehended before.

And yet—

Suddenly, something Emily had said to her years ago came to mind: "You've never needed Jesus the same way I have, Charissa. You've always had your life so well put together."

Emily was right. Charissa had worn her self-sufficiency as a badge of honor. For years her own pride had kept her from Jesus. She had never glimpsed her need for conversion or grace.

But now—

She had sat in worship on Sunday morning, listening to the Reverend Hildenberg's sermon about the sinful woman anointing Jesus' feet at Simon the Pharisee's house. Charissa had never liked that text.

"Which one are you?" he had asked the congregation. "Simon the Pharisee or the sinful woman who anoints Christ's feet with her precious ointment and her tears? What kind of host are you to Jesus?"

Now the question was pursuing Charissa again as she listened to her classmates openly discuss their own sense of resistance and attraction to the Host's invitation to intimate union and fellowship.

*What kind of host are you to Jesus? What kind of host are you to the Host?* Charissa was surprised to find her eyes burning.

*A lousy one,* she answered. *Absolutely lousy.*

Like Simon the Pharisee, she had welcomed Jesus into her home, but she had stayed in the position of control. She was polite and respectful, but she showed him no gratitude, no devotion, no—

Love.

*No love.*

*Did she actually love God?* The question startled her.

For as long as she could remember, she had dutifully performed all that was required and expected of her in leading a good Christian life. But why?

*Why?*

The answers came swiftly while her classmates' conversation swirled around her.

Because she didn't want to feel guilty. Because she wanted to avoid reproach and punishment. Because she wanted other people to respect and admire her. Because she knew it was the right thing to do.

But love for God did not appear anywhere on her long list of reasons and motivations for living an obedient Christian life. *How was that possible?*

She had been self-centered, even in her faith. Totally self centered.

She couldn't believe she had missed that. *How could she have missed that?*

She leaned forward in her chair, holding her head in her hands. Suddenly, she saw new depths of sin, and she was disgusted with herself. *How could she have been blind to that kind of self-centeredness?*

Hot tears began to splatter the page, and she hoped no one was watching. She wanted to run, to hide, to disappear and retreat in shame. *How could she have been so hard-hearted toward God? How could she have spent years priding herself that she didn't need Jesus?*

And now—

Now what? Where was she supposed to go from here?

"So when you hear Love's voice, gently pursuing you," Dr. Allen was saying, "what's your response? What do you lack?"

Was he inside her head?

Charissa stared at the blurred verses in front of her. *A guest,* she answered silently, *worthy to be here.*

And Love—

Love was bidding welcome, drawing near, and tenderly reassuring: "Charissa, you shall be she."

Charissa waited to speak with Dr. Allen until after the other students had left the classroom. "I had my aha moment today," she said, her voice quivering and her eyes filling with tears. "I see now."

"Tell me," he said gently, sitting down again.

She seated herself in the chair across from him, meeting his gaze. "I've been reading Herbert and the other poets the wrong way," she said. "I've been reading the literature the same way I've been reading the Bible all these years—clinically and critically, as an intellectual exercise and something to accomplish rather than as a devotional pursuit." She hesitated, wondering how to articulate what she had experienced in class that day. "I've been so frustrated with this class, Dr. Allen, feeling like I just didn't comprehend what you were asking us to do. I couldn't figure out what you wanted from me. But today . . . today the poetry actually became prayer for me." She lowered her voice to a whisper. "I've never had that happen before."

Dr. Allen's face lit up. "Beautiful, Charissa. That's a beautiful gift from God."

She went on, "You asked us to pay attention to our own sense of attraction and resistance, and I was right there, experiencing it while you were talking about it. Like this supernatural synergy or convergence or something. I don't know how else to describe it."

"Sounds like the Holy Spirit's stirring," he said, smiling.

She nodded. "I guess. There's just so much about God I don't understand."

"And that's the beginning of wisdom, Charissa." He paused. "May I offer you something, as one recovering perfectionist to another?"

She laughed and wiped her eyes. "Yes, please."

He leaned in closer. "God is always the first one to move in his relationship with us. Our movement is always a response to the Love which loved us first. It's not about being more perfect in your faith or in your love for Jesus, Charissa—it's about being more open to responding to his deep love for you. So no guilt or condemnation about not seeing things before now, okay? It's the Spirit who opens the eyes of the blind. Always at the right time."

"Thank you," she said. "Thank you for everything."

"You're on a great journey." He rose from his chair. "Sailing, remember?"

Sailing. She still wasn't sure she would ever prefer the unpredictability of the wind to the power of an engine, but she understood. "I actually thought of you this weekend," she said as they left the classroom. "I was at the lake, and there were still a few boats out."

"See? I'm not the only stalwart one," he said, chuckling. "Where were you?"

"A cottage near Lake Haven."

Should she tell him about the small world coincidence? Should she tell him they had a mutual acquaintance? What harm would it do? If he didn't remember Hannah, what difference would it make? And if he did—well, maybe he'd want to get in touch with an old friend. "Actually," she continued, "the woman who invited us said she went to seminary with you."

He raised his eyebrows inquisitively. "Is that right? Who's that?"

"Hannah Shepley. She said she didn't think you would remember her, though."

His face was inscrutable. "I do remember Hannah. Last I heard she was a pastor in Chicago. Is she living in Kingsbury now?"

"No, she's still pastoring in Chicago, but she's been given a nine-month sabbatical, and she's staying at a friend's cottage on the lake. We met in the sacred journey group."

"Well, when you see her again, tell her hello from me."

"I will."

Another student approached, waiting to speak to him. "God bless you, Charissa."

"You too, Dr. Allen."

As she watched him walk down the hallway with his student, she wondered if they were speaking about literature or faith. Knowing Dr. Allen, probably both.

Her mind kept whirling as she strode across the quad to the library. *Intimacy,* she thought. The spiritual life was all about intimacy. She'd just never seen it that way before.

She thought again about Herbert's imagery of passion and longing. Could she let her recognition of sin drive her into Jesus' arms? Could union and oneness with Christ be an even deeper kind of intimacy than what she was discovering with John?

Something unfamiliar and exhilarating was stirring within her. *Let me love you, Jesus, even as you first loved me,* she breathed. *Amen.*

Charissa hopped into the car and kissed John provocatively. "Hey!" he said. "Good day?"

"Excellent. I had this amazing aha moment in Dr. Allen's class today, and suddenly everything is shifting into focus."

John listened as she spoke excitedly about her new revelations, her need for Jesus, her longing for more. Somehow Charissa's awakening faith was stirring his own spirit. Truths he had taken for granted for many years were coming to life in new ways as he watched his wife grow and change. So much had happened in such a short time that it seemed hard to believe. But he was grateful—very grateful.

"So, I'm thinking I need to do some research tonight," Charissa said when they entered the apartment.

"Do you need to go back to campus after dinner?" He hung his keys on the ring.

She set down her backpack and gazed intently at him. "No, I don't need to go anywhere." She wrapped his arms around her body and pressed against him. "I was analyzing some sacred poetry at the library today—reading in the Song of Solomon, actually—and I started thinking that the best way for me to understand the text would be to explore the connections between intimacy with God and intimacy with a spouse. Can you help?"

He laughed. "Can I just tell you? I'm thanking God you signed up for Dr. Allen's class. And for that sacred journey group."

"An unexpected benefit, huh?" she said, smiling. "I told you—intimacy without defenses is a whole new world for me. Spiritually, emotionally, physically." She kissed him alluringly.

John breathed in the citrus fragrance of her hair. "So this research," he murmured. "When do you want to start?"

"The sooner the better." She guided his fingers to the top of her blouse. "It's urgent."

He grinned. "The work of a grad student, right?"

Charissa squeezed his hand and whispered, "It never ends."

October 15

7 p.m.

I'm sitting here on the deck at the cottage, watching the sun sink below the horizon. The sky is streaked with lavender and amethyst. Glowing, luminous, lovely. Sunsets are about the only thing I'm paying attention to these days—my only spiritual discipline.

I haven't had the energy or desire to write this week, but if I let this go on much longer, I know I'll end up disintegrating. And I don't want that to happen. My journal has always been a lifeline to me, and I can't let this go now. No matter how much I'd rather avoid writing, I can't. So here goes.

I've spent the past couple of days sleeping a lot. Don't know if I'm actually that tired, or if I'm just trying to escape. Meg was sweet to call Sunday night. She was worried about how I was doing. I just said I was tired, and thankfully, she didn't ask any questions.

I could never confess to her what a fraud I am—that I'm a pastor who can't even declare the simplest truths about God being great or good or loving. Meg wouldn't be able to handle my disappointment with God, and I'm not going to say anything that could hurt her growing faith. She doesn't need to know the darker truth.

I'm mad at God. I feel totally disappointed and betrayed and angry.

I used to tell people, "Give God your anger. He can handle it!" And what have I done? I've stuffed it. Totally stuffed it. I'm such a hypocrite. And now that it's out, where do I go? I can't talk to anyone in Chicago about it. Not even Steve. Even though he might understand. I don't know. I guess I could call Katherine and see if she'd be willing to talk with me, even though I'm not scheduled to meet with her again for another two weeks. I don't know where else to turn. And I'd say, "Help, Lord!" except I'm not speaking to him right now.

The fiery blaze of sunset is yielding to the cinder grays of twilight, and everything is in ashes. Everything.

October 16

1 p.m.

Slept in again today, and I'm still not dressed. Just sitting here staring out the window. Maybe I'll go for a walk later. Maybe. I did call New Hope. Katherine offered to see me this afternoon, but I'll go tomorrow instead.

Talked to Nancy a little while ago. She says she's worried about me—that I don't sound like myself. Guess I'm just too tired to fake it with anybody. No energy for faking anything. Hoping Katherine can help me.

October 17

11 a.m.

I'm sitting here in the labyrinth courtyard, trying to process everything that happened during my time with Katherine this morning.

I completely unloaded on her. Not about Nathan. I didn't mention anything about him. I just talked about disappointments in general. She didn't seem a bit shocked by my anger or bitterness. She just let me pour out all the ways God has disappointed me over the years. She didn't argue with me or try to defend God. She just listened. I was surprised that I didn't try to censor my words or my feelings. I just dumped it all out.

Her eyes filled up when I told her about the hysterectomy. That surprised me. Then she said something that took my breath away. "You've been bleeding on the inside for a long time, Hannah."

At first I didn't know what she meant. But then I began thinking about why I ended up having surgery. All those years battling chronic pain, not knowing what the source was. I just assumed it was normal to have such terrible cramps and horrific periods. I just dealt with it. I'd never even heard of "endometriosis" when the doctor finally said that's what he suspected I had. All that undetected bleeding tissue within my body, accumulating for years and years, fusing things together and growing in secret.

It works as a metaphor for my life, doesn't it? Katherine was right. I've always been an internal bleeder. I've always stuffed everything. And just like my body eventually began to hemorrhage, maybe that's what my spirit is doing now. The hysterectomy took care of my physical symptoms, clearing out the damaged tissue and organs and leaving an empty void behind. I never made the connection before, but Steve referred to the sabbatical as "radical surgery." Maybe this is what it's about. Clearing out the damaged, bleeding tissue within my spirit—years of accumulated toxicity, growing in secret, undetected.

That's it, isn't it? Even though that lectio of the wedding at Cana pushed me over the edge, I need to remember that Jesus didn't leave the jars empty. I don't have a clue what he's going to fill me with. But Katherine promises there's hope. She pointed out that it was a gift to be able to pour out my anger. She said that anger and resentment have been taking up space in my spirit for a long time. I just didn't know it was there. In that sense, then, the emptying is preparation for receiving something else. "Freeing up sacred space," Katherine said. I like that phrase.

No more secret hemorrhaging. Katherine said that my anger with God is a sign of my intimacy with him, even though it doesn't feel that way right now. She said that only people who really trust God can vent their anger at him. She's right. I've taught people that. I'm still not ready to talk to God. But maybe there's hope I won't be angry forever.

I'm being honest now in a way I never have been before. Guess that's part of cleaning out the toxicity. I've been so afraid. So afraid of disintegrating. So afraid of looking at my sorrow and being overwhelmed by it. I've still got things I shoved away years ago—things I've never talked to anyone about. And I'm still not ready to talk about them. Not yet. Maybe never. I don't know.

I have so far to go. So much to confront. I'm not going to be naïve about how hard the road will be. But there's hope. There's hope in the ashes.

I'll stop there. Someone has just entered the courtyard, maybe to walk the labyrinth.

Oh no. No no no.

Nate.

*Hannah spent weeks laboring over her inaugural sermon for preaching class. Choosing the John 4 text of the Samaritan woman at the well, she poured herself into the work of*

*exegesis. She studied cultural and historical contexts; she used her budding knowledge of Greek to dig behind English translations; she explored the theological implications of Jesus revealing who he was to an outsider and outcast. Then she wove all the "where, what, when, and why" into the "so what?" of personal application, inviting her listeners to contemplate the meaning of Jesus' promise to be Living Water in their own lives.*

*Though her hands trembled as she stood before her peers, she tried hard to make good use of all the speech tips and training she had received. When she finished, her professor congratulated her for a well-delivered, carefully crafted sermon. Hannah was relieved.*

*As she and Nate walked together to the student center for lunch, she asked him for his feedback. "Dr. Jenkins was right," he said. "You hit all the marks for careful exegesis and good technique. But it wasn't you, Shep."*

*Hannah was taken aback. "What do you mean, 'It wasn't me'? Maybe I was just nervous!"*

*"I'm not talking about nerves. We were all nervous. I'm just saying that Dr. Jenkins doesn't know you like I do. Your message didn't have any of your heart. You were so worried about getting things correct, you stripped the text of its life. And that's not you. You're full of passion and spirit. Your sermon wasn't." Hannah was quiet, contemplating her friend's accurate and perceptive observation. He smiled kindly at her. "I'm not being critical to be mean. You know that. I'm for you, Shep, remember?"*

*Hannah let go of her wounded pride. One thing she had learned about Nate Allen: she could always trust him for the truth.*

Nathan had arrived at Katherine's office for his monthly spiritual direction appointment at 11:30 a.m. Greeting his trusted mentor warmly, he sat down in a chair facing the window. "We keep getting these beautiful autumn days," he commented, looking out at the brightly colored courtyard.

Katherine smiled. "Haven't put the boat away yet, have you?"

Nathan shook his head and grinned. "You know that's one of my favorite spiritual disciplines. I'm hoping to get in a good sail with Jake tomorrow." His eyes fell to a woman sitting on the corner bench of the courtyard, writing in a notebook and repeatedly tucking her hair behind her ears. Normally, he wouldn't have paid much attention. Perhaps if Charissa hadn't just mentioned her trip to Lake Haven, he would have ignored the woman entirely. But his spirit quickened in recognition. Though he couldn't see her face, he knew the gesture.

*Hannah Shepley.*

"I think I see an old friend of mine in the courtyard," Nathan said. "Is that Hannah Shepley?" Katherine followed his gaze and nodded. "I'm sorry, Katherine. I haven't seen her since we were in seminary. Would you excuse me long enough to say hello?"

"Of course! Take your time!"

Nathan moved briskly down the hallway, praying as he went. What were the chances of their paths converging after all these years? He had spent the past several days debating whether or not he should try to contact her—just to say hello—and now here she was.

Hannah's voice from years ago rang in his ears. "A God thing," she used to say when speaking about God's providential workings. Nathan didn't know what purpose the Spirit might have in orchestrating a meeting after all these years, but he wasn't going to miss the chance to find out.

Hannah happened to look up just as he entered the courtyard. Their eyes met briefly before she looked down again and resumed writing. *She doesn't recognize me,* he thought. Not wanting to startle her, he approached slowly, saying her name tentatively. "Hannah?" She looked up again. "It's Nate. Nate Allen."

She was staring at him with the blank, amnesic stare of dark eyes ringed by dark circles. Her expression was opaque. He couldn't read her. Then she smiled slightly and rose from the bench. There was a moment's awkwardness as each one tried to determine how to greet the other. Handshake or embrace? A dance of gestures resulted in a casual one-armed hug.

"I can't believe it!" he exclaimed. "What a small world!" He was grateful Charissa had mentioned that she'd met Hannah. If Nathan had seen her anywhere else, he might not have recognized her. Her face was tired, and the fire that had once lit her eyes with life and passion had gone to ashes. He'd seen the signs of pastoral burnout many times over the years and wondered if Hannah's premature aging was the result of compassion fatigue. Or was there something else?

"Charissa told me she'd met you."

"Small world," Hannah agreed.

Nathan wasn't sure if her reserve was rooted in surprise at seeing him or regret over an old chapter being reopened. Though he kept trying to read her, she was unfathomable. The years had certainly given her ample opportunity for perfecting her mask.

"I was here to meet Katherine for spiritual direction and happened to glimpse you through the window," he explained. "After all these years it seems anticlimactic just to say hello. But that's all I wanted to say." Hannah didn't reply immediately, and he began to wish he hadn't come out to the courtyard.

"It's nice to see you," she finally said.

He decided to test how open she was to conversation. "Charissa said you're here on sabbatical."

She nodded. "Until June." He waited, but she said nothing more.

"You've got a generous church."

"Very."

Nathan cleared his throat. "I told Katherine I just wanted to come out and say hi." Hannah tucked her hair behind her ears. "Well . . . It's good to see you," he said. "Take care, Hannah."

"Thanks. You too."

This time Nathan was the one who walked away.

Hannah tried in vain to find her breath. The encounter had happened so suddenly that it took several minutes for her feelings to catch up with her; by then he was gone.

She couldn't stay in the courtyard. Not if he could glimpse her through Katherine's office window. So she gathered her things, went out to the parking lot, and disintegrated in the privacy of her car.

Of all the days for him to appear—why today? If only she'd had some warning. If only she had been the one to glimpse him from a distance. Then she could have decided whether or not to approach. But no. She had been cornered and trapped without any time to prepare. Not only did she look terrible, but she hadn't even been able to speak. She hadn't trusted herself to voice more than a few syllables.

What must he be thinking of her?

He had come to her without any hint of bitterness or resentment. Though he easily could have avoided her by choosing to remain in Katherine's office, he had deliberately come to the courtyard. Hannah had been given a chance to have a friendly conversation after all these years—a chance to ask questions about his life and to reconnect. Instead, she'd appeared cold, disinterested, and aloof. Here he was—less than fifty yards away from her—and she didn't know what to do. She was already so raw, so vulnerable.

But was their meeting in the courtyard purely coincidental? She would have to be a fool to believe that. She certainly didn't know what purpose God intended, but she would have to be blind to miss the divine fingerprints. Perhaps God was merely giving her an opening for closure, a chance to seal off any old hurts or regrets. What harm could result from a simple conversation?

She watched and waited. Shortly after twelve-thirty Nathan emerged from the portico and walked to his car. Calling out his name, she hurried to meet him. "Nate, I'm so sorry." She was struggling to find words even after rehearsing them in the car for almost an hour. "I didn't mean to be unfriendly. I was just so surprised to see you. Forgive me."

"Forgiven," he answered. "I was the one who had time to prepare. After all these years, I'm sure it was a bit of a shock." He was waiting for her to speak.

"I would have recognized you anywhere," she confessed, studying his face. In fact, he seemed to have grown younger even as he'd grown older. There was a lightness to him she couldn't quite describe or define, but it was palpable. "You haven't changed a bit—except for the goatee."

He rubbed his fingers along his chin. "It's required for academia," he replied, smiling. She could tell he was also searching her face for familiarity. She looked down. "Ministry has been hard on you, Shep," he observed gently. "I'm so sorry."

*Shibboleth*. She knew him. He had just revealed himself. Truly, he hadn't changed a bit.

If he had attempted to be flattering or complimentary, Hannah would have seen right through him. Nathan had never been one to be disingenuous. His honesty was one of the qualities she had most valued when they were friends. Now there was something warm and intimate about his artlessness, as if he were banking on their shared history of trust and openness.

*Shep*. He even felt comfortable enough to call her by the old nickname. No one else had ever called her *Shep*. She had forgotten.

Her eyes filled with tears.

"I'm so sorry," he said again. This time she wasn't sure if he was simply echoing his compassion or apologizing for speaking the hard truth. She wanted him to know he hadn't hurt her feelings. It was important for him to know that.

"You're right, Nate. My senior pastor saw warning signs I didn't see. I didn't want the sabbatical."

"No, I didn't think you'd choose that for yourself," he said quietly. "Forced rest, huh?"

"He called it 'radical surgery.' The disentangling of my personal and professional identities."

"Ouch. Death of the false self. That hurts."

Sixteen years melted away in a matter of minutes as Hannah realized how much she'd missed having a friend like him. Ministry had been so lonely, so incredibly lonely. Now she was face to face with someone who had known her as well as anyone ever had.

He glanced at his watch. "I don't have to be back on campus until three o'clock. Do you have time for lunch with an old friend?"

Hannah was conflicted. Part of her wanted to leap at the invitation. The other part was afraid. Nate saw.

"Don't worry, Hannah," he said, smiling kindly. "I'm not interested in reliving the past. You're safe. There's nothing that needs to be resolved on my end, okay?" She felt something catch in her throat as she nodded.

"Thank you," she murmured.

Oh, how dearly she had missed her friend.

"So you told Charissa you didn't think I'd remember you, huh?" Nate asked as they sat in a booth at the Corner Nook. Hannah confessed by nodding. "Trying to manipulate her into not revealing your whereabouts?"

Hannah laughed. "'Sir, I see that you are a prophet.'"

"You always had a scriptural response for everything, didn't you?" he teased. "And you still have a gift for seeing right through people. Charissa told me you have an excellent reputation for analyzing texts, including people's lives. I always said you'd make a good pastor." She hesitated, watching for nonverbal indicators that might give her permission to proceed. He was sitting with his hands openly resting on the table, looking relaxed. "What happened, Nate?"

"Lots," he replied. "I graduated from seminary and went into the ministry for a few years. But it destroyed my marriage."

Hannah flinched. "Oh, Nate—I'm so sorry." She was. She truly was. She could see the pain on his face, and it pained her.

"Thanks." He took a sip of coffee. "Ministry casualties. They warned us about those in seminary, didn't they? But I had too much pride to believe I'd become a statistic. I threw myself into the work of the church and forgot I was also called to be a husband and a father. By the time I woke up, it was too late. Laura had fallen in love with someone who actually paid attention to her, and she left." Hannah heard no hint of bitterness in his voice—no edge at all.

"Charissa told me you have a son."

Nate pulled out his phone and showed her some photos. "This is Jake. He's thirteen. A good, good kid. I don't deserve him." The photos showed Jake and Nate on a sailboat. Jake had his father's penetrating eyes and knowing smile. "Laura walked away from everything and gave me full custody of Jake when we divorced. I knew I couldn't manage being a single dad and a pastor, so I went back to my passion for literature. And I've been teaching at Kingsbury for a few years now."

"Jake's a handsome young man."

Nate put his phone away. "Thanks. Like I said, I don't deserve him." Leaning forward, he planted his elbows firmly on the table. "And what about you, Shep? Last I knew you were in Chicago." She was surprised he knew that much and raised her eyebrows. He grinned. "Internet search years ago," he confessed. "Curiosity." It had never once occurred to her to track him down. That's how thoroughly she had closed the door on their past.

"I've been at the same church for fifteen years," she said. "It's a wonderful place. I've been blessed to be there. But as you so aptly observed earlier, ministry has taken a toll. I've been totally devoted to the church in every possible way. You know how that goes . . . "

"Hiding behind your busyness, huh?"

He certainly hadn't lost his knack for being incisive.

"Busyness is my socially acceptable addiction," she replied, swirling ice cubes around and around with her straw. "If we're busy, we're important, right?"

He smiled. "The culture says it's all about productivity and achievement—even the culture of the church. It's so easy to wrap our whole identity around ministry—around being useful and thinking we're indispensable. Toxic, deadly, seductive stuff. I had to confront it in my own spirit. And it can have really deep roots. I'll tell you—Katherine has been a wonderful spiritual director for me. I've experienced so much healing the past few years."

*Peace.* That was the youthfulness Nate wore. He had been so driven, so agitated, so restless years ago. But he seemed grounded now, centered.

"You seem at peace, Nate. There's a stillness to you that you didn't have before."

"Thank you. You have no idea how much that means to me. It's the fruit of the Spirit's work."

Hannah sighed. "I'm hoping that's what these nine months will bring me: fruit of the Spirit's work. I sure need some."

"Hard pruning will do that," he said. "Our task is yielding and resting, saying yes even when God cuts off the parts we're convinced we can't live without." She felt her eyes fill with tears again. This was her old friend Nate across the table, and they were twentysomethings again, sharing all of their emerging insights about life and God and faith. "You okay?" he asked.

She bit her lip as his hand shifted on the table. For a moment she thought he was reaching toward her in a gesture of comfort. But she was wrong.

"I'm just trying to keep it all together, you know?"

"I know," he said, removing his glasses to breathe on them. Then he rubbed them slowly and methodically on his sweater. "Believe me, I know."

The next hour flew by. As Nate shared anecdotally about campus life, Hannah studied him carefully, eager to mentally photograph his gestures and facial expressions. She wanted to remember the way his eyes lit up every time he talked about his students—the way he clasped his hands together earnestly every time he mentioned how grateful he was to be teaching at a Christian university.

"They're so hungry for truth, Hannah. So hungry. And God gives me the privilege not just of discipling them in the classroom, but of being with them in the student center, sharing life and meals together. I thought when I left the church that I'd be walking away from ministry. But I just entered into a different kind. And I'm grateful for that."

"You don't miss the church?" How could he not miss pastoral ministry? She listened for any variation in tone, for any inflection that would contradict his smile.

"I do sometimes. But I know I'm exactly where I'm supposed to be for this season of my life, so I'm at rest. I'm just taking the opportunities God is giving me to be fully present to him and to my students."

At two-thirty she rose reluctantly from the table and walked with Nate to the parking lot. "So, Shep, where are you worshiping while you're here?"

"Nowhere." She knew he would press, so she quickly formulated an answer that would be honest without revealing the whole truth.

"Why?"

"Avoidance. I don't know who I am when I'm not pastoring, and I don't know how to worship when I'm not leading. So I haven't bothered. I can't turn off all the critical voices in my head, constantly evaluating all the elements of a worship service, so I haven't gone. I haven't wanted to battle the distractions."

"I'm going to challenge you about that."

She smiled wryly. "I figured you might."

"You're cutting yourself off from the very place where God can touch and heal you." He paused. "I've learned over the past few years how important the body of Christ is. Sounds dumb for a former pastor to say I've only just learned that, but it's true. We can't be lone rangers. You need to be fed, Hannah—not just in the sacred journey group or in your private devotions. You need other believers around you, worshiping with you and encouraging you. The very thing you've been avoiding is exactly what you need. Even if it's a struggle—even if it makes you feel lost and uncomfortable."

"I know." She sighed. "You're right." She wasn't ready to confess that she had even deeper reasons for avoiding worship. She wasn't sure she would ever be ready to admit that to Nate—not when the only Hannah Shepley he had ever known had been full of passion and devotion to God.

"I'll be praying for you, Hannah. And I'm not just saying that. I'm praying for this sabbatical to be healing for you in whatever way God chooses."

"Thank you. I need that." She slid into the driver's seat while he kept his hand on the door.

"You've got my number now, so call me, okay? I'd love to have lunch again. My schedule at the college is very flexible."

"Okay, thanks. Thanks again."

He had closed her door and was heading toward his car when he turned around, motioning for her to roll down the window. "You're not alone, Shep." His eyes were penetrating. "I think the Lord really wants you to know that you're not alone."

Since she couldn't speak, she simply touched his sleeve and nodded before driving away.

October 18

6 a.m.

I couldn't sleep last night. I kept tossing and turning, thinking about everything. I finally decided I might as well get up. So here I am.

What can I say? Yesterday took a turn I never could have predicted. I don't know what to make of it. I don't even know what I'm feeling. Less than twenty-four hours ago, I was sitting across the table from Nate, just like we used to, sharing at deep levels about life and faith. Of course, the deepest levels of my heart aren't visible to him. He has no clue where I am with God right now. Would he be shocked that Hannah Shepley—who was once so full of passion for Jesus—could feel so disappointed, distant, and angry?

But I'm not angry right now. The anger has passed. For now, anyway. At some point I'll confess it and ask God's forgiveness, but not yet. I'm not ready. Intellectually, I know I'm responsible for the choices I made years ago, but I made them for God. I made them for you, Lord, remember? I walked away because I honestly believed that's what you wanted me to do.

Just sitting at lunch with him yesterday, the years melted away. I felt like myself for the first time in I don't know how long. For the first time in years I wasn't hiding behind some role or trying to meet somebody's expectations. I was Hannah. Just Hannah. More than that—I was "Shep" again. I'd forgotten what that felt like, and I don't know where to go with it.

I had just come to realize how deep my grief really is. I had just embraced how hard it's going to be to confront these painful things from my past and bring them into the light. Now I'm afraid I'll be distracted by Nathan again—that his reappearing as a friend right now is going to ease the sorrow just when I need to be facing it. I don't even know if that makes sense. I don't want the easy way out of this. I'm not looking for an escape route. If I'm really going to grieve and let go of old things, then I can't be pulled off course.

But why would he reappear now? As a temptation and distraction, or as some kind of gift? I don't know.

How do I even feel about him? Yesterday made me remember what an amazing friendship we shared for those two years. He was my best friend—like a brother to me. We were soul friends. I loved him more than I ever loved any other friend. But did I ever feel more than that for him? I don't know. I don't even know my own heart. I'm so confused.

And lost. I feel totally lost.

Help. Please. Help.

9

# Found at the Crossroads

*Tempted to slide back into mud,*
*down to the bliss of oblivion,*
*yet I hear the lure of my Lover,*
*whispering through my story's confusion.*
*The God who draws me is urging me on,*
*and I discover my faltering Yes.*
*I stumble along the rough pathways,*
*surprised by a hand that is grasping my own.*

*To and fro, back and forth,*
*on the twists of the journey,*
*courage moves me onwards,*
*faith trusts in the future;*
*wisdom makes me pause,*
*I rest by the stream;*
*taking time to delve deep,*
*I listen for the Voice.*

From Psalm 121, Jim Cotter,
*Psalms for a Pilgrim People*

## *In the Wilderness*

It was still dark when Katherine arrived at New Hope on the last Saturday of October. She left her books and bags in her office, then made her way down the hallway to the chapel, where she seated herself beneath the large wooden cross.

Katherine had been directing the sacred journey groups for years, and she knew that by this point of the pilgrimage, some of the travelers were growing weary and discouraged. *Help me pray for them, Lord.*

Opening her Bible to Isaiah 40, she began to read: "Comfort, O comfort my people, says your God. Speak tenderly to Jerusalem, and cry to her that she has served her term, that her penalty is paid, that she has received from the LORD's hand double for all her sins. A voice cries out: 'In the wilderness prepare the way of the LORD, make straight in the desert a highway for our God.'"

Katherine prayed: *Lord, let me speak your words of comfort and encouragement today. Let your dear ones hear your voice. Let them know how tenderly you care for them, how deeply you love them. May they hear your words of healing and grace, reassuring them that you yourself have paid the price for their sin. You have purchased their freedom. Clear away any obstacles that hinder your coming into their lives. Meet them in the wilderness of their fear and shame and sorrow and regret. Come, Lord God, and make straight paths for them to travel more deeply into your heart of love. In Jesus' name. Amen.*

**Sacred Journey, New Hope Retreat Center**
***Session Four: Wilderness Prayer***
*Katherine Rhodes, Facilitator*

---

Read the following text from Genesis 16:7-10 slowly and prayerfully.

> The angel of the Lord found her by a spring of water in the wilderness, the spring on the way to Shur. And he said, "Hagar, slave-girl of Sarai, where have you come from and where are you going?" She said, "I am running away from my mistress Sarai." The angel of the Lord said to her, "Return to your mistress, and submit to her." The angel of the Lord also said to her, "I will so greatly multiply your offspring that they cannot be counted for multitude."

At a crossroads in Hagar's life, the angel of the Lord asked two fundamental spiritual formation questions that are worthy of prayerful pondering: Where have you come from? Where are you going?

As we pursue deep transformation in Christ, we need to name and contemplate what has shaped us in the past. We also need to consider how we are moving forward in our life with God. The answers to these questions are not easy. They must be discerned and explored in cooperation with the Holy Spirit. Before you begin to journal your responses, spend some time asking the Spirit to bring to mind the people and events that have significantly shaped you.

*Where have you come from?* Ask God to give you courage to name not only the times when you have experienced his intimate presence, but also the times when you have felt God's absence. What are the formative moments that have shaped your life with God?

*Where are you going?* Consider the invitations God is currently giving you. How is God leading and guiding you into a deeper awareness of his love and care for you? What promises of God are giving you hope for the future? How will you continue to be with the God who is always with you?

"Well, here we are at the midpoint of our pilgrimage," Katherine said as she welcomed the group to their fourth session. "I'm hoping you've already traveled some significant distance in your journeys with God."

"Amen!" Mara said quietly. Meg smiled at her and nodded.

"I'm glad," said Katherine, responding to nods and voices around the room. "Keep going! It takes practice to form new habits of prayer."

Charissa leaned over to Hannah and whispered something Mara couldn't hear.

Hannah smiled and nodded.

Mara frowned.

Katherine continued, "I also hope that you're experiencing the blessings that come from staying with what stirs you, whether you're paying attention to the joy and pleasure in God, or to the agitation and sorrow. The Holy Spirit is working in all things."

Mara was watching Charissa out of the corner of her eye, resenting that the stuck-up supermodel had become friendly with Meg and Hannah. Mara would be far happier, far less distracted if Charissa were sitting at a different table. Then again, Charissa had actually smiled and greeted Mara when she arrived. But Mara wasn't going to be influenced by something that superficial. Who knew what Charissa's motives were?

Shifting her weight, Mara turned her back toward Charissa and tried to concentrate.

Katherine said, "We're going to start by praying with a couple of verses from a text in Genesis: the story of God finding Hagar in the wilderness."

Mara raised her eyebrows in surprise. "My story," she whispered to Meg. "I know this one by heart."

Meg smiled and nodded.

Mara didn't have to listen while Katherine described the setting and context for the passage. She knew all about the Abraham, Sarah, and Hagar love triangle. Well, not exactly a love triangle. There was no evidence Abraham actually loved Sarah's servant Hagar—just that he and Sarah decided to use her to fulfill God's promise of descendants. After all, God was taking too long and clearly needed their help and ingenuity.

Their plan was disastrous, though, resulting in family conflict that rivaled anything Mara had ever seen on reality television: Sarah tells Abraham to get Hagar pregnant since Sarah can't have children; Hagar gets pregnant and flaunts it, enraging Sarah; Abraham doesn't want to get caught in the middle of a cat fight, so he takes the path of least resistance and tells Sarah to go ahead and do whatever she wants to Hagar; Sarah unleashes her anger on Hagar; and Hagar runs away with Abraham's child growing in her belly.

"There are handouts coming around to your tables," Katherine explained. "I've included the text and your reflection questions on the page: Where have you come from? And where are you going? For the next half hour or so, I invite you to consider these two questions. You may wish to journal a timeline of your life, identifying significant and formative events and influences. What has shaped you? Where have you perceived God's presence or felt God's absence? What are the significant moments of experiencing and knowing God? Don't rush this process. I don't expect you to finish this today. This is just a chance to begin pondering the scope of your own journey—to see how everything fits together in the larger picture of your life."

Mara took the handout from Meg and passed one to Hannah.

Katherine said, "Taking the time to slow down and journal our thoughts and feelings is one way of intentionally welcoming God into the process of reflection. In the safety of our journal pages, we have the freedom to be authentic, inviting the Spirit to help us listen to our lives. Be as truthful and honest as possible. No one else is going to be looking at what you've written."

Mara stared at the page. It would take her hours and hours to answer those questions. But at least she had already done some of the hard work of looking at where she had come from.

She wondered how Charissa would answer the questions. She supposed Charissa had come from a perfect family, never having to endure any kind of significant conflict or pain. Maybe that's why she was so hard-hearted, so condescending and judgmental. Maybe that's why she was such a . . . such a—

Mara gritted her teeth, bit her mind's tongue, and tried to listen carefully to Katherine again.

"Some of you are paying attention to the things that provoke you," Katherine was saying. "You're uncovering areas of sorrow, shame, guilt, or regret. Perhaps, like Hagar, you've been on the run, not wanting to confront painful things from your past. Maybe you're discovering God's invitation to stop running and to go back to the past with God's blessing, as difficult as that might be."

Mara wasn't sure, but it looked like Katherine's eyes were misty.

"Now, please don't misunderstand me," Katherine said earnestly. "I'm not talking about physically returning to situations of abuse, okay? I'm using this text metaphorically to help us with our sacred journeys, not as a command to return to something dangerous. It's extremely important that you aren't confused about that."

Katherine was quiet a long time as she looked out upon the group. "God always intends good for us," she finally said. "Always. There is nothing but love in God's heart for you. I promise. And because God loves you more than you can possibly comprehend, he will gently reveal areas of discomfort, pain, and agitation—not to cause you harm, but so that you can identify where it hurts and turn to him for comfort and healing.

"At the beginning of his public ministry, Jesus announced that he had come to preach good news to the poor, to open the eyes of the blind, and to set captives free. This is the work that Jesus devoted himself to. And it's the same work that God is still doing by the power of the Holy Spirit, our Counselor and Comforter. God comes into our lives to redeem our pain and set us free."

*I'd like to be free,* thought Mara. *Free from lots of things. Lots and lots of things.*

She sighed heavily.

Katherine continued, "We begin our journey to freedom when we go back to the places where we were spiritually, emotionally, and mentally wounded. But this time we go with God's presence, help, and strength. No matter how frightening and messy it feels, God invites us to trust him. The Lord does some of his most beautiful work in the midst of the messiness and brokenness of our lives."

Mara was watching Charissa again out of the corner of her eye. *Hear that, Princess?* she thought. *Sitting there so perfectly put together. You don't have a clue what Katherine's even talking about, do you? What mess have you ever had to deal with, Kristie?*

*Kristie?*

Charissa. Her name is Charissa.

So why was she thinking *Kristie*?

Kristie Van Buren had been coming to mind a lot lately. Far too frequently. Mara supposed that if she were to write a brutally honest timeline of her life, tracking her years of rejection and pain, Kristie would be one of the first people she would list as a significant influence. Did she really want to dig up those memories again?

No. Definitely not.

"Years ago I served as a chaplain at St. Luke's Hospital," Katherine was saying. "Sometimes I would visit the rehabilitation unit for burn victims. These dear people were enduring excruciating pain just to heal, submitting their bodies to grueling physical therapy. It was horrible. Absolutely horrible. Sometimes I would meet patients who refused physical therapy. Healing was too painful, and they wanted to avoid more pain. They desperately wanted to avoid pain."

Pain, Payne. Mara Payne.

Mara stared at the page while echoes of old familiar voices began to play on a continuous loop in her head.

*Go away, Mara! Can't you see that nobody wants to play with you?*

Nobody wants you. Nobody.

The words on the page were starting to blur together.

*Payne, Payne, go away. Don't come back another day!*

Singsong voices taunted her, encircling her and growing louder with her efforts to ignore them. They were swirling and whirling, the squeals of children's derisive laughter becoming the angry shouts of a lover's rage.

*Don't come back! Don't ever come back! You're a No-Good Whore! You hear me? A No-Good Whore!*

She put her hands over her ears, but the accusing, condemning voices didn't stop.

*Well, have you seen where she lives? She's so dirty, my mother didn't even want to have her in our house!*

She's so dirty, so dirty, so dirty . . .

Tears were splattering on the handout, and Mara could no longer see the words.

Why, why, why? Why did her same buttons get pushed over and over again? She wished her nine-year-old self would just grow up.

As she reached into her bag for a tissue, Mara felt the touch of a gentle, strengthening, empowering hand on her shoulder.

Meg's hand. No words. Just a hand.

Mara felt her body relax. She blew her nose and breathed deeply.

"Dear friends," Katherine said, her voice full of emotion, "healing can hurt. Deep healing hurts. But if you're uncovering pain and suffering in your life, the path to healing is not avoidance. You've got to go through it and confront it with God's presence and in the Spirit's power. And if you find you're facing something overwhelming, please remember that you aren't meant to travel the path to healing and transformation by yourself. We are never, ever meant to travel alone. God gives us the gift of his presence through the comfort and companionship of fellow believers—through friends, pastors, counselors, spiritual directors, teachers, and others who help us heal and grow. Don't walk this road alone. Please."

*Alone, alone, always alone.* Mara was always alone. She had always been alone. She would always be alone.

No.

No. No.

Not alone.

Somehow, not alone.

Mara stared at her tattoo, and her tattoo stared back. Unwaveringly. Incessantly. El Roi was watching. El Roi, the God who sees. El Roi, the God who saw her with tenderness and love. El Roi, the God who was still seeking, still finding her in the wilderness of her pain.

Meg's hand was still resting gently on Mara's shoulder.

*Not alone.*

Katherine was looking at the group with deep compassion. "I want to linger here for a while so you can ask questions before you go off to find a quiet place for prayer and reflection," she said slowly. "I know that for some of you, we are treading on raw and tender places. We're traveling on holy ground here. Remember that the Lord shepherds gently, always with a loving and steady hand. So just take the journey one step at a time, inviting and trusting God to bring to the surface what is ready to be healed."

Mara saw Hannah lean forward, hunch her shoulders, and rub her temples slowly.

*Headache?* Mara wondered.

Reaching into her bag again, she pulled out a bottle of aspirin and tapped Hannah on the shoulder.

Hannah shook her head and smiled broadly.

*Too broadly,* Mara thought.

"I'm okay," Hannah whispered, sitting upright in her chair. "Just tired."

But Mara didn't believe her. *Help her, Lord,* she prayed.

*Help us.*

As soon as everyone left the room to find quiet places to pray, Hannah packed up her things.

What had she been thinking, trying to come to the sacred journey group when she was still so raw, still so disconnected and distant from God?

Every word Katherine spoke pierced her, and she could hardly keep from bursting into tears. Determined not to lose control in front of the others, Hannah directed her dwindling reserve of mental and emotional energies into her mask. Then when she realized the mask wouldn't hold, she fled.

As she drove away from New Hope, the Spirit's questions pursued her: *Where have you come from? Where are you going? Where have you come from? Where are you going?*

She knew where she'd come from, and she was carefully navigating her way through the broken pieces of her past. She understood with new clarity why she had been stuffing her sorrow for so long: her fear of confronting her grief had been rooted in a fear of disintegrating. As long as she remained a helper and comforter in other people's suffering, she maintained her equilibrium. Being consumed with others' pain helped her live in denial about her own. As long as she stayed busy, there was no time to think about the things she wanted to avoid.

She saw that now.

But she was still afraid. So afraid.

Even if Jesus traveled with her into the pain of her past, she still wasn't convinced she could bear it. What if she discovered that the weight of regret crushed her? What if she discovered that she had walked away from a gift the Lord had wanted to give her in Nathan? What if the decisions she thought had been rooted in obedience had instead been rooted in avoidance and fear?

*What if?*

What if she had missed out on the life God had intended for her? What if she could never recapture all the blessings that might have been? What if she had made different choices?

The past was hard enough to face without contemplating the future. *Where are you going?*

She didn't have a clue. She had written several different versions of a resignation letter to the church, but she hadn't mailed one. Yet. She couldn't imagine ever being able to pastor again. She couldn't imagine emerging from her grief with restored confidence in who God was. She just couldn't.

Hannah had traveled several miles before she realized she had missed her entrance onto the highway. Suddenly surrounded by orange construction barrels and "Road Closed" signs, she became disoriented. Nothing looked familiar. Chiding herself for not carrying a map in the car, she finally turned into a restaurant parking lot. Maybe someone could direct her.

A smiling hostess greeted her. "One?" the young woman asked, grabbing a menu.

"No, thanks," Hannah replied. "I got lost, and I just need to get some directions."

"Where are you headed?"

"I'm trying to get to the highway—I'm heading over to the lakeshore—and I'm totally turned around. All the one way streets and construction got me all confused."

"I know. It's tricky around here," the hostess replied. "I can draw you a map. You're actually not too far." She took a paper napkin and scribbled some directions. Hannah thanked her and hurried back out to the parking lot.

As she approached her car, she reached into her coat pocket for her keys. Empty. She checked her other pocket. Nothing. Panicked, she pulled on each door handle, hoping she had been careless in locking them. No luck. As her tote bag and keys jeered at her from the front seat, all the emotion she had tried to suppress that morning erupted. *Enough! Enough! Enough! I can't take any more!* She pounded her fist on the car again and again, muttering a string of words she wasn't accustomed to using.

"Tough day?"

Hannah froze with her fist in midair. She knew that voice. She spun around to find herself face to face with Nathan Allen.

"Horrible!" she exclaimed, not sure whether to laugh or cry. She hardly registered the shock of his appearing or the embarrassment of being caught in the middle of a tantrum. She was just grateful to see a familiar face. "I've managed to lock my keys in the car."

"I hate it when that happens," he said, smiling.

Nathan didn't seem at all surprised by the serendipity of their meeting. Hannah, on the other hand, was beginning to think she was living on the pages of a Jane Austen novel. Talk about funny timing.

He looked over his shoulder as a teenage boy approached. "Jake, this is an old friend of mine from seminary. Hannah Shepley."

Hannah felt her face flush. She desperately hoped Jake hadn't overheard the content of her colorful outburst.

"Nice to meet you," Jake said, making eye contact as he gripped her hand with a firm handshake. He had his father's ridiculously long eyelashes and penetrating eyes.

"Nice to meet you too, Jake. I'm sorry I'm so flustered. I've managed to lock my keys and my cell phone in the car, and I was just trying to figure out what to do."

"Well, it's too cold to be standing outside, trying to figure it out," Nathan said. "Come on in with us. Saturday morning breakfasts at the Pancake House are a tradition for the Allen boys, right, Jake?"

Jake nodded.

Hannah hesitated.

"C'mon," Nathan urged. "You have to wait somewhere for a locksmith. You might as well wait with friends. You can use my phone, okay?"

Hannah yielded and followed them inside.

"Two?" the hostess asked, grabbing menus for Nathan and Jake.

"Three," Nathan replied, motioning toward Hannah.

Hannah buried her face in her shoulder and pretended to cough.

"I thought Charissa said there was a sacred journey group this morning," he commented as they walked together to a corner booth.

"There was. I left early."

He eyed her but didn't press. Thankfully.

"I was on my way back to the lake, and I missed a turn," she quickly explained. "By the time I realized it, I was lost. I came in here for directions and then discovered I'd locked myself out. And that's when you arrived. Just as I was throwing my tantrum." She shook her head. "I'm sorry about that. Not a very appropriate way for a pastor to behave, huh?"

"Effective, though," Nathan said. "I wouldn't have noticed you if you hadn't been assaulting your vehicle."

Hannah grinned in spite of herself, contemplating the strange turn of events. What were the chances of her running into him twice in a little more than a week? It seemed a ridiculous coincidence. Then again, Kingsbury was a much smaller place than Chicago.

Nathan reached into his pocket. "Here—use my phone. Have you got an Auto Club membership or something?"

"Yes, but my wallet's in the car."

"Shouldn't be a problem." He pulled out his wallet and handed her his card. "Call the number and explain what happened. And as for breakfast," he said, opening the menu, "I recommend the blueberry pancakes."

Nathan was right: the blueberry pancakes were delicious. For the next hour Hannah relaxed into comfortable conversation. Jake impressed her. Easygoing and articulate, he had his father's wry sense of humor. With undisguised affection and admiration, Jake talked about some of the adventures the two of them had shared. Hannah watched Nate's eyes light up with pride every time he looked at his son. *What a gift,* she thought. *What a gift.*

"So, Shep," Nate began as the waitress cleared away their dishes, "Jake's going out with friends for the next couple of hours, and I was going to head over to campus for a while. I'd love to give you a tour, if you're interested."

"I-uh . . . I don't want to take you away from your work."

"He's not working," Jake teased. "He just hangs out in his office when I'm not around to entertain him." Nate laughed, tousling Jake's dark hair.

"He's right, actually. I have no good reason to be on campus today. And maybe a tour of Kingsbury isn't all that exciting for you, especially in the cold."

Hannah smiled at him. "It's been a long time since I walked around a college campus. I wouldn't mind a tour."

"Good!" Nate replied. "The university isn't far from here, and our house is right near campus. Do you think you can manage following us?" There was a glint of playfulness in his eyes.

"I should probably program your number into my phone just in case I end up lost again."

By the time Hannah and Nathan reached the college, it was raining.

"Sorry!" he apologized as the two of them ran from the parking lot to Bradley Hall. The three-story brownstone building reminded her of Sullivan Hall, where she and Nate had attended Bible and theology classes together. As he held the door open for her, Hannah experienced a moment of déjà vu.

"This place reminds me of Sullivan," she said. "It even smells the same."

"I know. Feels like we ought to be heading to New Testament 101, huh?" He led her down the deserted hallway to his office.

"Have you been back to visit the seminary at all?" she asked, listening to her wet shoes squeak on the linoleum.

"I went back for a reunion about ten years ago. Most of the professors were still there, and it was fun to reconnect with them. But I've lost touch with people now. It was painful after the divorce." He unlocked his office door and ushered her inside. "Welcome to my home away from home."

The office was meticulously clean and well-organized, with a collection of nautical sundries interspersed with books on floor-to-ceiling shelves. Jake's face beamed from photos on Nathan's desk.

"I miss my office," Hannah said wistfully. "I miss my books."

"Well, help yourself to anything you find here. I'm happy to be a lending library during your sabbatical."

Hannah thanked him and began browsing the shelves while Nathan went to a file cabinet and shuffled through some papers.

If only she could spend hours with his books—especially with the pastoral care ones. She had forgotten what a prolific book-marker he was, and his margin notes were undressed windows into his mind and spirit. Reading his scribbling on the pages of his books was like poking around in his journals. Intimate. Revealing. She was peering into his soul, prying into the depths of his heart while he was thoroughly unaware.

"Hannah?"

She blushed at the sound of his voice and quickly shoved a book about forgiveness back onto the shelf. "Hmm?" She wasn't going to turn around until she was sure her face had returned to its proper color.

"How are you? Really?"

She kept fingering book bindings, pretending to be wholly absorbed in thought, while fighting the temptation to pull down a book on grieving and loss. Intuitively, she knew this book had been his particular companion, and she couldn't help herself. She took it and opened it. Not only were the pages filled with his notes, but there was an inscription in the front. A long one.

"Is this good?" she asked casually, holding up the cover for him to see.

"Fantastic. Go ahead and take it with you."

She felt guilty accepting what he so freely offered; nevertheless, she quickly thrust it into her bag, afraid he might suddenly remember the secrets he had disclosed on the pages and change his mind.

"The sabbatical has been really hard for me," she finally said, still scanning the shelves for anything else she might borrow. *Steal.* "You saw my outburst in the parking lot. What did they teach us in our pastoral care classes? That a 'disproportionate response reveals underlying sin or sorrow,' right?"

"You mean you weren't actually violently angry at your car?"

"No," she laughed, turning to face him. She owed him something in exchange for the book. "I left the group early because it hit too close to home today. And I couldn't risk breaking down in front of other people."

His eyes filled with genuine compassion and concern. "Still wearing the pastor's mask, huh? That's a lonely way to live, Shep."

*You have no idea,* she thought.

He sat down in one of the burgundy armchairs near the window and invited her to take the other. "What was Katherine presenting on today?"

Hannah stared at the rain pelting the glass and stripping the trees. The lawn outside his window was gilded.

She sighed as she sat down. "God finding Hagar in the wilderness."

"Ah," he replied knowingly. "Where have you come from? Where are you going? I remember sitting with those questions. They're complicated to answer under the best of circumstances and especially hard when you're in the midst of grief and change."

She was just beginning to wonder if she could match her skills of redirection and manipulation against his spiritual gift of discernment when Nathan generously steered the conversation away from her pain.

"I know from my own journey how hard it is to confront the pain of the past," he commented gently. "And some days it's impossible to see where you're going. But those were important questions for me a few years ago as I processed my own grief and transitions—hard as it was to be honest about it." He paused, smiling wryly. "I don't know . . . Maybe when we graduated from seminary, we were all given a pastor's mask along with the diploma. We've got to be strong and steadfast for the congregation, got to be the epitome of faith and hope, got to be perfect and holy. And then the mask just becomes the way of life. We don't even realize it's taken over. And it becomes an awful prison, doesn't it?"

Even a one-syllable answer seemed too dangerous to risk. Hannah wasn't going to disintegrate in Nathan's office. Was not.

She shouldn't have come.

Nathan was staring at his hands in his lap, lacing his fingers together. "My own sacred journey toward transformation and freedom hasn't been easy, but it's been good," he said. "God has been healing me from the inside out in ways I couldn't have imagined. I know I've still got a long way to travel. But when I look back on where I've come from, I'm grateful. There's so much to be grateful for."

As she looked into his guileless face, Hannah realized she didn't need to sneak away with his books to know his heart. He was opening the pages of his life and inviting her to read. She tried to conceal her voraciousness with the measured, steady tone of a journalist. "So how did you answer the wilderness questions?" she asked.

Nathan settled into his chair, crossing one leg over the other. "It was hard, Shep. Going back into the past was really hard. I had to take an honest look at my own sin and my own regrets."

Hannah felt herself stiffen. He had told her there was nothing unresolved between them. But was she a source of regret and pain for him? She hoped he wasn't going to revisit their past. Please, please no.

"Katherine was God's messenger in my wilderness," he went on. "When I arrived in Kingsbury, I had been on the run for a few years—running from all kinds of pain and regret about Laura. But Katherine helped me see that I wasn't alone in going back to the pain of the past. I started to see that the Lord went with me and gave me the blessing of his presence and his promises to heal and redeem."

Laura.

Laura was the source of his pain and regret. In that moment Hannah tasted a potent cocktail of relief and disappointment. She rubbed her forehead slowly, avoiding direct eye contact.

"When Laura walked away from our marriage into an affair, her sin was condemned. Publicly. But for years my sin had been congratulated and affirmed. I was such a good and faithful servant of the church, so passionate in serving God and others."

As an intimate silence began to descend, Hannah stared at the window again, watching raindrops compete in a race down the glass. She chose one particular bead against its rivals and cheered it on as it wound its way down, down, down the pane. *Go, go, go.* Just before reaching the bottom, it blended with another droplet and disappeared.

Nathan spoke again. "No one saw the hardness of my own heart," he said softly. "Or my determination to stay busy so that I wouldn't have to do the really important work of being a godly husband and father. No one saw that Laura and Jake only got my leftovers—emotionally, physically, spiritually. People looked at me and said, 'What a selfless servant of God!' And I was happy to have my ego stroked and my pride fed. I was consumed by a desire to project the right image, to control what people thought of me. I was full of self-righteousness, while secretly nursing bitterness that Laura didn't appreciate and honor me the way everyone else did."

Was he this open and honest with everyone, or was his vulnerability with Hannah a special gift, rooted in old friendship? She wished she knew. But then again, why was it important? She had no particular claim on him.

No claim at all.

She stopped staring at the window and made herself look at him.

"As terrible as it was when Laura walked away," Nate said slowly, holding her gaze in the steadiness of his, "it ended up being God's way of breaking me and revealing my own sin. I needed to be broken. It was God's mercy that brought me to an end of myself. The great mercy of God . . . " His voice trailed off.

Hannah said, "I don't hear any bitterness in you, Nate."

His shoulders moved up and down in a half shrug. "I was bitter and angry for a long time," he said. "Years, really, though I was too proud and pious to admit it. I was angry at Laura. Angry at myself. Angry at God. Katherine patiently walked that dark path with me, giving me the freedom to be honest about my anger and resentment so God could begin the process of draining out the poison in my spirit. Katherine pointed me to the cross and to my desperate need for forgiveness. She helped me see that my anger was taking up sacred space that belonged to God."

Hannah felt herself stiffen again. *Anger, resentment, and sacred space.* Nathan had no way of knowing how deeply Hannah connected with his words—no way of knowing that Hannah was now walking a similar journey with his mentor. She shifted in the chair.

"I just didn't want the toxic stuff taking up space anymore," he continued quietly. "So I let go. I took responsibility for my sin and asked for forgiveness. I forgave Laura, forgave myself. And with God's help, I've found a way to be an attentive father to Jake. Thank God Jake doesn't remember those early years of my absence. Or my anger."

"Jake is a wonderful young man," Hannah said.

"Thank you."

Hannah stared at her hands, listening to the muted tick of a clock somewhere in Nathan's office. It had been years since they had communicated to one another through shared silence, and she was out of practice. As long minutes passed, the quiet became threatening and ominous. She didn't want him to become the inquisitor. She didn't want him getting too close.

Did she?

She resumed her interview.

"What about the second question?" she asked. "Where are you going?"

Even though she told herself the answer had nothing to do with her, she was still ridiculously breathless. She bent over to pick up an invisible piece of carpet fuzz, just in case her expression was betraying her.

Nathan did not reply right away, and she became anxious. Maybe she had asked too much. Maybe the answer was too personal. Especially if it involved a relationship, or longings for one.

*Stop, stop, stop*, she silently commanded herself.

Why was her imagination sprinting in that direction? There were so many other ways for him to answer the question. Like whether or not he saw himself heading back into pastoral ministry. Or whether he thought he'd be staying at the college. Professional answers, not personal ones. She wished she could withdraw the question.

When she looked up again, she saw that he was studying her in the same manner with which she'd seen him study texts: with curious intensity.

"That was another gift from God through Katherine," he finally replied. "I began to see that there's really only one way for me to answer the 'Where are you going?' question, and everything else depends on my truly knowing and living it. My way forward is always about going deeper into God's love for me. That's where I'm going. Deeper into God's heart, deeper into union and communion with him. I'm walking the road to claiming my identity as the beloved of God. Nothing more, nothing less. And that hasn't been an easy or straightforward journey. But I'm getting there. Thank God I'm getting there." He paused. "You and Katherine have probably talked about the false self, right?"

Hannah nodded.

Nathan said, "For so many years I based my identity on how much I achieved and on what other people thought of me. I wasn't at rest in my relationship with God. I was always haunted by the thought that I should be doing more, that I wasn't a faithful enough servant. Then when God stripped everything away and pruned me down to a stump, I began to see all the false things I had trusted in." He lowered his voice ever so slightly. "I finally began to understand that I have the same invitation John the disciple had: to call myself 'the one Jesus loves.' To really believe it in a way I never had before and to live life from that center."

Clasping his hands together, he leaned forward. Hannah leaned back, tightening her grip on the armrest of the chair.

"You said the other day, Shep, that you saw a stillness in me that I didn't have years ago. That's where the stillness is coming from. I'm not trying to earn God's love and favor anymore. I'm just resting in Christ. And it's good. There's such freedom there."

Hannah's thoughts were still racing. "I never would have thought to answer the question that way," she said with a thin voice. "I was thinking about it in terms of guidance, direction, future plans—that sort of thing."

"I know," he said, nodding. "That's where I first went with it too. But all that is secondary, isn't it? I've learned one important thing: if I'm not resting in the core of my being that God loves me and intends good for my life, then I won't be able to discern his will."

How had he managed to overtake her in spiritual insight and maturity? She had once been the one mentoring him. Now their roles were reversed.

She didn't like it.

Or maybe she did.

She didn't know.

Everything seemed upside down.

Or right-side-up.

She wasn't sure.

She was dizzy and disoriented.

"You remember that spiritual theology class we had with Dr. Hendricks?" Nathan asked.

Funny. She had thought about that class a few weeks ago.

Aloud, she said, "I remember you were particularly uncomfortable with the medieval mystics' understanding of God as Lover."

He chuckled. "You're right. It was really unsettling to me. But I get it now. I understand what they were talking about. They had a deep awareness of God's passion for us and his longing for intimacy with us. And they wrote from the joy of discovering that kind of communion with the Lord."

His whole countenance was shining.

She looked away.

"It's still hard for me to speak about God being my Lover," he said. "I don't know—maybe it's my sense of masculinity resisting that image. But I understand the invitation God is giving me to live in his love—to really rest in it." He shook his head slowly. "I didn't have any idea how important that was until a few years ago, but it's everything. Trusting God's heart is everything. Like it says in the Song of Solomon, his 'intention toward me was love.' If I can always trust that God's intention toward me is love, then even when I don't understand the work of his hands, I can still trust his heart."

*His intention toward me was love. His intention toward me was love.*

See?

This was exactly why Hannah couldn't afford to rekindle a friendship with him.

Here he was, talking about God's heart, and all she could think about was Nathan's declaration of love years ago. He had intended love, and she had walked away.

She would have to walk away again before her heart journeyed somewhere she could not follow. Friendship with Nathan simply wasn't safe. She didn't have the strength to separate spiritual intimacy from emotional intimacy. And she couldn't risk being distracted from whatever healing work God wanted to do in her life.

She hardly heard him speaking from the faraway place in front of her. "Hannah, would it be okay if I prayed for you?"

"Sure," her voice replied.

At least, she thought it was her voice. It had come from her mouth without her mind's consent.

**Sacred Journey, New Hope Retreat Center**
***Session Four: Praying with Imagination***
*Katherine Rhodes, Facilitator*

---

For centuries Christians have used the imagination as a way of encountering God in prayer. Our minds are filled with stories, images, and memories which the Holy Spirit can use to bring us into deeper intimacy with Jesus. Praying Scripture with imagination allows the Spirit to guide us into places of insight about ourselves and God.

Begin by quieting yourself in God's presence. Invite the Holy Spirit to guide and direct your attention and imagination as you encounter Jesus in a scene from the gospels. Then slowly read the text several times to become familiar with the landscape and plot.

> They came to Jericho. As [Jesus] and his disciples and a large crowd were leaving Jericho, Bartimaeus son of Timaeus, a blind beggar, was sitting by the roadside. When he heard that it was Jesus of Nazareth, he began to shout out and say, "Jesus, Son of David, have mercy on me!" Many sternly ordered him to be quiet, but he cried out even more loudly, "Son of David, have mercy on me!" Jesus stood still and said, "Call him here." And they called the blind man, saying to him, "Take heart; get up, he is calling you." So throwing off his cloak, he sprang up and came to Jesus. Then Jesus said to him, "What do you want me to do for you?" The blind man said to him, "My teacher, let me see again." Jesus said to him, "Go; your faith has made you well." Immediately he regained his sight and followed him on the way. (Mark 10:46-52)

Begin to imagine the scene. What do you see? Hear? Smell? Feel? What do the outskirts of Jericho look like? Where is Bartimaeus? How big is the crowd? Who is there? What do they look like? What's the mood of the scene? Invite and trust the Spirit to guide you as you watch the movie play in your mind.

Once you have imagined the scene, picture yourself inside the story. Let go of any desire for historical accuracy, and actively enter into the text. Watch what the characters do. Listen to what they say. Where does the Spirit invite you to participate? Which character are you? What do you say? What does Jesus say to you? What do you want? Engage in conversation with the characters in the text. Don't worry about making things up. Trust the Spirit to speak and reveal God's truth to you as you pray.

Then prayerfully reflect on what you experienced in the text. What does God want you to know? How does this experience of prayer draw you close to Jesus?

## Praying with Imagination

Meg was worried. Where was Hannah?

At first Meg thought perhaps she had gone to the restroom. But she was away an awfully long time. Maybe she was sick somewhere. While Katherine led the group in a discussion about the wilderness questions, Meg slipped out the exit door.

Nobody in the bathroom. No one in the chapel. The hallways were empty. For a moment Meg considered going out to the parking lot to check for Hannah's car, but she didn't want to miss what Katherine was saying.

*Poor Hannah.*

She'd had such a shock at Charissa's apartment over Nathan Allen. And then when Katherine invited them to go back into the past to confront unresolved grief, it must have been too much for her. Meg knew what that felt like.

*Help her, Lord. Please help my friend.*

"We're going to look at one more crossroads text today," Katherine said. "I'm passing around another handout with a text from Mark's gospel and a description of praying with imagination."

Meg listened with nervous apprehension as Katherine walked the group through the process of imaginative contemplation. Though Katherine had encouraged Meg once before to see her imagination as a gift from God, Meg still wasn't sure she could trust herself to wander creatively inside a Scripture passsage. What if she did it wrong?

"I felt very anxious the first time I was invited to pray with my imagination," Katherine told the group. "I had such a deep respect and reverence for God's Word that I was reluctant to put any imaginary words into the text—especially into Jesus' mouth. After years of analyzing and studying biblical texts, I wasn't sure I could trust God to guide me if I started coloring outside the lines. But I began to see that the lines I'd drawn were my lines, not God's."

Katherine smiled and continued, "Imagination is a gift from God, and Jesus is still inviting us to encounter him face to face in the Word. After all, Jesus is the Living Word, breathing and moving and inspiring and revealing. So trust the Spirit to be with you as you freely and creatively wander with God. Let go of boundaries and constraints. Lay down your fears of doing it wrong. This isn't about 'right' and 'wrong.' This is about encountering God in the depths of our emotions, in the depths of our spirits. It's like peering into a deep well. You see the water, but you also glimpse images of yourself on the surface of the water. You see reflections of your hopes, fears, desires, and longings mirrored back to you. Trust God to meet you there in the depths. Trust the Spirit to reveal truth about who you are and who God is."

As the room fell silent, Meg quieted herself for prayer. *Holy Spirit, please guide me. Help me trust you while I wander in unfamiliar places. Guard my heart and my mind in Christ Jesus. Please.*

Slowly, Meg read the scene several times, getting a sense of the plot and movement of the text. Then she began to imagine the setting. She tasted the dust kicked up by herds of people and livestock traveling the dirt road in the noonday heat. She smelled the earthy stench of manure and sweat. She heard braying and bleating and the blending of voices in indiscernible conversations. She watched the pushing and the shoving of the crowd. So much pushing and shoving.

And suddenly, she was being pushed and shoved too.

She was trying to follow Jesus, trying to stay close to him so she wouldn't lose sight of him along the way. She could barely see the back of his dark head nodding up and down. Someone was talking to him, but she couldn't see who it was or hear what they were saying. Noise. There was so much noise.

And then Meg heard one voice shouting above all the others: a wail of desperate persistence, rising again and again. "Have mercy! Have mercy! Jesus, have mercy! Son of David, have mercy!" The agony in the man's voice pierced Meg and made her want to cry out with him.

Meg waited for Jesus to stop. But he kept walking. Couldn't he hear the man? Everyone could hear the man. He was getting louder and louder, screaming and shouting. Why wasn't Jesus stopping?

"Quiet!" someone yelled. "Just shut up!"

"Who is it?" Meg asked one of the people pressing against her. If she didn't keep walking, she was going to lose Jesus in the crowd.

"Ignore him," the man answered. "It's just Bartimaeus, the blind beggar. Pushy and obnoxious. There are dozens of them around here."

"Dozens?" Meg repeated.

Bartimaeus was still shouting.

"Give it up!" someone yelled again. "He's already gone!"

No no no! Jesus couldn't pass by. "Please stop, Jesus," Meg whispered, willing him to turn around.

But he kept moving.

"Jesus, stop!" she called. "Please."

But he couldn't hear her, not with the noise of the crowd.

Meg stopped walking, steadied herself, and shouted more loudly than she'd ever shouted: "Jesus, STOP!"

The people in front of her skidded to a halt, and she watched Jesus turn around and look at her with deep tenderness. The crowd parted for him as he made his way back to where she was standing.

"What do you want me to do for you, Meg?" he asked, taking her hand.

"Please, Jesus," she said, trembling. "Please let Bartimaeus see you, like I've seen you."

He touched her face, smiled, and told the crowd to bring Bartimaeus to him.

Meg opened her eyes and sat in the prayerful stillness of the room for a long time, wondering what to make of her imagination.

*What do you want me to do for you?*

It was the same sort of question Jesus had asked her at the beginning of her journey, wasn't it? *What are you looking for?* Now here she was, following Jesus along the way. She had found what she was looking for: she was with Jesus. And she wanted Bartimaeus to have the same joy she had discovered, the joy of simply being with him. Yes, to have blind eyes opened and to see who Jesus truly was. Meg longed for others to see and know; she longed for others to join in the journey with Jesus. Such intense longing.

Deep emotion welled up within her as she began to pray for the blind and the lost, crying out for God's mercy to be revealed to them. *Please, Jesus, please.*

Meg's heart was racing while she listened to the large group discuss their meditations on the text. She couldn't shake the sense that she was meant to speak up. But she was afraid. Maybe she could share her insights privately with Katherine.

No matter how she fought it, however, the impulse to speak became stronger, finally overpowering her fear. She raised a trembling hand, feeling heat rise to her neck and face.

Katherine was smiling encouragingly as she called Meg's name.

"I was so afraid Jesus wasn't going to stop and help Bartimaeus," Meg said in a small voice. "So I yelled for him to stop, and he turned around and asked me what I wanted him to do for me. And I told him I wanted Bartimaeus to be able to see him. Like I've seen him. And Jesus heard me. He did what I asked him to do." There was so much more Meg wished she could say, but words failed her.

"Beautiful!" Katherine exclaimed. "The Lord moved you to pray his heart for those who have yet to see and follow him. What a special gift of grace, Meg."

Meg felt faint as Mara grasped her icy hand. Though Katherine continued to shepherd the group discussion about how the Word of God had come to life, Meg hardly heard anything. Her heart was pounding in her ears.

Just before noon Katherine wrapped up the animated conversation in the room. "A few weeks ago," she said, "we prayed through the text in John 1 where Jesus asks the would-be disciples, 'What are you looking for?' Then Jesus invites them to 'come and see.' Now we meet a blind man, and Jesus asks the same kind of question: 'What do you want me to do for you?' Bartimaeus asks for sight. That's a courageous thing to ask for, isn't it? Sometimes it's easier to remain in our darkness and blindness. But Bartimaeus wants to see.

"I invite you to cry out for sight," said Katherine. "Cry out for God to shine light into the darkness of your lives so that you can be healed and set free to join Jesus on the way. And don't be afraid. 'Take heart; get up! The Lord is calling you.'"

Charissa's heart was pounding as she kept step with Mara down the hallway. Her meditations on the Bartimaeus text had revealed her toxic waste container.

Again.

As Charissa prayerfully listened to the Word, she knew where she was in the story. She was in the crowd telling Bartimaeus to be quiet. He was so loud, so persistent, so totally unconcerned with what anyone else thought of him. Jesus was on a mission, after all. He had to get to Jerusalem. He couldn't get derailed from his destination by some blind beggar.

But then Jesus stopped. "Charissa," he said, "go tell Bartimaeus that I'm calling him. Go and bring him to me."

She started to argue. They had to get to Jerusalem. They were on a schedule. But Jesus smiled and shook his head. "We have time, Charissa. Go and get him. Help him come to me."

Mara had shared with the group that she imagined herself as Bartimaeus, yelling and crying out because she was so desperate for Jesus. Mara claimed she didn't care what people said or thought. She just knew what she wanted and needed.

Now as Charissa walked beside Mara, she knew what she had to do. She needed to apologize for her judgmental and condemning attitude, much as she didn't want to.

At first, she rationalized her reluctance: it would only wound Mara more to know that someone else had rejected and condemned her. Wasn't it enough for Charissa to confess her sin privately to God? Mara never needed to know about it.

But the closer she got to the parking lot, the clearer the Spirit's voice became. Charissa knew she was being asked to lay down her pride and humble herself. She took a deep breath and long-jumped out of her comfort zone.

"I've been thinking the past couple of weeks about what you said at the cottage, Mara. About all the wells you've tried to drink from. I want you to know that God used what you said to help me."

Mara looked shocked. "Really?"

Charissa was tempted to leave it there. She could give Mara a gift of encouragement and then walk away. But the Spirit urged her forward.

"I also have some wells I've been drinking from," Charissa confessed. "Mostly about trying to be perfect and keeping up appearances so I can have everybody's respect and admiration."

Mara looked like she wasn't sure what to say.

Charissa cleared her throat. "Anyway, I'm beginning to see what a stuck-up Pharisee I've been. And I'm sorry. That day at the beach . . . " She had started the confession, and she had to finish it. "When we were together for the picnic that day—well, it was hard for me to hear your story. I felt really judgmental and uncomfortable. I've had such a terrible attitude about other people and their sin that it's kept me from seeing my own. I just wanted to say I'm sorry. Please forgive me."

Mara did not respond: not by word, gesture, or facial expression. As they walked together in silence, Charissa felt sick to her stomach. What else could she say? She had made things worse. She should have kept quiet. She had made things even harder for Mara.

No. She had made things harder for herself. Now what? She wanted a do-over. On everything.

They had reached the portico, and it was raining hard. Since John hadn't arrived yet, Charissa would have to stand there, either waiting for Mara to reply or bearing the discomfort of being scorned if Mara walked away. Did Mara know how vulnerable and exposed Charissa felt? Why wasn't she saying anything?

*C'mon, John, where are you?*

Of course, Mara knew all about being exposed and vulnerable, didn't she? She had suffered Charissa's astringent condemnation two weeks ago, not only at the beach, but in the forty-five minute ride home in Meg's car when Charissa had refused to speak to Mara, addressing only Meg in conversation. Wicked, cruel, juvenile. Charissa regretted it.

She scanned the parking lot for moving headlights. *C'mon, c'mon, c'mon.*

It wasn't just Mara, either. There had been others. So many others. Somehow, as she and Mara stood there side by side and miles apart, Mara became all of them—all the girls Charissa had rejected, judged, scorned, and ignored.

They lived in Mara.

If only Mara would say something. Anything. What was she thinking?

Mara was staring at the ground. "We're wearing the same shoes," she said quietly.

Charissa was startled, not sure what she meant. Symbol? Metaphor? Her mind was racing for an interpretation of the cryptic comment. "Sorry?" she asked.

Mara pointed to her feet. "We're wearing the same shoes."

Charissa looked down. She was wearing her favorite, most comfortable pair of navy and white sneakers. Mara's were identical.

Smiling slightly, Charissa shrugged and answered, "I guess even goody two-shoes need to find the right pair for sacred journeys."

Mara looked up into Charissa's eyes and laughed with a chortling kind of unrestraint that swelled up and made Charissa laugh too. "The Sensible Shoes Club, right?" Mara said, resting her hand on Charissa's arm. "That took guts for you to apologize, girl. Thank you."

A wave of relief and gratitude washed over Charissa. "You're welcome," she said. *Thank you, Jesus,* she breathed.

"I'd like to ask your forgiveness too," said Mara, her hand still resting on Charissa's arm.

Charissa raised her eyebrows. "What for?"

"For being judgmental and condemning about you. For thinking all kinds of nasty things about you. From the moment you joined our table that first day, I started judging you for your looks, for your name, for the way you carried yourself. I started blaming you for causing years of pain because you reminded me of some people who hurt me really bad. Crazy, I know . . ."

Charissa shook her head slowly as John pulled up to the portico. "Not crazy," she said, smiling. "I guess it's not surprising we have the same shoes, Mara. We're walking the same road."

Mara grinned and opened her fluorescent pink umbrella. "Amen, girlfriend."

"I'm proud of you," said Katherine as she and Meg cleaned up the room together. "That wasn't easy for you to speak up."

"No, I didn't want to. Then I kept feeling more and more nervous, knowing I was supposed to. I don't think I was very clear, though."

"You were perfectly clear! Not everyone connects with God's heart for the lost and blind, Meg. That's a wonderful gift."

The two of them continued in companionable silence for a while before Meg said, "My sister's coming to town next week. We haven't seen each other since our mother's funeral." She loaded the last coffee mugs onto the cart and wiped down the refreshment table with a damp cloth. "I guess I'd never really thought about it before, but Rachel is lost and blind. She just doesn't know it. I wonder if my insight today has something to do with her."

Katherine smiled but did not reply.

"I can't imagine talking with her about Jesus, though. She's kind of spiritually eclectic, and I've always been the little sister. Even at forty-six, I'm just the little sister who doesn't know much."

"I'll be praying for your visit."

"Thank you. Thanks for everything." Meg embraced her and then picked up her purse. "By the way, Katherine, did you see Hannah leave? I'm worried something happened to her."

Katherine gathered her papers together. "She told me she wasn't feeling well."

"I'll give her a call."

Katherine nodded. "God bless you, dear one."

On her way to her office, Katherine stopped in the chapel again. Quieting herself at the foot of the cross, she asked the Holy Spirit to help her pray for Hannah. Hannah was so afraid. So very afraid.

*Be tender to her, Lord. She's so frightened. There's a wounded child inside of her who is terrified and alone. So alone. Dear God, pour out your love and heal her. Heal her heart. Remove her resistance and overcome her fears with your perfect love. Take away her terror of intimacy—intimacy with you and intimacy with others. Meet her in the wilderness of her grief and fear, and show her that you see her. You see her, Lord. Please help her see you. Give her eyes to see you! And grant her courage—not just to confront the past, but to walk into the future you have for her without fear. In the strong name of Jesus.*

*Let it be, Lord. Let it be.*

"I saw something," Hannah said, opening her eyes and looking at Nathan. She hardly recognized her own voice. This voice was youthfully fervent—more like the voice she had used years ago when she and Nate were talking about God in her dorm room or at the student center. This voice was passionate and excited. "I saw something while you were praying for me."

She simply couldn't contain herself. She had to tell him. Nate was leaning forward in the armchair, his hands clasped and his elbows on his knees, still in a posture of prayer.

"Did I ever tell you about an image I saw years ago of me running in and out of God's throne room with flowers?"

"Remind me," he said.

Her words tumbled out. "I was praying in my college dorm room one day, and I saw an image of myself when I was a little girl, maybe four or five years old. My hair was in this little bob cut with a couple of plastic barrettes keeping it out of my eyes, and I was wearing one of those flowered sundresses my mom always loved, with a big bow at the back."

Nathan smiled.

"Anyway . . . I was running really fast, in and out of God's presence. Every time I ran in, I dumped flowers at Jesus' feet—armloads and armloads of beautiful, colorful wildflowers. Then I'd race out to gather more. I kept running in and out, back and forth to gather and deliver. And then finally, on one of my rushing trips in, Jesus leaned forward, scooped me up into his arms, and sat me down on his lap. He smiled at me with this wonderful, warm smile and said, 'Thank you for the flowers, Hannah. But what I'd really like is to hold you for a while.'"

Nathan still had his hands clasped together. "I remember now," he said quietly. "The perfect image for your desire to please God."

"Yes," Hannah said. "And a reminder that I was often so busy serving him that I forgot to be with him."

He nodded slowly.

She was breathless as she continued. "Well, as you were praying for me just now, I saw another image of the same scene. I was back in the throne room again. But this time I was grown up, and things were reversed. This time Jesus was the one with the flowers. And I kept racing in and out of his presence to grab the flowers and deliver them to people outside. I kept running in and out, back and forth, taking more and more flowers from Jesus so that I could give them to lots of people."

"God's delivery girl," Nathan said, smiling.

"Yes!" Hannah laughed. "And then . . . Then, something happened. On one of my trips in, Jesus stopped me. He took me by the hand and smiled at me and said, 'The flowers are for you, Hannah. The flowers are for you.'" Her voice caught, and her eyes filled with tears.

Nate's eyes mirrored her emotion. "Flowers," he repeated softly. "The lover's gift to the beloved. . . . What a treasure, Hannah. Thank you, Lord . . ."

Flowers. Lovers. Gifts. Beloved.

That wasn't what she had expected him to say.

And she was going to have to find a way to leave his office quickly so she could concentrate on Jesus without being distracted by Nate.

October 25

7 p.m.

I'm sitting here at the cottage, listening to the steady rain landing on the deck and trying to process everything that happened—everything God revealed to me today. Maybe the prayer of examen is exactly what I need to work through tonight in order to see the movement of the Spirit in today's events. I need to go back over the details in Jesus' presence and ask for his perspective on everything that happened.

I can see it now, though I didn't see it this morning. I see how God stopped me along my own wilderness road. I was so upset when I left the group. I couldn't risk breaking down in front of all of them. My pride was wrapped up in that—a pride that refuses to let anybody see me disintegrate.

Forgive me, Lord.

And then to wind up lost because I was so distracted. Not only lost, but locked out of my car and angry. So angry. What does it say about God's power and providence that even when I thought I was avoiding God and running away, I end up right where God wants me? That God sees me and finds me? I used to have an Einstein quote on a poster in my dorm room: "Coincidence is God's way of remaining anonymous." What kind of grace is it that finds me in my fear and disobedience and gives me the gifts God gave me today?

It was such a gift to hear Nathan's story. There's such freedom in him.

Freedom to be honest about where he's come from. And he has such joy and peace in knowing where he's going. He never had that kind of confidence in God when I knew him years ago. He's like a new person. A new creation. And if pain and sorrow have accomplished that in his life, then who am I to say pain and sorrow aren't gifts the Lord will use in my life? I want the kind of rest Nathan has. Rest in knowing God's love and enjoying the gift of being God's beloved. If stripping everything else away can bring that kind of gift, then help me trust you and yield, Lord.

I remember Katherine telling me at our first spiritual direction session that my journey toward healing and freedom will deepen when I truly understand myself as the beloved. What a beautiful image God gave me for that. If I can be confident in God's love for me, then maybe I can go back into the past without being so afraid. Maybe.

I deleted the resignation letters a little while ago. I don't know where I'm going when the sabbatical is done. I'd like to think that I'll be pastoring again, but I need to hold that desire with open hands. Those decisions aren't for me to make today.

Tonight, though, I have one other small answer to the "where are you going?" question.

Tomorrow I'm going to worship. Meg called earlier to invite me, and for the first time in a long time, worship doesn't feel like a "should." It's a desire. That's also a gift, Lord. Thank you.

10

# Deeper into the Wilderness

*I will lead the blind by a road they do not know,*
*by paths they have not known I will guide them.*
*I will turn the darkness before them into light,*
*the rough places into level ground.*
*These are the things I will do,*
*and I will not forsake them.*

Isaiah 42:16

## *Together*

On Sunday afternoon Hannah and Meg sat together in a Corner Nook booth, eating butternut squash soup and talking about the worship service.

"Thanks so much for inviting me," Hannah said. "It was good for me to be there."

"I'm glad," said Meg. "I've been worried about you. Praying for you."

"Thanks." Hannah knew she was standing at a crossroads. How much was she going to reveal? "I've had a rough couple of weeks," she began. "You've been so sweet to keep checking in with me. I really appreciate it."

"Well, you were there for me when I needed help and encouragement about Jim a few weeks ago." Meg's voice was soft. "I'd really like to support you, Hannah. If there's anything I can do to help . . . I know my faith isn't as strong as yours, but if there's anything I can offer you . . . I just wish . . . "

Meg's words pierced her. Hannah was no model of spiritual maturity. So why couldn't she confess that to Meg? Why was she so afraid to disclose the truth about her grief? Did she really believe Meg's faith would be harmed if she confessed her struggles or how disappointed she had felt with God? Was she protecting Meg or herself?

"Keep praying for me, okay?" Hannah said, stirring her soup methodically. "With everything I'm learning and processing, that's the best gift you can give me right now. I'm grateful for your prayers."

There. A confession of need without a confession of weakness. That was enough for today.

Hannah shifted gears smoothly and effortlessly. "I was thinking last night about what God showed you that day on the labyrinth," Hannah said. "About Jesus loving you even more than Jim did. I was so happy for you, thinking about what a gift the Spirit had given you. And yesterday God surprised me with the same kind of gift."

Meg's face lit up. "Really?"

"I saw an image as Nathan prayed for me in his office." Hannah broke off a piece of sourdough bread to dip into her bowl. "I was running in and out of the throne room of God, collecting flowers from Jesus to give to other people. Then suddenly, Jesus caught me by the hand and told me that the flowers were actually for me."

"Oh, Hannah—that's beautiful! Maybe you can keep some fresh flowers in a vase to remind you of that, especially during the winter."

*Flowers in winter.* Meg seemed completely unaware that she'd just said something profound.

"Flowers in winter," Hannah repeated slowly. "That works as a metaphor for the spiritual life, doesn't it?"

Meg looked puzzled. "What do you mean?"

"We have to hold on to God's declaration of love for us when we go through the trying and desolate seasons of our lives. We have to hold on to the promise of God's steadfast love during the 'winters of our soul,' when everything is stripped away." Hannah recognized her tone of voice. She was sliding into her comfort zone, speaking not only to herself, but seeking to bestow something on Meg.

For the building up of Meg's faith.

Meg had been shocked to discover that Hannah had run into Nathan—not once, but twice—and she was now convinced that Nathan's reappearance was God's providence and gift. But how did Hannah see it?

Hannah had commented that it was nice to reconnect with an "old friend" after so many years. But that was all. That was all Hannah said about him.

The same stirring that had prompted Meg to voice her insights about Bartimaeus now drove her out of her comfort zone again. She was praying as she spoke. "So, Hannah . . . What do you think God is up to, bringing Nathan back into your life again?"

She watched as Hannah almost choked on a piece of bread.

"Oh, I don't know," Hannah answered, avoiding eye contact by taking a long, slow sip of water. "I wouldn't say that God is up to anything in particular. It's just a gift to have an old friend reappear. I'm grateful for that."

*Help, Lord,* Meg prayed. "You don't think it's just a coincidence, do you?"

Hannah was still hiding half her face behind her glass of water. "A God-incident," she replied. "But I'm not reading anything special into it. Nathan's a friend. Just a friend."

"But—"

Hannah swiftly interrupted her. "I've got so much to process with God right now, Meg. I can't afford to be distracted by other things." Her tone was firm and resolute. "I'm walking this road toward understanding myself as the beloved, and I need to stay focused. I need to stay focused on what this whole sabbatical was all about to begin with. I've got to figure out who I am when I'm not pastoring."

Meg almost retreated and acquiesced. Almost. "I hear what you're saying, and I understand where you're coming from. But I'd hate for you to be so focused on what you think God's doing that you miss something else God might be doing."

Meg wasn't sure if the expression on Hannah's face was a look of astonishment, disagreement, or irritation. Nevertheless, she quickly spoke again before she lost her courage—before the ring of redness around her throat strangled her.

"I just don't think it needs to be an either-or thing, Hannah," she said quietly. "Maybe Nathan is part of the journey. Part of God's gift of love for you. Maybe Nathan is one of God's flowers. I'm just saying it's a possiblity . . . that's all . . . "

Meg wasn't a bit surprised when Hannah immediately steered their conversation in a different direction. She even cooperated by speaking about her upcoming visit with Rachel and her trip to England. At least Meg had done her part: she had said what she thought Hannah might need to hear.

Hannah had also spoken things Meg needed to hear. Meg had her own unconfessed, unresolved issues of grief, and at some point she would have to go back into the past with God's help and blessing.

On her way home Meg stopped at a local florist to buy herself a small bouquet. It wasn't a bad idea to keep her own vase of fresh flowers beside her bed.

Just in case it was a long winter.

## Hannah

There was still one box Hannah had not unpacked at the cottage. On the night she arrived in Michigan, she had removed it from her car and had immediately shoved it into a closet. The only reason she had even brought the box with her was because she hadn't wanted to risk the intern or anyone else finding it at her house.

As the days passed by, however, the contents of the box began to beckon her. Perhaps unpacking the box was the next step in her pilgrimage. Hannah had told herself that if she really understood how deeply God loved her, then she would have the courage to go back into the past without fear. This was her opportunity.

*Help, Lord.* She pulled out the box and carried it to the sofa by the picture window. It was time.

March 1

Dear Diary,

My name is Hannah Shepley, and today is my fifteenth birthday. Mom and Dad gave me this book, and it's my favorite present. I've never had a diary before, and I guess it will take some practice learning how to write in it. But I'm happy I have a place to write down everything I'm thinking and feeling.

So where do I start? I live in Oak Creek, California, with my mom and dad. I have a brother named Joey. He's five. I'm jealous of my friends who have sisters because I've always wanted one. I remember being so excited when Mom and Dad told me that we were going to have a baby, and I hoped and hoped for a girl. But Joey's cool, too. I love him even when he's annoying. And he's annoying A LOT.

We moved to Oak Creek last summer. I really hope we don't move again, but Dad's a salesman, and we move around a lot. It's hard, but I think our family is really close because of it. I'm lucky to have great parents because some of my friends have it really rough at home.

What else? I'm a freshman at Oak Creek High School. I like English, and I think I'd like to be a writer someday. My friends say I should be a counselor or something because I'm a really good listener, and I'm always listening to everyone's problems. They're always coming to me for advice about boyfriends and stuff. And that's really funny because I don't even have a boyfriend. I used to really like a guy named Brad, but not anymore.

Bye for now.

Sincerely,

Hannah Shepley

March 6

Dear Diary,

Had a good day at school today. Amy invited me to spend the night at her house on Friday night, and that will be so much fun. She was my first friend at Oak Creek, and she's my best friend. We have so much in common! I love hanging out with her. We'll probably stay up all night talking about boys and stuff. I seriously hope no one ever reads this.

Hugs,

Hannah

March 22

Dear Diary,

I thought I'd be able to write every day, but I haven't had much time. School is really busy right now, and Dad has been traveling a lot. That means I'm extra busy helping Mom take care of Joey. I hate it when Dad's away. Not that I mind helping around here. I just don't like it when he's gone. When I was little I used to cry to Brown Bear all the time whenever he was away. But I've been too old for Brown Bear for a long time. So I guess I'll use this diary for crying and sharing secrets and stuff. It still feels kinda weird to write down how I'm feeling, but I hope I get used to it. Even though my friends are always coming to me with their problems, I don't usually go to them with mine. Not that I really have any problems anyway. Not like some of my friends do. I'm really lucky.

I think my biggest problem is that I miss my dad when he's away. And I worry about moving. And sometimes Joey is really annoying. But that's what little brothers are for, right?

Love,

Hannah

March 27

Dear Diary,

Got a great surprise today—Dad came home unexpectedly! He wasn't supposed to be home until the end of the week. I was soooo happy to see him. I haven't really had a chance to talk to him much, though, because he and Mom are having a serious conversation in their bedroom with the door closed. I really, really hope this doesn't mean we're moving again. I'm just getting used to it here! I get worried when they have serious conversations. They're still talking, and they've been in there for a couple of hours now.

Better go. They just opened the door, and I can hear Mom crying. I really, really hope we're not moving again.

March 28

Just got off the phone with Amy. She told me that she likes Brad Sterling. I already suspected that, but I was waiting for her to tell me herself. I never told her that I used to like him, too. Besides, it wasn't like I was crazy about him or anything. He asked her to go out to a movie on Friday night, and I told her I was really, really happy for her. And I am! She deserves it! She's really awesome. I'm sure they'll have a fantastic time. They make a totally cute couple.

I still don't know what's going on with Mom. She was really upset last night, and Dad didn't seem like himself. He always comes in to have a serious talk with me whenever we're moving, and he didn't come in to talk last night. When I finally asked him what was going on, he just kissed me on the forehead and told me that everything's okay. He said I don't need to worry. We're not moving. I'm so glad!

Gotta go finish homework. I can't talk to Amy again until I'm done. And I want to hear more about Brad. I mean—I want to hear more about her and Brad! Anyway . . . bye for now.

April 8

Mom has been crying A LOT lately, but Dad keeps telling me everything is okay. But I know it's not. Something's wrong. Why won't they talk to me?? It's not like I'm a little kid who doesn't understand stuff. Why won't they tell me the truth?? I had a friend in Oregon whose dad died of cancer, but Daddy promised me he's not sick. So I don't know what's going on. Some of my friends have parents who have gotten divorced. But I've never even heard Mom and Dad argue. So I'm sure that's not it. I just wish they'd tell me the truth. I was going to mention it to Amy today, but then I decided not to. I don't want to dump my problems on her.

She had an AMAZING time with Brad at the movie, and now they're going together! I'm so happy for her. I don't get to see her as often now because they're always together. I mean, always! It's okay, though. I'd be excited, too, if I had a boyfriend. Not that I'm looking for one. I'm not. I've got too many other things going on to keep me busy. I seriously don't have time to be dating anybody. Seriously.

April 9

Mom and Dad are out to dinner with a client. I'm babysitting Joey. Gotta keep an eye on him because he can get into trouble really fast. I can't turn my head for a second. Dad says I never used to get in trouble when I was little—that I was always really responsible and well-behaved. Not Joey! I can't even talk on the phone while I'm babysitting him because he can get into trouble so fast. I still don't like to think about that terrible night in October—the Worst Night of My Life. It's bad enough he broke his leg, but it could have been much, much worse. Mom cried for days about that, and I felt terrible. It was all my fault because I wasn't paying attention. I swore it would never happen again. I'm extra careful now.

Gotta run. Can't see where Joey is.

April 11

Dad left on a business trip this morning. I was really upset, too, because I didn't even know he was going away. He always tells me when he's going away, and I can't believe he just totally forgot. And now he's going to be gone for a week! When he said good-bye to me this morning, he actually had tears in his eyes, and he never cries. So now I really don't know what's going on! He just asked me to promise him I'd take good care of Mom and Joey. And I told him that I always do. Then he kissed my forehead and said he knew I was so responsible and that he could count on me.

Mom is always sad when Dad's away, but it's worse this time. I asked her if she was feeling okay, and she told me she was fine. But she spends a lot of time in their room these days, just sitting in the rocking chair and staring out the window. I wish I knew what was going on. I just try to keep Joey from bugging her.

I used to get really upset whenever Mom cried because I was always afraid I'd done something wrong. I remember this one time when I broke one of

Mom's little ceramic birds, and I was so worried she would find out about it and be really upset with me. So I ran and hid behind a tree in our yard. Dad heard me crying and found me. He told me not to worry because he could fix the little bird. Mom never even knew it broke. It was just our secret.

I keep thinking hard about whether I've done anything to make her upset like this, but I can't think of anything. Dad promises me we're not moving. I really don't have a clue what's happening. And it makes me really worried. Help.

Gotta go get dinner ready. Mom says she's not hungry, but I fixed her favorite—homemade macaroni and cheese.

May 1

I haven't even been able to write the past couple of weeks because I've been too upset. And I don't even know what to say. I feel like everything has been turned upside down. And I don't know what to do.

I feel like I'm living in a movie—that nothing's real. Or like I'm living in a nightmare, and I just want to wake up. But I'm not going to wake up. Because it's real. It's all real.

I haven't even wanted to write because I keep thinking that maybe it will all just go away. And if I write it all down, then I'll have a record of it forever. Kinda like when Joey fell out of that tree, and I didn't want to think about it. But this is much, much worse than that. Oh, God, help. Please. I don't know what to do.

I promised Dad I wouldn't talk to anybody about it. I promised him—not even Amy. It doesn't even feel right to talk about it here. Like it's some kind of betrayal. So I won't. God, help.

He quit his sales job so he can be home. He said he didn't like traveling anyway. He says we'll get through this and that everything will be okay. But how can he be sure? There's nothing he can do to fix this. Nothing. And my heart hurts so bad I don't know what to do. Thankfully, I'm so good at hiding stuff, even Amy doesn't suspect there's anything wrong. And she knows me better than anyone.

*Enough.*

She had read enough.

Hannah placed the journal back into the box, shoved the box back into the closet, and crawled back into the bed to cry.

## *Meg*

Meg cleaned all Tuesday morning, readying the house for Rachel's visit. As she dusted the front parlor, her mind wandered to her father. Now that she had a single memory of him, she wished she had more. Why hadn't she pressed her mother for details about her dad? Why hadn't she insisted on knowing who he was?

She sighed. For the same reason Becca had never pressed her. Talking about her dad made her mother upset.

Meg remembered a conversation she'd had with Jim when they were teenagers. He had asked her about her father, and she told him about the accident. "The gun just went off?" he asked.

"While he was cleaning it."

"You're sure there isn't more to that story?"

Meg was confused. "What do you mean?"

"I don't know." Jim shrugged. "Nothing. Forget about it."

But Meg had gone home, pondering Jim's question. That night, while her mother was peeling carrots at the sink, Meg decided to be brave. "How did Daddy die?"

Mother never turned around. "You know how he died. He was cleaning one of his guns, and it went off."

In one of the more courageous moments of her life, Meg had persevered. "And it was an accident?"

Her mother kept peeling, never looking at her. "Of course it was an accident. Why would you ask such a ridiculous question?"

They never spoke about it again.

The next time Rachel came home for a visit, Meg decided to ask her too, just to be sure. But Rachel had reacted angrily. "What are you even suggesting?" she demanded.

"I-uh . . . I don't know . . . It's just—"

"Just nothing!" Rachel snarled. "Of course it was an accident! What—you think Daddy would have shot himself on purpose? That's the stupidest thing you've ever said!" Rachel had stormed out of the room, refusing to speak to Meg for the rest of her visit.

Meg had learned then that it wasn't worth asking questions. She loved her sister too much to make her angry. Peace in the Fowler family depended upon avoidance, and Meg wanted peace.

She was upstairs when she heard the front door open. "Anybody home?" Rachel's voice echoed in the foyer. Meg ran to the landing.

"I didn't expect you for another hour or so!" Meg bounded down the stairs to throw her arms around her sister.

"I made good time from Detroit," Rachel said, putting down her bag. "Hell, Megs! Put some weight on, will you? Do you eat?" She pinched Meg's cheek.

"You look great, Rache."

"Not bad, huh? Amazing what a bit of money can buy." She tossed her expertly highlighted hair, a fresh shade of strawberry blonde. "Like the color?"

Meg nodded. It was different every time Meg saw her.

Rachel walked into the parlor. "Dear God! I see you've kept the mausoleum as-is. Haven't you changed anything?" Meg shook her head. "You're surrounded by dead people's stuff. How in the world can you stand it? I would go absolutely insane."

Meg shrugged. "I guess I'm used to it. I wouldn't even know where to begin to change anything. Mother was so particular about having things 'just so.'"

Rachel laughed cynically. "Get her voice out of your head and gut the whole place. Better yet—sell it and be free. You know she only left it to you to keep you trapped here."

Meg flinched. Their mother's will was a sore spot for both of them: Meg felt guilty, and Rachel felt resentful. Meg tried to change the subject.

"I want to hear all about your latest adventures," Meg said, taking her sister's arm and guiding her into the kitchen. "I especially want to pick your brain about England while you're here."

Rachel whistled. "I still can't believe you're going. If I actually believed in miracles, I'd call it one." She seated herself at the table while Meg made coffee. "So how is Becks doing?"

Meg was happy talking about Becca and London. Anything to avoid the many landmines of more volatile topics. Meg stepped carefully, skillfully steering the conversation. Once Rachel started discussing her work and her travels, Meg relaxed.

They spent the next hour catching up, and then Rachel insisted on going out to eat. Meg pretended she hadn't already labored to plan and prepare a meal, telling herself she could freeze it for another time. Or she could deliver some more meals to Angel and the girls. Meg also pretended that she would be thrilled with spicy Thai food, convincing herself that heartburn was a small price to pay for avoiding a lecture about her "lack of adventure." She slipped some antacids into her purse when Rachel wasn't looking and cheerfully drove to the restaurant.

They were home by seven o'clock. Rachel's eagerness to explore the attic kept her from insisting on spending the evening at a bar. Meg was relieved. Another potential landmine averted.

"Smells exactly like I remember," Rachel said, climbing the stairs into the darkness. "Mold and mothballs. Ugh." She cast the beam of her flashlight around the perimeter of the room. "What a mess! We could get lost up here for weeks."

Meg was glad she had removed the box with Jim's letters. She wouldn't have wanted Rachel to find it.

"There used to be a light up here somewhere," Rachel said, scanning the ceiling. Meg found the bare, dusty bulb and pulled the chain.

"That helps a little," Meg commented, still shining her flashlight into dark corners. "So what are you looking for?"

"A box of photos, for one thing. Lots of pictures of Daddy. I used to sneak up here after Mother went to bed, and I'd spend hours looking at them." Rachel began to dig through some of the boxes. "She hated me talking about him. Sometimes I'd do it just to tick her off."

Meg cringed.

Rachel chuckled, saying, "That's one of the reasons I married Greg. She hated him. I only stayed married as long as I did to spite her. You knew that, right?"

Meg nodded. *Rachel the agitator; Meg the pleaser*. Rachel had never been afraid of a fight; Meg would do anything to avoid conflict. She hoped this wasn't the prelude to another one of her sister's long tirades against all the men who had ever wronged her. Or a diatribe against their mother.

"Hey! Found them!" Rachel pulled out a stack of photos and blew off a cloud of dust. "How'd such a good-looking guy end up with such a piece of work?" Rachel wondered aloud, shaking her head. "Here—check these out. Don't you think I look like him?"

Meg gazed at the many faces of her father, from small boy to grown man. She didn't see much resemblance between Rachel and their dad, but she wasn't going to disagree. Rachel had always been so eager to connect herself with him.

"Such sad eyes," Meg said simply, looking at some of the images from later years.

"Do you blame him? Imagine having to live here with her." Meg didn't have to imagine. "Okay," Rachel said. "Keep looking. Maybe there are more photos I don't know about."

Meg was quiet as she sorted through boxes. Their mother had kept decades of meticulous records: tax returns, bank accounts, receipts, and medical records, all carefully organized by year.

Rachel had moved to one of the corners of the attic. "Finding anything interesting?" she asked after a while.

"Nothing." Meg opened a box containing all the files from her childhood.

"There are boxes and boxes of books over here, Megs. And even some drawings of the house signed by Emmanuel Fowler. Oooh! Here's a box of Daddy's books. Old textbooks, storybooks. No photos, though." Rachel kept hunting. "Don't do anything with these boxes, okay? I'm gonna want to sort through all these books someday. Not now, though."

Meg took the file from the year she was born and flipped through a stack of receipts and canceled checks. "Boy, I sure was a bargain!"

Rachel stood up and wiped cobwebs from her sleeves. "Whaddya mean?"

"Mother kept everything. She knew where every penny went, and here's the record of every penny they spent the year I was born."

Rachel came over to look. "Daddy liked his drink, huh?" She smirked. "Like father, like daughter." Picking up the file from the year he died, Rachel began shuffling through receipts. "Funeral costs, flowers, dresses, coffin. I can still see it. I can still smell the lilies. To this day I can't stand the smell of lilies."

"Was I there?" Meg asked quietly. There was so much Meg wished she could remember.

"No. You stayed with one of the neighbors. With Mrs. Anderson, I think." Rachel continued to thumb quickly through the file. "Nothing exciting here. Not even an obituary. Mother certainly wasn't sentimental, was she?"

She handed the file to Meg and began opening other boxes, still searching for photos. Meg flipped through the papers, looking for anything that conveyed emotion about William Fowler's death. But the records and receipts were cold and sterile. Had her mother preserved nothing but these slips of paper to mark his passing? Nothing but a financial accounting of his life and death?

Meg was just about to close the file and move on to a more promising box when her eyes fell upon a single envelope marked with the return address of an insurance company. Intrigued, Meg opened the envelope and read the brief letter enclosed. It was dated three weeks after their father died.

Regarding Policy No. 1438
Insured: William G. Fowler
Dear Mrs. Fowler,

This letter acknowledges receipt of your claim for benefits under the above policy along with a copy of the death certificate. The claim is under review. Pending the outcome of the investigation, we are neither accepting nor denying payment of the claim at this time.

If you have any further questions, please contact me at the number below.

Sincerely,
Peter Michaelson
Claims Examiner

Meg's heart beat faster as she thumbed through the file. She didn't even know what she was looking for until she found it—a letter dated six weeks later.

Regarding Policy No. 1438

Insured: William G. Fowler

Dear Mrs. Fowler,

Regarding your claim for benefits under the above policy, we must inform you of our decision to deny coverage for the death of William G. Fowler.

Our investigation revealed the cause of death was suicide and not accidental. As you should be aware, under the terms of this policy, there is a clause denying coverage of death by suicide within the first two years of the policy coverage. Since your husband purchased this policy six months ago (see attached copy), we must deny coverage for this claim.

Should you have any further questions, please feel free to contact me.

Sincerely,

Peter Michaelson

Claims Examiner

Meg stayed on her knees. "Rache?" she quivered. The caves were closing in. The air was stale and stifling. She couldn't breathe.

"Find something?" Rachel asked, coming over to investigate.

Though Meg moved her lips, no sound emerged. Trembling, she offered the papers to Rachel, who flushed with anger as she read.

"Daddy didn't kill himself," she said, barely disguising her rage behind clipped syllables. "They just didn't want to pay out the money. What a load of crap." Kicking a nearby box, Rachel headed for the stairs, spewing profanity.

"Rache?" Meg implored, the tears searing her face.

Rachel didn't look at her. "I need a drink," she snapped. "Don't wait up for me."

Meg didn't sleep. At 2 a.m. the front door opened, and she heard the sound of Rachel's heavy footsteps plodding up the stairs. Though Meg wanted to call out to her, she kept silent, honoring her sister's desire for space. She watched from her bed as Rachel paused in their mother's doorway across the hall, muttering inaudibly. Then she stormed to her childhood room and slammed the door.

Meg waited until 5 a.m. before going downstairs to sit in the darkness of the kitchen. What other secrets had their mother kept? What other truths had been hidden away? Meg had spent another three hours in the attic after Rachel left, scouring files and boxes, seeking anything that might shed light upon their father's life and death. But she found nothing.

Not that she had expected to find anything.

In fact, she was surprised her mother had retained the insurance letters. An oversight. It must have been an oversight in her mother's attempt to conceal the truth. Or perhaps her mother's keeping them was simply part of the compulsion to document all the details thoroughly. She must have thought that no one would ever bother to sort through those files.

Of course, Meg knew what Rachel would say. If Rachel actually believed their father had committed suicide, she would accuse Ruth Fowler of deliberately leaving behind the record to torment her daughters after her death.

Meg breathed deeply. Had their mother managed to hide the secret from everyone, or just from her daughters? Who else had known the truth? And how could Meg possibly confront the pain of this new revelation? She wept as she heard her father's voice again, "I've got you, Meggie. Keep comin.'"

But he had abandoned them. For whatever reason, he had given up. *Why?* If he had ever given answers, they had been buried with her mother. Ruth Fowler had died with more secrets than Meg had ever imagined. *Heavenly Father, help me. Please.*

At nine o'clock Rachel appeared in the foyer, dressed and with her bag packed. "Are you leaving already?" Meg asked.

"I need to get going."

"Rachel, please—"

Rachel shook her head and waved her hand to cut off conversation. "Not now," she clipped. "Not now."

The room was spinning. Meg wasn't sure if she was going to faint or throw up. But she didn't argue. There was no use arguing with Rachel. "Can I at least get you some breakfast?" Meg asked weakly.

Again, a shake of the head. "I'll stop and get something on the road."

Meg rose to give Rachel an unreciprocated hug. "I'll walk out with you," Meg said, choking back her tears.

Meg stood in the driveway, staring up at the forlorn house. If only Mother had confided in her. If only Mother had shared the heartache, maybe things could have been different. Maybe . . . .

Maybe the attic revelation merely confirmed what Meg had always suspected: there was something deeper and darker to the sadness of her family. The specter of sorrow had never been named, and so it had become the air they'd breathed, poisoning them with its secrecy and silence. Now Meg had words. No reasons. No answers. But words for voicing the burden. Maybe that was gift enough.

Still—if only there were someone who could tell her about her father. If only there were someone who had known him. But there was no family left. And where would she even go to track down a friend? Her mother had lived such a secluded, solitary life.

As Meg trudged up the steps to the porch, her gaze shifted to Mrs. Anderson's house.

Dear Mrs. Anderson.

Her home had been a bright spot in Meg's childhood, a place of warmth and welcome. Mrs. Anderson had always shown so much kindness to Meg, and Meg had been sad when she moved away. They'd kept in touch with Christmas cards over the years, but Meg hadn't seen her since Becca was a little girl.

Dear Mrs. Anderson. *Thank you, Lord, for Mrs. Anderson.*

Wait.

Mrs. Anderson.

Was there a reason why she had come to mind? Had Mrs. Anderson known the truth?

Mrs. Anderson had known the Fowler family for decades. Was it possible that Mrs. Anderson could shed light on William Fowler's death?

Meg hurried inside and found her address book. *Loretta Anderson. Winden Plain, Indiana.*

Which was stronger? The impulse to confirm what she thought she knew? Or the guilt over betraying a family secret by asking questions?

As she sat at the kitchen table, she heard her mother's stern voice commanding her: "Don't you dare take this out of the house. You hear me? Don't you dare take this out of the house!"

Meg closed the address book, held her head in her hands, and prayed.

Loretta Anderson was thrilled to hear Meg's voice on the phone. She had often thought of her, ever since she'd heard the news that Ruth Fowler had passed away. Loretta had always loved the younger Fowler daughter. Rachel had been more independent and aloof, often angry and confrontational. But Meg—Meg had a purity of heart and sweetness of spirit that somehow persevered in spite of everything. Loretta had always marveled at Meg's lack of bitterness, especially when there had been so much to be bitter and resentful about.

But then, that was her outsider's view and assessment of things. Meg had never spoken about it being difficult. Nevertheless, Loretta had observed enough to know that Ruth Fowler had not reciprocated her daughter's affection and devotion. At least, not outwardly. So Loretta had seized every possible opportunity to show compassion to Meg while hiding from Ruth her motivation for doing so.

"I'm so happy to hear from you, Meg!" Loretta exclaimed. "I can't tell you how often I've thought about you the past few months. How are you, honey?" Loretta listened with keen interest as Meg spoke about Becca's adventures in London and how she had just received her own passport in the mail. "A world traveler!" Loretta marveled. "That sounds fantastic! I still can't believe Becca is in college. Where does the time go?"

"I know," Meg replied. "She's still a little girl in my mind."

"As you are in mine," Loretta said. "Do you remember coming over to help me bake cookies?"

"Cookies, music lessons, books. You were so kind to me, Mrs. Anderson. Thank you."

Loretta laughed. "After all these years, Meg, you can call me Loretta. And I always loved having you over. You were such a sweet little thing. So eager to help, eager to please. Of course, you didn't lose those qualities when you grew up."

They chatted comfortably for the next ten minutes, reminiscing about the neighborhood and swapping stories of things they remembered. "I hope you don't mind me saying so," Loretta said. "But you must be rattling around inside that big house. Don't you find it lonely?"

"I do," Meg answered. "It echoes terribly." There was a moment's hesitation. "In fact, Rachel was saying the other day that our father would have been alone in the house too after his mother died. I guess I'd never thought about my father and me being in the same situation. Alone in the big empty Fowler house . . . " Meg's voice trailed off.

"You're right," Loretta replied. "He was alone and very lonely. We used to have him over for dinner as often as we could. I don't think he did much cooking for himself. Then your mother came along, and—" Loretta caught herself before she said something negative. "Well, we didn't see him as often after that."

Though she could have said much more, she bit her tongue. She didn't believe in speaking ill of the dead. But as she had frequently remarked to her own dear husband, Ruth Dickinson had been a pretty little thing who knew how to turn on her charm when she wanted something. And she had wanted William Fowler and his house.

"Are you still there?" Meg asked.

Loretta reined in her wandering thoughts. "I'm sorry, honey. I'm here. What were you saying?"

"I was saying that I've been thinking about my father lately, realizing how little I actually know about him. I wish I knew more. And with Mother gone now . . . well . . . I was hoping maybe . . . I was hoping maybe you'd be willing to talk to me about him . . . to tell me what you remember." Loretta forgot that Meg was hearing only silence—not the racing of her thoughts—and she was silent a long time. "Mrs. Anderson?"

Years ago Loretta had promised herself she would never initiate a conversation with Meg about either of her parents. It wasn't her place. But now Meg was asking a direct question. She drew in her breath.

"What would you like to know?" she asked, begging God to help her answer.

Loretta was careful in what she said. Very careful. She knew the stakes as soon as Meg asked about her father. If Meg had known anyone else who could have answered her questions, she wouldn't have phoned. Loretta wasn't prepared to be Meg's sole source of information for something as important as her family history. That was too big a burden to bear.

So she restricted her comments to things she had personally known or observed to be true. She avoided offering her own opinions and speculations, though she had plenty of those. She loved Meg too dearly to say anything that might cause unnecessary heartache. After all, Meg had already had enough sorrow in her life, and Loretta wasn't going to add more. Not when there weren't people who could contradict or confirm what Loretta thought she knew. No, she would take her conjectures to the grave with her, and Meg wouldn't know the difference. Like the old saying, "What you don't know won't hurt you."

Determined not to hurt Meg, Loretta began with innocuous details, hoping those would satisfy Meg's curiosity. "I first met your father when Robert and I moved next door as newlyweds. Your grandmother was very kind to us. So was your father. He had a wonderful sense of humor and a way of telling stories that kept everyone spellbound. A 'gift for exaggeration,' your grandmother called it."

Loretta hadn't thought about William's stories in years. He had been a real entertainer—so likeable, so good-natured. She and Robert had been so very fond of him.

"He and your grandmother were very close," she went on. "He had moved home to help take care of her after your grandfather died, and he was the most eligible bachelor in the neighborhood. Handsome, full of life. Attractive in every way. After your grandmother passed away, he was lonely, like I said. And your mother was such a pretty little thing with a sharp wit. He fell madly in love. I remember him talking about her one night at our kitchen table. He was totally smitten, and they were married within six months, I think. Rachel was born a year or so after that . . . but you know that already . . . "

Loretta wasn't going to speak about what she had observed of Rachel. Rachel had kept her father tightly wrapped around her little finger. William had indulged and spoiled her, Loretta often remarked to Robert. But when your wife didn't return love and affection—well, he needed to pour his adoration somewhere, didn't he?

She continued aloud. "Then when you were born, your father fell in love all over again."

She wished she could see Meg's face. She wished she could know if her words were helping or hurting. She heard Meg blow her nose.

"Really?" Meg asked quietly.

"He absolutely adored you, honey," Loretta answered. "His face would light up every time he spoke about you. He would often bring you over to see us. He knew how fond I was of you, and we hadn't been able to have children of our own, you see. Your father was kind that way. Very kind. And I used to love to watch the two of you play together in the yard. He'd spend hours playing hide-and-seek with you. I can still remember you squealing with laughter whenever he found you. He'd scoop you up out of your hiding place and carry you around the yard, singing."

"Singing?" Meg repeated.

"Yes! Your father loved to sing. A beautiful voice. A songbird. Like you."

"I wish I could remember that," Meg said. Her voice was wistful. "There are so many things I wish I could remember."

Loretta did not reply. There were many things she was glad Meg did not remember.

Loretta had watched with sadness as William's joy and love of life gradually ebbed away. In his last years the laughter yielded to a persistent melancholy. He started drinking. Heavily. Loretta didn't know enough about alcoholism or depression to say which had come first. She just knew William battled demons.

Much as she had liked William when he was sober, he was a different man when he was drunk. Aggressive. Menacing. Not that he had ever hurt the girls. Loretta didn't think he had ever hurt the girls. But there were many things that happened behind closed doors, and she was convinced Ruth had died with secrets. Many of them. Loretta supposed she would die with secrets too, out of honor and respect for the dead.

Meg's voice interrupted her meandering thoughts. "Rachel was telling me the other night that she thought I stayed with you during the funeral."

*Here we go,* thought Loretta. She braced herself. "You did. You were so little, and you didn't understand what had happened. It was better for you not to be there."

"What do you remember about that?" Meg asked. "I mean—about when my father died?"

Loretta had known the question was inevitable. "Well, my memory's not as reliable as it used to be," she answered. That was partially true. Her short-term memory was fading, but her long-term memories lived on in high-definition clarity.

Meg pressed. "I know, but is there anything you remember about when he died? Any details at all?"

The details were precisely what Loretta had wanted to forget. How she had longed to forget! But they had haunted and pursued her for more than forty years. She could have played her mental movie back for Meg, scene by scene, frame by frame. In the long moments of silence, as Loretta frantically tried to figure out how much to reveal, she saw it all over again.

It was a hot, muggy August afternoon filled with buzzing mosquitoes. Loretta was kneeling in her flowerbeds, deadheading marigolds, her knees and hands covered in dirt. A window was open on the second floor of the Fowler house, with a sheer white curtain billowing in the breeze. She could hear the sound of voices raised in anger. She tried not to eavesdrop. She tried to concentrate on her weeding and deadheading. But she caught shouted words and phrases. Enough to know what the argument was about.

*No-good, useless drunk. Disgrace. Shame. Hopeless.*

She happened to look up at the window just as Ruth was peering down. Their eyes met briefly before Ruth slammed the window shut.

Loretta was still working in the flowerbed when she saw Ruth storm to the car, dragging Meg by the hand. Meg was crying. She wanted to kiss Daddy good-bye. *She always kissed Daddy good-bye.* Loretta could still see Meg standing in the driveway in her pink sundress, blowing kisses through her tears and waving at the house. Loretta didn't know if William was there, waving back.

She had never been able to erase the image of Meg's tiny face pressed against the car window, staring forlornly at the house as Ruth drove away. If Loretta had only known what would happen a few hours later, she never would have let Ruth drive away. Never.

"It was August," Loretta finally replied. "A very hot day in August. Rachel was playing at a friend's house, I think, and you and your mother had gone out. I was working in my flowerbeds when I heard what sounded like a car backfiring. I wouldn't have paid attention at all, except Robert happened to be standing next to me. When he heard it, he knew it was a gunshot. Robert was a hunter, and he sometimes went hunting with your father; so he recognized the sound, and he went running over to investigate." Loretta's voice caught. She wasn't sure she could go on with the story.

"Mrs. Anderson?" Silence. "Loretta? Please . . . if there's anything you can tell me . . . "

Grateful that Meg couldn't see her, Loretta gripped the table to steady herself. *God, help me. Please.*

"Robert found your father in your parents' bedroom," she said quietly. Loretta had seen him too, but she couldn't speak about that. The image was too painful, too fresh, even after all these years. William lay there lifeless on the bed, a blood-spattered photo of his little girls on his pillow.

But Loretta didn't reveal that detail. In fact, she gave as few details as possible, fervently hoping Meg wouldn't press for more. "Your mother got home shortly after Robert found him, and you came over to stay with me while Robert waited with your mother for the police. I don't remember Rachel coming home that night. I think she stayed at her friend's house."

She wasn't going to talk about the moment Ruth got home. Ruth had been icy and stoic, seemingly more provoked about the neighbors' intrusion than about her husband's death. But that was merely conjecture. Ruth had never been one to display any kind of emotion, and it could have been the shock of William's death that caused her to appear so dispassionate.

Loretta sighed. "And that's what happened," she said slowly. "It was terrible. A terrible tragedy, and my heart broke for your mother and for you girls." The seconds were ages as she anticipated the dreaded, inevitable question.

"Was it an accident, Mrs. Anderson?" Meg sounded like the little girl Loretta had adored, her soprano voice even higher than usual.

"I . . . I honestly don't know what to tell you, honey."

That was the truth. That was the honest-to-goodness truth.

## *Mara*

Mara sat in worship on the first Sunday of November, feeling sorry for herself. Though she had desperately hoped her spiritual growth would impact her family, nothing had changed. Nothing. Tom still wanted nothing to do with church, and she could no longer bribe or coerce Kevin and Brian into coming with her.

"They're good kids," Tom said whenever Mara mentioned her desires for Sunday mornings. "Don't you dare spread your guilt around. It doesn't matter if they go to church or not. Go ahead and do whatever you want, but leave us out of it."

Why had she thought anything would be different?

As she watched the Happy Families sitting together in worship, Mara wondered if they were grateful for the gift they had been given. She didn't like feeling bitter and resentful, but living out her faith was so much easier when there weren't other people involved.

So much easier.

"So, Mom, are you sure you don't mind that we're gonna be with Abby's folks for Thanksgiving?" Jeremy asked later that same day.

"No, of course not," Mara replied, avoiding eye contact by concentrating on stirring a pot of soup on the stove. Round and round and round with the wooden spoon. Circles, circles, circles.

"I mean . . . I figured we were with you guys last Thanksgiving, right? And with the baby coming in January, we're probably not gonna want to travel down to their place for Christmas. So plan on us spending Christmas Day with you, okay?"

Mara recognized his conciliatory tone. He had probably had a long conversation with Abby about how to keep the mothers-in-law even. "Sure, Jer. That sounds great."

At least Jeremy lived nearby. Mara was counting on having an advantage with the baby. Since she would get to see the baby more often than Abby's mother, maybe she would even become the favorite grandmother. She hoped so. She couldn't bear it if her granddaughter grew up preferring Ellen. After all, there was only so much love to go around, and Mara had spent a lifetime competing against people who could get there first. If she didn't get there fast enough, there would only be leftovers.

Or nothing at all.

"So . . . are you still thinking you want to serve Thanksgiving dinner at Crossroads?" Jeremy asked, dipping his finger into the saucepan. Mara good-naturedly slapped his wrist and handed him a spoon.

"I don't know. You know how Brian is about tradition. He's already got everything planned in his head about how the meal should be."

Jeremy shrugged. "But you could probably manage both, right? I mean, maybe you could have your dinner later that night. Or have it on Friday. I just know how much Crossroads means to you."

Mara nodded. "We spent a lot of Thanksgivings together there, didn't we?" she said quietly, remembering glowing, candlelit tables set with paper plates and plastic utensils.

"I just remember the pies," Jeremy said, grinning. "They let me have as much as I wanted."

Mara ladled the soup into bowls and took bread from the oven. "I'd love to be there. But I'm not gonna go by myself."

"So ask Tom if he'll go."

Mara snorted.

"I'm serious, Mom! Ask him to go with you. It would be good for Brian and Kevin to experience it. They need to get out of their suburban bubble."

Jeremy was right. Brian and Kevin had no comprehension of the life she'd had before they were born. Mara had sheltered, shielded, and protected them as much as possible.

"Tell you what, Mom. You've been talking so much lately about how God is answering prayer in your life. Why not ask God for a Thanksgiving gift? I'll pray for that for you, okay?" Mara's eyes filled with tears as she looked at her son. "You're the one who keeps telling me nothing's impossible with God," he said. "Right?"

Mara sighed. "Right, Jer. Right."

So why did she struggle to believe that life with Tom would ever change?

Charissa had never been late. Never. Like everything else in her life, her monthly cycle had always been under her careful control, especially after she and John got married. Though John sometimes teased her about her rigorous discipline, Charissa took The Pill at precisely the same time each day. Being meticulous and exact prevented anything unexpected.

So when she sat staring at a faint blue plus sign, she was sure it had to be a false positive. In fact, she was so certain that she retook the test three times over three days with three different brands. But dots, lines, and plusses all confirmed the truth.

She was pregnant.

"Now what?" she exclaimed, finally revealing the truth to John.

John was shocked, thrilled, exuberant. "What do you mean, 'Now what'? We're going to be parents! This is amazing!" He went to embrace her, but she drew back.

"It's not amazing—it's terrible! I can't believe this!" She started to cry.

John looked as if he had been kicked. "Are you kidding me?"

"No, I'm not kidding! Do I look like I'm kidding? I can't believe this! After all the hours I've put into that Ph.D. . . . for this to happen? This wasn't part of the plan!" She began to cry harder.

"Whose plan, Riss? Whose plan?" John was shaking. "I can't believe you. I can't believe you're acting like this. This is a baby we're talking about—our baby!"

She wasn't listening. "I can't believe this," she said over and over again. "I've worked so hard. So hard! And now this? I'm going to have to give up school. I can't believe I'm going to have to give it up."

John stared at her, frozen in disbelief and hurt. "All you can think about is your precious Ph.D.?" he asked, his eyes brimming with tears. "I knew you were self-centered, Charissa, but this is unbelievable." He went to the kitchen and grabbed his keys. She didn't look at him. "I'm leaving before I say something I regret."

She heard the door slam behind him.

When John arrived home three hours later, Charissa had gone to bed. As he watched her lying there, he wasn't sure if she was really asleep or not. She did not move, and he did not try to speak to her. He changed his clothes in the bathroom, grabbed his pillow, and went out to spend the night on the couch.

This was not the way he had imagined it would be. He had lived in joyful anticipation of the day when he would become a father. Granted, he hadn't thought it would happen for a few years—especially since he knew how important Charissa's education and career were to her. But as careful as Charissa had been about her birth control, couldn't she see God's hand in this? John had witnessed so much evidence of spiritual and emotional growth in her the past few weeks, and now it seemed to have completely evaporated. In an instant—gone.

Who could have imagined that a simple plus sign would have the power to reveal so much about his wife's heart?

He turned off the light but didn't sleep.

## *Meg*

Meg tried for a week to reach Rachel by phone, eventually receiving a brief e-mail in reply to her increasingly anxious voice mail messages.

> Meg,
>
> Just want you to know that I'm okay. You don't have to freak out just because I haven't had a chance to return your calls. I'm really busy right now with work and travel, so we probably won't connect for a while.
>
> I'm not interested in having a conversation about Daddy. Believe whatever you want. You didn't know him like I did, and I know for a fact that his death was an accident. I don't want to discuss it with you any further.
>
> I left without taking the photos I wanted. Just leave the box in the attic, and I'll pick it up the next time I'm in town. Probably sometime in January after you get back from England. Have a good trip.
>
> Rachel

Meg had hoped the revelation about their father's death would be enough to bind their hearts together in a new way. But there would be no changing Rachel's mind about having a conversation. She had their mother's stubbornness, much as Rachel had spent a lifetime vehemently denying any similarities between them. That's probably why they had always had so much conflict. They were too much alike.

Then again, maybe it was better that Rachel refused to consider the possibility of their father's suicide. She would only end up blaming Mother for driving him to it, and then Rachel would have one more reason to stay bitter and angry with the dead.

At least Meg wasn't bitter. Even though she was convinced her father had made the decision to end his life, at least she wasn't bitter.

*Please, Lord, don't let me be bitter. Please.*

Later that afternoon Meg sat in Katherine's office, recounting what she had discovered about her father. Katherine listened carefully and then asked, "Do you know anything about your name, Meg?"

Meg was surprised by the question. "My grandmother's name was Margaret, and I'm assuming my dad named me. But I only got called Margaret when I was in trouble."

Katherine smiled. "Do you know what *Margaret* means?"

Meg thought for a moment and then answered, "'Pearl,' I think."

Years ago Mrs. Anderson had given her a mug with her name and its meaning printed on it. She wondered if she still had the mug.

Katherine was sipping her tea slowly. "What do you know about how pearls are formed?" she asked.

"A grain of sand in an oyster, right?"

Katherine nodded. "Sometimes sand," she replied, setting down her mug. "And sometimes a parasite or other irritant. At first the oyster tries to get rid of it. But if it can't, it encloses the intruder into a sac. Then the oyster begins coating the sac with mother of pearl—the same substance that lines the shell. The oyster adds layer after layer for the rest of its life." Katherine grinned. "So the next time you look at your natural pearls, consider the possibility that they're tombs for parasites."

Meg laughed. "I think I was happier imagining myself as a precious gem."

"You are! That's the miracle of the process. Life's painful intrusions aren't negotiable, are they? They happen. It's what we do with them that matters."

They shared the silence while Meg gazed outside at the labyrinth courtyard. The roses were gone, and the fiery colors of autumn had disappeared. Only the brown of the oak trees and the green of the pines remained. It was good to remember that the pines were always green. Even in November—especially in November and especially *this* November when she missed Jim more than ever—there was still evergreen.

Her eyes filled with tears.

Katherine spoke gently. "I've met many people over the years who coat their suffering with bitterness, resentment, and self-pity, and nothing fruitful comes of it. And I've met just as many people who try to pretend that the pain isn't there. They think that denying their pain is God's command—that denial is somehow the evidence of faith. But Jesus invites us to name our pain and to receive his grace for our suffering so that nothing is wasted." She handed Meg a tissue from the box on her coffee table. "Jesus is the perfect Redeemer of our sorrow and suffering, if we entrust ourselves to him. The miracle is that Christ has the power to make something precious and beautiful out of it."

"A pearl," Meg murmured.

"A pearl," Katherine echoed, nodding slowly. "I'm watching God form you into a beautiful pearl, Margaret," she said with deep feeling. "Your father named you well."

*Her father.*

Meg sat a long time in Katherine's fortifying presence, allowing her mind to wander into dark and difficult places. "I don't know why I'm so upset about my dad," she finally said. "I mean . . . what difference does it make to me now? Does it really matter how he died? It doesn't change anything about growing up without him."

Katherine paused before answering. "Everything you thought was true about his death has just been shaken upside down," she said slowly. "And that's worth grieving."

"But it happened more than forty years ago."

"I know . . . And you grieved in your own way as a little girl. But I suspect that you've never grieved the loss of your dad as an adult."

Katherine was right. That had never even occurred to her.

"You've just discovered that there's a real possibility your father's death wasn't an accident. That's a profound thing to grieve, Meg. A hard and profound thing. And with all the unanswered questions swirling around, this will take time. It's not something to be rushed. And God is never impatient with us. So take your time . . . Take it slowly and reverently. We need to be reverent with our pain."

Grieving, grieving, grieving. Meg wasn't sure she had the strength to grieve anything else right now. She breathed deeply.

Katherine leaned in closer. "Think about the process of grieving your beloved Jim and how much courage you've shown just to allow his memory to live again," she said gently. "It's easier to stay in denial. We can hear voices in our heads, saying, 'Remember how painful it was the first time? You certainly don't want to go back and go through it all again!' But the path to freedom and healing takes us right through the heart of the pain. Jesus the Good Shepherd walks with you through the darkness, Meg. You're not alone. Never alone."

Meg blew her nose delicately and sighed. "I still hear my mother's voice inside my head, telling me to just get over it. I should be strong enough to just get over it."

Smiling, Katherine shook her head slightly. "God never says, 'Just get over it,' Meg. Never. God says, 'Give it to me.' And there's an enormous difference between the two."

Meg was taken aback. She had spent years trying to stuff and contain her grief. She had spent years trying to be strong enough to get over it. She had never thought about offering her sorrow to God in prayer, and she felt something shift in her spirit.

"It takes courage to grieve well," Katherine continued, reaching for her mug of tea again, "and God is able to give you the courage. Look how much courage the Lord has already given you in such a short amount of time!"

Meg looked down at her boots. "I guess it's easy to lose sight of how far I've come if I'm only looking at how far I have to go," she murmured.

Katherine nodded. "The process of transformation is never complete this side of heaven. But the Good Shepherd faithfully and lovingly leads and guides us as we say yes to him. These things have come to light now because God is working to heal you. And you're ready to receive the healing. That's good news, isn't it? The Spirit of God is moving."

Moving, stirring, revealing, shaking.

Meg was beginning to wonder if the Spirit offered a remedy for motion sickness.

## *Mara*

Mara sat in Dawn's office on Wednesday morning, staring at a two-dimensional painted figure on top of the bookcase. The little girl had her arms raised high above her head, her outstretched hands open wide in a posture of trust and joy.

"Is that new?" Mara asked, pointing.

Dawn turned around, following her gaze. "I put it there about six months ago."

"Seriously? I'm surprised I didn't see it before." Mara kept staring at the little girl.

Dawn watched her and then asked, "So, what do you think, Mara? Is she receiving or letting go?"

Mara wasn't sure. "It's impossible to tell," she replied after a while. "It's the same gesture for both."

"Go on," Dawn urged.

Mara sighed. "And I still don't know how to live with my hands open. I still have tons of junk to dump, and for some reason I keep clinging to it. Some days I feel like I'm not getting anywhere."

"But you are getting somewhere, Mara. I've watched you take huge strides forward! Think about what you've just managed to do with forgiving the woman in your group. That was really significant."

Mara shook her head. "But it just kicked up all kinds of old crap too."

"Like what?"

"Like all the girls who teased and rejected me and made my life miserable. All the ones who never apologized and probably never even realized what they did to me. I mean, it was one thing to forgive Charissa. She said she was sorry. But I just can't seem to let the other ones go. And that's crazy. It shouldn't be a big deal, but it is. And now that I'm thinking about them again after all these years, I'm even angrier. It's like the thing with Charissa just brought all the old wounds out again. And it sucks to have to remember all the things I've been trying so hard to forget." She paused. "Even though I know what Katherine would say. I know what you're gonna say. You're gonna tell me that they've come to mind for a reason, right? That God is stirring up all the junk so I can see it, let go of it, and be healed."

Dawn smiled at her. "See how far you've come?"

Mara exhaled slowly and sat back heavily in the chair. She knew what was coming next.

"So, Mara. Let's talk about these girls."

## *Together*

Hannah, Meg, and Mara sat together at the back corner table on Saturday morning, waiting for the group to begin.

"I was talking to my therapist, Dawn, the other day," Mara said, "telling her how I'm having all this old crap from my past kicked up. Not the relationship and sin stuff I was talking about at the beach, but junk from my childhood. Girls teasing and rejecting me and making my life absolutely miserable. I guess I'd just been trying to stuff it all down. I didn't want to think about it, you know? And then when I did think about it, I kept telling myself that it shouldn't be a big deal and that I shouldn't still feel angry and upset about it because it happened . . . when? Like forty years ago? More than forty. It's crazy. Sometimes I feel like I'm stuck at eight or nine years old."

Meg nodded. "I was talking with Katherine about the same kind of thing this week, saying that I still hear my mother's voice inside my head, telling me to just get over the pain. And then Katherine told me that God never says, 'Get over it.' God says, 'Give it to me.'"

"Oooh . . . that's good," Mara said, reaching for her notebook.

"It sounds like you've got some things to grieve, Mara," Hannah said. She tried hard to ignore the pestering internal voice that was defying her to take her own advice. "It's not a small thing to be rejected as a child. That can have some pretty significant consequences into adulthood, affecting how we see ourselves and how we see God."

"I know. You're right. Dawn and I talked a long time about how I need to forgive those girls, even though they never apologized. They probably never even realized how much they hurt me. But I still need to make the decision to let them go with God's help because otherwise they just stay hooked to me, you know? And I sure don't need to be lugging around that extra weight. So I've been praying about that the past couple of days."

"It's wonderful you're letting go of so many things," said Meg. "I'm really proud of you, Mara."

Mara smiled. "Thanks. I feel like I'm traveling more 'freely and lightly,' like we talked about at the beginning of the group, right? I've actually started writing some letters—not anything I'll send, obviously, because I don't have a clue where Kristie and the others are. And frankly, I'm not interested in tracking them down. But Dawn suggested I write letters and name exactly what they did to hurt me so that I know what I'm forgiving. And that's been helpful. Not easy, though. I've been crying a lot just remembering the details, but I feel like God is setting me free. It's good."

Mara reached into her bag and rummaged around. "By the way," she went on, "I picked up some info on my way in about all the different prayer and spiritual growth stuff they do around here. I was thinking maybe we could sign up for another group together sometime."

"That would be great!" Meg said, studying the pamphlets. "Look at this. Katherine is leading a pilgrimage to the Holy Land next year. Have you ever been there, Hannah?"

Hannah shook her head. "No. I always wanted to and never had the opportunity."

"Well, you've got plenty of opportunity now, girlfriend!" Mara exclaimed. "You should do it!"

"I think so too, Hannah," Meg said. "What a wonderful way to spend some of your sabbatical!"

Hannah's thoughts began to whirl. *What if?*

She had spent years looking longingly at photographs of the places where Jesus had walked. What if the culmination of her nine-month interior journey were an actual pilgrimage?

Meg and Mara were right. There was nothing to prevent her from going—absolutely no hindrances. Years of disciplined frugality meant there was money to pay for a trip, and a trip like that would certainly enhance her teaching when she returned to Westminster.

As Hannah read the paragraph describing the three-week trip in May, her heart began to race. She hardly even heard Katherine invite people to take their seats.

She was imagining herself walking in the footsteps of Jesus.

# 11

# Lightening the Load

*The people who walked in darkness have seen a great light;*
*those who lived in a land of deep darkness—*
*on them light has shined. . . . For the yoke of their burden,*
*and the bar across their shoulders,*
*the rod of their oppressor, you have broken.*

Isaiah 9:2, 4

## Confession

When Charissa arrived at the New Hope Center half an hour late, she made her way to the back corner table as inconspicuously as possible. "Sorry," she mouthed to the others, removing her laptop from its case.

"You okay?" Mara whispered.

Charissa nodded and pulled down the rim of her baseball cap to cover most of her face.

"It's always a gift when the Spirit shines the light of truth into the dark corners of our lives," Katherine was saying. "It's mercy when God reveals areas of blindness to us. God never shows us these things to condemn us, but to free us. The Lord gently coaxes us out of hiding so that he can heal and restore us."

Charissa leaned forward, unsure if her nausea was spiritual or hormonal.

Katherine said, "Years ago I was telling a group of friends about someone who had criticized me—unjustly, I thought—and I was upset about it. I was angry, defensive, and bitter, and I was looking for people to sympathize with me. My friends were all very sympathetic and nurturing, affirming my right to be angry. Except for Sheri. Sheri listened carefully and then said to me, 'Katherine, I'm hearing a lot of sin in your response. Maybe God is inviting you to look at that.' I was stunned. I hadn't expected to be confronted with sin. At first I was hurt and offended. But as I prayed it through, I realized Sheri had discerned the situation correctly. God was asking me to examine myself, and Sheri was doing the loving thing by pointing out cancer in my own spirit. She didn't point out my sin to shame me. She wanted to help me be free. She loved me enough to speak the truth into my life—truth I needed to hear.

"Friends, there's such freedom in being able to say, 'Yes, that's my sin. And yes, I have a Savior.' No need to hide. No need to be defensive. No need to be ashamed. No need to carry the burden of trying to be perfect. We have freedom to confess what's true about ourselves and receive God's grace."

*Spiritual*. Charissa's impulse to be sick was definitely spiritual.

Of all the topics Katherine could have presented, why sin and confession? *Why?* If she'd had a syllabus, Charissa would not have come. If she'd known they would be inviting God to reveal more areas of captivity, sin, and resistance, she would have stayed home. The only reason she'd even come to the group was because it gave her an excuse to be away from the apartment.

She should have gone to Castleton Park to power walk a couple of miles. But no—she didn't have the energy to work up a sweat. Besides. Ever since she discovered she was pregnant, she saw pregnant women everywhere: glowing, happy pregnant women pushing shopping carts up and down supermarket aisles, standing in line at the bakery, walking rainy day laps at the mall, ordering decaf lattes at Starbucks. Castleton Park was a gathering place for the smiling sorority of mothers-to-be, and Charissa didn't want to join them.

Maybe she should have gone over to campus for a while. There were no happy, smiling pregnant women there. But she didn't want to risk bumping into Dr. Allen.

She sighed slowly, cradling her chin in her hands.

"I'm going to give you some extended time for prayerful self-examination and confession today," Katherine said, passing around some handouts. "Let me be clear that when we're talking about self-examination, we're not talking about self-scrutiny for the sake of perfecting ourselves. Self-examination isn't about being perfect. It's about listening and responding to the Spirit. It's about allowing God to reveal where we are hiding and resisting his love so that we can come out from hiding to receive grace and mercy and wholeness. This isn't about beating ourselves up, and it's not an invitation to obsessive introspection. We can't make ourselves whole or holy. That's the Spirit's work. Our work is simply to cooperate with the Spirit by saying yes to God's movement in our lives.

"Remember, it's a gift when the Holy Spirit exposes areas of darkness, captivity, and sin. When you can actually see the ugliness, it's because the light has come, revealing what was already there. So ask for the courage to be uncomfortable, uneasy, and provoked so you can confess and release these things. The Lord is full of compassion and love for you. God wants to reveal truth so that the truth sets you free. Don't be afraid. The Lord God is with you, walking with you. May you have ears to hear the Spirit's gentle voice."

Charissa didn't want to have ears to hear, and she was tired of seeing her sin. She already knew her sin—some of it, anyway—and she didn't want light shining into any other dark corners of her toxic waste container.

She and John still weren't speaking beyond minimally necessary syllables. She couldn't bear to be with him. She couldn't bear the pained and wounded expression on his face every time he looked at her. She was still too consumed with her own grief to consider the sorrow she had caused him. And though she knew she was only making things worse by refusing to communicate, she couldn't help herself. She didn't trust what she might say.

Shutting her eyes, she pulled her cap even lower over her face, hoping the others would think she was deep in prayer.

**Sacred Journey, New Hope Retreat Center**
***Session Five: Self-Examination and Confession***
*Katherine Rhodes, Facilitator*

---

Read the following text from Genesis 3:1-9 slowly and prayerfully. Then journal your responses to the questions below.

> Now the serpent was more crafty than any other wild animal that the Lord God had made. He said to the woman, "Did God say, 'You shall not eat from any tree in the garden'?" The woman said to the serpent, "We may eat of the fruit of the trees in the garden; but God said, 'You shall not eat of the fruit of the tree that is in the middle of the garden, nor shall you touch it, or you shall die.'" But the serpent said to the woman, "You will not die; for God knows that when you eat of it your eyes will be opened, and you will be like God, knowing good and evil."
>
> So when the woman saw that the tree was good for food, and that it was a delight to the eyes, and that the tree was to be desired to make one wise, she took of its fruit and ate; and she also gave some to her husband, who was with her, and he ate.
>
> Then the eyes of both were opened, and they knew that they were naked; and they sewed fig leaves together and made loincloths for themselves. They heard the sound of the Lord God walking in the garden at the time of the evening breeze, and the man and his wife hid themselves from the presence of the Lord God among the trees of the garden. But the Lord God called to the man, and said to him, "Where are you?"

1. In what ways have your "eyes been opened" to your sin? What do you see about yourself? How do you feel about what you see?
2. With what tone of voice do you hear God ask the question, "Where are you?" Why do you think you hear God that way?
3. What fig leaves have you fashioned for yourself? What are you hiding

from God? From others? From yourself? What keeps you from coming out from hiding?

4. James 5:16 reads, "Therefore confess your sins to one another, and pray for one another, so that you may be healed." If you could be convinced of unconditional love and acceptance, what burdens of sin, temptation, regret, and shame would you confess to someone else?
5. David prayed, "Search me, O God, and know my heart; test me and know my thoughts" (Psalm 139:23). Do you trust God to search and know you, revealing your sin? Why or why not? What does your longing or resistance show you about your life with God right now?

"You okay, Charissa?" Mara asked as they packed up their things.

Charissa stretched her lips into a broad smile. "Absolutely. Thanks."

Mara reached into her bag. "I keep thinking about that story Katherine told us about her seminary prof," she said. "I'd never thought about hearing God's question in the garden that way before."

Though Charissa didn't know what Mara was talking about, she didn't want to call attention to the reasons why she had been late.

"Katherine was telling us a story before you arrived, Charissa," Meg explained, accepting Mara's offer of cinnamon Altoids. "She had a seminary professor whose older sister ran away from home when he was a little boy. His parents searched for her for months—they scoured the country for her—and couldn't find her. One day he got home from school early, and he heard his mother weeping upstairs in his sister's room, crying over and over again, 'Where are you, Karen? Where are you?'"

Mara said, "Yeah—Katherine told us he preached this amazing sermon about Adam and Eve hiding from God. He talked about how God's heart broke over Adam and Eve, just like his mom's heart broke over his sister. And Katherine said she's never been able to hear God's 'Where are you?' question the same way again."

"I don't think I'll be able to, either," said Meg quietly.

Mara offered the mint tin to Charissa, who shook her head slightly. She was beginning to feel nauseous again.

"I was writing down my answers to those questions Katherine gave us on the handout," Mara said, "and I realized I've always heard it like God was angry at them . . . like he was trying to smoke 'em out from hiding to punish them. But hearing it this way changes everything. I think I'll be spending the next two weeks just sitting with those questions from today."

Mara paused, rattling around the Altoids container before putting it back into her bag. "You know," she went on, "I put so much energy into hiding over the years, and now suddenly, everything's breaking loose, and I'm not afraid like I was before." She smiled at Charissa. "I'm not terrified of rejection anymore. How amazing is that?"

A single question was swirling around in Charissa's mind: *Where are you, Charissa? Where are you?* John's wounded face rose before her, pleading with hurt and sorrow.

She felt her cheeks flush. Blasted hormones.

"You sure you're okay?" Hannah asked, looking at her with the sort of curiosity that threatened Charissa's already fragile equilibrium.

Charissa gave a slight nod. She didn't trust herself to open her mouth to speak. *Where are you? Where are you?*

She had wounded John more deeply than ever before. What if she had done irreparable damage to their marriage? What if he'd never be able to forgive her for her selfishness?

Mara was flipping through the pages of her spiral bound notebook. "I can't believe the junk I've dumped since we started walking this path," she said. "I've got tons more crap to give up, but at least I'm seeing some of it. And like Katherine says, it's a gift when light comes, right?" She read from her notebook. "I wrote down what she said: 'The exposure of sin is the beginning of its destruction.' That's good, isn't it?"

Meg rested her hand on Charissa's arm. "Are you sure you're okay, Charissa? You don't seem yourself."

"Headache," Charissa said simply.

*Where are you? Where are you?* Her eyes were filling with tears without her permission.

"Can we pray for you?" Mara asked.

How could she politely refuse an offer of prayer? And what was she so afraid of, anyway? Charissa took a deep breath.

"I'm pregnant," she confessed. Before anyone could make things worse by congratulating her, she quickly added, "And I don't want to be. John and I aren't even talking right now because he was so excited when I told him the news, and I was so upset. All I can think about is everything I'm probably going to have to give up. All my plans, all my hard work. Everything. And I hate being so selfish." Meg squeezed her arm in a gesture of encouragement. "And now I'm worried I've hurt John so badly that he'll never be able to forgive me."

"Let's pray," Meg said, looking at the others and reaching for Charissa's hand.

Charissa was surprised by the strength of Meg's grip.

"You sure you won't join us for lunch, Charissa?" Mara asked as they walked out to the parking lot together.

"No, thanks. I've got to get home. I need to talk with John."

"We'll keep praying for you," Meg said. "If you need anything, you've got my phone number, right?"

Charissa nodded. "Thanks. I feel like a load has lifted off my shoulders, just by being honest with you guys." She paused, jingling her car keys. "You know, I've spent years investing energy in keeping up appearances—wanting everyone to think I've got everything put together. Dr. Allen calls it, 'impression management.'"

"The proverbial mask, huh?" Hannah asked, smiling broadly.

"Yes," Charissa replied. "And I'm starting to see just how exhausting it is to wear it."

Hannah nodded vigorously.

Perhaps it was Charissa's imagination, but something in Hannah's eyes didn't seem to match the rest of her face.

"I just don't know how to say I'm sorry this time, John. There aren't words to describe how self-centered and selfish I am."

John was sitting in the recliner, and Charissa was on the floor, kneeling in front of him.

"We don't get a chance to relive that moment," he said quietly. "We don't get a second chance of experiencing that joy together. You took something really precious away from me."

She felt sick to her stomach. "I know. I'm sorry." Her whole body was trembling.

"I'm still not getting the impression that your heart has really changed about having a baby," he said. "I get that you're sorry for being selfish, and I forgive you. But what hurts is that you're not seeing parenthood as any kind of gift."

"I know," she said. "You're right. I just need some time, John. Change is really hard for me. You know that. Like I told you: I'll go see Dr. Allen on Monday morning and withdraw from the program. I don't know how else to show you that I'm committed to this baby. To our baby."

She didn't want to cry. She didn't want tears to manipulate him into embracing her, so she bit her lip. *Help, Jesus,* she prayed. *Please.*

John was silent a long time. "I never asked you to walk away from school, Riss," he finally said.

Placing his hand upon her head, he slowly stroked her hair. The tenderness in the gesture opened the floodgates of her emotion. He loved her. He forgave her. How much grace was too much grace? Her shoulders began to heave in silent sobs of relief.

"I'm not asking you to give it up, honey," he said, kissing her on the forehead. "You do this all-or-nothing, black-and-white thing, and maybe there's something in between. I don't know. But we don't need to rush into any major decisions right now, do we?"

She loved him, truly loved him.

"Besides," John said, smiling, "wouldn't Dr. Allen tell you that you can only walk a sacred journey one step at a time?"

"Yes," she breathed.

That was exactly the sort of thing Dr. Allen would say.

## *Meg*

On Monday, the tenth of November, Meg sat by herself in a secluded booth at the Timber Creek Inn, sipping soda in the candlelight.

She had not set foot in the Timber Creek since the night she and Jim had celebrated their ultrasound glimpse of Becca. Now, exactly twenty-one years after his death, Meg decided it was time to revisit the past. Listening to Mara talk about writing letters had given her an idea. Maybe she needed to write a letter of her own.

Breathing deeply, she pulled her journal out of her purse and prayed, asking God to help her find the words she had been too frightened to say.

*My dearest Jim . . .*

Could she really do this if those first three words caused her to cry? She inhaled and exhaled again, fixing her gaze on the small vase of flowers on the table. *Walk with me, Jesus. Please.*

*My dearest Jim,*

*I'm writing this letter for myself. If you were here, I know you'd understand. You always told me I needed to be kind to myself. You tried to help me understand that loving myself wasn't a selfish thing, but a way of opening up to God's love for me. You always knew God's love in a way I couldn't comprehend, and you used every day of our life together as an opportunity to show me what it meant to be loved and treasured.*

*Thank you, Jim. I understand now.*

*I'm letting go of you in a new way tonight. Or maybe I never truly let go before. Maybe I just buried you so deep within me that over the years I forgot you were there. But tonight I'm saying I love you, and I miss you.*

*By admitting how much I still love you, I'm also saying how much it hurt when you died. I died that day, too. Except I had to go on living. I just didn't know how. I wish I could have done it differently. I wish I hadn't been so afraid. But you'd be so proud of your beautiful daughter. She's not afraid. She has your love of life and love for other people. I'm praying she'll come to know your love for God, too. Or rather, that she'd come to know how much the Lord loves her. You would have shown her that, Jim. You would have lived in such a way that Becca would have never doubted how much her Heavenly Father loves her. I'm praying I'll be able to point her to God's heart. Lord, help me.*

*I remember you told me once that you were praying I would come to know how much the Lord loved me. You said you hoped someday I'd realize your love for me was just a shadow of God's love for me. I'd forgotten about that until recently. I can't believe I forgot that. But in the years after you died, I forgot so many things. I lost my way.*

*I'm found now, my love. I'm found. I just wanted to say thank you for this, your last gift.*

*And I love you. Always.*

On the way home from the restaurant, Meg stopped at the florist to buy herself twenty-one white long-stemmed roses.

It was the sort of thing Jim would have done to tell her how much he loved her and missed her.

## *Hannah*

Hannah stood at the kitchen sink, washing her breakfast dishes. She couldn't stop thinking about the list of questions she had been accumulating: Who are you? What do you want? Where have you come from? Where are you going? And now, where are you?

Such simple questions to ask, such complicated questions to answer. Was she really making any progress at all?

She reached for a red checkered towel and slowly dried her cereal bowl.

*Who was she?* She was God's beloved, the one Jesus loved.

*What did she want?* Well, she wasn't going to examine that. She would just skip that question.

*Where had she come from?* She'd started unpacking some of the sorrows from the past, even though significant mental and emotional boxes were still duct-taped shut. At least she was acknowledging she saw them.

She put her mug and bowl back into the cupboard and wiped down the kitchen counter.

*Where was she going?* She was meant to be journeying deeper into the heart of God, deeper into trusting God's good intentions toward her.

*Where was she?*

She walked over to the picture window, curled up on the sofa, and began to write her reply.

Wednesday, November 12

10 a.m.

Where are you, Hannah? Where are you? That's the Holy Spirit's question to me right now. I'm just not sure how to answer it.

Hiding, I guess. Still hiding things from others, hiding things from myself.

I sat there at the Corner Nook after the group on Saturday, presuming to counsel Meg and Mara about grief and forgiveness, and all I could think about was what a fraud I am. Physician, heal thyself! Meg and Mara have both been so courageous, not only to confront the past, but to talk about it so freely and openly.

Can I just say how much energy it takes for me to listen to Meg talk about her dad? It hits too close to home. Way too close. Not ready to go there. Not even in the safety of these pages. I can't, Lord. I'm sorry. But I can't.

No. "Can't" isn't the right word, is it? I won't. It's an act of my will. I've got way too many things I'm trying to process. I don't need that one piled on top of everything else. Don't ask me to do that, Lord. Please. Not now.

Then there was the whole thing with Charissa on Saturday. There she was, bravely confessing her sin, and all I could do was sit there and feel resentful and sorry for myself. She was talking about being upset over being pregnant, and I was feeling angry. She has what I wanted and never got. And even though I confessed all that to God, even though I poured out my anger and disappointment, my circumstances haven't changed. It still hurts. I don't know if it will ever stop hurting.

When I put on my pastor's hat, I understand Charissa's grief process. I understand that the pregnancy wasn't part of her plan, and her other dreams are coming to death. But I was still so upset when I heard her talk about it. I felt so angry. So incredibly angry and resentful.

So I confess it all again, Lord, and ask you to help me. I confess that I coveted Charissa's life. I coveted her loving husband and the gift of a baby. Forgive me, Lord. I need your grace to help me live in my reality. I need to know your presence and love even when I don't have what I want. Please, Lord. Help me want more of you. Will I always want your gifts more than I want you? I have moments of hope, but my buttons get pushed so easily. Like I've always told others, maybe part of my progress is realizing what triggers me and catching it more quickly each time. Help, Lord. Help. I can't change myself. I spiral so quickly into regret. Please help me fix my eyes on you. Please.

So where am I? Still grieving and trying to let go. A few steps forward, a few steps back.

I can't help thinking about Meg pushing me a few weeks ago after the worship service. She surprised me by asking point-blank about Nathan, and I gave all sorts of evasive answers. I haven't wanted to answer the "Where are you?" question with regard to him either.

He and I have talked a few times by phone and have another lunch set up for next week. On the one hand it's all very casual. He's very easygoing about reconnecting with an old friend. I think he's eager to help me navigate through my own "spiritual wilderness," if I'll let him. But where am I with that?

Scared. More than scared. I don't trust my heart. Every time I talk to him, I want more. There. I guess that's honest. And that terrifies me. Because I didn't come to Michigan to fall in love. So I'm trying to guard my heart.

He told me the other day that he and Jake have already signed up for the pilgrimage to the Holy Land. I had no idea he was going when I mentioned I was considering it. Now I'm afraid to go. Much as I'd love to walk in Jesus' footsteps—much as it would be a dream come true for me—I'm not sure I could manage it with Nathan. I'm afraid of getting too close. That's where I am.

Help, God. I'm a mess. I wish I had the courage to come out from hiding like the others have done and share my burdens. No, that's not exactly true. I have to take one step back from that. I suppose I could ask for the desire to come out from hiding and have courage. Because I don't want to stop hiding. I don't really want their courage. That's where I am.

Nancy phoned the other day. She invited me to come down for Thanksgiving. It was a very sweet offer, but I think that would be too hard right now. I don't trust myself. Even if I were there for only a couple of days, I'd be trying to reconnect with the church. I need to stay away. Hard as it is, I need to stay away. Of course, Nate also invited me to have Thanksgiving dinner with him and Jake. It's just the two of them. But I made an excuse about that, too. Lied, actually, and said I already had plans. It's better for me to be by myself. For all kinds of reasons. That's where I am.

Phone's ringing. More later.

"I don't know why I felt so strongly that I needed to call Hannah," Charissa told John as the two of them lay in bed together that night. "I guess I was wrong."

"Why do you say that?" he asked, stroking her hair.

"I mean, there I was, after the sacred journey group, talking about how selfish

I'd been over the pregnancy . . . how I'd been unhappy about it and how much I'd wounded you in that. Then today I suddenly remembered our picnic at the beach when Mara was trying to find out about Hannah's relationships, and it came out about her having a hysterectomy last year. She changed the subject pretty quickly, but there was this look on her face when Mara told her it wasn't too late for her to fall in love and have kids. I don't know how to describe it."

"Upset?"

"No. Completely stoic."

"Maybe it didn't bother her," John commented.

Charissa shook her head slowly. "I don't know. I'm not sure. Anyway, I was trying to put myself in Hannah's shoes. I mean, if I were her age and didn't have a family, I might feel really resentful about someone coming in and complaining about being pregnant. So I just wanted to apologize."

"What did she say?"

"She told me not to worry about it—that it hadn't even occurred to her. She said how happy she was for us and that I'd shown real courage in confessing my sin to them. Then she changed the subject."

John shrugged. "Maybe it isn't a big deal for her. There are lots of women who are single and happy."

"I know," Charissa sighed. "I just don't think she's one of them."

## *Meg*

On Thursday, the thirteenth of November, Meg sat at her kitchen table, reading a handwritten letter she had just received from Loretta Anderson.

*My dear Meg,*

*I've second-guessed myself a thousand times after our phone conversation. I don't know if I'm doing the right thing now or not. I just know I haven't had any peace since I spoke to you. Please forgive me if my writing this to you now causes you more pain. What I'm revealing to you, I reveal in love, hoping God will use it in whatever way He sees fit to bring you help and healing.*

*I remember the day your father died as if it were yesterday. The images are seared into my mind. I wish they were not, but perhaps it has been for such a time as this. Maybe God always planned for me to tell you the truth about what happened, though I cannot tell you how much it pains me. Maybe my desire to protect both the living and the dead has been an obstacle to the truth God wants you to know.*

*As I told you on the phone, I have such fond memories of watching your father play with you. You were a bright spot in his life, and he loved you. He often told us how proud he was of his girls. I am quite sure he would be extremely proud of the woman you have become. Your gentleness and compassion for others are gifts your father would have admired. Your father was gentle and compassionate, too. That was the real William we knew and loved.*

*In his later years he fought a losing battle against alcoholism. I don't pretend to know the reasons why your father began to drink so heavily. I just know that Robert and I both watched in sadness as he lost more and more control over his life. Your mother, as you well know, had a certain degree of pride in maintaining appearances, and his drinking became a source of shame and embarrassment for her. Especially when it was visible to others.*

*About six months before he died, he crashed his car into a tree in our front yard. We were relieved he wasn't hurt, but it could have been very serious. You were playing in the yard, and he barely missed hitting you. He didn't remember a thing about it afterwards, but of course, he was frightened and heartbroken when he realized what he'd done. He was scared when he thought about what could have happened. He told Robert one night that he couldn't forgive himself. He said he was worried he'd lost control to alcohol and that he couldn't stop drinking. He was terrified he'd do something to harm you or Rachel. He was extremely worried about that. He became more and more depressed, and I think he lost hope that he'd ever win the battle against his demons. He truly was a tormented soul.*

*The day he died I was gardening along the side of our house. I could hear arguing upstairs through an open window. I tried not to listen, but I heard enough to know that your mother was upset about his drinking. I don't know what set off the fight, but your mother ended up leaving the house with you. A few hours later, Robert and I heard the gunshot.*

*Thankfully, your house was unlocked, and Robert and I both ran in, frantically calling for your father. When we found him upstairs, he was lying lifeless on the bed with a photo of you and Rachel beside him.*

*I'm so sorry if this causes you more pain. You have already endured so much heartache in your life. Though many questions remain unanswered, I wanted you to know that your father's last thoughts must have been of you. For whatever reason, William must have believed that he did what he did because he loved you. Because I know how much he loved you, Meg.*

*Your mother never disclosed her thoughts or feelings to me about what happened. I don't know who your mother's confidantes were, or even if she had any. She was a very private person, and we did what we could to protect her privacy as much as possible. Robert and I agreed we would never speak about what we saw, except for what was necessary to disclose to the proper authorities. People who knew William knew he liked to drink, and it was widely assumed that he was intoxicated when the gun went off. In any case, we never corrected anyone who referred to your father's death as an accident. I suppose that was out of love for him and a desire to protect his reputation. We also were determined never to contradict what we knew your mother had told you and Rachel.*

*This is what I know—what I have known. Please forgive me for whatever pain either my secrets or my disclosures have caused to you. As I've written this letter, I have prayed for you. I have continued to pray for you in anticipation of your receiving it. May you know the steadfast love of your Heavenly Father as you grieve what remains to be grieved. You are in His heart—and mine always, dear one.*

*With deep love and affection,*
*Loretta*

Her hands trembling with emotion, Meg inserted the letter into the envelope and carried it upstairs to her parents' room. She placed it on her mother's pillow and shut the door tightly behind her when she exited. Then she staggered into her own room—her childhood room—and collapsed onto the bed, sobbing.

## *Sunday*

Hannah awoke at 4 a.m. on Sunday morning with the same dream that had provoked her every night for a week.

She was trying to talk. She was trying to say something really, really important, but she couldn't form the words in her mouth. Then she'd become more and more frustrated until she finally realized she was wearing a retainer. Why was she wearing a retainer? She didn't need a retainer. She had gotten rid of her retainer years ago.

If she could figure out what the dream meant, maybe her subconscious would stop screaming at her.

Rolling over, she tried in vain to go back to sleep.

Mara sat in worship on Sunday morning, trying to let go of her resentment toward Tom. As Pastor Jeff preached, Mara mentally replayed their dinner table conversation from the night before.

Over and over again.

She had finally broached the subject of Thanksgiving, expressing her desire for the family to serve together at Crossroads House. "I just think it would be a wonderful thing for us to do together," Mara had said. "We have so much to be grateful for when there are so many people who have nothing."

"What? You mean give up our dinner here?" Brian asked incredulously, loading his plate with a second helping of spaghetti and meatballs. "No way!"

"Yeah, Mom," Kevin agreed. "We've always had Thanksgiving here. And besides—we always watch football with Dad. I'm not givin' that up just to go somewhere we've never been and hang out with a bunch of homeless people."

Mara chewed on a fingernail and counted to ten before she replied. "We could still have our dinner here, just later in the day. We could do both."

Tom tousled Kevin's red hair. "I'm with the boys," he said, reaching for more garlic bread. "Not interested."

Mara had stewed in silence the rest of the meal, waiting until the boys went down to the basement to play video games before she spoke to Tom again. "You know how much that place means to me," she said quietly. "Crossroads saved my life."

He did not reply.

"Why can't you do this for me? It would be good for the boys to serve other people."

Tom leaned back in his chair. "Your life back then was your life," he said. "It has nothing to do with me." His lips curled into a sarcastic smile. "I know—why don't you call Jeremy and see if he'll go with you? You obviously had such happy memories there, just the two of you."

Mara's eyes burned. "This isn't about me and Jeremy."

Tom rose from the table. "Do whatever the hell you want. We're not going with you. Just make sure your plans don't affect ours."

Mara was startled out of her thoughts by the sound of the worship band playing the first bars of the final song, and she stood with the rest of the congregation to sing.

Meg sat cross-legged on her bed Sunday afternoon, staring at the white roses on her nightstand. It was almost time to throw them away. She pulled off one of the wrinkled petals and rubbed it slowly between her fingers.

"I mailed a note to Loretta this morning," she said to Hannah, wedging the phone more firmly against her shoulder. "I just wanted to thank her for telling me the truth, as hard as it was to hear it." She paused. "You know, I had closed the door to my parents' bedroom after I first talked to her on the phone. And now that I know even more details about my father's death, I just don't know if I can open it again. I can't bear the sight of the bed."

"I think that's perfectly okay," Hannah replied. "What happened in that room was horrific."

Meg was still gazing at the roses. "I know. But I'm also feeling like there's something I need to do to get it all out of myself. I've been thinking about the letters Mara has been writing to the girls who hurt her. And then I wrote that letter to Jim last week. As hard as it was for me to sit there in the restaurant by myself and name the pain and the deep sense of loss I've been feeling, there was something so healing in it. I don't know . . . " Her voice trailed off, and there was silence on the other end of the phone.

"I often tell people that we can only let go of the things we first hold on to," Hannah finally said quietly. "Maybe someday you'll find yourself writing a letter to your dad, as a way of turning it all over to God in prayer."

After she hung up the phone, Meg lay a long time on her bed, staring up at the ceiling. Maybe a letter was the right next step to take. Maybe there were many difficult things she needed to be able to say to her father.

Maybe.

John lay on the bed Sunday evening, holding Charissa's hand while he listened to one side of her phone conversation. They had finally decided to call and tell her parents the news about the baby, and from the pained expression on Charissa's face and the tension in her voice, he could tell it wasn't going well. Though John had assured her she had nothing to worry about, Charissa had evidently predicted their reaction accurately.

"I don't know, Daddy. I'm not sure yet," she said, stiffening her posture. John let go of her hand, sat up, and began gently massaging her shoulders. She did not relax. "No, I haven't wasted everything. There are lots of women who manage to juggle lots of things, and Dr. Allen says we don't have to decide anything about the Ph.D. right now." Pause. "No, I know . . . I know how hard I've worked . . . " Her voice was beginning to break, and her lips were quivering. It was time to end this conversation.

"Hey, Riss," John said, loudly enough for her parents to hear his voice, "we've gotta go."

She turned a grateful face toward him, her eyes brimming with tears. "Hey, Mom? Daddy? I've got to go. John's calling me. I'll call you later, okay? Love you . . . "

Shutting her cell phone, she buried her head against John's chest and started to cry. "I'm sorry, honey," he said quietly, wrapping his arms around her and stroking her hair. "So sorry."

## Meg

For the next three days, Meg prayed fervently, asking for the courage to set foot into another swirling eddy of grief. Though she continued to hear her mother's voice belittling her for being too sensitive and commanding her to be a grown-up, Meg also began to hear the persistent voice of the Spirit inviting her to take the next steps into freedom.

Sitting down at her desk on Wednesday night, Meg asked the Good Shepherd to walk with her into the darkness of her family's past. For a long time she sat staring at a blank piece of paper, praying from Isaiah 43: *Don't be afraid, Meg, for I have redeemed you. I have called you by name, Meg. You are mine.*

Finally, with an icy hand, she began to write.

*Dear Daddy,*

*Tonight the little girl who grew up without a father needs to write this letter. I don't even know where it's going to go. I'm asking God to help me find the words. I guess this is just my first attempt to walk toward a new kind of healing. I don't know where this road will take me. But I'm walking it.*

*I wish you had chosen a different path, Daddy. Loretta said that your last thoughts must have been of me and Rachel—that whatever reasons you had for taking your life, you must have believed you were doing what was best for us. I don't know if that's the truth or not. You didn't give us the gift of revealing your heart. I'll never know the reasons why you chose to leave us. You didn't tell us why. I could drive myself crazy the rest of my life asking the unanswerable question. A friend told me I need to find a way to ask a different question. I'll never get answers to "why?" so I need to start asking, "what now?"*

*But before I can even ask, "what now?" I need to look at how sad I feel. All these years I thought your death was a horrible accident. Now I discover you chose to abandon us. You of all people knew how hard life was with Mother. You knew that. And you left us without your help. You betrayed us, Daddy. Your presence and love could have eased our lives. Maybe you thought you were protecting us by killing yourself. I don't know. Loretta said you were terrified you'd do something to harm us. But the moment you shot yourself was when you harmed me in the worst possible way.*

*So tonight I say out loud that my life would have been different if you had made a different choice. Tonight I confess that I'm angry and sad. So sad, Daddy.*

*But I'm not bitter.*

*I'm so sorry that you were so overwhelmed by your despair, sorrow, and hopelessness that you saw no other way forward. I'm so sorry that you didn't have eyes to see a future and hope for you. For us. I'm so sorry. It must have been pure hell for you. I don't even pretend to know what that kind of despair is like. I've never felt it. Not even in my darkest of days. And I've had some dark days. So I'm not judging you, Daddy. I forgive you.*

*The Lord gave me a precious memory of you to treasure, and I hold on to your words as God's very words to me: "I've got you, Meggie, keep coming." Even though you let go, Daddy, I know the Lord grips my hand and helps me to keep going, no matter what comes. I can't describe the deep sense of peace I have as I remember that. I know with all my heart that God's love never fails, and His faithfulness is my strength. The Lord is my Shepherd, my Friend, my Love, and my Father.*

*Loretta gave me the gift of describing moments I shared with you that I do not remember. I wish I could remember playing with you. I wish I could remember you singing. Tonight as I write this, one more shadowy image emerges. I don't even know if it's real. I guess it doesn't matter. I have an image of myself standing in the driveway, looking up at the house, watching for your face. Even though I can't make out your face, I do see a shadow in the upstairs window, waving to me.*

*Good-bye, Daddy.*

*Again.*

## Hannah

"So . . . last group tomorrow, huh?" Nathan said as he and Hannah ate lunch together at the Corner Nook on Friday afternoon.

Hannah nodded and poured a bit more honey-lime dressing onto her grilled chicken salad. "Now I need to figure out what to do with the rest of my sabbatical."

"Have you thought any more about the Holy Land trip?"

"Not much," she lied. She had spent hours thinking about it.

He dunked a corner of his French dip sandwich into a cup of au jus. "What would keep you from going?"

"I don't know. I need to pray about it. I'm not sure if it's something the Lord wants me to do." There. A pious sounding excuse for being evasive.

"What do you want, Shep?"

He had seen right through her. Sometimes she hated his gift.

"I don't know what I want," she lied again. She knew what she wanted and didn't *want* to want it. She moved quickly to change the subject. "Tell me about your classes, Nate. When do you finish for the semester?"

"A couple more weeks." He pulled at a carmelized onion that was dangling from his sandwich. "I can't believe Thanksgiving is next week. Where did the fall go?"

They chatted awhile about incidental things. Normally, Hannah hated small talk. She found it exhausting. But today small talk served the useful purpose of keeping Nathan from plumbing the depths of her spirit. She wondered how long he'd let her continue. After all, she knew he didn't like small talk either. He considered it a waste of time.

Once the waitress had cleared away their empty plates, Hannah heard him take a preparatory breath. She braced herself. She recognized that breath. He was leaving the surface to dive deep.

"So, Hannah, while I'm not your spiritual director or your pastor, I am your friend. And I'm actually interested in knowing how you're doing. So far today I've seen nothing but the mask. Where are you?"

Even with a moment to prepare herself, the question still startled her. "Do you keep track of the texts Katherine uses with the sacred journey groups?" she asked.

"No. Why?"

"Just wondering."

Nate took a slow sip of coffee. "You can always opt out of the question," he said. "I just don't like playing games."

"Okay. I'll opt out. I'm just processing a lot right now, and I'm not ready to talk about it."

"Fair enough."

He stopped talking. Evidently, he was no longer going to give her the gift of small talk. If there was going to be conversation, Hannah would have to lead it. She knew him too well to think he was punishing or manipulating her through silence. He was simply waiting.

Hannah wished she still had a plate of food in front of her—something to distract her and keep her hands occupied. She reached for her glass of water and drank more than she wanted.

*Where are you? Where are you? Where are you?* The question was hovering between them in a dense, stifling, swirling cloud. She was suffocating.

"I lied to you about Thanksgiving," she confessed quietly.

His expression was even, just like his voice. "Why?"

"It wasn't that I didn't appreciate the invitation, Nate. I . . . It's just . . . "

He set down his coffee mug. "I didn't have any ulterior motives in inviting you. I just didn't want you to be by yourself. That's all."

So that's where his heart was. Her disappointment revealed where she was too. She mustered a smile. "I'm sorry," she said. "Forgive me."

"I'm just glad to be your friend again," Nate replied. "I told you at the beginning that you didn't need to worry about me going back into the past. In fact, maybe it would help you if I told you that you made the right decision by walking away."

Hannah wasn't sure if his words were a gift or a burden. Could she trust herself to speak?

"What do you mean?" she finally asked.

He leaned forward, folding his hands in front of him on the table. "We were so young. I thought I knew what I wanted. You were my best friend, and I cared more about you than I'd ever cared for anyone else. You made me love God more, and that was important to me. Very, very important. I was devastated when you left."

She flinched.

He saw.

"I don't say that to wound you, Hannah. It's just the truth. But as much as it hurt when you left, I'd hate to think what might have happened if you'd stayed."

She took her hands off the table so he wouldn't see them trembling and began tightly wringing the napkin in her lap.

"I wasn't ready for a relationship," he said slowly. "Look what I did to Laura. I'd hate to think what I could have done to you."

Hannah fixed her gaze on the basket of jam packets on the table, determined not to cry. She was not going to cry. Was not, was not, was not.

"Anyway," Nathan said, "I just hope your reluctance to go on the pilgrimage doesn't have anything to do with me. You can trust me, Shep. I promise."

*Oh, God,* she prayed. *Help.*

"I've been talking your ear off ever since you got here." Meg looked at Hannah from across her kitchen table. "Enough about my father. I want to hear about your day too."

Hannah shook her head. "Not much to tell, really. After I had lunch with Nathan, I spent all afternoon at the bookstore, salivating over all the books I want to read. And for the first time in years, I have time to read everything. No excuses." Hannah laughed ruefully. "So I came away with a bag full."

She stared at Meg's mug as Meg poured each of them some more Earl Grey tea. *Margaret, a pearl.* She wondered if Meg had ever contemplated the meaning of her name. "A pearl," Hannah remarked, gesturing toward the inscription. "That seems perfect for you."

"Thanks," Meg said shyly. "It was Katherine who first talked to me about the meaning of my name, and then I remembered that Mrs. Anderson had given me a mug when I was a little girl. I can't believe I found it in a box in the attic." She poured some milk into her tea. "My mother wasn't sentimental about keeping things from my childhood, so finding this was a special gift."

Hannah stared at the pot of purple mums on the table, trying to decide how best to keep Meg talking. "I think it's wonderful how you're processing and praying through all your grief, Meg—not just about your father, but about Jim. It takes real courage to do that."

Meg smiled. "It's all the Spirit's work. I just keep putting one foot in front of the other, remembering that Jesus is walking with me." She paused. "You know, I managed to do something today that I haven't been able to do in a really long time."

Hannah shifted forward, placing her elbows on the table.

"I actually drove by our old house this morning, where Jim and I lived for six years. It's not far from here—just a couple of miles. But I hadn't driven by it in years. It was just too painful for me."

Hannah nodded in encouragement.

"Anyway," Meg continued, "there's a 'for sale' sign in front. For a moment I would have given anything to go inside and walk around. I'm half-tempted to find out when they're doing an open house and just walk through it. I don't know. Maybe it's another way for me to say good-bye. Does that seem weird?"

"Not at all," Hannah replied. "We all have different ways of bringing closure." *And some of us prefer leaving the boxes duct-taped shut,* she thought.

"Jim and I loved that house." Meg offered Hannah the plate of homemade brownies. "I think that's why it's been so painful to think about it—because I was so happy there. Maybe if I'd had more courage about raising Becca on my own, I would have stayed. I made my choice, though, and I'm still here." She exhaled slowly. "But lately I've been thinking about selling this place. I don't know. Maybe that would be the next step in letting go . . . of getting rid of my guilt about disappointing my mother. Maybe that's the next step of freedom I need to take."

Was this really the same woman who could hardly make eye contact two months ago?

Hannah picked up a stray chocolate chip from her plate and idly rotated it between her fingers before she put it in her mouth. "Where would you go?" she asked.

"I don't know. I guess I'd stay in Kingsbury. Kingsbury has always been home for me, and I don't have any reason to go anywhere else." Meg shrugged. "I guess I have some thinking to do when I get home in January, and I'm trying not to become overwhelmed by too much before I leave. I'm just trying to take it gently and not push myself too hard."

"That sounds wise."

The only sounds in the house were the low hum of the refrigerator and the chiming sigh of a grandfather clock. As the house pressed in with somber stillness, Hannah found herself hoping that Meg would sell it and escape.

Meg cradled her mug and said, "I remember you told me once how kind the Spirit is to reveal what we need to know, when we need to know it. And I don't want to resist what God's doing. I want to stay attentive."

"'Stay with what stirs you,' right?" Hannah commented.

"Right. Both the positive and the negative things. I'm seeing how God is working in all that movement, and I just want to keep going deeper. I can't tell you how amazing it is not to feel afraid of digging deep. Knowing the Lord is with me makes all the difference. Like you've taught me, Hannah. It's all about knowing where we're going. I'm going deeper into the heart of God, and that keeps me safe. I'll never forget that."

Meg's words pierced and convicted Hannah. Meg had been so open, so honest, so vulnerable. But Hannah was still hiding behind her mask.

Why? What was she so afraid of?

Here she was, listening to someone testify to the freedom God had given—freedom to look hard at the ugly details of her past and to bring the pain into the light of God's healing love. Hannah had been shepherding Meg along a path she had refused to walk for herself.

In fact, she'd spent years shepherding people along paths she had refused to walk for herself.

Why? What was she so afraid of?

"You seem tired, Hannah," Meg commented as they put away the last of the dinner dishes. "Don't feel like you need to stay up on my account. I've got Becca's room all ready for you."

"Thanks. I think I will head up, if that's all right. Maybe I'll get some journaling done before group tomorrow."

Hannah went into the foyer, picked up her duffel bag, and followed Meg up the stairs. When they reached the hallway, her eyes fell upon a closed door across from Meg's room. Fixed to the door was a framed pencil sketch of Jesus tenderly embracing a little lamb with his nail-scarred hand. Hannah had the same sketch on a wall in her office.

Meg saw her gazing at it and smiled. "I saw it in the bookstore a few days ago, and it spoke to me. Beautiful, isn't it?"

"One of my favorites," Hannah replied.

"I know it's a little odd to have it nailed on the door, but—" Hannah heard Meg's voice falter. "My parents' room," she explained softly. "It just seemed like the right place to hang it for now. As a reminder of being held."

Hannah nodded slowly, contemplating the tragedy and sorrow that had occurred behind that closed door. She imagined the sheer horror of walking in and discovering him, lying on the bed—

She felt herself grow faint.

"Are you okay?" Meg asked, her face filling with concern. "You look pale."

Hannah closed her eyes and steadied herself by reaching out to touch the wall. "Dizzy," she murmured.

Meg took her bag and held it for her, waiting. "Here, Hannah, let me help you," she said, gently extending her hand.

Hannah shook her head. "I'm okay. Thanks." She followed Meg down the hallway to Becca's room and sat down on the bed, shutting her eyes again.

But when she shut her eyes, she saw the scene unfolding in high-definition detail. *No no no.* She opened her eyes.

Meg had seated herself in a chair by the window. "I'm sorry, Hannah," she said, leaning forward with her hands clasped together. "When I invited you to stay here tonight, I wasn't thinking about what I've uncovered about my dad. I didn't know about his suicide the last time you were here, and I'm so sorry if it's upsetting to you. I'll understand if you don't want to stay."

*No no no.* That wasn't it. That wasn't it at all. She just couldn't tell Meg what "it" was.

*No no no.*

Meg's face was etched with lines of deep compassion. How could Hannah reassure Meg without betraying the truth?

Hannah smiled weakly. "No, no—I'm happy to stay here. That's not it at all. I'm grateful that you invited me. Thank you."

The house was pressing in again, and the silence dragged on uncomfortably. Meg finally said, "Did something happen with Nathan today?"

*No no no. Of course not. No.* Nathan had nothing to do with it. Except—

Maybe a discussion about Nathan was the perfect diversion.

Hannah answered, "I'm just struggling with some regret, I guess."

Meg's tender expression was the narrow edge of the wedge, opening Hannah's spirit to more disclosure. She owed Meg something, didn't she?

"I'm afraid of falling in love with him."

She hadn't expected to be quite that direct, but Meg didn't look at all surprised.

Hannah soldiered on, not even sure what she was going to say. "I didn't come on this sabbatical to fall in love," she explained. "This was all about figuring out who I am when I'm not serving, when I'm not playing a role. If I get distracted by Nathan, I'll miss what the Spirit is trying to say to me. Besides. I missed my chance with him. I missed it years ago when I walked away."

*Why?* Why had she walked away?

She had walked away because Nathan had seen her too clearly. He had glimpsed the No Trespassing signs surrounding her internal high security area. Not only had he glimpsed them, but he had asked her why they were there. And she couldn't tell him. She just couldn't tell him.

*No no no.*

Could she tell Meg?

No.

*Yes,* the Spirit said. *Yes.*

Hannah sat, her mind whirling, envisioning the closed door down the hallway. She also had a closed door—a door she had firmly shut almost twenty-five years ago. Did she believe she would be safely held if she opened the door and entered the room again?

*Did she?*

Meg had come over to sit cross-legged beside her on Becca's bed.

"There's so much I haven't said, Meg." Hannah's voice sounded faraway as she felt Meg grasp her hand.

"It's okay," Meg said softly. "It's okay, Hannah. Don't be afraid."

Meg's strength had arrived stealthily, and now she was pulling Hannah to solid ground, not with a rope, but with a firm and steadying grip.

Breathing deeply, Hannah fixed her eyes on a vase of fresh flowers that Meg had placed beside the bed in a kind and thoughtful gesture of hospitality.

She heard herself whisper, "You know what Nate said to me years ago?"

Meg waited patiently for the answer.

"He told me I had secrets I wouldn't even tell myself. And he was right. I don't even know anymore what I'm afraid of. I just know I feel sick to my stomach every time I even think about disclosing the truth." She paused, still staring at the flowers. "But I know God has been trying to tell me to let it go. I've made it far worse by hiding it. It's taken on this life of its own inside of me, and I need to release it. There's a part of me that's trapped at fifteen years old."

How could she have spent years leading and guiding other people toward spiritual and emotional health while staying imprisoned by her own fear and sorrow? Katherine's words came to mind: *Trust God to bring to the surface all that is ready to be healed.*

Was she ready? Was she really ready to confront the past in order to let it go? If she was going to speak the words out loud, she needed to do it now before her courage failed.

Hannah closed her eyes.

"I was fifteen," she murmured. "A freshman in high school. One day I got home from school late. My mom's car was in the driveway, and I knew she was home. But she didn't answer when I called for her. And my brother, Joey, was sitting there in front of the television by himself. I asked him where Mom was, and he kept staring at the cartoons. He said she was really tired, and he couldn't wake her up."

Hannah was narrating someone else's life, speaking without emotion.

Meg tightened her grip.

For the first time in years Hannah was watching the scene unfold again: a slow motion horror movie of her teenage self standing in the doorway of her parents' bedroom.

*She was staring at her mother lying facedown on the bed with her left arm dangling over the edge, an empty prescription bottle on the nightstand. Now Hannah was moving slowly toward the bed, whimpering.* Mom? Mommy? *No movement. No response. Hannah was screaming, crying, shaking her, trying to rouse her.*

"I couldn't wake her up either," Hannah said. "I tried and I tried, but I couldn't wake her up. She had taken too many pills. And I was frozen. Totally frozen. I couldn't even think straight—I didn't know what to do. I was just standing there, looking at her lying facedown on the bed. And Joey kept yelling that he needed a snack. He was hungry, and I was screaming for him to shut up. And he was crying hysterically."

Hannah was still watching the movie play out in her mind.

*Daddy was home. Thank God Daddy was home! He was racing through the doorway to the bed.* Jane? Janie? Oh, God! Janie! *He was searching for a pulse, looking for breath. He found it, and he was crying. Daddy was crying. Joey was screaming. Daddy was sweeping her mother's limp body up into his arms and racing down the hallway to the car. He was shouting,* Stay here, Hannah! Take care of your brother!

"Dear God," Hannah breathed. "If my dad hadn't gotten home right then, what would I have done? Oh, God, what would I have done? I didn't know what to do . . . I just didn't know what to do! My mom probably would have died. I would have watched my mother die. I was paralyzed. Totally paralyzed. The hospital was right around the corner from our house, and I don't think I would have gotten the ambulance there in time. I was completely, utterly numb."

"But your dad *did* get home," Meg said, earnestly squeezing Hannah's arms with both her hands. Hannah opened her eyes and gazed into Meg's tearstained face. "Your dad got home in time, Hannah."

How could the "what if" of that moment still haunt her after all these years? Why was she tormented by what might have happened?

*Let it go,* the Spirit directed. *Let it go.*

Hannah nodded, wiping her eyes on her sleeve.

"My mom was in a psychiatric facility for weeks," she whispered. "I didn't talk to anyone about it. Not even my best friend. Dad wanted to protect my mom. He wanted to keep it a secret. I told everyone she was away in Arizona, taking care of my grandparents. I guess people thought my parents were separated. I don't know . . . I remember telling Dad I was worried people would think that, and he said it was better for people to believe their marriage was struggling than to know the truth. So I put all my energy into pretending that everything was okay. And to this day, right up until now, I kept the secret. I never told anyone."

"Oh, Hannah," Meg said soothingly. "What a terrible burden. I'm so sorry."

Hannah had started the story now, and she needed to finish it. She was going to bring as much as she could into the light.

"I wasn't allowed to go see her in the hospital, and I didn't know what was going on. I didn't understand anything about depression then. I just thought maybe I'd done something to upset her. I kept trying to figure out what I'd done to make her so sad. Then one night, while my mom was still in the hospital, my dad heard me crying in my room. I'd been trying not to show how upset I was. I knew he was tired and worried about Mom, and I didn't want to add to his burden. But he heard me sobbing uncontrollably, and he came into my room and found me curled up on my bed, clutching my old teddy bear. He wanted to know what was going through my head. So I told him I thought it was my fault. I thought it was all my fault."

Hannah hesitated, closing her eyes again. "That's when I found out that my mom had already had three miscarriages, and she'd just lost another baby. I never even knew she had been pregnant. And she couldn't cope with the grief of it. It broke her. After that I lived in terror of doing or saying anything that would break her again. I was afraid of how fragile my mom was. Really afraid."

They shared the silence.

"You never talked to your mom about what happened?" Meg finally asked softly.

Hannah shook her head. "It was just easier to take it into myself. I couldn't risk causing harm to her. I promised Dad I would never talk about the miscarriages either. To this day I don't think my mom even realizes I know the truth about the pregnancies." Hannah pressed her palms against her eyes.

"You've been living with a lot of fear, too," Meg said. "I'm so sorry, Hannah."

Hannah nodded slowly. "Katherine called it 'internal bleeding.' Hemorrhaging. She didn't know the details. She just sensed I'd taken things into myself that I was never meant to absorb." Hannah paused, massaging her temples. "This was the next step for me to empty it out, I guess. Dear God, help! I've been treating the surface stuff without going after the roots." She took another long, deep breath. "Now I need to discern where to go from here."

Meg's gentle smile was full of warmth and sunlight. "It's all one step at a time, remember?" she murmured. "You don't need to have it all figured out. Maybe it's enough to lay the burden down. You've been carrying so much for so long. Just rest, Hannah. Rest."

But resting was such hard work.

12

# Walking Together in the Love of God

*As the Father has loved me,*
*so I have loved you;*
*abide in my love.*

John 15:9

## *Rule of Life*

"Welcome to our last sacred journey group," Katherine said.

There was a chorus of wistful protests around the room.

Katherine smiled. "It's been such a joy and privilege to witness the Holy Spirit's work of healing and transformation in your lives, and I know the Spirit's work will continue."

Meg glanced in Hannah's direction, but Hannah was sitting with her shoulders hunched forward, cradling her head in her hands, and Meg couldn't see anything. *Please help Hannah,* Meg prayed. *Please help her find true rest in you.*

Katherine said, "We're going to spend time today celebrating and giving thanks for some of the ways that the Spirit has been stirring you these past few months. But before we move into a time of storytelling, I want to give you an opportunity to reflect on some of the spiritual practices that are helping you grow in love for God and love for others. Some people call this a rule, or rhythm, of life.

“Rules of life are like trellises,” Katherine explained, “helping branches grow in the right direction and providing support and structure. They can be as simple or as detailed as you wish. I’ve known some people who benefit from having specific spiritual patterns and rhythms for each day; others prefer more of a free flow. What’s important is that you discern what brings you life. Which disciplines help you keep company with Jesus? Which practices create space where God can dwell deeply within you?”

Meg thought about all the different ways of prayer that were bringing her life: simple breath prayers, walking the labyrinth, lectio divina, the examen, praying with the imagination, personalizing Scripture. Her awareness of God’s presence was becoming more habitual, like breathing. She was grateful. So grateful.

“Each of us has our own unique spiritual rhythm,” Katherine went on. “What brings life to me may not bring life to you. Not only that, but we have our own cycles and seasons in the spiritual life that we need to pay attention to. A discipline that may be right for me when I’m parenting young children might have no meaning for me when I’m retired. What may help me during a season of spiritual dryness may not be as useful to me during a season of abundance. I might have a few daily spiritual disciplines that help me develop intimacy with Christ, and I might have several monthly disciplines that I practice in order to keep company with God. This is all about discerning what draws you close to the Lord in this particular season of your life. Nothing is set in stone.

“So I invite you to take the next thirty minutes or so to begin to consider the practices that help you cooperate with the Spirit’s work of transformation. Think about the disciplines that help you be lovingly attentive to the God who loves you. When we string moments of God-ward attention together, soon we discover that our well-lived hours are stretching into well-lived days, weeks, months, and years. And that’s the kind of life worth living, isn’t it?”

**Sacred Journey, New Hope Retreat Center**
***Session Six: Rule of Life***
*Katherine Rhodes, Facilitator*

---

In the early centuries of the church, many spiritual communities developed "rules of life," which helped structure individual and corporate life around Christ as the center. The most well-known rule was developed in the sixth century by Benedict of Nursia, who wrote a practical, balanced, and down-to-earth guide to help form rhythms of work, prayer, and study. This guide addressed needs of the body and the spirit, the individual and the community—all for the purpose of being formed and transformed by the love and grace of God.

A rule, or rhythm, of life is an intentional structure designed to free us to respond to the movement of the Spirit. Like a trellis, a rule helps us grow in the right direction as we orient our lives toward Christ. It can be intensely practical: not checking e-mail after 9 p.m., finding three nights a week to share a leisurely meal with family or friends, exercising regularly as a way of stewarding our bodies, etc. It includes both the practices that are life-giving to us and the ones that help us stretch beyond what is comfortable and easy. It can include daily, weekly, monthly, and seasonal practices that are well-suited both to our temperaments and stages of life. Unlike a New Year's resolution or a personal growth plan, a rule is not focused on efforts to fix and control our lives. Rather, a rule of life is first discerned and developed after listening prayerfully to the Spirit. It focuses on deepening intimacy with God, not the improvement of self. Paul wrote that while all things are lawful, not all things are beneficial, and we are not to be enslaved by anything (1 Corinthians 6:12). While a rule of life can help free us from the habits or patterns of sin that enslave us, it must not become another burden or yoke. A rule of life is meant to breathe. It's not a rigid list of duties or obligations. It needs to reflect who we are becoming in Christ at this moment in time.

As you begin to pray about developing a rule of life, here are some questions to ask:

What regular practices help me to receive, remain in, and respond to the love of God? What brings me life and helps me stay close to God? What practices help me deepen relationships and love others?

What habits and patterns of sin impede my growth and formation in Christ? What regular practices can address these patterns and help me to cooperate with the grace of God?

So here's what I want you to do, God helping you:

> Take your everyday, ordinary life—your sleeping, eating, going-to-work, and walking-around life—and place it before God as an offering. Embracing what God does for you is the best thing you can do for him. Don't become so well-adjusted to your culture that you fit into it without even thinking. Instead, fix your attention on God. You'll be changed from the inside out. Readily recognize what he wants from you, and quickly respond to it. Unlike the culture around you, always dragging you down to its level of immaturity, God brings the best out of you, develops well-formed maturity in you. (Romans 12:1-2, *The Message*)

"I was thinking about how much solitude and quiet I have in this season of my life," Meg said as they shared their reflections in small groups during the second hour. "And I'm glad that my alone time is becoming more life-giving to me, because it was absolutely terrifying after Becca left." She paused to read through the list she'd made of the disciplines that had helped her draw close to God.

"I'm finding I'm becoming more aware of God's presence with me even as I'm doing ordinary things throughout the day," Meg continued, gently stroking her neck. "I'm grateful for that. Really grateful. But I'm feeling like maybe the Spirit is stretching me out of my comfort zone and showing me that I really need to be involved with a community. I don't know how to do that yet. Maybe a group at my church, or something else here. But I need to find ways to intentionally connect with other people, apart from worship on a Sunday morning. Being in community needs to be part of my regular rhythm if I'm going to keep growing. And I want to keep growing."

"You go, girl," Mara said, grinning. "You're not the same woman who came here in your high heels in September! Or, like my therapist would say, you're becoming a truer version of yourself."

"I like that," Meg said. "Thank you." She folded her hands in front of her. "Enough about me. Who's next?"

"Go ahead, Charissa," Mara urged. "What did you come up with?"

Charissa said, "Well, I'm glad Katherine mentioned that the rule can be as detailed and structured as possible because as you guys have probably figured out, I really like order." Meg and Mara laughed. "I need to get the balance right, though—especially since it seems that discipline and control are two sides of the same coin for me. I need to watch that. I'm such a control freak that I could easily strangle the life out of my relationship with God if I get too rigid. I'm trying to learn how to relax and take myself less seriously, but it's hard for me." Charissa smiled. "Is 'letting go' a spiritual discipline?"

"That 'palms-up, palms-down' prayer was a way of doing that, right?" Meg offered. "Releasing and receiving?"

"Oh, yeah! I forgot about that one! I hated that when we did it. But maybe that's a good way for me to start off the day." Charissa scribbled herself a note. "I guess one of the most important things I'm learning is that the spiritual formation journey is about transformation, not information. So I'm trying to let that shape the way I read God's Word."

She paused, fingering the open pages of her Bible. "I'm starting to find some life in lectio divina," Charissa went on slowly. "I've abandoned all my Scripture reading plans for right now—I need to back away from my compulsion to just tick Bible reading off my to-do list. And I'm trying to read slowly and prayerfully, listening for what the Spirit is saying. That's really new for me."

"I think that's wonderful, Charissa," said Meg.

"Thanks. I'm also realizing that everything's in flux now with the baby. The things that may work for me now may not work after the baby's born, and I want to be okay with that. I want to keep letting go of my desire to control everything." She twirled a strand of hair around her finger. "I suppose the other big piece is about finding ways to serve other people, especially John. He's so good at laying down his life for me, and I need ways to confront my own selfishness and self-absorption. I don't know what that looks like yet, but it's something for me to pray about."

Mara smiled at her. "As far as letting go and laying down your life, I think you'll find that being a mom is the perfect spiritual discipline for that."

Charissa laughed. "I'm sure you're right! Anyway . . . Thanks for your encouragement and your prayers. I hope we can keep connecting together."

Mara glanced at Hannah. "You're awfully quiet, Hannah. You okay?"

"Just processing a lot." Hannah was thumbing through pages in her journal, avoiding eye contact. "I wrote down lectio divina, journaling, and the prayer of examen as daily disciplines. I put down spiritual direction as a monthly discipline—that one is key for me. I need someone sitting prayerfully with me and helping me discern what God is doing in my life. And even though I've got lots of silence and solitude right now, I know that if I'm not intentional about cultivating those disciplines, I'll fall right back into old habits once I'm working again. So I'm going to read a lot about Sabbath-keeping and see if I can become a better steward of my time. And that's about it."

Charissa was studying her hands. Meg was staring at her lap. Mara was trying to figure out how much she should say.

"Those things are great," Mara finally ventured, "but they're all pretty personal, aren't they? I mean, you need community too, right? Worship or a small group . . . Some place where you're connecting with other people, like Meg was talking about. I just hope you won't spend the rest of your sabbatical by yourself, you know?"

"You're right," Hannah said simply. "That's something for me to pray about."

But Mara wasn't sure what her matter-of-fact tone actually meant.

"How about you, Mara?" Meg asked. "What gives you life?"

Mara leaned back in her chair and exhaled slowly. "Sounds crazy to say it, but confession. I want to keep confessing my junk to people I trust. That's been life-changing for me. Totally life-changing. And you guys have been part of that healing process for me. So thank you." She looked around the circle and smiled. "Now that I've tasted the freedom of dumping the junk, I don't want to pick it all back up again, you know? So I need to keep practicing laying those burdens down. And speaking of that . . . I'm trying to let go of all my disappointment about Tom and the boys not coming to Crossroads House with me on Thanksgiving. I was really hoping they'd see how important it is to serve other people, but that's a no-go. Still . . . Tom doesn't care if I go, as long as it doesn't affect our dinner plans."

Mara had been confessing her bitterness and resentment to God all week. She had fervently hoped that Tom would change his mind and agree that the boys would benefit from the experience. She had imagined herself phoning Jeremy to tell him the good news about how his prayers for a Thanksgiving gift had been answered. But it wasn't going to happen. Not this year.

Katherine was inviting everyone to finish discussion around the tables so that they could transition into a large group time of storytelling and prayer.

"Anyway," Mara said, "if any of you guys are looking for a place for Thanksgiving, you'd be welcome to join me at Crossroads. I've got the details."

"I wish I could," said Charissa. "My parents are coming to town, though."

Meg rested her hand on Mara's shoulder. "I was just going to be on my own, Mara. I'd love to be there with you."

"Great! How 'bout you, Hannah? Have you already got plans?"

"I'm not sure what I'm doing yet. But thank you. Thanks for the invitation. I'll let you know."

Mara gazed at her intently. "Just don't stay by yourself, girlfriend. Okay? It's not good for you to be alone."

Hannah smiled weakly but did not reply.

Just before noon Katherine brought the large group time of sharing and prayer to a close. "In one of our early sessions," she said, "I invited you to consider Jesus' question in John 1: 'What do you want?' I'm hearing many of you respond the same way the disciples responded. You want to be with Jesus. I hope some of these spiritual practices will continue to help you do that.

"Remember: even though we sometimes experience significant breakthroughs and tangible evidence of the Spirit's work in our lives, spiritual growth is often imperceptible. I encourage you to be patient. Just as parents don't notice physical changes in their children from day to day, we don't often see immediate fruit from our disciplines. But think of grandparents coming to visit a child they haven't seen in six months, and they'll tell you how much that child has grown and changed. Months from now you'll look back and perceive ways God has been transforming you, all because you're saying yes and cooperating with the Spirit's work in your lives.

"God is faithful," Katherine said. "So faithful. And there's so much joy in the journey! My prayer for each of you is that you grow in trust. May you grow in the knowledge of God's deep love for you. May you learn to relax into God and rest in his power and faithfulness. May you find opportunities to love God and love others. And since God made us for life together, may you find trustworthy companions to walk with you along the way."

"So, Meg," said Charissa, looking into her planner. "I've got us down for being at the airport at noon a week from Monday."

"Thanks," Meg said. "You guys don't have to come, you know."

"Are you kidding?" Mara exclaimed. "I wouldn't miss this for the world. We'll pray you off in style!"

Meg's eyes filled with tears. "Thank you. Thank you so much. I'm so grateful for all of you." She looked down at her shoes. "What a road we've walked so far."

"And so much farther to go!" Mara declared, laughing.

"I still wish there were a straight line, without all the spirals and switchbacks," Charissa commented, putting her laptop away. "But maybe the twists and turns make the journey more interesting." She smiled at Mara's raised eyebrows. "Maybe."

Mara said, "You guys sure you won't join Meg and me for lunch?"

Charissa replied, "I can't. I've got tons of work to finish."

Hannah shook her head. "I've got such a headache. I think I'll just go back to the cottage and rest. Thank you, though."

Meg embraced her. "Praying for you," she whispered.

"Thanks," Hannah mumbled. She said good-bye to the others, then hurried to her car.

## Revelation

Hannah waited in the parking lot until she saw the others leave. Then she wrapped her scarf tightly around her neck, put on her hat and gloves, and made her way back to the courtyard. She wanted to walk the labyrinth alone.

Had it really been less than three months since she'd been exiled from her world in Chicago?

She had lived years since then, and she wasn't even halfway through her sabbatical. What else was God going to bring to the surface?

As she followed the winding path toward the center, she thought about everything the Spirit had already revealed: her false self rooted in productivity, her need to be needed, her hiding behind busyness. She thought about the death of her images of God, her disappointment and unconfessed sorrows, her anger, bitterness, and regrets. And now that she had actually spoken her family's secret aloud—

Where was that path going to lead?

She kept walking back and forth, back and forth. It was so easy to become distracted by the twists and turns along the way, so easy to lose sight of where she was going.

*Where was she going?*

She was going deeper, deeper into the heart of God. She needed to stay focused on where this journey was taking her, especially when the path seemed disorienting and circuitous. She needed to pause and remember where she was going.

So she stopped walking the path and turned to face the middle of the labyrinth.

That was her destination: being held in the heart of God, knowing herself as the beloved, understanding at a deep level that the flowers really were for her. Even when she had her back turned toward the center—even when she couldn't glimpse the goal—she needed to stop, turn, and face the middle. She needed to stop and remember that the Lord was inviting her to comprehend the breadth and length, height and depth of Christ's immeasurable love for her.

If she could stop and remember that the flowers were for her . . . If she could receive the Lover's gift to the beloved . . . If she could continue to treasure that image as a particular gift of grace in her life . . . If she could—

*Oh, Lord.*

*Dear God—how?*

*Why hadn't she seen it before?*

As Hannah stared at the middle of the labyrinth, the memory of Mara's comment from the first meeting floated back to her.

"It looks kinda like a flower in the center, doesn't it?"

The center of the labyrinth was shaped like a six-petaled rosette.

Hannah stood, wide-eyed and open-mouthed, as a wave of warm electricity coursed through her entire body. *The flowers are for you, Hannah. The flowers are for you.*

When she reached the center of the labyrinth, she had no words.

She simply fell to her knees and offered her tears to Jesus.

Nate. She wanted to see Nate.

She wanted to tell him how the Lord had spoken in love again, confirming that she was heading in the right direction.

The flower: the Lover's gift to the beloved.

Jesus was treasuring her and inviting her to savor it. She wanted Nate to know about the joy she felt as she walked the outward path—skipped, actually—saying over and over again, "All for me! All for me! The flowers are all for me!" In that holy moment Hannah knew she had the undivided attention of the God who had flung galaxies into space.

It was good.

It was very good.

And she wanted to share it with Nate.

She glanced at her watch: one o'clock. He had told her that Jake was going to be out of town for the weekend, and he was planning on working in his office. "Drop by if you've got time after your group," he'd said casually. Just drop by unannounced like friends do—like intimate friends who can show up without calling first—like the two of them used to do years ago.

She pulled her map from the glove compartment and followed the route to the college.

Nate removed his glasses and leaned back in his chair, staring at the slowly diminishing stack of ungraded papers on his desk. He glanced at his watch: one thirty. Where had the hours gone?

Just as he was standing up to stretch, there was a knock on his door. "C'mon in!" he called, expecting to see a student. The door opened.

*Hannah.*

"Did I catch you at a bad time?" she asked, looking tentative.

"No . . . no." He walked toward the door to greet her. "Come in! I'm glad to see you!" Stunned, actually. He certainly hadn't expected her to drop by. He reached for her coat. "Here, let me take that for you," he offered.

"You're sure I'm not interrupting anything?" She removed her scarf and gloves.

"Positive. I was just going to have some lunch. Have you eaten?"

"Not yet."

"Good! I happened to pack two peanut butter and jelly sandwiches this morning, and I'd be happy to share one with you. Or we can go over to the student center if you'd prefer something more sophisticated."

She smiled. "I love peanut butter. Thank you."

Nate closed the door behind her and went over to the dorm-sized fridge in the corner of his office. "Have a seat," he said, handing her a sandwich, an apple, and a water bottle. "I was just thinking of you this morning, wondering how your last sacred journey group was going." He took the other armchair by the window, praying silently as he looked at her.

Something had shifted. He'd seen it as soon as he took her coat. Her eyes were actually bright. *Thank you, Jesus.* Nate didn't know what had actually happened, but something had changed.

"So . . . how are you?" he asked cautiously.

Hannah was gushing and breathless as she told him what she had seen on the labyrinth. The flowers were for her. The flowers really were for her. "And I feel like something has broken loose in me, Nate. Or opened up. And I couldn't wait to tell you about it because you've been part of the journey . . . and . . . I just wanted to say thank you. Thanks for your prayers."

Nate made sure he had control of his voice before he replied. "You're welcome. I'm so glad you're walking that road, Hannah. You've spent a lifetime giving flowers away to other people. It's time you started receiving some yourself."

"It's hard for me," she said.

"I know."

He just wasn't sure why it was so hard for her. Fear. It all came back to fear. But why? What was she so afraid of?

Nate sat back in his chair and put his feet up on the small coffee table, determined to communicate how comfortable he was—how completely nonthreatening and safe he was. She could trust him. She didn't need to be afraid.

"Maybe that's the next part of your sabbatical, huh?" He took a bite of his sandwich. "You spent the first part unpacking some of your grief points and sitting with some of the sorrow. Maybe the next part is about entering into rest and joy and really basking in God's particular love for you—whatever that looks like in your life."

Nate paused, weighing his next words carefully. "Let me suggest something radical to you, okay?" he said slowly. He saw her stiffen momentarily, almost imperceptibly. She probably wasn't even aware of it. "When's the last time you did something to pamper yourself?"

Hannah looked at him as if he'd spoken in tongues. "Like what?" Clearly, *pamper* was not a word in her vocabulary.

"I don't know," he replied. "I doubt you're the kind of woman who covets manicures or facials."

"You're right about that."

Good. At least she was smiling. He kept going.

"But what about something entirely frivolous and luxurious?" he asked. "The image I'm seeing is Mary of Bethany pouring out that costly ointment to anoint Jesus' feet in this beautiful, extravagant act of love." Nate waited long enough to let her see it before he turned the picture upside down. "What if Jesus wants to pour out something totally extravagant into your life?"

Hannah laughed. She actually laughed, and her laughter was water rippling lightly over smooth stones. He hadn't heard her laugh like that since—well, since before she'd walked away.

Hannah said, "I guess if Jesus offered to do that, I'd argue with him and tell him to use it to help somebody else."

"Exactly," Nate said. "That's exactly my point. You don't have a clue how to be anything other than a giver in relationships. It's time to start receiving. You need to find ways to practice receiving."

This was all feeling familiar. Very familiar. And Nate was about to ask Hannah the same kind of question that had once driven her away.

He was praying as he spoke. "Hannah, what do you think will happen if you focus on yourself for a while? Why are you so afraid?"

She didn't answer.

She also didn't walk away.

If she hadn't just disclosed to Meg about her family, Hannah might not have known the answer to Nate's question. *Why was she so afraid?* Suddenly, she saw. As soon as he asked the question, two memories converged in her mind. She'd never seen the connection before.

She was fourteen, and she was on the phone with Brad. He was asking her out to the movies, and she was excited—so excited. Her first date! Then she heard the screaming. Joey had fallen out of the tree, and it was her fault. All her fault. If she hadn't gotten distracted by Brad, her brother wouldn't have gotten hurt, and her mother wouldn't have gotten upset. Her mother had cried for days afterwards over what might have happened to Joey. If Hannah hadn't gotten so distracted, she could have spared her mother that trauma. At least she could have spared her that one.

And then there was that awful day when she'd found her mom.

Hannah had decided to go to her friend Amy's house after school when she should have gone straight home. She had promised Daddy she would take care of Mom. She'd promised him. But she broke her word. If she'd gone straight home—if she hadn't been so self-absorbed—she could have been there for her mother. She could have prevented her mom from taking the pills. If she'd been more focused on her mother's needs instead of having fun with her friend, she would have gone straight home. And everything would have been different. Everything, everything, everything.

Now Hannah was getting a second chance. Nate was giving her a second chance to answer the same kind of question that had driven her away years ago—the question that had revealed he'd seen too much. Nate actually trusted her enough to ask her again.

And Hannah trusted him enough to tell the truth, now that she saw the truth.

She whispered, "People I love get hurt if I'm not paying attention."

Nate's heart broke as he listened to Hannah describe the details of her mother's nervous breakdown. The traumatized little girl within her still felt responsible. She'd never been able to let it go. She'd never forgiven herself for getting distracted. She'd never forgiven herself for being irresponsible and selfish. She merely became all the more determined never to get distracted again—never to put herself first again.

Because someone might get hurt.

Hannah had poured all her undivided, undistracted attention into serving God's people, terrified that if she turned her back for a second, one of them might get hurt. That was her burden.

Now Nate understood. He understood why she had walked away so many years ago. He saw. And if he'd been alone, he would have wept for her. He wasn't even sure she could hear the tragedy in her own story. But he heard it and grieved for her.

"You've been carrying a terrible load, Hannah," he finally breathed. "I'm so sorry. If you had told me years ago . . ."

Hannah pulled another tissue from the box he'd given her. "I almost told you once," she said. "But then I remembered the promise I'd made to my dad, and I couldn't break it. Not even with you. Then as the years went on, I guess I just stopped thinking about it. I stuffed it all deep inside, never even considering what kind of stronghold had been created, or how I was being impacted. I didn't see. I just didn't see."

"Thank God Steve did," Nate said softly. "Thank God." Nate leaned forward in his chair but did not reach for her hand. Any gesture of intimacy might scare her away. "Can I pray for you?" he asked.

He was glad when she answered, "Yes."

"So . . . Where do I go from here?" Hannah asked, opening her eyes. Even as she spoke the words, she knew how many layers there were to the question. "I mean . . . I know I've got a lot of stuff to work through with my parents, and maybe I'll be taking a trip to see them at some point. But I don't feel like I'm ready for that yet. Not yet."

Nathan was silent a long time, and Hannah desperately wished she knew what he was thinking. But he was giving nothing away. Nothing.

"Maybe now your sabbatical can become what it's meant to be," he finally said. "A rest. Now that you've been able to discern some of the burdens and lay them down, you can begin to rest. And play. When's the last time you played, Shep?"

"Played what?"

"C'mon. Are you serious? Wait! Yes, you are," Nate teased. "Being serious is one of your strongest qualities." Hannah tossed her empty sandwich wrapper at him. "What did you like to do for fun when you were little?" he asked, crumpling the wrapper and shooting it into the wastebasket.

"Reading, writing . . . "

"Solitary things."

"Yes. Mostly."

"You spent a lot of your childhood being very grown-up."

She'd never thought about it quite that way before, but he was right. Hannah had spent her childhood being responsible. She'd spent a lifetime being careful, disciplined, and vigilant. That was her comfort zone, as burdensome as it had been.

"So," Nate continued, "what if part of this sabbatical is all about learning to play? What if God wants to teach you how to stop taking such good care of everybody else and start looking at what brings you life and joy? Like Katherine says, learning how to 'relax into God.'"

"I don't know how to do that."

"I know," he said. His voice was gentle. So gentle. "You've spent a lifetime being the burden-bearer. What will you do if you're not carrying the heavy loads anymore?"

"Stand up straighter?" she quipped.

He laughed. "See? There's still life in there." Nate finished off his water bottle and went to the fridge for another. "Too bad I've put the boat away. I'd take you out for a day of sailing and show you a good time. In the spring, okay?"

He had his back turned toward her, and Hannah couldn't see his face. She was glad he couldn't see hers. He was so easygoing. So comfortable. Did he have any idea what that invitation meant to her? How could she continue to guard her heart?

"In the meantime, Shep . . . " He sat back down again as she bent forward to fiddle with a shoelace that had not come untied. "It's back to the question of how you're going to open yourself up to receiving God's extravagant love for you. Sounds like your sacred journey is about learning how to celebrate the flowers and play with joy. And that's a great journey. Not easy, but good. Who knows? Maybe God reconnected us again so I can help you learn how to play." He wasn't looking at her as he twiddled the water bottle lid between his fingers. "After all, I've been practicing how to play for a few years now, and I've gotten pretty good at it. I'd be happy to teach you."

Hannah wanted to say yes. She had so much to learn from him. But if she said yes to this, she was committing her heart to much more. Meg's voice was echoing in her head, and she couldn't tune it out. "Maybe a relationship with Nathan is one of God's flowers," Meg had said.

*But he just wants to be my friend,* Hannah silently argued. *That's all he wants. Help, Lord. Please.*

Nathan had stopped twiddling and was now looking at her with an odd expression of tenderness and bewilderment. Or was it woundedness? Hannah couldn't tell. But there was something very vulnerable in his eyes. "You still look like you're afraid of me," he finally said quietly. "What are you so afraid of?"

What was she afraid of?

She had already revealed so much truth to him. She had already removed many of the defenses and retaining walls that had held her life together for so many years. Retaining walls. Retaining walls. *Retainers.*

The dream.

In the dream Hannah was trying to speak really important things. She just couldn't get the words out because she was wearing a retainer. But the retainer didn't need to be there. She'd outgrown it years ago, and she needed to remove it in order to speak.

That was it.

That was the interpretation, wasn't it?

Her coping strategies had served their purpose for a season, helping her hold her life together. But she had outgrown them years ago, and now they were only hindrances and obstacles to her freedom.

As Hannah sat on the verge of tears, she knew the last bit of truth she needed to speak aloud. She met Nathan's eyes and prayed for the courage to say it.

"I'm afraid of falling in love with you, Nate. Again."

There.

A single word could make all the difference. One little word revealed everything. One little word brought the whole truth into the open. No more hiding. No more mask. She placed the final burden of fear and regret at his feet and waited.

Neither one of them moved. She wasn't even sure she was still breathing.

And then, "Don't be afraid, Hannah."

Nathan was leaning toward her, touching her face with the feather-light tips of his fingers, sending volts of electricity through her entire body. "Don't be afraid." He moved a single finger to touch her mouth, and she found her breath again in his breath as he hovered near her lips.

Hannah lost herself in one sacred moment of all-consuming peace, found in the gentleness of one holy kiss.

And it was good.

It was very good.

# Epilogue

"You're sure you've got everything, Meg?" Mara asked as they sat together in the Kingsbury Airport lobby on the first of December.

"I think so." Meg looked at her boarding pass before tucking it into her carry-on bag. "I got a funny email from Becca last night, reminding me to pack good walking shoes. 'I know you like your high heels, Mom,' she said, 'but leave them at home. You won't need them here.'"

Hannah laughed. "I love it!"

"She's not gonna recognize you in your cute sensible shoes," Mara teased.

"I know. I just can't believe I'm going. I keep having dreams I can fly. It's scary and exciting at the same time." Meg took a slow sip of coffee. "So, Mara, tell them what happened at Crossroads last week."

Mara breathed deeply and leaned back in her chair, shaking her head slowly.

"I had an amazing God-encounter while I was there," Mara began. "You know how I was saying that I hoped God would be able to use some of the stuff I've been through to help somebody else?"

Charissa and Hannah nodded.

"Well, there was this young girl there, maybe eighteen or nineteen. And she had a little baby boy, just a couple of months old. She'd left home because her parents were so upset about the baby, and the dad was a deadbeat." Mara's voice broke. "We had the best conversation. And I was able to tell her about Jesus."

As her face filled with emotion, Mara touched her tattooed wrist to her eye and held it there. "I was able to tell her how much Jesus loved her. I told her that there was hope, even if it didn't feel like it." Mara paused and gazed at her wrist. "Anyway . . . It was one of the most incredible experiences of my life, just being able to share my story of what the Lord has done for me. We ended up praying together for a long time, and the next day she boarded a bus and went back home again."

"Oh, Mara!" Hannah exclaimed. "What a wonderful gift."

"I know," Mara said, rummaging around in her oversized bag. "Here I was, feeling sorry for myself because Tom and the boys wouldn't come with me, and all along God had something else in mind. A totally different kind of Thanksgiving gift."

"I'd like to serve with you at Crossroads sometime," Hannah said, handing her a tissue.

"That would be fantastic! I'd love that." Mara wiped her eyes and looked intently at Hannah. "You didn't end up spending Thanksgiving on your own, did you?"

"No," Hannah answered. "I ended up having dinner with an old friend and his son."

Hannah's voice trailed off, her attention drifting. A little girl was walking toward the security checkpoint, holding an older woman's hand and repeatedly blowing kisses to a man in the waiting area. "Bye, Daddy!" Hannah heard her call out. "Love you, sweetheart!" he called back. As the child proceeded through the screening process, she kept turning around to make sure her father was still there, as if his steady wave of benediction was giving her the courage for whatever journey she was about to take. Even after his daughter disappeared down the concourse, the man didn't move.

Hannah pulled her attention back to the table and said, "Mara, I don't think I ever told you about my small world experience here in Kingsbury." Mara looked puzzled. "I found out a while ago that one of Charissa's professors is an old friend of mine from seminary: Nathan Allen."

"Seriously?" Mara asked, sounding tentative.

Hannah nodded. "Seriously."

Mara did not reply. Hannah suspected that given Mara's prior experience of inserting her foot into her mouth, she was probably reluctant to ask any probing or inappropriate questions.

Hannah smiled at her. "Turns out you were right, Mara. About me being in a relationship. Maybe it isn't too late for me after all."

"Seriously?" Mara asked, sounding a little more animated.

"Seriously."

Mara waited a moment and then exclaimed, "Then c'mon, girlfriend—details! Gimme the details!"

Hannah laughed. "Well," she began, placing her elbows on the table, "I'm getting a second chance with a very dear friend. And I'm grateful. Very grateful. I spent Thanksgiving with Nate and his son, Jake, and we had a great day together. Turns out Nate is a fantastic cook. I had no idea what a good cook he is!"

"Like John," Charissa commented.

Hannah nodded. "Yes. Like John. We spent the day eating great food, telling stories, and playing lots of games." She chuckled. "Nate is hyper competitive, though, and I'm not sure I'll be able to play Scrabble with him ever again."

The others laughed.

"I wanted to thank you, Charissa," Hannah said.

Charissa replied in Eyebrow.

Hannah answered, "For not being manipulated by me. For telling Nate you'd met me. Thank you."

Charissa shrugged slightly. "I figured it wasn't causing any harm to let him know. Funny how it all works together, isn't it?"

"Definitely a God thing," Hannah said. "And it took me completely by surprise."

"I'm so happy for you, Hannah," said Mara, beaming. "I'll be praying for you guys, for whatever God has planned for you."

"Thank you. I'm trying not to think too far ahead, you know? Like what happens in June when my sabbatical is up?" Hannah was trying hard not to think about that. She kept telling herself it was enough to say yes to the flowers today without worrying about what would happen with her life in Chicago.

"A lot can happen in six months," Meg said, reading her thoughts. "Look what's happened in only three."

"Just one sensible shoe in front of the other," Mara added. "One baby step at a time."

Hannah nodded. Yes, what a perfect image. She was learning to walk. Again.

"Thinking of baby steps," said Meg, "how was your time with your mom and dad, Charissa?"

Charissa stirred her decaf latte methodically. "Well, it was interesting."

"Good interesting or bad interesting?" Mara asked.

Charissa sighed. "I guess I'm starting to see some stuff I've got to work through with them—in terms of their expectations and my fear of disappointing them. I didn't even know all that was inside of me. Next steps of the journey, I guess. I'm paying attention to why my buttons are getting pushed right now and trying not to be so quick to blame it on hormones." She smiled faintly. "Although that would be a convenient excuse for everything, wouldn't it?"

Mara narrowed her eyes. "They're upset about the baby?"

Hannah heard something agitated—or maybe protective—in Mara's tone. She wasn't sure what it was, but there was something there. Perhaps the Holy Spirit had connected Mara and Charissa together for deeper purposes, for deeper healing. After all, there was always the opportunity for deeper healing.

Charissa said, "They aren't upset, exactly. Just surprised. They have all sorts of questions about what decisions I'll be making about grad school and my career, and I have to keep telling them that we're trying to trust God with the timing of everything. I keep saying that John and I aren't going to be making any decisions about that right now. It's enough to take it one day at a time. Dr. Allen's happy with that too. He said there's no rush to decide anything. So that feels right."

*Yes,* Hannah thought. That was exactly what Nate had been saying to her too. "We don't have to figure any of this out right now, Hannah. I think the Lord wants us just to enjoy the journey together, without having to figure out where it ends."

She had figured out one part of the journey, though: she was going on the pilgrimage to the Holy Land. She would be walking in the footsteps of Jesus alongside Nate.

A blur of movement in the corner of her eye caught her attention, and Hannah turned her head. A young woman was running into the arms of someone waiting for her with flowers at the gate. Husband? Boyfriend? She wondered how long they'd been separated. What a gift to have someone waiting to meet you at the end of a journey. *What a gift.* After a lingering embrace, the two of them walked away together, hand in hand.

"I think we all have quite an adventure ahead of us," Meg was saying.

"Amen, sister," said Mara. "The journey goes on."

Charissa and Mara walked out toward the short-term lot together, stopping at the exit kiosk at the end of the terminal to pay for parking. "Have you got class this afternoon?" Mara asked, inserting her ticket into the machine.

Charissa shook her head. "No. I've actually got some free time before I pick John up from work. It's weird. I'm not used to having free time."

Mara smiled at her as she swiped her credit card. "Well . . . enjoy it." She paused. "I hope everything works out really well for you, Charissa—with the baby and the Ph.D. and your parents."

"Thanks." Charissa reached into her purse and removed her ticket. "I don't do well with the one step at a time thing, you know? I've spent my whole life planning things out. I just don't handle uncertainty very well." Charissa stared at her hands while she spoke. "I'm also not great with spontaneity," she said tentatively, "but . . . well . . . Would you like to go out for lunch or something?"

"Right now?" Mara asked, looking surprised.

Charissa nodded. "If you're free, that is . . . "

Mara beamed. "You bet, girlfriend!" she exclaimed. "I'm free."

Meg sat with her head resting against the cabin window, watching the rain pelt the glass. As she waited for takeoff, she opened the envelope Hannah had given her when they hugged good-bye at the security gate.

*Dear Meg,*

*I was reading Psalm 91 this morning and couldn't shake the sense that it's for you today. I think you'll know why when you read it. Here are the first few verses: "You who live in the shelter of the Most High, who abide in the shadow of the Almighty, will say to the Lord, 'My refuge and my fortress; my God, in whom I trust.' For he will deliver you from the snare of the fowler and from the deadly pestilence; he will cover you with his pinions, and under his wings you will find refuge; his faithfulness is a shield and buckler."*

*I've watched you grow in quiet trust and confidence in God, Meg. You have made the Lord your refuge and your fortress, and I'm watching you dwell in peace. You've been so brave to confront so many difficult things from your past, and your courage inspired me, too. Thank you. God truly has delivered you from the fowler's snare, and you're free to fly. What a wonderful adventure you have ahead of you!*

*I'm proud of you, and I thank God for bringing you into my life. God bless you, Meg!*

*Love,*

*Hannah*

Meg smiled to herself and gripped the armrest as the plane gathered speed along the runway. Moments later she was airborne, watching the slate-colored skies give way to a glorious sunlit world above the clouds.

Meg Fowler Crane had found her wings.

"I hear so much freedom in you," Katherine said as she and Hannah stood together at the threshold of her office. Hannah had stopped by New Hope after she left the airport so that she could sign up for the pilgrimage.

"I certainly couldn't have predicted all this when I came here in September. It's been an incredible adventure so far."

Katherine smiled. "You're saying yes to love, Hannah. Yes to all God's invitations to travel deep into his heart. There's no greater adventure. And you've found such lovely traveling companions to walk with you."

Hannah nodded. "I know. Now that I've finally given up trying to honor God by suffering as much as possible, maybe I can learn how to relax into something new and different. Nate is determined to teach me how to play."

"He's a good teacher."

"Like you, Katherine. Thank you."

Katherine reached out her hand and touched Hannah's cheek. "I'm so proud of you. God bless you, dear one."

As Hannah made her way down the hallway, she glanced at her watch. She still had time for one more brief stop before she met Nate at the college.

Apart from the chickadees and cardinals flitting among silvered branches and red-berried shrubs, the courtyard was still, hushed and cloaked under the softness of a gray flannel sky. Hannah approached the center of the labyrinth slowly and knelt to trace her hand along the petaled outline on the pavement. *Thank you,* she prayed. *Thank you. For everything.*

*Remember,* said a still small voice. *Always remember. The flowers are for you.*

"The lover's gift to the beloved," she whispered.

And deep in her spirit, she heard the tender invitation: "My beloved, walk with me."

# With Gratitude

My words are inadequate to express my love and appreciation for all those who have walked with me in the writing of this book.

To my husband and dearest friend, Jack—the very best of John, Jim, and Nathan all wrapped up in one man. God blessed me with you. I love you! I couldn't have done this without you.

To our son, David, who is full of patience, love, and grace. I love you, and I'm so proud of you.

To the real Sensible Shoes Club (Jill, Shalini, Cherie, Cynthia, Jan, Jennifer, Nahed, Eleanor, Connie, Sue, Diane, and Nancy). Your stories of life change and transformation are far more stunning than anything I have described in these pages. Thank you for sharing the journey with me.

To the wonderful faith community of Redeemer Covenant Church. What a joy and privilege to share life in Christ with you.

To Sister Diane Zerfas, my trustworthy spiritual director, who has encouraged my imagination and helped me to pay attention. Thank you.

To my early readers who cheered me on: Ruth, Krisha, Yu Chen, Vaneetha, Katie, Mary, Catherine, and my dear Aunt Sally. You gave me courage. Thank you.

To Todd and Holly, whose early input and suggestions made this a better book. Thank you for your gentleness and your persistence.

To Celeste, who brought me flowers at exactly the right moment. Thank you.

To Betsy, who invited me to the cottage where the story began. Thank you.

To Martie Sharp Bradley, who edited my manuscript with deep affection for my characters. Thank you for climbing into my spirit and imagination to draw out the best in these women.

To Colleen and Kathleen, who never stopped talking about Jesus. I am eternally grateful.

To Steve, who spoke timely words of wisdom and helped me to let this book go with open hands. Thank you.

To Dr. Robert Jacks (R.J.), who taught me to write for the ear; to Mr. Don Shultz, who taught me to write what I know; and to Mr. Art Farr, who told me to write. Thank you.

To Cindy Bunch and the wonderful team at InterVarsity Press. Thank you for glimpsing the vision and saying yes.

To the Dominican Center, where I have explored many of the disciplines described in the book, including the labyrinth and its three-fold movement of releasing, receiving, and returning.

To mentors and teachers I have never met, whose wisdom breathes in these pages: Hannah Hurnard, Richard Foster, Henri Nouwen, Robert McGee, Eugene Peterson, Gerald Sittser, C. S. Lewis, Philip Yancey, John Ortberg, Adele Calhoun, Teresa of Avila, Brother Lawrence, Julian of Norwich, Ignatius of Loyola, the desert fathers and mothers, and too many others to name.

To my sister, Beth, my faithful friend and companion in the journey. I love you.

To Mom and Dad, with gratitude and love beyond words. Mom, thanks for being such a careful editor and proofreader. You saw things I didn't see.

And finally, to the Holy Spirit, my faithful Ghost-writer, who patiently and gently answered and overcame all my objections and fears about why I couldn't write this book.

This is my offering of love to You.

*I pray that, according to the riches of his glory, he may grant that you may be strengthened in your inner being with power through his Spirit, and that Christ may dwell in your hearts through faith, as you are being rooted and grounded in love. I pray that you may have the power to comprehend, with all the saints, what is the breadth and length and height and depth, and to know the love of Christ that surpasses knowledge, so that you may be filled with all the fullness of God. Now to him who by the power at work within us is able to accomplish abundantly far more than all we can ask or imagine, to him be glory in the church and in Christ Jesus to all generations, forever and ever. Amen. (Ephesians 3:16-21)*

# Discussion Guide

For further book club resources and more information about *Sensible Shoes,* please visit the author's website: www.sensibleshoesclub.com.

1. If you could sit and have a conversation with one of the characters, who would you choose? Why? What would you want to talk about?
2. Which character did you most identify with? Least identify? Did your opinion change as the story unfolded?
3. Think about some of the childhood experiences for each character. How did some of these events shape each woman's sense of identity?
4. Identify some of the turning points for the main characters (Hannah, Meg, Mara, and Charissa). Why were these moments significant?
5. Name some of the images or metaphors that were significant in each character's process of self-discovery and transformation. Which of these images connect with your life or your longings?
6. What are some of the important growth points or unresolved issues for each character? What next steps do you hope each one takes?
7. Mara says, "I hate the word 'discipline.' I already feel guilty." What is your reaction to the concept of spiritual disciplines?
8. How do you define "spiritual formation"?
9. What do you find either appealing or frightening about taking a sacred journey with other people?

10. Dr. Allen says, "The things that annoy, irritate, and disappoint us have just as much power to reveal the truth about ourselves as anything else. Learn to linger with what provokes you. You may just find the Spirit of God moving there." What provoked you as you read the book?
11. Meg says, "It's easy to lose sight of how far I've come if I'm only looking at how far I have to go." When do you feel overwhelmed or discouraged by the distance you still have to travel? What helps you keep a God-ward perspective on your journey?
12. How would you respond to an invitation from New Hope?
13. What is God stirring in you as a result of reading this book?

*Excerpt from*

# Two Steps Forward

A STORY OF
PERSEVERING IN HOPE

Sharon Garlough Brown

IVP Books
An imprint of InterVarsity Press
Downers Grove, Illinois

# one

## *Meg*

Meg Crane clutched the collar of her turquoise cardigan, her knuckles cold beneath her chin. Ever since takeoff, the well-dressed, gray-haired woman beside her in seat 12-B had been casting appraising glances in Meg's direction. Was she breaching some sort of airplane etiquette? Transmitting neon messages of first-time-flyer anxiety? Maybe the woman was examining the scarlet, telltale blotches that were no doubt creeping up her neck. If only she had worn a turtleneck. Or a scarf. Her shoulder-length, ash blonde curls provided a meager veil.

The woman extracted a plum-colored Coach bag from beneath the seat in front of her. "I swear they keep stuffing more rows into these planes," she said. "Flying isn't much fun anymore, is it?"

Meg cleared her throat. "It's my first flight."

"Really! Well, good for you."

Meg supposed she deserved to be patronized. There probably weren't many forty-six-year-old women who had never been on an airplane before.

"Where are you headed?" the woman asked.

"London."

"No kidding! I'm going to London too! Overnight flight tonight?" Meg nodded. The woman pulled her itinerary from her purse. "Flight 835 at seven?"

"Yes." Meg had studied her ticket so frequently, she'd memorized it.

"How about that! Small world!" She tapped a heart-shaped pendant dangling from a gold chain around her neck. "I'm taking a bit of my husband's ashes to scatter in Westminster Abbey."

She carried her husband around with her in a necklace? Meg had never heard of such a thing. Was she allowed to scatter ashes like that? Surely there were rules against that, weren't there?

The woman leaned toward her in the sort of confidential way normally reserved for friends. "Before my husband died he made a bucket list—not of all the things he wanted to do before he kicked the bucket, but of all the places he wanted to be taken after he kicked it. So, ever since he died, I've been traveling all over the world and sprinkling him here and there. The Taj Majal, the Grand Canyon, Paris—right off the top of the Eiffel Tower! My daughter thinks I'm terribly morbid, but I told her, 'No. Morbid would mean shutting myself up alone at the house and crying over old photos into a gin and tonic. That would be morbid. And I refuse to be morbid.' So this month it's London, and next spring it's the Bolivian rainforest. And then next summer I'll be heading to Machu Picchu to hike the Inca trail. My husband always hoped we'd make that trip together, but the cancer got him first. So I'll sprinkle a bit of him there on top of the mountain, right in the middle of the ancient ruins."

Meg replied with a courteous smile and "hmmm" before casting an envying glance at the solitary and silent passengers across the aisle, their books establishing a definitive Do Not Disturb zone, her books tucked in her carry-on bag, now stowed securely in an overhead bin. Just as she was about to reach for the in-flight magazine, the flight attendant arrived at their row with the beverage cart. "Something to drink for you?" She handed each of them a miniature bag of pretzels.

"Ginger ale, please," said Meg. Maybe that would help settle her stomach.

"I'll take a Bloody Mary." The woman opened her wallet, then pivoted again toward Meg. "Do you live in Kingsbury?"

Meg nodded.

"You look really familiar. I've been sitting here trying to figure it out. Have we met before?"

"I don't think so." She definitely would have remembered someone this gregarious.

"Do you happen to go to Kingsbury school board meetings?"

"No."

"How about the gym on Petersborough Road?"

"No."

"It's going to drive me crazy until I figure it out."

"How about Kingsbury Community Church?" It was the only place Meg could think to offer as a possibility.

"Definitely not." The woman squinted hard. "Art museum, symphony, gardening club?"

"Afraid not."

She snapped her fingers. "Got it!"

Meg tilted her head.

"You look like someone my husband worked with years ago. Beverly something. Beverly, Beverly, Beverly . . . Beverly Reese! You're not related to a Beverly Reese, are you?"

"No, sorry. Doesn't ring a bell."

The woman patted her cheeks and neck with her left hand while holding her drink in her right. "I suddenly remembered because she had really fair skin like you and used to get the same kind of hives whenever she got nervous. Have you tried acupuncture?"

"Uhhh . . . no." How long was the flight to New York?

"I think she did acupuncture. And yoga. Just a thought." She pressed the button to recline her seat a few inches. "So what takes you to London?"

Meg teased open her bag of pretzels, careful not to spill them on the tray table. "My daughter's studying there for her junior year. She's an English literature major."

"Ahh. What a wonderful opportunity for her."

"Yes."

"And how long will you be staying?"

Honestly, of all the people to end up sitting next to. "A couple of weeks. Through Christmas."

"Christmas is lovely there. Are you staying right in London?"

"Not far from the college."

"How nice for you."

Yes, it was going to be wonderful. She had been dreaming about their visit for weeks now. She had planned to dream about it during the flight. She chewed slowly on a pretzel.

Without taking a breath, her seatmate launched into detailed and colorful narratives about her own family: her name was Jean, her daughter was an unmarried actress currently starring in an off-Broadway production, her husband had died of pancreatic cancer, her son was going through a messy divorce. "I always knew it wouldn't last," she said. "At least they didn't have kids. She was a nightmare. An absolute nightmare. I'm glad he finally woke up and said, 'Enough! No more!'"

Eventually, either because of the effects of alcohol or a loss of interest in one-sided conversation, Jean drifted off to sleep. Careful not to bump her, Meg shifted position in her seat and slipped off her shoes.

Her sensible shoes.

What a journey she'd taken since September, when she first met Hannah, Mara, and Charissa at the New Hope Retreat Center. They had happened to sit together at a back corner table near an exit door, and Meg had used the excuse of her high heels to avoid walking the prayer labyrinth. "I'm afraid I didn't wear very sensible shoes," Meg told them. "Guess I wasn't taking 'sacred journey' literally, huh?"

"I like it!" Mara had exclaimed. "Sacred journeys need sensible shoes! What shall we call ourselves? The Sensible Shoes Club?"

Over the past three months, they had learned to travel deeper into God's heart, sometimes with reluctant and stumbling steps. Meg had grown to love and appreciate each of them: Mara, a fifty-year-old wife, mother of three sons, and soon-to-be grandmother; Charissa, a married and newly pregnant graduate student; Hannah, a pastor on a nine-month sabbatical from ministry in Chicago.

All of them had come to the airport to pray for Meg and offer their encouragement. She was grateful. So grateful for companions on the spiritual journey.

"It's gonna be an awfully long month before we can all be together again," Mara had said while they drank coffee in the Kingsbury Airport terminal. "I don't want to fall off the track, you know? I just hope I remember some of the stuff I learned during the retreat. Me and my menopause brain. Remind me, okay?"

"Me too," said Charissa. "I wrote down a whole list of spiritual disciplines that I wanted to keep practicing, all kinds of things that could help me grow in the right direction and be less self-centered. But I always get even more obsessed about school this time of year, with final papers and projects and everything. Lately, I haven't been doing much of anything from that list. My rule of life right now is just 'Survive.'"

"So start smaller," Hannah suggested. "Maybe choose one thing that will help you stay connected with God in the midst of the stress, and then there may be other practices you can gradually weave in."

"I just wish there were a quick fix," Charissa said. "It's the whole letting-go-of-control thing. I don't know if I'll ever get there. Maybe I'll always be a control freak."

"At least you see it, right?" Mara said. "That's progress! Even if it feels slow. Guess I have to keep remembering that it's okay if it's two steps forward, one step back. 'Course, sometimes it feels like a few baby steps forward, then a few big steps back. And I still get dizzy from walkin' around and around in circles, same old baggage again and again."

Meg had recorded some of their prayer requests in her notebook: for Charissa to find ways to love and serve others well, even in the midst of her busyness; for Mara to know God's peace and to persevere in faith while battling chronic frustration and disappointment with her husband and their two teenage sons; for Hannah as she continued to settle into the rhythm of rest and a new relationship.

"How about you, Meg?" Mara asked. "How else can we pray for you?"

"I think 'hope' is my word right now," Meg replied. "Especially with all the hopes I have for this trip, for my time with Becca. We lit an Advent candle in worship yesterday—the hope candle—and my pastor talked about how true Christian hope isn't about wishing for things, how there's a big difference between hoping for something specific to happen versus trusting God to be faithful, no matter what happens." She had written down some sermon quotes in her notebook so that she would remember: *Our hope isn't uncertain. Christian hope doesn't fluctuate according to circumstances. True hope is about having confidence that God's good and loving purposes in Christ can never be thwarted, no matter how it appears.*

"I'll pray for you every day, girlfriend," Mara had said.

Meg knew she meant it.

She rotated her feet in several slow circles, then pressed the button on her armrest to recline. Her seatmate was snoring softly, mouth draped open. Meg stared at the pendant around her neck. She had been quick to judge the widow for carrying her husband's ashes in a locket, forgetting that she also carried part of her husband with her. She had tucked Jim's last card into her carry-on bag, the card he'd given her on the day they saw their baby on the ultrasound. He had written about his love for Meg, his love for their unborn child, his eagerness to be a dad, his certainty that Meg would be a wonderful mother. But weeks later, on a dismal, gray November afternoon, Meg's world imploded when Jim's car slid off an icy highway and slammed into a tree. He died at St. Luke's Hospital before she could get there to say good-bye. On Christmas Eve, with anguished sobs, Meg returned to St. Luke's and delivered their baby, a beautiful girl who had her mother's large doe eyes, just as her father had hoped. And now that baby girl was turning twenty-one, and she and Meg would celebrate together in England.

So much to celebrate, so much to share.

Out of necessity, Meg had mentally and emotionally locked Jim away after he died. Unable to face the prospect of raising Becca alone, she left the beloved home she had shared with Jim and returned to her childhood house, where tears were not tolerated. Her mother, widowed when Meg was four years old, had no patience for weakness or self-pity and offered an ultimatum: If Meg was going to live under her roof, she would need to pull herself together and move on. Fearful of disintegrating under the weight of her grief, Meg swallowed her sorrow and complied with her mother's demands as best she could. Becca, meanwhile, learned early in life that asking questions about her daddy made Mommy sad, so after a while, she stopped asking. And the years rolled on as if Jim had never existed.

But after twenty-one years of repressing her grief, Meg had recently discovered the courage and freedom not only to mourn, but to let Jim live again in her mind and heart. Though it was difficult to feel the pain of his absence, she was also remembering the joy of their life together, and she wanted to share some of those joys with their daughter. She wanted Becca to know how much her father had loved her, even before he knew her. She wanted to look Becca in the eye and tell her how sorry she was for withholding him, how she wished she had done things differently. Now that Meg was remembering his life and love, she hoped he would come to life for Becca too.

*Hope.* That word again.

She had fixed her gaze on the flickering hope candle during worship, her prayers focused on the fears that had paralyzed her, the regrets that had consumed her, the longings for God that had begun to emerge, awakening her to new possibilities, new opportunities, new courage, yes—to new hope. Katherine, Hannah, Mara, and Charissa had accompanied her on the first steps of that journey toward transformation and healing. Now there were more steps to take.

In England.

Jim would be so proud of her for traveling by herself across the ocean. And he'd be so proud of his daughter, their winged and confident, lively and spirited daughter, who had not inherited her mother's fears. *Thank God.* With a contented sigh, Meg leaned her head against the window and closed her eyes, eventually lulled to sleep by the gentle vibrations of the plane.

## *Charissa*

Charissa Sinclair twirled strands of her long dark hair around her fingertips and listened to the rhythmic squeak of the windshield wipers. What was keeping him? She'd already been idling the car for seven—now eight—minutes outside John's office building, and she didn't want to turn off the engine now.

C'mon, c'mon.

She never should have spent three whole hours away from her doctoral work, especially with the end of the semester rapidly approaching. But she was serious about her desire to be less self-absorbed, so she had decided to give herself a break from paper revisions and spend her class-free afternoon by going to the airport to say good-bye and offer support to Meg. And then, rather than eating by herself, she had invited Mara to join her for lunch. Until recently, Charissa had regarded Mara only as an overweight, middle-aged housewife with a tabloid past. Mara was the sort of person Charissa had spent a lifetime avoiding. They had nothing in common.

Scratch that.

They actually did have something significant in common, hard as it was to admit. They both "needed grace." Charissa had begun to learn that difficult lesson through their Sensible Shoes group over the past several months.

To her surprise, Charissa had discovered that she enjoyed being with Mara. Despite being crass and tactless at times, Mara, with her dyed auburn hair, brash wardrobe colors, and clunky costume jewelry, had her heart in the right place. "Anything you need, call me," Mara had said at lunch. "You know, since your mom is so far away. I could be like a whatchamacallit . . ."

"Surrogate?"

"Yeah. Surrogate mom. Or grandmother. I love babies!"

That was another thing they didn't have in common. Charissa had always been allergic to babies. An only child, she had never been subjected to young children, had never even babysat as a teenager. While her friends trained in Red Cross CPR classes and invested long hours in childcare to earn extra money for clothes and car insurance, Charissa spent her time investing in her future. "It's much more important for you to spend your time studying," her father had always insisted. "Your mother and I will take care of everything else."

Now the very future she had strived for was being jeopardized by an unexpected pregnancy. She was less than halfway through her Ph.D. program in English literature at Kingsbury University, and despite Professor Nathan Allen's assurances that the program could be flexible enough to accommodate her needs, Charissa didn't like detours. Didn't like them at all.

A rap on her window startled her, and she turned to see her husband's jovial face pressed against the wet glass. "Go around!" she mouthed, pointing to the passenger seat. He dashed in front of the car and hopped in, spraying Charissa with water droplets.

"Enough of the rain already. It's December! Gimme some snow!" John leaned in to kiss her cheek. "Sorry I'm late. Got caught on the phone." She brushed the moisture off her face and drove forward while he fastened his seat belt. "Good day?" he asked.

Lately a "good day" meant being able to eat without feeling sick. So in that regard, she supposed it had been fairly decent. "I'm wishing I had spent all afternoon working on my Milton presentation."

"You've been working on that presentation all semester. I thought you were done."

"Well, the first draft's done. But I've still got lots of revision work to do." And less than two weeks left to complete it. Dr. Gardiner had instructed them to view these final presentations as if they were conference papers, and Charissa was determined to be primed for any possible question from her peers or department faculty. One couldn't be too prepared for these things.

"You'll be fine," John said. "You always do great. More than great. How was Meg?"

"Nervous. Excited. She'll have a good time once she gets there."

Charissa flipped on her left turn signal when she reached the road.

"Turn right, okay?" John said.

Charissa raised her eyebrows. "Why?"

"Trust me. Just turn right."

"What for?"

"Just humor me, okay? It won't take long. Promise."

"I told you I'm already feeling behind today—"

"And this will take half an hour, max. Turn right here, then left at the light on Buchanan."

Charissa hesitated, then with an exaggerated sigh, switched the left turn signal to right. "Where are we going?"

"It's a surprise."

"I hate surprises."

"I know."

She followed his verbal instructions, eventually arriving in a suburban neighborhood filled with ranch-style houses. "Okay, we're looking for Columbia Court." John pressed his face to the window. "There!" He gestured toward a stop sign. "Turn right and go slow." Charissa was already doing twenty-five; she slowed to fifteen just to make a point. He didn't seem to notice. "464 . . . 468 . . . 472—okay, there—480! Where the For Sale sign is. Go ahead and turn into the driveway."

Charissa pulled in behind a black sedan. John leaned forward in the passenger seat, his hand on the dashboard. "Whaddya think?"

Charissa stared at the nicely landscaped, beige single-story house, trimmed with twinkling white lights. "What do you mean, what do I think? Whose house is it?"

He grinned mischievously. "Ours, maybe. What do you think?"

"What are you talking about?"

"Well, you know how we were crunching our numbers, trying to figure out if we could afford to buy a house?"

Was he being deliberately obtuse? They'd had this conversation several times over the past couple of weeks, and she wasn't going to have it again. Buying a house simply wasn't feasible, particularly a house in a desirable neighborhood with excellent schools, she reminded him.

"I know," he said. "But I was on the phone with my folks earlier today, talking about the baby and how we weren't sure how we were going to manage with the one-bedroom apartment, and when I said we might need to lease a two-bedroom or maybe rent a duplex, my dad offered to help us with a down payment on something."

She gaped at him. "Are you kidding me?"

"Would I kid about something like that?"

"A down payment. On a house."

He grinned even more broadly. "You know how excited they are about having a grandchild, and they want to help. You're not going to let pride get in the way of saying yes, are you?"

"No—of course not—it's just—"

He reached for her hand. "Listen. Just because your folks aren't enthusiastic yet doesn't mean other people don't want to help and support us."

"Unenthusiastic" was a mild way to describe her parents' reaction to the news of her pregnancy. And honestly, Charissa wasn't ready to say much about her own desires, except that she had moved beyond her initial shock and resentment to a place of ambivalence that she hoped would eventually become acceptance, gratitude, even joy. Some days were better than others.

The front door opened, and a woman in business attire beckoned to them. Charissa furrowed her brow. "John?"

He shrugged. "Well, after I talked to my dad, I did a search online, and when I saw this one, I couldn't resist. I called the listing agent and set up an appointment."

Any impulse to chastise him for bringing her here on false pretenses receded as she considered what his parents' extravagantly generous gift could mean for them. Though John's income was enough to keep them going on a no-frills budget while she was in graduate school, they had only recently begun to squirrel away some money for a future down payment. This unexpected twist changed everything.

"What if I'd insisted on turning left?" she asked.

"I can be very persuasive."

"Hmmm," she said, looking into the visor mirror to check her makeup. "We'll see."

All of Charissa's attempts to communicate nonverbally with John while they toured the house with the realtor were futile. Whereas she thought it would be a good strategy to remain reserved, he couldn't contain his boundless enthusiasm: the three bedrooms were huge; the family room had a large walk-out deck; the kitchen had been recently remodeled. After years of dorm rooms and then a one-bedroom apartment, this house of almost two thousand square feet—plus a finished basement!—felt like a palace. "And there's a big laundry area next to the mudroom," the realtor said.

John elbowed Charissa. She often complained about lugging laundry down multiple flights of stairs to a dark and musty apartment basement. "No more stashing quarters," John said. "No more waiting in line for a machine! Sign me up!"

"Well, we're certainly not signing up for anything tonight," Charissa declared, both for his and the realtor's benefit.

"Oh, of course not," she said. "Go home and sleep on it. And if you decide to make an offer, you can call me in the morning. Remember, though, I've got some other couples coming through in the afternoon. And I have a feeling they're going to love this place."

"You don't seem very enthusiastic, Riss," John said when they pulled out of the driveway. "What didn't you like about it?"

"It's not that I didn't like it. But you've had all day to think about this, and I had it sprung on me an hour ago. You know I don't like making quick decisions, and now I'm going to feel pressured." Her tone sounded more irritated than she intended. "Sorry. I just don't want to rush into anything, okay?"

"I know, I know. But I've been crunching the numbers ever since I talked with Dad this morning, and with their help on the down payment, this one is right in our price range. I really think we should jump on it. It's perfect. Don't you think?"

He chattered about how perfect it was all the way back to their apartment and all the way through dinner and all the way through cleaning up the kitchen. While Charissa tried to compile footnotes and a bibliography for her Milton presentation, John parked himself across from her at the dining room table, perusing online photos of the house, peppering her with questions, then apologizing for interrupting her work, then imparting what he'd discovered about neighborhood comps and school district ratings. It was no use. She saved her document and closed her laptop.

"Sorry," he said. "I'll shut up now."

"No—you're right. Call your dad and see what he thinks."

"Really?"

"Yes. Call him."

"But do you like it?"

"It's great, John. Let's figure out what kind of offer to make. Call your dad, show him the link, and get some advice." Had she really just agreed to purchase a house?

John jumped up from his chair to embrace her. "It felt right as soon as we walked in, didn't it?"

Unlike her husband, Charissa had never been one for gut-level decision-making. Nevertheless, the rigorously thorough, practical, list-making part of her knew that the pros would far outweigh any cons she might identify over the next few days. Hadn't she just confided to the group at the airport about her desire to grow in letting go of control? Maybe this was a perfect way to practice. To use one of Dr. Allen's favorite metaphors, maybe it was time to unfurl the sails, catch the wind, and see where they might go.

# *The Sensible Shoes Series*

*Sensible Shoes*

*Two Steps Forward*

*Barefoot*

*An Extra Mile*

## STUDY GUIDES

For more information about the Sensible Shoes series,
visit ivpress.com/sensibleshoesseries.
To learn more from Sharon Garlough Brown or to sign up for her newsletter,
go to ivpress.com/sharon-news.

AVAILABLE AUGUST 2019

Formatio books from InterVarsity Press follow the rich tradition of the church in the journey of spiritual formation. These books are not merely about being informed, but about being transformed by Christ and conformed to his image. Formatio stands in InterVarsity Press's evangelical publishing tradition by integrating God's Word with spiritual practice and by prompting readers to move from inward change to outward witness. InterVarsity Press uses the chambered nautilus for Formatio, a symbol of spiritual formation because of its continual spiral journey outward as it moves from its center. We believe that each of us is made with a deep desire to be in God's presence. Formatio books help us to fulfill our deepest desires and to become our true selves in light of God's grace.